Knights Errant

MERELY PLAYERS – BOOK ONE

IAN D SMITH

www.sincyrpublishing.com
sincyr.submissions@gmail.com

Published by SinCyr Publishing, University Place, WA 98466
Copyright © 2021

Knights Errant Copyright © 2021 Ian D. Smith, combined novel
reprinted and expanded from two novelettes; "Knights Errant"
Copyright © 2015, and "The King's Captain" Copyright © 2016
published by Fireborn Publishing

Print ISBN: 978-1-948780-32-2

Edited by Haley Isleib
Copy Edit by Sienna Saint-Cyr
Cover by Lee Moyer

DEDICATION

Dedicated to the real Otto, a beautiful, gentle giant with a huge heart, who we've missed since he went to his final sleep at the end of August 2020.

Thanks to Jackie for being patient when I wander off into my own little writing world to see what my imaginary friends are up to.

I'm indebted to both Haley Isleib and Sienna Saint-Cyr for their constructive and thoughtful comments which helped me to tell this story far better than I thought I ever could.

Many, many thanks to Monti Shalosky, Lucee and Sam for their encouragement and constructive feedback on the earlier version of this story, and all the members of the Erotica Readers and Writers Association, whose generous and constructive feedback on my writing has always been incredibly helpful. You are a constant source of encouragement.

CONTENTS

1

As usual, I was early for my dinner-date, so waited in the bar area where I could keep an eye on the entrance. The restaurant was decorated in soft pastel tones with fairly bland artworks on the walls. The room lighting was soft, with a small lamp on every table, and the staff moved quietly and efficiently. The atmosphere was relaxed, just the usual background hum of multiple quiet conversations and cutlery on plates.

Kathy arrived exactly on time. She was easy to spot; good-looking, a little over six feet tall, and nicely dressed in a cream short-sleeved top and a pale green, light summer skirt, both of which suited her height and build. Her light brown, collar-length hair briefly glowed as she walked in the light cast by a downlighter. She'd walked in looking confident and waved as soon as she saw me.

I approached, and gave her hand a gentle squeeze. "You look lovely." She did, too. Her hair framed her face well and she wore only a little make-up. She had a single fine silver chain necklace, two tiny stud earrings, and a couple of rings, but neither on the third finger of her left hand.

Her smile made her seem a little nervous and excited. I felt the same, but over the last eighteen months, I'd learned how to hide my true feelings and look relaxed, happy and confident. For a while anyway. I wanted more than anything to actually *be* happy and confident—to find real love again—but I was still recovering from an emotional train wreck of loss. For the time being, a convincing act was all I had.

She blushed ever so slightly. "Thank you." She didn't pull her hand away before I released it a couple of seconds later. Right then, I knew there was a pretty good chance she'd already decided our evening might last well into the morning.

We sipped pre-dinner drinks and made our choices from the menu, then chatted about the conference. She was organising one for the following year, and was keen to learn from my experience. I'd been impressed by her talk on medieval domestic life, but, as a horror film fan, I was more intrigued by her poster presentation outlining medieval myths and folklore about werewolves and vampires.

I selected an excellent wine from the list, better quality and far more expensive than my usual choices from whatever supermarket was convenient. I half-filled our large glasses and made an effort to drink at the same pace she did. With her to focus on, I didn't feel any reason to drink myself into numbness.

She quickly relaxed. As a lot of people had done at the conference, she asked about the jousting displays I did, and said she'd been impressed by the action photos and video clips on the team's social media pages and website. I was flattered that she'd taken the trouble to check them out.

"So, which is your true passion?" I asked. "Domestic history or mythology?"

"My academic specialism is domestic history, but I've loved supernatural stories all my life." She took a sip of wine. "Folklore about revenants and shapeshifters is ancient, but modern writers have changed them so much. King Canute's eleventh century legal codes had rules restricting werewolves, believe it or not. Vampire stories only developed their modern romantic edge in the nineteenth century. We don't take the supernatural seriously today, of course, and we're nowhere near as superstitious."

I encouraged her to tell me more, as I found it interesting and she was clearly enthusiastic. We discussed some of the TV shows and films featuring vampires and werewolves, agreeing that "American Werewolf In London" had the most plausible transformation scene.

The safe topic of shoptalk soon became happy general conversation, then friendly flirting. Her smiles became laughs and our fingers brushed over the basket of bread rolls. Our eyes held contact for longer and longer periods. She let me take her soft, warm hand in mine as we went back to the bar for brandy. We shared a comfortable sofa in a quiet corner and sat so close our legs pressed together. She leaned against me as she laughed, looked up, and our eyes locked. We shared a first tentative kiss, a gentle touch of her lips against mine.

"Can I make a gentlemanly offer to see you back to your room?" I asked.

She blushed again and looked away for a second. I thought I'd overstepped the mark, but she looked up, smiled shyly, and nodded. "I'd like that, Paul. Thank you." She paused, then looked me in the eye. "It's been a few years, so I'm a bit nervous."

"Don't worry," I murmured. "I know what 'no' means."

Our second kiss, in an alcove in the corridor, was far more passionate. She pushed me against the wall and ground her hips against me, giving me an unmistakable message.

"It's great being with a guy so much taller than me," she murmured.

"You're tall for a woman, but there must be plenty of men taller than you."

"I've not met many. What are you, six four, six five? It probably sounds silly, but it's lovely wearing heels and still having you taller than me. That's a real novelty."

"Doesn't sound silly at all." I stroked her hair and tucked some behind her ear. "I bet you want me to pick you up and carry you to your room."

Kathy raised her eyebrows a fraction of an inch and gave me a teasingly dirty smile. "Come off it, I'd put your back out."

"Not a chance."

She stretched up and kissed me. "If you're sure," she whispered. "I've always wanted to be carried and laid on the bed."

"Always happy to help a dream come true," I said. I picked her up and she snuggled against me as I carried her the last few yards to her door, where she had a fit of the giggles.

"You'll have to put me down, the key's hiding somewhere in my handbag," she said.

She opened the door and walked in backwards, towing me by my jacket lapels. "What was that about dreams coming true?"

I pushed the door shut behind me.

"You know it's only tonight, don't you?" she asked.

"Yes," I said gently. "But I'd be flattered if we could stay in touch as friends and colleagues."

She put her arms around my neck and kissed me. "Well, better help me get undressed," she whispered.

"Then carry you over to the bed?"

"Oooh, yes please."

We undressed each other hurriedly, both knowing what was coming and eager to start. I picked her up again, shuffled towards the bed and laid her down gently. She pulled me down beside her, then we hugged, kissed, and explored each other. Her full breasts were sensitive to my touches and kisses, and her pussy tasted hot, salty, and so exciting. Her first orgasm arrived quickly and was clearly intense. She was deliciously vocal as her climax approached and she moaned loudly as she crested, holding my head firmly in place with her hands.

We cuddled while she got her breath back, then she stroked my cheek. "Come on, you big hunk, fuck me."

I quickly put on a condom and slid inside her soft, warm

wetness. She felt gorgeous, her pussy hot around my cock, her arms around my back, her legs writhing around my thighs and her tongue against mine. We were both eager in our shared lust and want. I thrust hard, over and over again. She gasped and pushed her hips up against me. Her nails scratched and dug into my back as she came again with loud cries.

"Wow, that was amazing." She lay back and panted for a few seconds. "You going to come or what?"

"Pretty damn soon," I murmured.

"Oh, good." She purred as she wrapped her legs more tightly around mine and squeezed my backside with her hands, urging me on. "Get that cock right down inside me."

We ground against each other, so I was as deep inside her as I could be. My climax was a burst of intense pleasure as I shot hot pulses into my condom.

We cuddled and giggled while our sweat dried. We lay on top of the bed in the warm room. The duvet had been thrown aside in our haste.

"Wow," she said. "I'd almost forgotten that sex can be this much fun. Like being a student again." She leaned her arms across my chest, rested her chin on them, and grinned at me. "Fancy some sparkling wine? I left a bottle in the basin in the bathroom, in cold water."

She'd planned for this. I felt flattered. I removed the condom and folded it in a tissue. "Any glasses?"

"On the table. I'll get the wine," she said.

I watched her hips sway as she scampered across the room. She had a lovely figure with generous curves. I think men who don't appreciate watching a naked woman with a fuller figure as she moves around are really missing out.

Unbidden, my memory replayed a brief scene from my past, when I was watching Helen's naked bottom as she hurried across our bedroom, pink where I'd playfully spanked her. She'd leapt onto our bed, giggling. "I've been far naughtier than that, you should spank me again." We didn't do that often, as I wasn't completely comfortable hitting her, even as part of lovemaking and at her suggestion. I preferred things we could take turns in, like being tied to the bed and driven crazy with lust.

Kathy returned, wearing only a happy smile and carrying the wine. She passed me the bottle to open, and retrieved the glasses. We stood together, her tucked naked under one of my arms as we clinked glasses and sipped the wine. Which reminded me of something fun and a little silly Helen and I used to do.

"Put your glass down," I murmured and took a long sip from my own before putting it beside hers. I put both arms around her and she grinned up at me. I leaned down to kiss her and let the sparkling wine trickle from my mouth into hers, where it exploded into a fizzy shared experience.

She was startled for a fraction of a second, then burst out laughing. "The bubbles went up my nose."

"Want to try it again?"

"You bet. At least I know what to expect this time."

She giggled as we shared another sip of wine. When we finished the kiss, she looked up at me. "Right, you're in trouble now." She arched an eyebrow. "On the bed please. And no fidgeting."

Intrigued, I lay on the bed. She produced a fancy-looking box of chocolates and opened it, then selected two and put them on my nipples. Then she straddled me, bent down and slowly ate each one, licking and teasing my nipples with her lips as she did. As she moved, her pussy brushed against my cock, which started to swell again.

She moved to my side and placed four more chocolates in a line down my body, starting in the middle of my chest, then slowly ate each one. The fourth, placed on the tip of my cock, had melted a little before she got around to dealing with it. She had an exciting way of using her tongue.

"My turn." I gasped as she released me from a delicious teasing.

She rolled onto her back and I placed one chocolate on each of her nipples, one between her breasts, another on her tummy and the last one on her pubic hair just above her clit. Then I held one between my lips and leaned close enough for her to bite half of it. I chewed the other half, then kissed her, which made her giggle again. I took my time eating those on her body, which meant the one near her clit had started to soften.

"Oh, dear," I said. I looked up into her eyes and grinned. "It's melting down here. It may need some serious work to clean up."

"Oh, dear, indeed." She sounded a little breathless. "We wouldn't want to make a mess of these sheets."

She sighed happily as I enjoyed the chocolate slowly. She gasped when I got distracted by her lovely pussy and my tongue found her clit. Her next climax got us both in the mood for more sex.

"Can I be on top?" she asked.

"Of course." I quickly donned another condom, then lay on my back.

Our second bout was slower and good fun, with tickling and laughter. She slid down on me, sat astride my hips and eased up and down me, playing with her clit.

While she rode me, I was torn between wanting to play with her breasts and watch them jiggle and sway with her movements. She watched me until the last moment, when she had to close her eyes. Watching her face as she climaxed was a lovely sight, as she seemed so completely carried away. Then she lay on my chest and I held her loosely. She watched my face intently as she pumped me with her hips until I erupted again. I felt relaxed and happy. I could step further back from the edge of the pit of depression I'd been struggling out of. Our lovemaking was a brief, blissful reminder of what had been. And which seemed a lifetime ago.

Afterwards, she curled up beside me, with my arm around her.

Her head was on my shoulder and we shared a quiet and incredibly personal conversation. We were open with each other about our lives. She told me about her painful divorce, her two young children, and the male friend she knew was keen on her, but she was holding back from as she was scared to try again. I told her about Helen, something I'd not shared with anyone except my immediate family and closest friends.

"Someone special will want you in their life," she whispered. "You'll be perfect for each other."

All I knew for certain was that Kathy wouldn't be in mine after we parted in the morning.

She slept peacefully, her fine, light brown hair spread across the pillow and an arm across my chest. I lay awake beside her, feeling the fleeting contentment fade as I grew angry with myself and empty inside. Whatever it was I wanted wasn't here with Kathy, but that was my problem, not hers.

She was curled up with her back against me when we woke. My morning hard-on was touching her backside.

"Hard already?" She giggled, a lovely happy sound. "Well, shame not to make the most of it, since you're obviously keen for more of me."

"That's true," I said. Which it was.

She took a condom from the pack I'd left on the bedside cabinet and passed it to me. When I was ready, she manoeuvred herself and slipped over the tip of my erection, then bore down until I was deep inside her again.

We shared delightfully tender sex as I screwed her with slow, deep thrusts, nuzzled her back and shoulders, and stroked her breasts and tummy.

She guided my hands over her body. "I love your hands," she said, "So big, but so gentle on me." She half-rolled onto her back and guided my right hand between her legs. "I'd love you to bring me off while we're screwing." She left her hand on mine as I stroked her clit, giving me hints about where and how fast to move. We twisted a bit so we could kiss as we moved together. Her climax seemed to be a huge rolling wave for her, pulses from her internal muscles rippling against my cock, and she moaned into our kiss as she came.

"I love being screwed from behind," she whispered. "Take me hard. Fuck me into this mattress." She rolled onto her front, stretched her hands up and gripped the edge of the bed.

I slid into her again. She felt so hot and wet. The mattress was a little soft and bouncy for really vigorous humping, but we managed well enough. She came twice more before I couldn't hold back any longer, then we held each other close while we got our breath back.

When it was time to go, I kissed her tenderly. "Thank you so much, Kathy; that was absolutely lovely."

She stroked my cheek and looked touched. "And for me, too. Rather special." Was that a hint of a tear in her eye? She gave me a smile tinged with sadness and went for a shower. I dressed and slipped out of the hotel.

2

Standing under the shower in my flat an hour later, I didn't want to think about Kathy. So of course, I could think of nothing *but* her. In a few hours, she'd be back home, probably visiting her parents to collect her children, who were staying with them. No doubt she'd talk about the conference, how her presentation had gone, and all the interesting people she'd met. I guessed our night together would be her little secret, and I couldn't blame her for that. I was always puzzled why some people don't think women should actually enjoy sex, let alone have one-night stands.

So I beat myself up for being a stupid bugger yet again, falling into bed with a woman I knew could never be a part of my life. I'd found her genuinely interesting and attractive, and maybe, if things were completely different... In a few hours, I'd be alone in the bed I'd only ever shared with one person. At least I wouldn't have to keep up my act, pretending that I was coping and almost back to my old self.

I dressed, then went to grab some breakfast.

My sister Claire was there, leaning against my kitchen unit, sipping a mug of coffee. She gave me her single-raised-eyebrow treatment. "What time do you call this?" She turned and slipped some thick slices of bread into the toaster.

I filled a mug from the cafetière and slumped into a chair, too tired to argue. I looked up at her and let my weariness show. "Breakfast time." I felt guilty; I knew she'd come up to my flat because she was worried about me. I hadn't remembered to warn her I might not be coming home after the last day of the conference.

She looked at me. "So she didn't give you any?"

I kept my expression bland. "Breakfast? No. I left before the restaurant opened."

She fought to suppress a grin. "I don't want to know what she *did* give you."

I remembered moments from the previous night as I sipped my coffee, which was strong and bitter. I wondered if there was a silver lining in the black clouds filling my mind. More like looking for a silver needle in a field full of haystacks. I had to cut down on my drinking; alcohol was an evasion, not an escape.

Claire put a plate of toast in front of me, then sat down across the table. "Seeing her again?"

I shook my head. "Here for the conference. Divorced with kids. She stayed for the post-conference organiser's meeting, as she's running one next year and wanted to learn how we'd organised it." I took a bite from the toast and realised she'd put butter on the toast rather than the low-fat spread she kept putting in my fridge. She was definitely worried about me. And I felt as guilty as shit all over again.

"So you both had a bit of fun?"

I spread some homemade raspberry jam on the next piece. "Yeah, same as usual," I murmured.

Claire reached for my hand and squeezed it. "Why do you do this, Paul? You know chasing unavailable women will only hurt you in the end."

I knew that all too well. I didn't dare speak, not while my eyes and throat were burning.

Claire stood up, walked behind me, and wrapped her arms around me. "Look after that big soft heart of yours. Sleeping around isn't you. Helen would want you to find someone else and be happy, like we do. But you won't find anyone who'll save you until you're ready to try to save yourself."

I knew the truth when I heard it. And that truth hurt. Tears spilled from my eyes.

"I loved Helen, too, Paul," Claire whispered. "She was a good friend as well as a pretty darn good wife for my dopey brother."

"I know," I whispered. Even saying that was a struggle.

My big sister sighed, kissed the top of my head, and hugged me a little more tightly. "Go for a ride on Otto, that usually cheers you up. I've got enough escorts for this morning's ride, so clear off on your own. You can always go the gym later, as I don't suppose the one at the hotel was too good."

"Might do," I said. "Theirs was small but well-kitted out."

I knew it was good advice, and, as I wasn't in much of a mood to be with other people, I made Otto the first part of my plan for the day. I finished my breakfast, changed into jodhpurs and riding boots, and ventured outside. It was a lovely morning.

Otto was happy to see me and nickered as he trotted over to meet me at his paddock gate. I led him into a stable, where he munched hay while I brushed him down, then checked his legs, feet and shoes. His dark brown coat had dapples and a rich gloss which emphasised his muscles. He nudged me with his nose and leaned his chin on my shoulder, both ways he showed affection. He knew I was in pain. I hugged his neck for a few seconds, then tacked him up, put on my hat and body protector, and led him out into the yard.

The teenage girls preparing horses for the day's first escorted ride gave me their usual collection of wolf-whistles and applause when I vaulted from the ground across Otto's back and slid into the saddle.

"Jealous?" I shouted.

"Yeah, we all want eighteen hands between our legs," one called back, to chorus of giggles and laughter.

I patted Otto's neck. "They're definitely jealous," I told him. I waved to the girls, then let Otto set off at a gentle amble.

I saw no-one else on the moors, and enjoyed the scenery in peace and quiet. A few white clouds floated in a blue sky and I felt a gentle breeze on my face. Birds of prey hovered high above, ever-alert for their next meal. I went through the routines of warming Otto up, paying attention to his walk, trot and canter rhythms. They all felt right, so I let him have a gallop, lifting my backside out of the saddle so he could freely use his back muscles. The wind in my face and the slightly acrid smell of his sweat helped calm me and I tried to empty my mind.

When Otto stopped, I returned to the present and looked around. I hadn't given a thought to where we'd go, but he'd taken me to be with Helen again. Or at least, to the spot on the high moor where I'd scattered her ashes two years earlier. He stopped as if waiting for me to decide what we were doing next. I listened to the breeze and a sudden burst of bird song so loud it drowned out the snarl of a distant motorbike on the main road.

Was it the breeze and birdsong? Or was it Helen? Maybe it was my subconscious telling me to grow up? Something about the moment told me change was coming. In my heart-of-hearts, I knew I couldn't keep up the act—the only thing that kept me functioning—for much longer without the wheels coming off.

"I need to sort myself out," I told Otto. "I'll start with a thorough medical, cut back on drinking and get myself back on the right path."

Otto turned his head to look at me and I patted his neck. "But first of all, let's have another gallop."

An hour or so later, Otto was grazing in his paddock and I was back in my kitchen. I felt far happier as I waited for the kettle to boil and cut myself a slice of cake. Mum had excelled herself with that lemon drizzle sponge. I'd decided to go to the university gym late that afternoon, my usual time. I'd not made any effort to get to know anyone yet, but I liked seeing a few familiar faces when I was there.

"Yo, Romeo."

I turned to see my brother-in-law walking through my living room towards the kitchen. "Morning, John. Claire tell you to give me some stick?"

He laughed. "Me? Criticise all-night-Paul? Where d'you get the energy?"

"I don't have two young kids and a stressful job." I held up a mug and he nodded. I got my larger cafetière out, spooned in ground coffee and filled it with boiling water.

He cut himself a slice of cake, pulled out a chair and sat down. "True, but I ain't swapping. If anything happened to Claire, I'd be as fucked-up as you."

I ignored his little jest. Well, I treated it as a jest. I poured two mugs of coffee and sat across the table from him.

"Where did you meet her?" he asked around a mouthful of cake.

"At the conference," I said. "I knew her by reputation, an expert on medieval domestic life. She's a bit of a rising star, gave an excellent presentation. It was great to talk with someone so knowledgeable and enthusiastic." And her frequent eye contact and body language had made me confident an invitation to dinner on her free final evening would be welcomed, but I didn't say that to John.

"What's she like?" he asked.

I paused for a second, deciding how to describe her in the snappy way John liked. "Mid-thirties, good-looking, curvy, very bright, confident and articulate. Spoke and dressed well. Privately educated, read history at Oxford."

"So, you earned brownie points for being one of the organisers of a successful conference and got a bonus night of bonking a cuddly, posh, sexy historian?"

"One way to look at it." I looked at him and realised he hadn't come up just to tease me. He had something he was itching to tell me. He could keep a pretty straight face, but I knew him well enough to spot when he was excited. "Do I spot a 'good news' smile trying to creep over your face?"

He grinned broadly. "The Royal Cornwall Show booked our loony jousting show, six performances over three days. Major-league chance to show a large audience what we can do. Probably have a few seconds shown on local TV, too. We're replacing some daredevil act, which pulled out due to injury."

An exciting opportunity, but it would be hard work for all of us. "That's great." I sipped my coffee and immediately started running through the practicalities in my mind. "Bit too far to travel every day," I mused. "And as I'm the only single guy, it'd make sense if I stayed over with the horses and kit, wouldn't it?"

"You're psychic, mate. Should do a fortune telling act."

"Nah, I'm a mug."

"Three nights camping at the showground. Bound to be plenty of salespeople with stalls there, and then there's all those young lady farmers and farmers' daughters looking after livestock, and a bevy of shapely lady show-jumpers. Nudge, nudge, wink, wink."

I grinned behind my mug. I knew where this was going.

"You might even shag the same woman on two nights," he teased.

"What, like in a relationship?"

He sipped from his mug. "Claire's bet me twenty quid you score with two women at the show."

"What did you bet?"

"Thirty that you have the same woman two nights running."

I thought about that moment earlier, up on the moor with Otto. "Suppose I don't pull any women?"

He looked at me for a few seconds, surprised. But he knew I wouldn't lie to him about it, as we were always honest with each other.

"Let's make it no shagging between now and the last morning of the show," I said. *Where the hell did that come from?*

"A hundred," he said. "Charity of your choice."

I held my hand out. "You're on."

He snorted. "Might as well write your cheque out now; easy money." But we shook on it. This wasn't gambling, but an old-fashioned matter of honour.

You will win. It was as if I heard Helen whispering. But it might be a real challenge, as I hadn't been able to help myself for the last eighteen months.

"Better get the guys together," I said, switching back to business. "We'll need to figure out what we can do for that many shows, and practice, practice, practice to get it all rock-solid."

John nodded. "They're coming this weekend so we can start. Show's the first week of June."

"What? Bollocks. That's only six weeks. I'll check our kit over. Bound to need a few repairs."

"You need to get your head down, Paul," he said gently.

I shook my head. "Tonight, when I'm too tired to think. Otherwise, I'll be awake for hours." I'd had far too many sleepless nights, and many more when I'd drunk too much in a futile attempt to avoid dreaming. It was time to take a deep breath and try another way. Claire was right, as ever. I knew my current lifestyle wasn't doing my physical or mental health any favours. I had to save myself, even if it meant letting myself be vulnerable again.

But my first priority now was preparing for these six displays. There was time enough for John and I to get ourselves fit and ready to be the two lead performers, and to make sure all our horses were prepared too. But we had a lot of work to do to figure out how the team could put on six entertaining shows safely, ideally with noticeable differences between them all.

"Already got some ideas for new scenes," he said. "Want to grab some weapons in a bit and start working on them?"

"You bet, I'll take any chance to beat you up." I leaned my

chair back and, without looking, scrabbled for a notepad and pen in a drawer behind me. "Right, let's get started on some plans."

3

The herald's voice carried across the arena. "Our final contest today will be this third and deciding joust between John of Tavistock, wearing black, and Paul of Wadebridge, wearing white. The score is one lance each. With no love lost between these two noble gentlemen, we can expect a fine clash to settle matters."

I hoisted my lance, signalling readiness. The herald, in his red and gold tunic, acknowledged me. John neglected any courtesy and galloped down his tilt lane, his lance already levelled.

I grinned, closed my visor, tucked the lance under my arm and urged Otto forward. He took off like a racehorse. He loved jousting.

We met in the middle of the tilt, exactly as we'd rehearsed. I felt John's lance strike my shield and slide harmlessly up and over my shoulder. The first foot of my lance splintered against his shield, and he fell to the ground a few seconds later, landing flat on his back.

I threw the shattered lance well to one side, drew my sword and cantered around to stop beside the man lying on the ground. Otto was having the time of his life and showing off for the audience. He snorted loudly, tossed his head, then scraped at the turf with a front hoof.

I lifted my visor and hoped the radio microphone inside my helmet was still working. "Yield, or continue combat on foot?"

John raised both hands, then let them fall. That wasn't good and my chest immediately tightened with anxiety. He was my best mate as well as my brother-in-law.

"I yield," he replied, sounding distinctly breathless even over the PA, "but we will meet again and on that day, victory will be mine."

I saluted the herald, then rode Otto clear while two of the team rushed over. They helped John to his feet and supported him as he slowly walked away. At least he was on his feet. John's horse had been safely caught, and was quite calm as she was led out of the arena.

Half-listening to the herald as he wound up the show, I made a couple of final fast gallops around the edge of the display area, mere feet from the audience, almost all of whom shrank back. An armoured knight is an impressive sight, but on the back of a large horse, galloping towards you with a broadsword in his hand… We generally got lots of photos and video clips posted on our social media pages after a performance.

I heard the herald's final speech. "Thank you, boys and girls, lords, ladies and gentlemen. The Knights Errant hope you enjoyed the show. We'll be performing twice every day of the show, with different displays each time. If you're coming back to the Royal Cornwall Show tomorrow or the day after, we hope to see you again."

I slowed Otto to a trot and then a walk as we went towards the exit from the arena. I halted and Claire, my squire for that show, took my reins. "Looked great, Paul. The audience really enjoyed it."

I dismounted and took off my helm. "How's John? Did he land badly?"

"Only winded. Muttered something about being owed a pint."

"More than fair, that new fight he choreographed went down well."

"You two dump your armour, then go for a wander and relax, we'll tidy up," said Claire, in her no-nonsense tone. "You've not had a decent break all day. Go chill, pat yourselves on the back for two great shows."

I made a fuss of Otto, fed him a few treats, then hurried over to help clear the arena for the next event. Claire gave me a pointed look, but even though we weren't short of helping hands, I wasn't going to leave packing up to everyone else.

The show's main announcer came on the PA system. "We'd like to thank the Knights Errant for that excellent display." His voice was slightly nasal, his accent plummy. "It's their first time here at one of Britain's oldest, biggest, and best county agricultural shows, and what a fantastic show they put on for us."

Half an hour later, John and I sat down at a picnic table in one of the refreshment areas, each with a pint of chilled cider. Wearing brightly coloured replicas of fifteenth century gentleman's clothing, we'd been popular with anyone with a phone or a camera. We always had handouts with us for anyone who wanted one and happily signed them if asked.

"Excuse me, are you with the Knights Errant?"

I turned towards the clear, nicely-articulated voice and saw two pretty women, both smiling at us. I felt something like a shock when I saw them; I immediately found them both attractive.

One seemed to be a sort of gothic elf in black leggings and a black strappy top. She was slender, with stylish short brown hair and grey-green eyes. She had a cheeky smile and a small, slightly turned-up nose. She was probably in her mid- to late-twenties, but I found it difficult to guess her age. The sun had caught her face and shoulders, bringing out some freckles. She had a few tiny silver rings and studs in both ears. My instinctive impression: bright, full of fun and mischief. I definitely wouldn't have said no, and probably gone back for more, even if my fingers got burned.

Her companion had blue eyes, long blonde hair tied back in a ponytail, and sunglasses perched on top of her head. Her skin had a lovely glow from the sun, which suited her classic English rose look. I thought she was a little older than her friend, maybe around thirty. She wore faded jeans, a sleeveless blue tee shirt, and a loose scarf. She was slim too, but with a slightly curvier figure than her friend. I felt I should recognise her, but couldn't say why.

I immediately knew I wanted to get to know both of these women, even if took time, effort and a willingness to let my emotional guard down. That was an interesting and novel feeling, which I pushed aside to think about later.

"Yes," I said. "I'm Paul and this is my brother-in-law John. We manage the team."

"I do hope we're not interrupting, but we'd like to talk to you about some possible TV stunt work," the blonde said. She was the one who'd spoken before. She had a typical upper middle-class southern English accent, and struck me as being confident and professional.

John raised his eyebrows. "Please join us, ladies. Would you like a drink?"

"It's okay, thanks, I'll get some," said the gothic elf, who darted off to the bar.

The blonde sat down next to me. She seemed to be eight or nine inches shorter than me, the same as her friend. "I'm Hayley, Becky's my best friend," she said. "I'm an actress, she's mostly a stylist, doing hair and make-up for TV and fashion shoots."

I offered Hayley one of our fliers which she scanned, folded neatly, and put in her handbag.

Becky was back with two tumblers of white wine almost immediately and sat next to Hayley. From the way the two women behaved and looked at each other, it was obvious they were close friends.

"We thought both your performances were excellent," said

Hayley. "We're developing an early-evening family TV show, an hour-long romantic story with a medieval theme; dashing knights, damsels in distress, almost fairy-tale stuff. We're looking for some period stunt performers willing to get on board. We were really impressed by your display and wondered if it'd be okay for the director to meet you and see your show? We came down here with him to scout some locations for filming."

I glanced at John, who was trying not to grin too broadly. His daydream was to do some TV stunt work.

"Absolutely delighted," I said. "Would you like some guest passes? We were given some for our team and their families."

They both nodded. "Yes, please," said Becky. "We're staying nearby."

I looked at the two women, then glanced at John. "About the same size and height as Libby?"

He nodded, catching my drift. "Yeah, that might be a good idea." He turned to the women. "How about joining our show tomorrow, as the noble ladies we try to impress? We can lend you costumes so you'll be able to watch us at work from close-up. Libby usually plays that role; she's married to David from the team. But she's pregnant and stayed at home today; she's suffering morning sickness."

Becky gave Hayley a nudge with her elbow. "Yeah, go on, let's do it, Hayley. Be a laugh and a chance to see how we all get on." From her accent, I guessed she'd grown up in a middle-class family in the London area.

Hayley smiled at us both. "That's a great idea. I'm the female lead, so it'd be useful to see how well we can work together."

The two women exchanged a glance, then Becky sipped her wine and looked at me. "So how did you get into this, Paul?"

"It's an idea John and I talked about for a few years. When my wife died in a car crash, I took voluntary redundancy, moved here, got a couple of part-time academic jobs, and we set up the

Knights Errant with some equally potty mates. Mostly for fun, but we've been building up the show and had a few bookings. It'll never be a full-time thing, but we enjoy it and the reaction of the audiences always gives us a real buzz."

Hayley squeezed my arm. "Sorry about your wife."

I felt touched at her simple act of thoughtfulness. I looked at her, and realised her fine eyebrows and eyelashes were only just darker than her skin tone, which gave her an interestingly smooth appearance. "Thanks, it's been a tough couple of years."

"What did you do before?" asked Becky.

"Professionally, I'm a metallurgist," I said. "I've been interested in ancient arms and armour for years. I make our armour and weapons, and between us we make most of the other equipment and costumes."

The two women exchanged glances. "I'll be honest," Hayley said. "This is a pretty low-budget production, so any help with realistic props and costumes would be a huge relief. We're hoping an eye-catching pilot show will make a big enough splash to get funding for a short series with better budgets."

John grinned at me. "Claire and Libby love making medieval costumes."

"What about other periods?" Becky asked. "If this first one goes down well, the idea is to move on to what are basically just-for-fun rip-offs of popular movies and stories, all aimed at the Saturday early-evening family audience."

"We'd have to check," said John. "So long as they have time, designs, and fabrics, I guess they'd be able to do it. They've made some costumes for fancy dress, local amateur dramatic groups, living history people—stuff like that."

I poked around in the leather pouch on my belt and found some business cards. I gave one to each of the women. "Our social media details, email, and phone numbers."

"Great." Hayley quickly wrote her number in a notebook, tore out the page and passed it to me. Her handwriting was neat and rounded.

"The longer I look at you, the more familiar you seem," said John, looking thoughtfully at Hayley. "What is it I can't quite remember you from? Some ads? A show?" He closed his eyes for a couple of seconds. "Oh, I know, that children's series. My kids absolutely love it." He rapped the table with his fingers in concentration, then looked at her again. "Hayley Terence?"

Hayley nodded.

I looked blankly at John. "Hayley's on TV?"

He shook his head and looked at the women. "Don't mind Paul, he's bloody hopeless. He's usually working, riding, or exercising when kids' stuff is on TV. When you've finished your drinks, come and meet the rest of the team."

Back at our vehicles, John made introductions, and everyone was interested to hear about the possible TV work. I tried to be subtle about admiring Hayley's shapely backside, courtesy of her nicely fitting jeans, while she chatted with the team.

Becky came over to me and put her arm through mine. She didn't have to try that hard to get my attention, but I enjoyed it nonetheless. Helen and I had been very tactile with each other, and I missed that sort of simple human contact. "You've got a lovely team here, Paul."

"Thanks, the guys and I have all known each other for years, from school, college, or university. They've been helpful for me over the last year or so." I held up our envelope of guest passes. "One each for you two, what about your director?"

"Two, please. He and his wife are location scouting while we skive here." She looked at me. "You really don't know who Hayley is, do you? Or who her family is?"

"Not a clue," I admitted. "I've probably seen her on TV, but don't remember. She's just the friendly person I met today. I've had a pretty bad patch since Helen… Well, the world rolled along without me noticing much for a while."

Becky gave me a sympathetic smile. "Don't worry, she won't be bothered. I think it'll make a refreshing change for her. She gets a bit pissed off with people assuming she's the same person as one of the characters she's played. Or sucking up to her because she's been on TV. At least I don't have that problem, not being in front of the camera."

Hayley practically skipped over to us, looking happy. "Your sister's a sweetheart, isn't she, Paul? I'll have to make friends with her and find out your embarrassing secrets."

"She won't tell you any real dirt," I said airily. "I know plenty about her. We've got a sort of mutual benefit arrangement."

"We'll see," she said casually and exchanged a glance with Becky. They both grinned. I've never understood how close female friends in particular can share things so easily, and I suspected Claire would jump at the chance to wind me up a little with the odd tale she thought would make me cringe.

"When do you want us tomorrow?" Becky asked, raising one eyebrow.

"First show's at eleven, but allow at least an hour to get into costume and for us to run through our show with you. Local traffic will be heavy and slow, so it'll be a good idea to set off early."

"The dresses. Are they long enough to hide modern shoes?" Becky asked.

I'd not thought about that. "Hmm, not sure. Depends on your height. Leather ankle-boots would look about right. Ideally brown, if you've got any."

Hayley grinned and opened her mouth, but before she'd said anything, Becky sighed and rolled her eyes theatrically. "Okay, I give in; let's go shopping for bloody shoes. I know there are a few stands you want to go back to."

"We'll do the jewellery and craft stands, too," Hayley said. "See you tomorrow, Paul. We won't be late, promise."

Becky winked at me, then they wandered away together, arm-in-arm, towards the main retail area.

John wandered over to me. "So, what d'you think?"

"Chance of a lifetime. And you know I'll give it my best shot."

He gave me a what-are-you-like look. "I meant your new lady friends."

"Mine? Come off it, only just met them."

He grinned. "Might be mistaken, but I reckon they both seemed interested in you. You did a decent job keeping your tongue off the floor, though."

I probably gave him one of my better gormless expressions. "You what?"

He rubbed his finger and thumb together. "I can see you writing that cheque for one hundred pounds. If either of them snapped their fingers, you'd jump."

I couldn't deny that, but it seemed pretty bloody unlikely. I felt sure they both already had boyfriends, and even if they were up for a bit of fun, I didn't think either would abandon even a half-decent hotel room for the chance to share the cramped and stuffy sleeping area in the horse transporter cab with me. I gave him my long-suffering look. "I'm pretty sure I can last another two nights."

He raised one eyebrow and levelled a finger at me. "No porkies. I can always spot it when you try to hide something."

Annoyingly true. I wondered if I could persuade Hayley to give me some tips on acting so I could pull the wool over John's eyes now and again, if only for the hell of it.

He nudged me with his elbow. "Come on, let's get the horses settled and everything packed away. We're all keen to get away before the local roads go into gridlock."

"Yeah, worth getting rid of you all," I said. "I'll get some bloody peace and quiet."

I was struck how the atmosphere in the showground changed as late afternoon became early evening. Apart from the modest audience avidly watching the end of the day's show jumping, the public had gone home. The stallholders tidied up and restocked. The animals in the livestock marquees, sheds, stables and horseboxes were fed, watered, fussed over, and settled. I watched the show jumping for a while, as I knew a couple of the competitors, then went to find something to eat.

Everyone staying overnight seemed to congregate in the catering areas to relax and mingle. The bars and food stalls did good business and the air filled with chatter and the aromas of fast food. As the evening progressed, the chatting involved more and more flirting. It had been the same the evening before, but being dog-tired after a long day of getting everything arranged, I'd eaten, had a couple of drinks, then gone to bed early.

It felt a little odd, avoiding anyone who showed an obvious interest in me, pretending not to notice the encouraging smiles and other come-ons. But it also felt as if I'd taken an important step in my life, one which had given me an unexpected sense of peace and pushed the black cloud of my depression a little further away. Before this, I'd have been deciding which opportunity to pursue that night and which to defer until the next. But all that felt stale. Predictable. Uninteresting. Even so, I could easily have been tempted into a fun fling for the night after a few drinks too many.

Maybe I was simply tired. Like the rest of the team, I'd put my all into our two shows that day, after a poor night's sleep in the horse transporter cab. And I had to get up early the next morning to prepare myself and six horses, and be fit and ready for another two shows.

I bought some hot food, drank a couple of pints of cider and chatted, then slipped away before the come-ons got too obvious to plausibly ignore.

4

I woke in the small hours. I'd had an incredibly vivid dream, in which I'd woken beside Helen in the tiny bed in the pitch-dark horse transporter cab. We'd been lying face-to-face, and she was slowly stroking my very hard cock. "Hmm, wondered if I could get you to come right as you woke up," she'd murmured.

"You've tried that loads of times," I'd mumbled sleepily.

"Oh? And how does it usually work out?"

I'd run my hand down her body and slipped it between her legs. She was hot and wet. "With both of us coming."

She'd lifted her leg over mine and guided my cock into place against her body. "Well, we could have a quickie, I suppose. Better be gentle so we don't get the truck rocking too much."

I'd eased into her and we'd clung on to each other tightly, kissing deeply as I'd steadily thrust in and out of her. I'd known she was going to come from the way her grip tightened and her kissing became clumsy. Just as she'd climaxed, she'd leaned her head against my shoulder and I'd felt her teeth against my skin, coming myself a few seconds later. We'd held onto each other as we breathed deeply, sleep creeping up on me unusually quickly.

"You're a naughty boy," she'd whispered. "Just how I like you."

The last thing I remembered happening in the dream was her gentle kiss.

Before falling asleep again, I thought about it for a minute or so. I felt strangely comforted by the dream, which had been so realistic that it felt like a memory. Even though it was pretty much what we'd have done in the circumstances, I'd not owned a horse transporter until after she'd died.

I surprised myself by waking shortly after dawn that morning, feeling rested and happy, both of which were a welcome novelty. I realised I was looking forward to seeing both Becky and Hayley again and getting to know them better.

After our successful first day, everyone had arrived in good spirits. My parents were there too, to take Claire and John's children around the show. Libby and her modest baby-bump turned up with David, curious to meet the two new women she'd heard about. She and Claire shared a rather squicky compare-and-contrast discussion about the early stages of pregnancy. I was pleased to see her, and not just because she was a paramedic; she was great fun, full of life, and had a really macabre sense of humour.

Becky and Hayley were far earlier than I expected and looked eager to join in. The rest of the team were pleased to see them again, too. Becky seemed like one of the gang already; joking, teasing, and flirting light-heartedly.

"How do I look? Is this okay? How's my hair?" Hayley looked comfortable in the costume, but anxious. I was surprised to realise that a professional actor could suffer from nerves before a public performance as much as I did when I stood at the front of a lecture theatre full of students for my first lecture of a new academic year.

"You both look spot-on for your parts," I said. "Absolutely perfect in every way."

Claire had found her a cream-coloured undergown and pale blue overgown, both ankle-length, and it all seemed right on her. A silver-coloured chain around her waist gathered in the fabric to hug the curve of her hips. Lengths of her hair had been neatly braided to form a sort of headband; the rest was pulled back and plaited. I guessed Becky had done that, as Hayley had told me she did hair and make-up for actors and models. I could plait horse tails and manes pretty well, and recognised a good job when I saw it.

Becky was delighted with the more gothic look Claire had suggested, and flounced around happily in a black undergown and a bottle-green overgown with a long, flowing skirt, and a long black veil hanging down her back. She chatted happily with Claire. It looked like all three women had already hit it off. Was that good or bad?

All morning, I'd found myself watching one or the other, Hayley a little more often than Becky, who I knew was teasing me. She'd pointedly catch my gaze, hold it briefly, then look away. But I often found Hayley looking at me. I'd soon have to concentrate on our performance and try not to gawp at these two intriguing and attractive women.

I fancied them both pretty much equally, but in different ways. Becky was cute, more confident, outgoing, and liked being the centre of attention. She appealed to the overgrown child inside me. Hayley, more of a beauty, quieter, and a little more reserved, brought out the protective side of me, the one I'd been hiding from the world for the last two years.

I tried not to stare as Hayley smoothed out some almost invisible creases in her costume, as the movement of her hands emphasised the way the fabric flowed over her breasts and down to her stomach and hips. "Do you put the same show on each time?"

"We always start with demonstrations of skill-at-arms, horsemanship, and some of the training exercises knights did: bashing quintains, picking up rings, and stuff like that." I passed her a small coronet and a white veil. "We finish with a fight of some sort in the mornings and jousting in the afternoons. John and I take turns to lose, to share the chance of injuries. Even a planned and rehearsed landing can easily knock the wind out of you and leave bruises."

It was almost time to set up. I looked around, noticed that Becky and Claire were talking intently, then glanced out at the arena. The last of the show-jumping fences were being cleared away from the arena and our tilt fence, quintains, and other equipment were loaded on trailers ready to be taken out.

"Two of the guys still aren't confident enough with their riding to join in with the mounted displays," I said. "Two others can ride well enough, but not joust safely yet, so only John and I do that. We've choreographed and rehearsed a number of combat routines, both on horseback and on foot. This morning, we'll end with a mêlée, which should look like a manic, full-on free-for-all. This afternoon we'll do something different."

As we walked out, I pointed towards a low platform which had been set on one side of the arena. "You and Becky can sit on those little thrones and look all important and disinterested. We'll try to impress you with our skill and daring."

Forty minutes later, they both sat anxiously on the edges of their seats. Hayley had a hand over her mouth and her eyes were wide open, while Becky peeped between her fingers and jumped every time our swords clashed. The fight ended when John appeared to kick me in the groin. I bent forwards and his sword struck the back of my helm. I slumped theatrically to the ground, then lay still. I grinned when I heard booing mixed with applause. He loved playing the bad boy, always cheating, and breaking the rules. Gave him a complete change from real life.

The herald's voice came over the PA. "As the last man standing, Sir John is the victor in the mêlée, and may now claim his prize from Lady Hayley." John sheathed his sword, swaggered over to the platform, bowed graciously, and accepted the gold-coloured goblet offered by Hayley, to applause from the audience.

A few seconds later, the herald drew our performance to a close.

"Now by the magic of tourney, the fallen may rise."

I rolled over and climbed to my feet. I needed a cold drink and a fresh T-shirt. It was a hot day and we'd put some energy and enthusiasm into our well-rehearsed mayhem, in heavy armour well-padded for safety. I'd already swallowed some ibuprofen tablets, hoping to offset the aches and sore muscles I expected to have later.

I picked up and sheathed my sword, then walked over to Hayley and Becky. "So, how was it for you, ladies?"

"Bloody scary," said Becky. She jumped off the platform and squeezed my arm. "Bloody near peed myself a couple of times. You don't half go for it, don't you?"

"All carefully rehearsed, so we know what's coming next. It looks vicious, but we always hold back and the weapons are blunt. So it looked okay?"

Hayley nodded her head vigorously. "God, I'll say. You work really well as a team, it looked so realistic. I'll be amazed if Phil doesn't offer you the job on the spot when he sees you tomorrow."

"That's great, thanks." I offered Hayley my hand and she accepted it as she stepped elegantly off the platform. "We've only got a few minutes to clear the arena for the next event, then we'll untack and settle the horses."

"Come on, Becky, let's help. I want to see those lovely horses again."

A couple of minutes later, they walked past me out of the arena, their arms laden with rolled-up banners. They both seemed anxious, and looked intently into the crowd over near the row of corporate stands on the far side of the arena.

"It can't be him, he's in London," I overheard Hayley say.

Becky shrugged. "I'm sure. He was proper looking daggers at you. Let's keep out of the way."

A little later, I found Becky in the truck, rifling through our collection of costumes. "Don't want to seem nosey, but I overheard you and Hayley, and you seemed to be worried about someone. Anything I can help with?"

"Hope not. I thought I saw Hayley's ex in the crowd." She shrugged. "He's the sort of dickhead who'd make a scene, but he worked in London the last time I heard about him."

"There's always someone around, so shout if you get worried."

She smiled. "Thanks. He's a big guy and has a bit of a temper; I wouldn't be able to do anything to stop him."

I left her to find John and tell him. As I walked past our horse transporter, I heard voices come from inside it.

"Tony, please no…" It was Hayley. And she sounded afraid.

I looked in and saw her in the far corner, looking scared and cowering. An overweight man in a dark grey business suit towered over her. His fists were clenched and his upper body was tense.

"It's your fault my career stalled," he shouted. "This was my big chance to move on. And you have to show up here and make me blow it." He raised his right hand.

I didn't think, just reacted. I ran in and caught his wrist as he started swinging his hand down towards Hayley. He turned towards me and punched out with his other hand, then gasped as it slammed hard against the steel breastplate I still wore. The guy's breath was aromatic from alcohol. His eyes widened in shock when he took in my appearance, an armoured warrior a few inches taller than him.

"Fucking hell." He pushed past me and stumbled out of the vehicle, rather unsteady on his feet.

Despite being tempted to catch the guy and kick his arse, I turned to Hayley. "Are you okay? Did he hit you?"

She moved towards me and I put my arms around her. She trembled and sobbed for a few seconds.

"No, because you arrived in time." She sniffed. "He's my ex-boyfriend. We split up last year, when I finally realised he's a bully. He works in their Oxford office now, but he's on his firm's stand here. Something about an opportunity to prove himself. But he's been drinking."

She sat on a trunk, pulled a tissue out of her handbag and blew her nose. "He said he spotted me in the crowd yesterday and accused me of trying to make him mess up an important property negotiation."

I took off my gloves and squeezed her hand. "Tell you what, you get into the transporter cab and draw the curtains. The back seat is completely hidden. You'll be safe there. I'll get Becky to sit with you. Give me a few minutes to check up on things. I'll be back as quick as I can."

I saw Hayley safely into the cab, found Becky, and explained.

"That arsehole wanker tosspot," she muttered. "I'll fucking kill him." Then she hurried off to join Hayley.

I wanted to teach Tony an unpleasant lesson. I always tried to control my temper, being conscious of my size and strength, even as a youngster. At school, I'd scared the shit out of a lad with a single thump on the nose because he'd been upsetting Claire. I was furious with Tony for harassing Hayley and felt relieved I'd stopped him from hitting her. But I wanted him to pay for his boorish petulance.

I didn't know what I was going to do, but set off in the direction he'd gone. I spotted him almost immediately as that area of the showground was fairly empty. He was easy to follow from a distance as he tottered across an exhibitor's car park. He unlocked a car and climbed into the back seat, apparently oblivious to the large armoured knight trailing him. He had a couple of quick drinks from a half-bottle of something and lay down.

I waited for a minute, but nothing happened, so I approached and cautiously glanced into the car. He was flat-out on the rear seat, apparently fast asleep. I walked around the car. From the registration number, it was only a few months old, and the number plates bore the name of a leasing company, so I guessed it was a company car. I thought about letting all the tyres down, or covering him with fresh horse dung while he slept. Then I saw he'd dropped his car keys in the rear passenger footwell.

I had an idea and pulled out my mobile phone. "David? I need to do something underhanded and disreputable to help damsels in distress. Any chance you can help? I'm in the exhibitor's car park nearest to our transporter. Can you bring Libby? Don't say anything to John, though."

Ten minutes later, I dropped David's chain mail off in the back of the truck, shook out both my arms for a couple of seconds to restore the circulation, then knocked on the transporter cab door. Becky peeped through the curtains, then opened the cab door to let me in. Half-way up, I realised it would have been sensible to dump my own armour first, but silly male pride won the day.

Hayley still looked upset. "Paul, thanks for helping. It's not your problem though, and I don't want to involve you or anyone else."

"I'm already involved," I said. "Tony was trespassing in our transporter, he hit me and threatened you, but I don't think he'll bother you here again."

"Why? How?"

I shrugged. "Well, if you're a damsel in distress and I'm wearing shiny armour, why can't there be a fairy-tale happy ending?"

They looked at each other, then at me. "You've not done anything to him, have you?" asked Becky, rather suspiciously.

"Hand on heart, I've not touched him. I saw his car leave the showground a few minutes ago. I'm sure he's perfectly safe. He'd clearly had a few drinks and, unless he's pulled over for drink driving, will probably be sleeping it off before long."

They both gave me a "yeah, right" look, but I kept a straight face. They looked at each other again, that funny telepathy thing some close friends can do.

"The least I can do is buy you all lunch," said Hayley. She smiled at me shyly. "But to say thanks…" She slid onto my lap and kissed me gently on the lips.

I was surprised and delighted. She felt lovely in my arms, even through my padding, mail, and plate armour.

"Bet you've never snogged anyone wearing armour before," Becky said.

"Don't knock it, Becky," said Hayley. "It's not far off a chastity belt for the guy."

"Come on," I said. I felt awkward, but flattered by the kiss. "Let's all get something to eat and drink. You won't need to buy anything, so don't worry."

Mum had brought along a huge collection of sandwiches, pasties, sausage rolls, pastries, doughnuts and soft drinks, and Dad's propane water heater was already up to temperature for tea and coffee. Claire was eager to chat with Becky and Hayley, which I was sure gave them both a welcome distraction.

Fifteen minutes later, David and Libby quietly reappeared, looking innocent as babes.

"And where have you two been?" Claire had more than a hint of suspicion in her voice.

"Running a little errand," Libby said casually. She and Claire went off a short way, spoke quietly, then parted in giggles.

David ambled over to me. "Libby checked and he's medically fine, but out for the count, safe and sound in the recovery position, as best we could manage it. His car's in the middle of a field a few miles away. Took some backroads, and didn't pass any police or highways cameras, so no comebacks. The police have had an anonymous phone call and he'll soon be in safe hands."

"Thanks, David, bloody good work. I'll get you a couple of bottles of something nice from the food hall."

"Pity Libby's not drinking at the moment," he said. "She loves mead, and this is a great place to buy some."

"It'll keep," I said. "I'll get you some this afternoon. You're sure no-one saw you?"

"Certainly no-one official," he said. "There was a guy walking a huge grey dog in the area when we left and he was still there when we got back, but he didn't seem to pay us any attention."

Becky walked over to us, stopped right in front of me, put her hands on her hips, then raised both eyebrows pointedly. Somehow, I managed to keep a straight face and said nothing.

5

After the afternoon show, I was in the truck checking our armour and weapons for damage when Hayley climbed in and beamed at me, still in costume.

"I've had a brilliant day, even with the Tony thing this morning. I hope Phil likes what he sees tomorrow, it'd be great to work together properly."

"We'd all jump at it."

She gathered up her skirts, sat down on a trunk, and looked at me with interest. "Ever acted?"

"Other than playing around in these shows, only some minor roles in a couple of school plays." I sat down opposite her. "How did you get into it?"

She shrugged. "I'm basically an insecure, attention-seeking show-off, I guess. Both my parents act, so what else could I do?"

Becky and Claire walked past, engrossed in conversation. "It sounds like they're as bad as each other," Claire said.

Hayley and I looked at each other.

"Up to no good?" I whispered.

Hayley nodded. "Plotting and scheming, without a doubt. Becky can be a major pain at times, but she's a total sweetie. She reckons I need to find a new boyfriend who isn't a dickhead, and I can see her point."

"Claire's much the same. She's a big sister in a million."

Hayley sighed. "I was so hurt by Tony. And that was on top of a couple of other bad choices before him. Guess I need to meet someone prepared to let me take my time and learn to trust them."

I nodded. "Yeah, I can understand that. I've not dated anyone since, well, you know. All my girlfriends had been friends first. And Helen was…" I trailed off, my throat suddenly tight.

"A tough act to follow?"

I swallowed and nodded. That was as good a way to put it as any other.

Hayley looked down. She linked her fingers together tightly, then looked up at me. "Met anyone who you think might fit the bill?"

I thought she sounded more than a little nervous. I paused, wondering how to say it. My mouth suddenly going dry didn't help. I felt nervous, too, and wasn't keen on making a fool of myself, or messing up what might be the chance of a lifetime. But I felt I had to clearly hint that I found her attractive and would very much like to spend more time with her. "I rather think I have. Very recently. Someone I want to get to know a lot better. She's interesting and I already know I like being with her. Totally different from anyone I've met before. And you?"

She swallowed and nodded, smiling shyly. "Yeah, I'm beginning to think so, too," she said.

My tummy did a brief skippy dance. "Come on," I said, "the showground's a great place for an aimless wander." We both stood, I offered her my arm and she put hers through it.

Becky and Claire gaped open-mouthed at us as we walked past, arm in arm. Their faces were a picture.

"Going for a quick wander," Hayley told Becky. "I've got my phone."

Half an hour later, I'd become more comfortable about people staring and taking photos as we wandered around in medieval clothing. We were watching a judge trying to decide which of six identical sheep was the best in its class when Hayley snuggled up against me. My arm seemed to fit around her perfectly and she slipped her arm around my waist. She looked up and I looked down. I swallowed hard and had to ask the scariest question I knew. I'd always found it hard, and I'd not asked anyone this for eight years.

"Hayley, can I see you again? Other than for the TV show, I mean?"

She smiled at me and nodded, all the answer I needed. I let out the breath I'd been holding.

Our first kiss was soft and gentle, the lightest touch of our lips. The second was longer and more confident, our lips parted and our tongues met tentatively for a few seconds. She giggled and I felt all nice and warm inside.

"How long does it take to drive between Devon and Sussex?" she asked.

"Hmm, probably around four hours, I reckon. Slower in the school holidays."

"Oh, well." She sighed. "We'll have to take it in turns. It'd only be fair. Assuming you think I'm worth the effort."

I put my arms around her waist and picked her up off the ground so our faces were level, to her surprise. "I'll be grown-up, Hayley. No games. I've had more than my fill of that and I guess you have, too. You don't need to fish. I think you're absolutely lovely, all right? You're worth a bloody long drive."

She grinned and kissed my forehead. "Okay, message received. I'm not used to guys with emotional intelligence. Or ones who can literally pick me up."

"You do live in Sussex, don't you?"

She slapped my shoulder playfully and I put her back on the ground.

I spotted a bar nearby. "Fancy a drink?"

"Ooh, yeah. What's the cider like?"

"The usual mass-market stuff, but at least it's cold. A pub near me does a few local ones, some you can't see through."

"That's the sort I like." She grinned up at me. "A headache waiting to happen."

I squeezed her hand. I felt happier than I had for a couple of years. I'd met two interesting women and made a tentative start on a relationship with one of them. I had no reservations about that, so maybe that moment on the high moor when I sensed impending change had been a premonition.

I felt Hayley's hand in mine. I'd been prepared to get into a fight to protect her, without a second thought. And realising that gave me an idea…

"Could you and Becky hang on a while this afternoon? We always have a quick meeting to sort out what we're doing tomorrow. I've got a plan I want to run past the guys."

She grinned at me. "A plan, Sir Knight?"

"Verily, Madam. A cunning plan."

She hugged my arm. "How cunning?"

"More cunning than the cunningest plan by a Professor of Cunningnousnous."

"Cunningnousnous?" She raised an eyebrow.

"It'll involve Becky, too."

"If it sounds like fun, causing trouble, or being the centre of attention, she'll be up for it, drink or no drink."

*****

The women were both curious by the time I addressed our end-of-the day team talk. Becky had tried to tease some hints out of me, and had even pouted rather theatrically when I wouldn't give in.

"Okay, Hayley's producer is planning to be here tomorrow," I said. "And I've been wondering how we can make the best possible impression. What do we all think about doing a slight variation on our brand-new routine?"

Everyone nodded in agreement, except John, who looked doubtful, even though I'd discussed it briefly with him earlier. I guessed he was playing Devil's advocate, to encourage anyone else with reservations to speak up. "We've only rehearsed it with Libby, remember," he said. "I know there's nothing the guys particularly need to rehearse, but, well, with your new idea, too…"

He paused, then looked at Hayley and Becky. "Are you two up for a much bigger role tomorrow morning? Right in the thick of the action? Little bit of improvisation?"

They didn't even look at each other before nodding.

"Do I get a sword?" asked Becky, a little too eagerly.

"Sorry, not this time," I said. "Insurance and all that. We'll run through it in the morning, but one of you can be a princess kidnapped by this gang of despicable rogues and outlaws." I waved my hand at the team around us. "The other can be her lady-in-waiting, who fights back, escapes, then finds me. I proceed to be all heroic, rescue the princess and leave a pile of bodies behind me."

The two women grinned at each other. "You fancy being the princess?" Becky asked Hayley. "I've always wanted to do a fight scene."

Hayley grinned. "So long as it's not me you're attacking. You fight dirty."

"Can either of you ride?" John asked.

"I used to," Becky said, "When I was a youngster."

Hayley looked uncertain. "I could sit on a quiet horse without falling off. Probably."

John nodded. "Not a problem, just thinking about how to start off." His brief grin at Becky's enthusiasm had been enough to show me that he'd decided we'd do it.

We looked up at the sound of a new voice. "Hi, John." A uniformed police sergeant walked over to us.

John looked surprised, but pleased as they shook hands. "Greg. What's up?"

Hayley sidled over to me and put her arm through mine.

Greg took his cap off and ran a hand over his bald patch. "Patrol car followed up an anonymous call," he said, in a broad local accent. "Found some guy from up London way sleeping like a baby in a fancy car, in the middle of this field a few miles away. The police surgeon reckoned he'd had a bad reaction between alcohol and some prescription drugs he's been taking for stress or something."

John offered Greg a cold bottle of a soft drink, which he gratefully accepted and took a long drink from.

David looked questioningly at me and I discreetly shook my head. I felt Hayley tense beside me, and I squeezed her hand to reassure her.

"Anyhows," Greg continued, "he couldn't remember how he got there, but swore blind he'd not driven. He was over the drink-drive limit and we found a trace of cocaine in a plastic bag hidden in the car, too. He's here on one of them big corporate stands, offering rental property management services, and his boss was proper pissed about making a late-evening trip to the station to collect him."

"What are you going to do?" asked John.

"His boss ripped him a new arsehole in front of everyone at the station, and told him to clean up his act or else. He offered to sort out some counselling, a last chance sort of thing. We were discussing what to charge him with, then it got a bit odd. This bloke from something called the National Investigation Task Force turned up, questioned him and had a word with the inspector. No idea who they are, but they obviously have some clout. The inspector says no evidence of an offence other than possession, first offence and piss-all coke anyway, so just caution him and send him on his way."

John looked rather surprised. "Fair enough," he said. "So how can we help?"

"Checking a minor detail. He said something about knights, but his recollection was proper confused. I was on duty here today and knew you were doing your show, so wondered if you'd seen him."

"Found a guy in one of our transporters after our show this morning," I said. "He seemed drunk and unsteady on his feet. He got a bit aggressive and hit me, then wandered off."

Greg looked at me with obvious surprise. "He hit you?"

"Yeah, on the chest, but I was wearing armour. Didn't even feel it."

Greg grinned. "See where he went next?"

I waved an arm. "That way, towards an exhibitor's car park, I think."

"Did anyone else see him?" He looked around.

"I did." Hayley raised a hand tentatively.

Greg looked at her. Still in costume, she was probably just one of our team as far as he was concerned. "Is that right, miss? Did he appear to be drunk and aggressive?"

She nodded. "Yes, and I saw him hit Paul."

Greg nodded. "Thank you, no need for statements, I think. It all fits. I'll mention it to the inspector and that's that."

John nodded. "I'll catch up with you next week, Greg."

After he walked out of earshot, Becky and Claire leaned against the truck together in a fit of giggles.

John looked at me. "And what was that all about?"

I shrugged, trying hard to keep a straight face and look innocent. "We answered his questions truthfully. It seems a fair outcome for whoever that guy was."

He raised his eyebrows and looked around. David and Libby deserved Oscars for their innocent looks, and everyone else looked non-plussed. "So why didn't you tell me about it at the time?"

Hayley squirmed and blushed. "I asked Paul not to, it's embarrassing."

"No big deal," I said. "Doing my knightly duty."

"Yeah, right." John looked at Hayley.

"He's an ex who wanted to blame me because he messed up a business deal he was negotiating. It was all over in seconds." She calmly returned John's stare. "How come you and that sergeant were so chummy?"

"I'm a detective in my day job," he said, managing not to seem embarrassed. "I've known Greg for years; met him when I started in uniform, taught me a lot. Good old-fashioned copper. Decent, solid guy."

That released the tension, and the team and their families wandered off to their cars a few minutes later.

When the others had left, Hayley gave me a hard look, then stomped over to Becky and Claire. "We need to talk," she said firmly. She took their arms and dragged them both around the side of the truck.

Later, right before John and Claire left, my sister pulled me to one side. "Don't mess it up, okay? If you do, I'll kick your arse so hard you won't be able to sit down for a week."

I looked at her in genuine puzzlement. "What?"

She gave me her "are you for real" look. "You really do need help, don't you?" She squeezed my hand and looked at me intently. "Give it a chance, Paul," she urged. "Let your guard down for once. Please."

6

When Becky and Hayley arrived the next day, there was something of an atmosphere between them, as Hayley seemed quieter and Becky a little more over the top than the day before. My rational brain quietly told me it would blow over quickly, but my fragile self-confidence loudly proclaimed that I'd done something wrong, upset them both, and blown my chances out of the water.

Claire spotted it, muttered something and grabbed the two women. "Come on, we're off for bacon baguettes and coffee."

Twenty minutes later, things were back to more like normal. John always said Claire would have made a great police officer with her knack for sorting things out.

From their behaviour and body-language, I had a hunch that Becky was annoyed with Hayley. My anxiety level went down a few notches, but I felt worried that by making a move on Hayley, I'd caused a rift between them.

We talked the women through the scene, then Claire made sure they were both happy sitting on the two quietest horses we had with us. The time for our first show arrived. It went like a dream from my point of view; we all got the timing spot on, nothing went wrong, and no one was injured. While Becky's character was looking for me, Bonnie Tyler's "I Need A Hero" was played over the PA. The audience reacted well, which was a great confidence boost for all of us.

Hayley introduced us to their producer, Phil, and his wife, Sarah, after our performance.

"That was fabulous. I'd love to use exactly that scene," he said. "It would fit the storyline well. And you all look like the real deal, used to the combat and weapons, and you've got impressive costumes and kit. The audience response around us was great."

Sarah nodded. "How much rehearsal did you all do? When Becky kicked that guy between the legs during the kidnap, everyone around us winced, laughed or cheered, it looked so realistic."

David, the guy in question, muttered. "I'm glad her aim wasn't better."

Becky blushed with embarrassment. "Sorry, I did get a bit carried away, didn't I?" She turned back to Sarah. "No rehearsals for us, we just played along with the guys. They made it easy."

"That thing when you took on six armed guys one after the other looked great, Paul." Phil looked thoughtful. "You all really went for it, didn't you? With the right camera work, that could be an amazing single-take sequence."

"Thanks. John put a lot of thought and time into choreographing it. Everyone put in an awful lot of work. The whole show's a big team effort."

Sarah nudged Hayley. "And you looked so lovely, sitting up there with him as you rode off. Classic happy ending, nice move."

Behind her, Becky mimed sticking two fingers down her throat, but I kept a straight face. I was pleased to see both she and Hayley were behaving more like they had the day before.

"Well, it's a fairy-tale ending, which means we can ride around the arena and wave at the audience," I said. "It goes down well, particularly with children."

Hayley shuddered slightly. "You try looking happy when you're terrified. The ground's a long way down from the top of that horse and we were going way too bloody fast."

"Well, I was convinced." Sarah winked. "And I don't think your dashing knight would have let you fall."

"Any chance I can get some video?" Phil asked. "Impressive stunt performances like yours will help me when I try to sell the show to the networks."

John nodded. "We've got quite a lot of action stuff on HD I can e-mail you."

Phil looked around the team. "We're confident we'll get the finance in place next week. I'll email John as soon as I can and formally offer John a role as combat consultant, and all of you contracts as stunt performers and extras." We all shook hands.

Phil took Hayley and me to one side. "Paul, I need a leading man who can convince a family audience he's the real deal. Hayley says everyone's happy and settled in regular full-time jobs, except you. Have you ever acted? Or thought about it? You really do look the part and it's not likely to be a challenging role. We've not cast it yet, and I'd struggle to find a professional actor who could do a fraction of what I saw today."

Hayley snorted. "You can act better than you think, keeping a perfectly straight face after pulling that stunt the other day." She put her arm through mine and looked up at me with what seemed to be an anxious, silent appeal. I wondered how much she knew about what David, Libby and I had done, but if she knew, it didn't seem to bother her.

No harm in trying, I told myself. I nodded at Phil. "I'd give it my best shot. Not sure how I'll compare to the professionals you're used to. I have been on TV before, though, one of the experts in a documentary about swords, presented by the actor Trevor Western."

Phil nodded. "I've worked with him." He gave Hayley a brief questioning look, but she said nothing. I guessed something had gone way over my head, but it probably wasn't important.

Phil carried on. "This'll be a low budget production, working fast with a small crew and using filming techniques often used in sports and reality TV shows. Cameras hidden in the set, on boom arms and even on drones. I want to do some long single takes, let the cast improvise a bit. I want to engage them and the audience in the story. Your team's high-energy on-the-run combat stuff is ideal. It won't be easy to record, but it'll look bloody fantastic."

"Why not set up a screen test?" Hayley looked at me. "We can improvise a scene or two from the storyline and it'll give your confidence a huge boost to see yourself on-screen. You can clearly do complicated and demanding physical routines, and, as you're a university lecturer, you can learn and deliver material, or improvise around an idea." She turned to Phil. "I'll organise some coaching for Paul if you sort out Equity memberships for them all."

With that agreed, we returned to the team, where Sarah was chatting with the rest of the gang. "So what's your afternoon performance?" she asked.

John answered. "The first part will be broadly similar, but followed by a joust. How would you like to join Hayley and Becky as our guests of honour? Best seats in the house."

Sarah glanced curiously at Becky's and Hayley's outfits.

"We've some great costumes," David said.

"That sounds rather fun," Sarah said to Phil.

"We'd be delighted," he said. "Any chance I can be a lord?"

Behind me, I heard Claire talking on her mobile phone. "Yeah, in the main arena, about three this afternoon…" She looked up and saw I was watching, then blushed, turned away and lowered her voice.

She's up to something, I thought.

"Come, Sir Knight." Hayley tugged my arm. "Tarry not, we must hasten hither."

I grinned. Messing about with mock Shakespearean English sounded like fun. "Hasten hither? Why, madam, what distresseth you thus?"

She put on an overdone exasperated expression, and waved towards the nearest catering area. "Why, sir? Yonder cider barrel is nigh ready to rupture, save that we drink a flagon thereof."

Sarah giggled and Phil shook his head. "She's as mad as her dad," he said. "His weakness is gin."

"Pray join us, gentles," I said, bowing to Sarah and Phil. I turned to Hayley. "Make full haste to yonder cider barrel, mistress, that we may yet relieve its suffering." I held one arm up for her, the other for Becky, and we set off for the bar.

Ten minutes later, Sarah was giggling into her wine and I was struggling to keep up with Hayley, but didn't want to give in first.

Becky spluttered and coughed after laughing while trying to drink. "For God's sake, give it a rest you two." She wiped her face with a tissue. "I'm laughing so much I've just snorted cider down my nose."

Phil shook his head and grinned. "If you two can improvise nonsense like that in front of us, no need for a screen test."

Hayley squeezed my arm. "Welcome to the world of acting, Paul."

An hour or so before our final show, Becky wandered over to me. "Come on, you can help me pick out costumes for Sarah and Phil."

I felt a little surprised that she'd asked me rather than Claire, but she wasn't in sight. I got the impression she had something on her mind, as she seemed a little reserved, and I hoped it wasn't bad news.

We rifled through the costumes in the lorry and picked a few suitable items out, then we both stood up and Becky looked a little nervous. "Can I say something?"

"Of course."

She grabbed my arm and pulled me around so the costume trunk was right behind me. I took the hint, shut the lid and sat down.

"I've been talking to Claire," she said. "It's obvious she and John have been worried about you, but they think you're turning yourself round." She took a deep breath. "I'm pretty sure you fancy both me and Hayley, but don't know what to do. It's kinda lovely that you're being such a gentleman about it."

She hitched up her long skirts and sat astride my thighs, which completely took me by surprise. I instinctively put my hands behind her back to keep her steady. Up close, her eyes were lovely, hazel with dark flecks. She cupped my face with her hands and I suddenly felt nervous.

"Hayley's insecure at the moment and won't push her luck. She had a huge boost when you asked to see her again, and I was surprised you did it so quickly. I'll do what I can to encourage her, but it's down to you two to figure it out." She paused for a second, then took a deep breath. "She's not forward, like me. I was planning to try and pull you today." She bit her lip. "Look, if it doesn't work out with Hayley, so long as she's okay about it, I'll grab you like a shot."

She leaned forward a few more inches and kissed me on the lips. Very gently. "And you won't know what's bloody hit you," she murmured.

We kissed again, her tongue briefly tickling mine. I felt awkward, as it seemed a very intimate thing to do with Hayley's best friend.

She leaned back and grinned. "But if I ever think you've intentionally done anything at all which hurt Hayley, I'll personally remove and pickle your testicles, then make earrings of them, okay?"

"Don't worry about that," I said. "I've stopped acting like a selfish shitface."

"Good," she said. "Then your assets are safe from being made into unique but tasteless jewellery."

She leaned forward again, put a hand around the back of my neck and kissed me hard, pressing me back against the inside of the van. I was surprised, but put my arms around her and we spent a short while implicitly acknowledging that we fancied each other. And naturally, I got a hard-on, which she pressed herself against.

"Claire and John were both pretty convinced by your selfish shitface act," she murmured. "Maybe you're a natural actor." She wriggled on my lap, pressing herself against me very pointedly for a second. There was no way she'd have not noticed my erection. "I'm convinced by your 'I fancy Becky' act and I've worked with lots of actors." She then stood up, rearranged her long skirts, and picked up the costumes we'd selected for Sarah and Phil. "Pleased to see you're in proportion all over, too," she said, almost conversationally. "The only other really tall guy I've been with was a let-down in that department." Then she calmly walked out.

I had to spend a few seconds ensuring my tunic hid my erection before I could follow her. John was a few yards away, doing some stretches and twists to loosen up his muscles. His knowing grin showed me I should have waited until I'd got over my surprise, too. His training and experience of police work made him annoyingly sharp at spotting clues from facial expressions and body language.

*****

We'd finished the final performance and were packing everything into our trucks. Phil and Sarah had enjoyed themselves and gone away happily. The team would leave as soon as we'd loaded up. There was always a lot of show-related traffic at that time in the afternoon, and no one wanted to hang around any longer than necessary.

I overheard Claire talking with Hayley and Becky. "Look, it'll be a long journey, why not stay with us for a day or two? We've no guests at the moment. Be a good chance to get know each other better. Our place is easy to find, but just follow us if you want."

"If the two of you don't mind sharing a king-sized bed, you can stay in my flat," I said, carrying another box towards the truck. "It'll save Claire making up any rooms. We're all knackered, after all."

Hayley looked at Becky. "I'm not sure. We don't want to impose."

I saw Becky look at Claire, who discreetly glanced at her watch. Something was up, but I didn't have a clue what it was. I put the box down in the truck and untied my ponytail, as much from nerves as wanting to relax.

"Paul, come here you big sexy hunk."

Surprised, I turned towards the voice. I recognised the speaker right before being seized in a ferocious bear hug.

"Heather, how are you?" I gasped.

The tall, well-built, curvy brunette beamed at me, kissed me on the cheek and whispered, "Play along."

She stood back and took both my hands, looking me up and down. "Didn't know you were back in the area," she said more loudly. "Wish I'd tracked you down earlier. You make a dashing romantic hero."

I grinned. It was lovely to see Heather again, even if it was some sort of set-up. We'd been friends at college and dated for a while. We'd messed about a lot, but not slept together. She went to a local further education college when I moved away to a more distant university. I had a huge soft spot for her and we'd kept in touch sporadically. She and Claire had been firm friends for years.

"How did you know I was here?" I asked.

"Fair guess you'd be involved in something this bonkers, so I wasn't surprised to spot you."

John and the guys grinned at each other, then carried on shifting equipment. Claire was trying hard to hide what I always thought of as her scheming-and-plotting face, while Becky looked rather smugly amused. Hayley looked a bit put out.

Heather stretched up and ran her hand through my hair. "Rather suits you, makes you look rather hunky and dangerous as well as tall, dark, and handsome," she said. "It's years since I went riding. You do lessons and rides out on the moors, don't you? I'll have to pop over and we could catch up."

She looked at her watch. "Oh, my God, must rush. Look, lovely to see you again." I got another hug, a brief kiss on the lips, then she darted off. After she'd gone about twenty yards, she turned and held her hand up in the universal give-me-a-call gesture, a finger and thumb stretched out.

Her strappy top revealed the edges of a couple of tattoos she'd not had when she was eighteen, and she was way curvier now, filling her shorts very nicely indeed. I watched her as she slipped away into the crowd. I thought she overdid the wiggly bum thing a bit, but didn't mind too much. She had a shapely backside.

Out of the corner of my eye, I saw Becky give Hayley a meaningful glance and a sharp nudge with her elbow.

"Claire, I'd love to stay," she said. "Even if Hayley doesn't want to."

"Oh, don't be daft, Becky, of course I'd love to. I'll ring Mum and let her know."

"No snoring if we're sharing in Paul's flat."

"What do you mean? I don't snore."

It seemed to be a long-running joke. While Hayley went to get her mobile phone from the transporter cab, Becky and Claire both looked at me with deadpan expressions.

"What a coincidence, my only local ex-girlfriend just happens to drop by," I said.

Claire shrugged nonchalantly. "Stranger things have happened."

"Seems odd, considering we all went to her wedding last year. Oh, look. She's right over there. With her husband, a pushchair, and their toddler, and they're all waving at us." I returned the wave with a big grin.

I went back to help John put the last crates and trunks in the truck. When we finished, he offered me his hand. "Never thought you'd manage six nookie-free weeks, and I take my hat off to you, mate. You've even seriously cut back on your drinking, too. Which charity gets the hundred quid?"

I'd also made changes to my diet, set myself more challenging work-outs, had a thorough medical, and even been tested for STIs. The result had been reassuring, as I'd had a slight anxiety after a few impulsive bareback encounters.

"Air ambulance," I said. "You never know, I might need it one day."

John nodded. "Funny old life, isn't it? You wait two years and two nice women turn up at the same time. They're like chalk and cheese, but Claire and I like them both well enough." He looked at me thoughtfully. "I'm pretty sure you fancy them both and they both fancy you. You'll have to choose. And I ain't going to bet either way."

7

As soon as everything was packed and we were confident the horses were settled, we set off. John and Claire drove the truck, I had the horse transporter. Show traffic meant a slow journey, but there was no way I would have driven fast with six horses aboard. John and Claire easily beat me back home, and Becky and Hayley had followed them. By the time I got back, they'd met my parents, my niece and nephew, and the household dogs. It was chaotic, in a nice, comfortable way.

Our first priority was to turn the horses out into their paddocks for a run around. Then I gave Becky and Hayley a quick tour of my flat, found them some towels, and left them to shower and change. John and I unloaded the tack and equipment, then I had a shower and change of clothing.

John did a fine job with his propane barbecue, turning out good food for the eager group, chatting around a large wooden table in the garden. I was grateful that he and Claire had spent some time the previous evening preparing everything. I really wanted simple, plain food and a pile of crispy fresh salad after a few days of eating an unbalanced and heavily seasoned diet, even with the fruit Claire had brought me every day.

The sun was low in the sky by the time we'd eaten. My parents had gone home. The two Jack Russell terriers were content, full from scrounged leftovers. My three-year-old niece Vicky was struggling to stay awake, perched on Hayley's lap. My five-year-old nephew, Daniel, was fascinated by the tiny skull ornament hanging from Becky's necklace.

Hayley glanced at me, then turned to Claire. "So, what was Paul like as a youngster?"

I glared at my dear sister. "Don't you dare." I recognised the look on her face.

Becky grinned. "Go on, Claire, I dare you. Make him cringe, please."

She smiled at me innocently. "Come on, Paul, you know the rules. Big sisters have to tease their horrible little brothers. You've coped for almost thirty-five years."

"Oh, shit," I mumbled, and put my head in my hands. I couldn't really die from embarrassment. Could I?

"Paul, can you get some more wine from the fridge? I'd better put the kids to bed; otherwise they'll be insufferable tomorrow." Claire stood up and ruffled my hair when she walked past me. "Then maybe a few family tales."

A couple of hours later, the sun had set, and John had said goodnight, as he was back on duty the next morning. Claire looked ready to join him soon. Becky, clearly feeling mellow, had stretched out on the wooden bench beside me and rested her feet on my lap. The solar lamps around the courtyard cast a soft blue-white light over us.

"How come you get so bloody many stars?" Becky asked. "Hardly see any where I live."

"Almost no light pollution," I said. "I'd forgotten about it too until I moved back. Hope I never get used to it. This area is probably pretty different from what you're used to. Rural and quite old-fashioned, in good ways."

Hayley had folded her arms on the table and rested her chin on them, apparently happy and relaxed. She raised her eyebrows and looked at me. "So, any thoughts about what to do with your unexpected guests?"

Becky snorted. "Hey, don't go making offers I ain't prepared to live up to."

Hayley looked embarrassed, then giggled.

I looked at Claire. "A drive across the moor? Pub lunch?"

She nodded, then turned to Hayley. "Some fantastic views and we'll think of some more spots you might want to tell Phil about as possible locations."

"What sort of places?" Becky asked.

"Lots of rugged landscapes," I said. "Weird-looking tors, prehistoric stuff, ruined farmhouses, ancient bridges, standing stones, rivers with spectacular rocks in them, herds of ponies, sheep and even Highland cattle."

"Sounds good," said Hayley. She reached across the table and prodded my forearm. "You're exhausted, Paul. And I'm not much better. You ready to retire, Becky?"

"Half-asleep and at least half-pissed." She lifted her feet off my lap, swung her legs over the edge of the bench and sat up quickly, in a single smooth movement. "Come on, you two. Take me to bed."

I stood up. "Best offer I've had in months."

"Even with Heather around?" asked Hayley. She stood and walked around to my side of the table.

"Without a doubt," I replied, leaning forward to kiss her on the cheek. She smiled and kissed me on the lips.

Over Hayley's shoulder, I saw Claire and Becky exchange grins. Scheming and plotting, bless them.

Becky and Hayley followed me up the stairs into my flat, a conversion of the upper floor of an outbuilding. I grabbed a blanket and pillows from my old pine ottoman, stripped to my underwear, stretched out on my sofa and went out like a light. Three days of living off takeaway food, jousting in hot sunshine, and sleeping in the cramped transporter cab had left me a tad weary.

When someone woke me by grabbing my hands, it was pitch dark.

"Come on, we're not leaving you on that uncomfortable sofa," a woman whispered.

I couldn't work out who it was. I realised that each of my hands was held by a different person, their hands small and soft in mine. This seemed surreal enough to be a dream, but what the heck. A minute later, I was in my own bed, with a woman curled up on either side of me. They both wore a tee shirt, as far as I could tell.

"You shouldn't leave things lying around when you have nosey guests," Becky said, from my right.

"Things like this," Hayley said, from my left.

Something was put over my eyes. I realised it was the blindfold Helen and I used to play with. I'd left it in the top drawer of the bedside cabinet on the left of the bed, as we had when we were together. We'd alternated taking charge in erotic games, ones I'd only ever played with her.

"Is that okay?" Becky asked. "Just say no if it isn't."

I swallowed, aware that I was being offered a step into unknown territory. But I was curious, too. "It's fine," I said.

"And then we have these," Hayley said. I heard a metallic sound and realised she had the play handcuffs, which I'd left wrapped up in the blindfold. She clipped one bracelet around my left wrist, then pushed my arms up towards the metal bars of the headboard. I cooperated and slipped my hands between the bars, then felt Becky move up to secure my other wrist. I felt nervous and vulnerable, even though I knew I could reach the release mechanism easily enough. But with Helen I'd learned that a little anxiety could really help things get hot and exciting, but I was out of practice at letting anyone put me in that situation.

I heard a click and guessed someone had switched on a bedside light. It had a low power bulb. Helen had a thing for candlelight, so

I'd bought bulbs which were about as dim, but not a fire hazard.

I heard the duvet falling to the floor. It was difficult not to feel nervous, blindfolded, handcuffed, and almost naked on a bed with two women I fancied but didn't yet know all that well. There was a soft rustling sound and then two pairs of naked breasts were pressed against my chest.

"You don't mind, do you?" Hayley asked, from my left.

"We thought you might like to share a little fun with us," Becky whispered, so close I felt her breath in my right ear. "Just remember you can say no anytime."

They both snuggled up against me and ran their fingertips over my chest, so lightly it almost tickled. One of them had slightly longer fingernails than the other, but I was too distracted to figure out minor details right then; it was bloody erotic. It only took a couple of seconds for my underpants to feel uncomfortably tight, valiantly trying to contain my erection.

Becky sat up and leaned over to lick and tease my right nipple with her lips. Hayley turned my head towards her and kissed me. I let her take the lead, and enjoyed the feeling as her tongue explored my mouth. The forcefulness and intensity of her kiss surprised and excited me. She seemed to have a less restrained side to her that she kept hidden away.

Hayley ended the kiss and the girls swapped roles. Becky was a great kisser, too, but that didn't quite stop me gasping as Hayley nipped my other nipple with her teeth.

"Someone's getting excited, Becky," Hayley whispered.

Becky stopped kissing me and started nuzzling my neck. "I know I am."

Hayley giggled. "I meant our cooperative victim," she said, then I felt her move beside me, and she stroked my tummy with the same feather-light touch as she had my chest. From how it felt, I was sure she had the longer fingernails.

I felt the bed wobble as both girls sat up and moved down.

From the movement of the mattress, I knew they were kneeling on either side of my hips. Two sets of fingers ran slowly and teasingly over my tummy, brushing the hairs and driving me ever so slightly bonkers with anticipation. I didn't know who touched my cock first; all I felt was a fingertip press against it through my underpants. Then more fingers joined it, ran along the length of my shaft and over my balls. I might have arched my back, possibly even gasped. All I knew was that two attractive women were playing a teasy, sexy game with me. And I didn't want it to stop.

I just heard them murmuring, but couldn't make it out. They both jumped off the bed, leaving me restrained, blindfolded, and nearly bursting with anticipation. I heard feet on the floor, so I guessed they were swapping sides. Or pretending to...

Suddenly, the mattress moved again and they were both beside me, one on either side. At the same instant, the elastic hem around my tummy was eased down by two pairs of hands and my cock sprang free. The hands slid my underpants down my legs and I lay there, feeling more than a little awkward, exposed, vulnerable, and distinctly turned on. The fingers returned, soft, warm and small, with more pressure, and I sighed with delight as they teased my sensitive skin. One hand wrapped around my tip and squeezed me, slowly and rhythmically. Another grasped my shaft and stroked slowly, pulling the skin tight then releasing it rhythmically. The most frustrating and exciting thing was that I couldn't identify or touch either of them, as they'd clearly made an effort to confuse me. But I so wanted some direct contact with them while they teased me, and to know who was doing what. I felt out of control, but excited about it.

There was a whispered exchange I couldn't hear. The mattress shifted again as they moved. One straddled my hips and pressed her naked pussy against my cock. The other moved up and kneeled on either side of my head, so her pussy was right above my face. I heard her grip the iron frame above me. Whoever was on my hips teased the tip of my cock with her fingertips, while the woman above my face lowered her pussy until I found it with my tongue. She opened her lips with her fingers, then sighed as my tongue explored. Her natural flavour and scent were mild, salty, and feminine. She wriggled around a little, so I kept my head still to allow her to get my attention exactly where she wanted it. Helen had trained me well, to our mutual delight.

It felt as if the woman who sat on my cock was playing with me and herself at the same time, something I'd have loved to watch as well as feel. I felt her open pussy lips press against my shaft and a distinct sense of movement as she stoked herself. Then she moved herself and me, stroking my tip along the length of her hot, moist cleft.

I tried to stay aware of everything happening to and around me, but it was difficult. I guessed the woman above my face wanted my tongue inside her. She gasped as I pushed it into her over and over again. Then she slid back so my tongue was directly on her clit. I lapped all around it, trying to work out where she was most sensitive.

Then I was suddenly distracted in a major way. Whoever was playing with my cock changed her game. She stopped playing with me and ground her pussy against my cock, sliding up and down it. I gasped in surprise against the pussy pressed to my face. Whoever was on my cock stopped with the tip of my cock near her entrance, then moved around a little until I was firmly and teasingly placed. As tempted as I was, I didn't dare ease into her. I wasn't wearing a condom, and didn't want to spoil the moment for any of us. Then she almost broke my resistance when I felt her body move as she fiddled furiously with her clit.

Whoever I was teasing with my tongue had started creeping up on her climax, and I felt the muscles in her thighs and tummy quiver. The woman almost riding me leaned back a little and made a series of stifled cries, her hips twitching and pressing against me.

The woman hovering over my face tensed for a couple of seconds, then she gasped several times, thrusting herself against my face each time.

Then they were both still and all I heard was heavy breathing. After a few seconds, they both moved off me and stepped off the bed. I heard and felt the duvet being pulled up, then one lay on either side of me again. They both lay an arm across my chest and kissed me on the nearest cheek.

"Considering you were tied up, you were very naughty," Hayley said, from my left-hand side again.

"But it was very nice, too," Becky added.

Their hands simultaneously slid down my body and their fingers interlinked around my shaft.

"Time to say thank you," Hayley murmured.

"But we'll say it slowly," Becky added. "It's only fair to get you back nicely."

Their slow, steady wanking action was amazing, teasing, exciting, and frustrating all at the same time. I writhed and wriggled on the bed as my orgasm started to build, ever so slowly. They both giggled and nuzzled my neck and shoulders, then one would kiss me deeply and passionately for a few seconds.

I reached a delicious state of arousal where I was only aware of my inevitable and tantalisingly near climax. They threw the duvet back again when it was clear I was getting close. I whimpered and arched my back, but didn't care. Then I felt it start; my balls tightened, warmth built up where my cock met my body and moved up my shaft. Two hands together wrapped around my tip as I spurted, which gave me an intense wave of pleasure for a couple of seconds.

Then I was panting in my bed, feeling spent and dreamy. Slight movements by the women's hands proved that the tip of my slowly subsiding cock was still incredibly sensitive, and I couldn't help twitching as their teasing continued. They giggled and let me kiss them, then I heard tissues being pulled from a box on the bedside table and my tummy was mopped clean.

"Did we get our own back, Becky?" Hayley asked.

"I think so," Becky replied.

"You two are in trouble," I said. "As soon as I can move again."

The handcuffs were released and the blindfold slipped off my eyes. I looked up at two smiling women looking down at me. I reached a hand up to each of them and stroked their cheeks. Becky pulled my fingers to her mouth and licked the tips one at a time, which I found unexpectedly erotic. Hayley leaned forwards and we kissed slowly, our tongues engaged in a slow and teasing dance. Then she snuggled down against my side and I kissed Becky just as slowly and tenderly.

"Thank you both," I said. "That was one of the most amazing things I've experienced."

Becky pulled the duvet back up, turned the light off, then snuggled under my right arm. "So far, anyway," she murmured.

"Who was it who said something about making promises the other wasn't prepared to keep?" Hayley teased.

"I might keep him all to myself," Becky said, sounding sleepy.

Hayley moved close to my ear. "No way," she whispered, so quietly I only just heard her.

"No secrets," Becky mumbled. "We're mates, remember."

"No stealing Paul away, then. Or else."

I lay back, each of my arms around a lovely naked woman and smiled at the dark ceiling. *No more one-night stands either*, I promised myself. *So long as I can win one of these two.*

My hidden doubts and anxieties had other ideas. *Win either of these two?* a chorus of inner voices mocked. *Not a chance. You're a loser. Face reality. You can't escape that depression forever.*

I swallowed hard and tried to ignore those voices.

8

I sensed none of the embarrassment I'd feared when we woke. It was still early and none of us were that lively. We cuddled and dozed. Hayley tucked herself against my side, facing away from me, and pulled my arm around her. I spooned against her and liked feeling her hair against my chest. Becky snuggled up against my back, her arm around my waist, and I felt her steady, slow breaths against my back. There wasn't much that beat an early-morning cuddle, but doing it with these two women did. And It felt delightfully natural.

It struck me that I'd not cuddled with a slender woman of average height for years. Helen, like Kathy, had been tall, and, like most of my recent lovers, well-built. It didn't bother me either way, but these two smaller bodies beside me both seemed fragile and precious, which brought out my protective side.

I had an erection, which Hayley lazily pulled between her thighs, pressed against her rather hot pussy. She squeezed her thighs together every few seconds and I tried not to react to the stimulation or temptation. Becky nuzzled my back and idly played with one of my nipples, teasing it with her fingers. I was pleasantly surprised how sweet it all was, and how comfortable I felt about this odd situation.

I moved my hand to cup one of Hayley's breasts, and she moved her arm to let me, covering my hand with hers. Her small, pert nipple was hard against my fingers. I nuzzled the back of her neck where her hair had fallen away. After a minute, she giggled and rolled onto her back.

"God, much more of this and I'll want you to shag me," she said.

"Please do, I'd love to watch," Becky mumbled against my back.

Hayley turned and grinned at her friend over my body. "You'd make rude comments."

Becky snorted. "As if. I'd be diddling myself silly, hoping Paul would get hard again soon and give me a good seeing-to."

I turned onto my back and hugged each of them close to me. "Are you two like this all the time?" I asked.

"Yeah," Becky said. "We pick up random men, bewitch, and mistreat them." She stretched her arms and looked contented.

"In a manner most foul," Hayley added. "Particularly single men from jousting teams."

"So when do I get mistreated?" I asked.

"What, you enjoyed that?" Becky tried to look worried.

"Shit, I think he did," Hayley said, her expression of mock concern more convincing.

"No, I bloody loved it," I said.

They both sat up and exchanged comic looks of surprise over my chest.

Becky lifted the duvet and ducked her head down to peer underneath it. "Oh shit, Hayley, look," she said. "It's grown again."

Hayley ducked under the duvet. "Yeah, I was teasing him a little. We might be in trouble, Becks."

I felt pleased that we were all relaxed and happy, but completely unsure where this was all going. I'd only ever been intimate with one woman at a time, and I'd usually been in control, or at least allowed to feel that way. Well, unless Helen wanted to play. This was fun, but felt uncomfortable as well. I didn't feel that I had any control right then.

"Roll onto your side, facing Becky," Hayley whispered. "You play with her while I play with you. Then we can swap over."

Becky was certainly a good kisser and massaged the back of my scalp with her fingers while our tongues met in her mouth. Hayley reached around and wanked me with long, slow strokes. Her hand felt hot and tiny around my cock, which added an extra novelty. She pulled my skin tight at one extreme, then squeezed my tip at the other. I pushed the duvet down to reveal Becky's breasts, small and shapely, with large, dark nipples. I cupped one breast, then the other, fingered her nipples, then leaned down to tease them with my lips and tongue. Becky purred and pushed her breasts into my mouth. It was all rather intriguing and exciting.

"I love having my neck nibbled," she said.

"How can we manage that?" I asked.

Becky rolled onto her back with her shoulders and neck twisted away so I could nuzzle the back of her neck. Her hair felt lovely against my face. She took my hand and guided it between her legs, past a patch of downy pubic hair, to her cleft. I opened her lips and found she was temptingly hot and wet. I stroked her up and down, slid a finger as far into her as I could, then moved it up to circle and stroke her clit.

She reached down again and took my hand in hers. "Like this. It drives me insane," she whispered, demonstrating a circular movement with one of my fingers lightly touching her. I carried on the movement and the nibbling and nuzzling. Despite me using my clumsier left hand, she was soon carried away, writhing and moaning, her eyes closed.

Hayley hadn't changed what she was doing to me, which felt great, but I wasn't close to coming yet; focusing on Becky kept me distracted. Hayley nuzzled my back and shoulders, licked a spot then blew gently on it, a combination which was quite stimulating.

Then Becky's whole body tensed and she slowly lifted her hips off the bed. She seemed to hover for a second, then came with a loud cry. Her hips twitched as I carried on moving my finger over her clit, and she gasped each time her body moved. Then she relaxed completely, sighed and turned to smile at me.

"That looked fun." Hayley giggled.

She'd sat up and leaned on my chest to watch Becky's expression as she came.

Becky stuck her tongue out at Hayley, then rolled towards me. "He learns too bloody quickly," she murmured. I hugged her, she put her arms around my neck, and we kissed slowly and tenderly. "You were gorgeously naughty," she whispered.

"My turn?" Hayley asked.

"You bet, I'm good to go," Becky said. "All change."

Hayley stroked my face. "I hope you'll be as wicked to me."

I rolled over and Hayley lay on her back, smiling up at me. Becky got on to her knees and leaned on me. Her hand grasping my cock felt as small and exciting as Hayley's had. Her wanking action was shorter and faster, with more sense of movement over the rim of my tip, which was exciting, but made me worry I'd lose control.

Hayley gave me an irresistible *kiss me* look. As we kissed, she stroked the stubble growing on my face. "I'd love you to swap between licking my nipples and kissing me," Hayley murmured. Her hand guided mine down under the duvet and I found her pussy was as invitingly open and wet as Becky's had been a few minutes before. Her breasts were as firm as Becky's, slightly larger, but her nipples were smaller. I nuzzled one with my lips as I started exploring her pussy with my fingers. She moved her legs further apart as I found her soft, warm, wet entrance, then she pressed my hand with hers. As I slid two fingers into her, she closed her eyes and sighed. I finger-fucked her slowly, alternating between licking and nuzzling her breasts and kissing her mouth deeply. Each time I pushed my fingers into her, she lifted her hips slightly and pressed down against my fingers.

She ran her fingers through my hair as we kissed. "I'm so jealous of your hair," she murmured.

"Yeah, and me," Becky added. To make the point, she gnawed on my shoulder.

"I'm jealous of your boobs," I said. "If I was suddenly a woman, I'd never stop playing with them."

"Only until you discovered your clit," Becky said.

"Is that true?" I asked Hayley's right nipple.

"Multiple orgasms," she murmured.

Becky giggled and squeezed my shaft with her hand. "Yup."

I slid my fingers up between Hayley's pussy lips. She let out a breath as they touched her clit, then I moved them in a tight circle around it, touching her as lightly as I could.

"Any hints?" I asked.

"Carry on," she whispered. "That's bloody lovely."

She came more quickly than Becky had, holding me tight with an arm around my neck and making urgent little gasps and moans. Becky giggled against my back and wanked me faster, which almost distracted me. Hayley tensed, arched her back, then let out a long sigh, rolling her head from side to side. She relaxed and stopped my hand. "That was fab. I could carry on for hours, but I'd kinda like to walk today."

"Which leaves naughty Paulie to deal with," Becky said.

"Yeah, it does." Hayley agreed.

She reached both her arms around my neck and pulled my head down to hers. We kissed intensely and she ran her hands over my breasts and nipples while Becky's hand worked its magic.

I came while I was kissing Hayley. Our mouths parted and she licked my nose as I moaned. The nerve endings in the whole of my erection went into delicious overload, a brief taste of ecstasy.

"Ooh, that's done it," Becky said. Her hand still held my cock in a gentle grip.

I looked down and saw splashes of my semen over Hayley's tummy and some on Becky's fingers. I took Becky's hand and licked it clean. They exchanged a surprised look. I leaned down, licked my splashes and spots off Hayley's tummy, then we all snuggled down for another group hug. I'd not tasted my own semen for a couple of years; salty and with a slight numbing quality. Helen had always loved me cleaning her up on the occasions I'd made a mess, which I was happy to do.

"You two are deliciously wicked," I told the girls. "Please don't ever feel you need to change."

We cuddled and kissed for a while in a comfortable silence. I wanted to appear confident and relaxed, but I actually felt confused and out of my depth. A couple more hours of sleep would have been good, too.

"I'm ready for some breakfast," Becky said.

She slid out of bed and walked over to the window, apparently completely blasé about being nude. It was the first time I'd clearly seen her body and liked what I saw. Lithe and slim, with small, pert breasts, long legs, narrow, rather square hips, an almost boyish bottom, and a neatly-trimmed mid-brown bush, her pussy lips shaven. She stuck her head through the curtains, letting bright daylight spill into the room.

"Another lovely day." Her voice was slightly muffled by the curtains. "An amazing view, too."

"Let's see," Hayley said.

She hopped out of bed and walked over to the window. Hayley's bottom was fuller than Becky's, a more classically feminine shape, and her breasts a little larger. Her bush was similarly trimmed, but honey-coloured. Looking at them, I thought that they both looked after themselves, staying fit and trim.

They stood together, their heads through the gap between the curtains. They seemed completely comfortable together, nude and with their bodies touching. Hayley whispered something I couldn't hear, which made Becky giggle. I slid out of bed and joined them at the window. It faced eastwards, and we looked over open moorland towards a distant hill crisscrossed with drystone walls in various states of repair, the rough grass peppered with scrubby thorn trees, patches of bracken and pale grey granite boulders.

"I'm jealous of you," Becky said. "Waking up to this every morning."

I suddenly felt nervous, but decided to say what was in my mind anyway. "You're both welcome to see this view any morning you want to." Hayley put an arm around my waist and hugged me, and Becky squeezed one of my arms. I'd meant the invitation, too.

Hayley grinned. "How big's your shower?"

"Might be tight for three."

"Let's see," Becky said, with a mischievous smile and raised eyebrows.

We made a cosy crowd under my shower head, but the cubicle was big enough for three people happy to be physically very close. It was amazing having the two of them lather my body at the same time. Quite enough for me to get another erection. The girls washed each other's backs and hair. They let me do their fronts slowly, then retaliated while I shaved, distracting me by using all four hands to soap my cock. That was definitely something I could suffer any morning.

I hoped the childrens' reaction to meeting their new friends again over breakfast would distract Claire. She'd know I felt something amazing had happened to me. We both knew each other far too well not to see something like that in each other. But I hoped to avoid being teased about it just yet.

9

"This area's amazing," Hayley said. "Any chance of some photos to show Phil?"

I jogged back to my Range Rover for my camera bag. On the way back, I fitted my long zoom lens and took a couple of photos of Becky and Hayley standing together between the twin rows of standing stones. Through the lens, I saw Hayley sit heavily on one of the stones and cover her face with her hands. Becky squatted on her heels and put a hand on Hayley's shoulder while they talked, then Hayley abruptly got to her feet and walked away.

You've fucked it up, my brain told me. *They've argued and fallen out. And it's your fault.*

A cold wash ran through my body and pain stabbed my chest. I leaned forward and rested a hand on my thigh, struggling to draw breath for a few seconds. I'd not had an anxiety attack that bad for well over a year. My self-confidence curled up and hid in a corner of my mind.

Come on, keep up the act. Keep it up long enough and it'll stop being an act.

I stood up, closed my eyes, and made a concerted effort to take a few deep breaths. When I looked again, Hayley had walked over to a nearby small circle of stones and had leaned against the huge, upright standing stone in the middle of it. Becky had sat on one of the stones in the row, with her head in her hands.

My throat suddenly hurt and I fought back tears as my self-doubts overran all other thoughts. I'd kept them pretty well suppressed for about eighteen months, thanks to bloody mindedness and maintaining an act of confidence. I'd almost convinced myself it wasn't an act. But it evaporated as fast as a drop of water on red-hot iron.

You can do it. Just a little longer. Be the good host and pretend nothing's wrong. They'll go and that'll be the end of it.

The sensible part of me spoke up, audible despite the tumult of fears. *You need to reach out and trust. Don't give in and let that depression back.*

I slung my camera over my shoulder and walked the fifty yards or so to Becky. My legs struggled to move heavy feet. Sensible me knew why. *It's only fear, just a feeling. You can do feelings. You really can.*

As I got closer, Becky stood up, wiped her face with a tissue and blew her nose.

"It's almost spooky. How old is all this?" Hayley shouted. She reached as far up the tall standing stone as she could, but it was almost three times her height.

This was something I could deal with far more easily than an uncomfortable, emotionally charged conversation. I'd studied all I could about this area as it fascinated me. Time for my teacher act.

"Bronze Age," I called out. "Three to four and a half thousand years old."

Both women walked towards me and we stopped close together. Hayley looked distracted and I thought Becky was putting on a brave face.

It's my fault. My fears told me so, over and over again.

"What can you tell us about it?" Becky asked. "I guess you've looked into the history."

"The area was probably forested at the start of that period, until farming arrived." I pointed up at the hill on the other side of the road. "The uppermost stone wall marks the highest level of farming." I pointed my arm in specific directions around us. "The remains of some Victorian farm buildings are over there, those rings of stones are the foundations of Bronze Age round houses, these two double stone rows are unique. And then there's that standing stone and circle, more standing stones over that way, and some burial cairns."

"What was it all built for?" Becky asked. "Is it Celtic? Something like a mini Stonehenge?"

I shrugged. "No records, we can only guess. We don't know anything about who lived here, not what they called themselves, their languages, or cultures. The commonly-held idea of the Celts was invented by a modern historian who got carried away. Genetic studies show a wide diversity in so-called Celtic populations. It's only used as an adjective now."

Hayley pointed at the empty cist on the edge of the double stone row. "Why bury someone there?"

"Again, we don't know. Their society evolved and changed, and things important once were forgotten about."

"How do you mean?" Becky asked.

"Okay. The Bronze Age lasted around fifteen hundred years. That long ago from now, the Romans hadn't long left Britain and Saxons were settling in Kent. Think how much our society has changed since then. These people traded with the continent, sharing cultural ideas. There were probably a few invasions, or at least one warrior elite replacing another, each bringing a new culture."

Hayley slowly turned around. "So beautiful. Just us and the breeze. Pity we didn't bring a picnic." She waved towards the standing stones. "This could make a great spot for some outdoor scenes. And those huge rocks up on the hills over there, too."

I switched my camera on again. "So, what do you want photos of?" *Keep calm, play it cool. They'll never know.*

Becky squeezed my arm, which suddenly made me feel comforted and wanted. "Can you take a picture of me and Hayley by that big stone?"

"Sure."

Becky grinned. "I'll tell everyone it's a life-size replica of your willy."

Hayley shook her head. "Your jokes never get any better."

*****

A few hours later, Hayley and I sat close together on one of the huge granite outcrops of Haytor, for me Dartmoor's most impressive and intriguing hill.

Becky was about twenty feet away, taking photos of us with her phone. "Go on, kiss him or something. I need a nice pic to show your parents why you wanted to stay on a couple more days."

We kissed in an exaggerated and chaste manner. I was conscious of being physically close to her, and felt like I was fourteen or fifteen again, next to a girl I fancied, and wondering if I dared hold her hand. At the same time, I felt stupid for imagining I stood a chance of happiness with either of these women.

You can only find women who want a quick fuck, my doubts taunted me again. *Ones who want a bit of fun, not a relationship.*

I pushed my anxieties back enough to put on my act again. "Is she always like this?"

Hayley nodded. "Like an embarrassing sister, but I love her."

"Yeah, I know that feeling."

Hayley laughed. "Claire's great, she really loves you. And John. Their kids are great." She smiled. "Your parents are lovely, too. Less outrageous than mine."

Becky came and sat beside Hayley and we all looked out at the view. It was a bit hazy, but in the distance, I made out the sea.

"I'll bet you were a bit surprised last night," Becky said.

"That's putting it mildly," I said.

I felt surprised at the conversational jump. I'd convinced myself I'd totally blown the chances of anything more between us.

"You didn't mind?" Becky looked at me intently.

"No, far from it. It was the most amazing experience."

Becky smiled, then leaned back on the granite and closed her eyes. "I loved it, too."

I looked at Hayley, who seemed to be lost in thought. "You okay?"

She sighed, took my hand, and squeezed it. "Yeah, way better than okay. I loved it, too. I felt…powerful. Like exciting and scary at the same time."

"I felt that, too," I said. "Sometimes it's nice to surrender, sometimes nice to be in charge."

"How long is it since you surrendered?" Becky asked, still lying on the stone.

"Two years, four months, and a few days," I said quietly. The loss I'd felt for every second of that period abruptly weighed me down.

Hayley put her arm through mine. "Not since Helen?"

I couldn't speak. My mind took me back to the day the receptionist at work rang me to say a police officer needed to talk to me urgently.

Becky came up behind me, and wrapped her arms around my shoulders and chest. "Don't worry, we might play games, but we don't want to hurt you," she said. "We've both been let down and hurt, too."

"Helen didn't hurt me," I whispered, my throat burning. "It wasn't her fault at all. But I felt so lost when she suddenly wasn't there anymore." I wiped at the tears which had escaped from my eyes and run down my cheeks. "I've been trying to convince myself ever since that it wasn't my fault."

"Why?" Hayley looked concerned. "Were you there?"

I shook my head. "Couldn't get the day off work."

Hayley put her hands on my cheeks and turned my face towards hers. "Then it wasn't your fault, was it? Stop beating yourself up."

My throat burned. I wanted to walk away, to find a quiet place where I could be alone.

"Claire and John have been worried sick about you ever since it happened," Becky said, her face pressed against my shoulder. "You know they think you're bottling it up."

I nodded. "They're right, of course. And I feel like a shit for doing it. But, well…" *Say it. Tell them.* I opened my mouth. "Helen was the only woman I trusted enough to see the real me." *Wimp.*

"But you've already trusted us," said Becky. "You hardly know us, but you let us tie you up. Like that's not trust?"

"Yes, I trust you," I said. "But…" I sighed. "I'm still an emotional mess and my reactions can confuse the hell out of me, even now. For the first few weeks, I was like a zombie, going through the motions. The company wanted people to volunteer for redundancy. I said yes, to escape. I moved here and, well, it was like I'd started again in some ways. Found enough confidence to put on an act, and got the academic work through Dad and his contacts." I paused and took a deep breath. "I've spent the last eighteen months or so behaving like a real shit. I know John and Claire have worried. Part of me felt guilty, but most of me ignored that part. Sometimes the guilt gets a bit too much. But I don't know what to do."

I heard Hayley sniff and turned to look at her. Tears ran down her cheeks, just like those on mine. Becky rooted in her handbag and passed us each a tissue.

"I'm still scared of ending up with another domineering bully," Hayley said. "Tony was great at first, then tried to take my life over. Undermined my self-confidence, which is the last thing anyone needs, let alone an actor. I relied on goodwill and my track record to get any work since him. This new project is the first exciting offer

I've had in about a year."

I squeezed her hand. "I'll do whatever I can to help. Anything at all. Just ask. All the guys are excited about it, too. We know we're amateurs, but we're not bad at what we do."

She smiled. "Thanks. It didn't take me long to realise you're one of the good guys."

I patted the stone beside me. "Come on, Becky."

She sat next to me and took my hand. "I feel like the odd one out, no major trauma recently."

"You were cut up about Mikey," Hayley said.

"Yeah, well... we'd run out of steam. I was only hurt that I didn't end it first. Silly pride."

"Since then?" I asked.

The two women smiled at each other. "My priority has been Hayley's pathetic self-confidence," Becky said. "If you think she's a loser now, you should have seen her a year ago."

Hayley glowered at Becky for a few seconds, then they both burst out laughing. She was the first professional actor I'd spent much time with. I was struck by how quickly she could put on almost any act she wanted and be convincing, which made me wonder whether I could ever know what she really meant or wanted.

"You didn't mind that we just, um, played?" Hayley asked.

Of course they only played with you, my doubts said. *That's all any woman wants from you.*

I told my doubts to fuck off.

"Not in the least," I said, honestly. "Anything more would have been too much. It was really close to the edge of my comfort zones as it was."

"Not too close?" Becky asked.

I smiled and shook my head. "Close enough. If we do anything like that again, maybe yellow for far enough, red for stop."

Becky nodded. "Good for me."

Hayley hugged my arm and leaned her head against it.

Becky patted the rock we'd all sat on. "This hill," she said. "Is it an ancient volcano? The rock was obviously molten, since it's all droopy-looking."

"It's an intrusion," I said, appreciating the change of subject. "The molten rock didn't reach the surface, which would have made it a volcano, but cooled underground and was left behind when softer stuff around it was eroded."

Becky jumped up and pulled my hand until I stood up, then I dragged Hayley up off the rock. She tried to stop me and we ended up having a play fight.

We set off downhill towards the car park. It felt a little weird holding hands with two women, but comforting. I liked that. If they gave me nothing else, I'd felt happy briefly.

"Do you mind if I ask if you played games with Helen?" Hayley asked.

"Don't mind," I said.

And waited.

They grinned at each other. "Did you?" they chorused.

"Yeah, sometimes. Bit of bondage, teasing, toys, role play. Just fun really. We liked making love outdoors sometimes. Easier when we stayed here; the moors are lovely and it's easy to find a private spot."

There was another, almost telepathic exchange. "Might come and visit you again," Becky said casually. "All this great outdoors."

Hayley squeezed my hand and briefly stroked my palm with a fingertip.

Yeah, right, my doubts said.

But I hoped they would. I wanted them to. I wanted to be saved from myself.

10

When I parked in the farmyard, Daniel ran over to meet us, followed by both the terriers, yapping with excitement.

I'd unlocked my front door and ushered everyone in when John drove up and got out of his car. He looked tired and deflated, not like his normal self. I guessed he had a new investigation. He always told me and Claire a little of what was going on at work, to help him cope with the stress.

"Can you make me a coffee?" I called up the stairs. "I'll be up in a minute."

I walked over to John. "What's up?"

He sighed and shook his head. "Just given a new case. Suspicious death. Woman found this morning with nasty injuries."

"Shit, that's awful. Any clues?"

He shrugged. "Might be gang-related. Known sex worker and drug user."

"So you're heading the team?"

He nodded. "Yeah." He was silent for a while. "Still, you can cheer me up and tell me all about your day later. I need a few minutes to myself and a large mug of tea." He looked at me appraisingly. "Then you'll tell me what's on your mind." He squeezed my upper arm. "And no bullshit, okay?"

I nodded and walked over to my flat.

"Or I'll set Claire on you," he called out after me.

I saluted him with my middle finger.

Daniel clattered down the stairs as I reached my front door. "Mum said to tell Hayley and Becky that dinner's in an hour, Uncle Paul."

"Am I invited?"

He looked at me as if I was mad. "Of course, silly."

Then he ran off to his dad. I stood aside as both dogs flew down the stairs, raced over to John, barked in their excitement, and jumped all over him.

Becky had collapsed on the sofa. Hayley was in the kitchen area, spooning instant coffee into three mugs.

"Jeez, kids," Becky said. "Thirty seconds of him and I'm exhausted. Where do they get the energy?"

"Maybe you'll find out one day," I said.

Becky grimaced. "Me? A mum? No way. No maternal instinct. I'm planning on being a bad influence on Hayley's kids."

I felt an emotional stab and saw a pained expression flash across Hayley's face before she got herself under control. "I'd set social services on you," she muttered.

Seeing them there, I had a flash of insight from my doubting inner voice. *Both these women could break your heart, and you could break Hayley's. If you let them get close.*

"Paul," Hayley said, "I don't want to seem rude, but you've got no books here."

"It's a small place, I have to be tidy." I pointed at what looked like a cupboard door. "They're all in the study, have a look."

Becky jumped up and they disappeared through the door together. "Bloody hell," Becky said. "This is like a compact version of your dad's study, Hayley."

I sipped my coffee. I kept all my reference books there, as I didn't have a permanent office at either of the universities I taught at. I had mixed feelings, but knew it was the right time to be more open.

Letting them into my office was part of that, revealing more of me.

When I joined them, they were looking at the framed photos on one wall. Photos of me in my bachelor's and PhD graduation gowns and caps. Some huge frames with a jumble of everyday snapshots; family photos, me and the team at jousting shows, holiday photos. A lanky teenage me on a horse at show jumping and endurance riding competitions, or being presented with prizes for fencing or archery. A formal studio photo of me with Helen, and one of our wedding photos.

"She was pretty," Hayley said quietly. "Love her hair, almost black. And you look so happy together in every one."

"We had our arguments," I said, "but worked through them. We were happy. She was my best friend in a way John never can be."

Becky put her arms around me. "Maybe you'll find another special person and be happy again, in a different way."

"I hope so."

Becky studied the wedding photo. "You're what, six-foot-three or four? So, Helen was six feet tall."

"I'm six-five, she was six-one." I remembered the feel of her, my arms around her broad shoulders, my hands on her ample hips, her full breasts against my chest. Her smile which always made me feel better. The rich tan she got every summer. The way her brown eyes showed me when she wanted to fuck me senseless.

Hayley looked out of the window, her shoulders tense. She let a breath out and relaxed. Becky saw it, too, and went over to hug her friend. They had a brief whispered conversation, then both turned to the nearest bookcase.

Hayley touched one of the books. "Your PhD thesis? I've never seen one before. Can I look?"

"Sure."

She pulled it down and flicked through the pages.

Even ten years later, I still felt a glow of satisfaction for the effort I'd put into that single book. It was the first time I'd seen someone other than my family look at it, and it felt a bit odd.

She flicked back to the title page. "The metallurgy and metalworking techniques of arms and armour in fourteenth century England."

"No home should be without a copy," I said.

"You said you make your own stuff," Becky said. "Ever done that experimental archaeology, recreating old things to work how they were made?"

"I did some for my thesis, and for some of the things I sell to reenactors and collectors."

Hayley circled one of my forearms with her hands. "From the shape of these, I guess you do your own forging?"

I nodded. "More fun than the gym."

Becky pulled out a large book about medieval clothing, put in on my desk, and starting flicking through it, intently studying some of the illustrations.

"You okay?" I asked Hayley, in a low voice.

She nodded. "Just being silly," she murmured.

"Want to talk about it?"

She looked uncertain for a second or two, then turned towards me. "You said about hoping you'd meet someone special again," she said quietly. "Me, too. Hoping there's someone special for me who'll make it all better."

I took her hand and squeezed it. "I wonder if there aren't dozens of people like that, but you don't realise it when you meet them. Or you can't connect long enough for it to take."

She started to say something, then paused and bit her lip. "You know the other day? When we both said we thought we might have met someone with promise?"

I nodded.

"Is it always scary?"

I smiled. "Might be. It's only happened to me twice."

"Helen was the first?"

"Yeah. I was terrified. She seemed to be too good to be true."

"The second time?"

I took a deep breath and jumped in, hoping I wasn't making a complete fool of myself. "I'd forgotten how scary it is, hoping I'm right and don't screw it up."

She gave me a shy smile. "It is, isn't it?"

The flush of hope and optimism I felt gave my doubting inner voices an emphatic kick into a dark corner.

She stretched up to kiss my cheek. "What's it like with two of us?" she whispered.

"Terrifying and fun," I whispered back. "Not quite sure what to make of it yet."

She raised an eyebrow, but said nothing.

Becky closed the book and put it back on the shelf. "Brilliant illustrations. I'd love to borrow that sometime and steal some ideas from it." She looked at the two of us, standing close together, and gave us a lovely smile. "You'd make a great couple in photos, you know. Perfect for publicity shots for the show."

*****

Later that evening, Uncle Paul read the children their current favourite bedtime story yet again, tucked them in and turned off the lights. When I walked into the huge farmhouse kitchen, all the women were huddled around one corner of old pine table. As they all looked at me, grinned at each other, and stopped talking, I guessed I'd interrupted a girlie chat. I poured myself a glass of red wine and sat next to Claire.

Becky looked at us alternately for a few seconds. "I can't get over how similar you two are," she said. "It's like seeing the male and female versions of the same person."

"We think we're identical twins," Claire said. "I'm twenty-three minutes older than Paul."

"I thought identical twins were always the same sex," Hayley said.

"They usually are," I said. "According to my internet research, if we're identical, Claire's a mutant."

Claire jabbed me with her elbow. "Watch it, or I'll get us DNA-tested to see who's the mutant." She turned to Becky. "Paul got the muscles and a few extra inches in height, I got the looks and the brains."

Hayley grinned, enjoying the banter. John was used to it. He joined us with another couple of bottles of wine and topped up any glasses that needed it.

"I think you're both good-looking," Becky said, almost absently. "Amazing cheekbones. Paul's more masculine, obviously. Square jaw and he's built up his body with exercise. But you're a very feminine woman, Claire. Nice round face, great complexion, good figure, classic waist to hip ratio. You're, what, about three inches different in height?"

"You must excuse her," Hayley said. "Her masters in art looked at how ideas of beauty have evolved."

"Sounds like more fun than qualifying as an accountant," Claire said. "Paul's four inches taller than me."

"Try studying for a detective inspector's exam," John added. He nodded at me. "My revision makes Paul's bloody thesis seem riveting."

I tried to look offended. "It *is* riveting." Maybe one day someone would get the pun.

Hayley laughed. "That was a pretty convincing expression, Paul. We might make an actor out of you yet."

Claire nudged my foot with hers.

John nodded his head at me. "I'll embarrass Paul now, but it's in a good cause. When he first moved down here, he was a right bloody mess. Sometimes, we'd go out and end up in a rough pub. When things got rowdy, just as it was all about to kick off, he'd turn into this 'don't fuck with me' macho character and walk into the middle of it."

John was quite right. I was embarrassed. I wanted to forget about that. I'd wanted to get into hard, nasty fights. I'd not wanted to hurt anyone else, but to be hurt myself, so I could feel something other than my inner pain and loss.

"The weird thing was he scared the shit out of everyone and it all calmed down in no time. I can only remember a couple of people who even threw punches at him." John sipped his wine. "Whoever he turned into scared me, too. I reckon so long as the character you want is one he can be, he'll really be it. Not act it, but be it."

Everyone looked at me, which I had to tolerate, as the ground completely and utterly failed to open up and swallow me in the way I rather hoped it might.

"Maybe I can get a job as a security guard," I said, wanting to change the subject. "Wander around a supermarket, making people feel guilty."

"Make sure you get a nice uniform," Becky said. "All the girls like those."

"Couldn't possibly comment," Claire muttered, exchanging a smile with John.

Hayley leaned forward and reached her hands across the table towards mine. I reached forward and took hers.

"Do you always read the children their goodnight stories?" she asked me.

"Not always. They ask for whoever they want. I enjoy it, though."

She smiled at me. "I've narrated some children's audiobooks. It's good fun. Makes a refreshing change from regular acting sometimes."

"Do a lot of actors do that?" John asked.

"Not many. I think you need the right sort of talent. A few are amazing and make a good living. In my case, I didn't have any other work at the time. I'm okay at it, I think. It's work, and something fun to do."

I knew John was itching to ask both women lots of questions, something he said all police tended to do. He'd learned not to when off duty, as Claire had told him years before, in no uncertain terms, to behave like everyone else or he had no chance with her. He leaned forward a little, looking at Hayley with interest. I recognised this as his usual slightly sneaky conversational technique, subtle enough for Claire to tolerate. "So, this show you want us to work in?"

Hayley fiddled nervously with the stem of her wine glass. "It's a big deal for me," she said, looking down at the table. "I'm thirty-one, so can't play teenagers any more. Unless I can make a name for myself, major roles will probably be thin on the ground until I'm old enough for middle-aged characters. If this show doesn't lead to a series, it'll probably be ads, one-off parts in dramas, or if I'm lucky, a regular part in a soap. I might have to look for work in regional theatres again. That was fun when I was in my early twenties, but, well…I've got to the point where I want a life, if that makes sense."

She looked up at John and the light caught tears in her eyelashes. "So, finding a group of bloody good stunt performers with eye-opening routines is the most amazing luck."

John looked at her with genuine warmth. "We'll open their eyes, Hayley. Don't you doubt that." He nodded his head towards me. "And I know Paul will do his best to be a great leading man for you."

Hayley looked at me. I saw a mixture of hope and anxiety in her expression, which touched my heart.

I nodded. "Kick me into shape, Hayley. I'm here for you."

She smiled, then wiped her eyes.

Claire nudged me with her elbow, an *I approve* gesture.

Becky leaned her head against my arm and looked up at me, like a child asking for a huge favour of some sort. "You're a big, soft bugger, aren't you?"

Claire laughed, then looked at Hayley. "So what's next for you?"

She brightened up as she replied. "Pretty decent gig actually. Three weeks of outdoor Shakespeare; *Midsummer Night's Dream* and *Twelfth Night*. All around the country, staying in budget hotels, so it'll be intense and exhausting, but it's with a good company. Phil's confident he'll be able to start production in five or six weeks, so it works out for me."

"And I'm going too, makeup and wardrobe," Becky added. "Hayley got me the work."

John looked at me. "So, what happened today?"

Hayley looked from me to John. "Today?"

John nodded. "Paul wasn't himself when you all came back. I know something happened which rattled him."

Becky and Hayley looked at each other. "Yeah," Becky said slowly. "You seemed to change a little this morning. By those stones."

I swallowed. I didn't want to talk about it, but I'd promised John I would. "I had an anxiety attack, first one in ages. Knocked my confidence a bit."

Hayley looked at me sympathetically. "I had some when it all blew up with Tony. They were awful. What brought it on?"

I paused, feeling stupid and embarrassed. "When I came back with my camera, I saw you two talking and it looked like you'd argued and..."

"You thought you'd done something to upset us?" Becky asked.

I nodded, feeling about an inch tall.

Hayley got up, rushed around the table, and hugged me. "Becky told me to grow up and I threw a hissy fit."

"I might have been a bit blunt," Becky admitted.

"But you do it so well," Hayley said, with a laugh.

Becky nudged me. "Just to prove it, Paul, you're a lovely, gentle, thoughtful guy, one lots of women would seriously consider as a keeper." She paused and I turned to look at her. "So stop being so fucking oversensitive and insecure," she added, pointedly.

John laughed and stood up. "And so say all of us. Anyone fancy a stronger drink? Gin, brandy, or scotch?"

11

Later, we were in bed together, Becky on my right and Hayley on my left again, talking quietly like new lovers might; relaxed, open and trusting. We were all naked and it felt natural for us to be together like that. I loved it.

Becky had sat up and ran her fingers through my hair. "I meant what I said earlier."

"She did, too," Hayley added. "I've not heard her say many nice things about guys, but we agree about you."

"Thanks," I said. "Right now, I feel like I'm the most stupid, hopeless case ever."

"Come off it," Becky said. "You're not even in the top ten."

"Why are you so insecure, Paul?" Hayley asked.

I paused, then decided to tell them. "Remember I said I felt guilty about Helen's death?"

"Yeah," Becky said.

"I'd asked for the day off, but my boss said no. I was working on something critical for a big deadline of his. He was a sneaky, domineering bully who picked on me, and I didn't know how to deal with it. He wanted me out and made my life very uncomfortable."

Hayley reached an arm across me and Becky slid down and rested her chin on folded arms on my chest. It felt reassuring and comforting, these two women so relaxed and comfortable with me.

"The weather was awful; snow, ice, and slippery roads. Helen's mum had a hospital clinic appointment and she went to give her moral support. Her dad was driving. This huge lorry jack-knifed right beside them, then overturned, crushing their car almost flat. They all died immediately, I was told. I always blamed myself for not standing up to my boss and driving them. They'd have been in my Range Rover and I've far more experience of driving on shitty roads."

Hayley squeezed her arm around me. "It wasn't your fault. It might have happened just the same, but with you there, too."

I sighed. "I know." I paused. "Sometimes, at dark moments," I said quietly, "I've almost wished I had been there."

Becky jabbed me with a fingertip. "Don't ever think that. Never ever ever. You've too much to offer the world. Give us a chance to help everyone else see that."

I reached an arm out and pulled her close. "Thanks. But I wasn't there, through my own weakness. And that's what I can't forgive myself for."

"If you'd been there, maybe it would have been four tragic deaths, Paul," Hayley said. "It wasn't your fault."

I swallowed, trying to shift the hard lump from my throat. "Five," I whispered. "Helen was pregnant. Only a few weeks, but she was carrying our baby."

I was smothered by two embraces, arms around me in a confusion of movement. They held me as I sobbed and kissed my cheeks as tears poured from my eyes.

When I recovered my composure, Hayley asked if I wanted a drink. We all agreed on scotch, so she padded off to the kitchen.

"I wish I'd not said I didn't want kids," Becky said. "That must have hurt."

"You didn't know."

She stroked my face, then leaned forwards and we kissed in a tender and loving way.

"If I change my mind, you're top of the list," she whispered. Then she stroked my cock, which was partially erect. "I'm sure this could do the trick. Eventually."

"Suppose Hayley and I are together then?" I asked.

Becky giggled. "She's my best mate, we borrow things from each other all the time."

I puzzled about that for a couple of seconds, then Hayley came back with our drinks. We rearranged the pillows and sat up.

"So, how did you end up here?" Hayley asked.

"There's a week or so I simply can't remember, or don't want to. There were police enquiries, inquests, cremations for me to organise. I was given redundancy without any questions, probably in the hope I'd go quietly without beating up my boss. With that, life insurance and inheritance, I was financially secure." I sipped my drink. "Claire, John and I had a few long talks, and, cutting a long story short, I bought Mum and Dad a smaller house a few miles away and we all moved into the old family farm. Claire took redundancy from her big city bank and started her dream equestrian business, John got a promotion by moving to the local police force, and I've got my work and interests, and help Claire out."

Becky reached out and squeezed my arm. "You all made big changes."

"We did, but so far, it's working out for us."

"All you need now is to be happy."

"I'm getting there," I said. "Things have picked up lately."

"Anything to do with being in bed with two naked women in bed?" Hayley took my drink and put it on the bedside cabinet with hers. Then she straddled my thighs. "Two pairs of boobs to play with." She got up on her knees and leaned forward, then wriggled her breasts in front of my face.

I held her and kissed each nipple in turn. They puckered up as my lips touched them. "Maybe it's you two I like, naked or not," I said, well aware that I had an erection rapidly growing very close to Hayley's pussy.

"Right answer," Becky said.

She got to her knees and pressed her breasts against my face as well, one after the other. I took each nipple into my mouth and teased them with my tongue and lips.

"What's the time?" Hayley asked.

Becky peered at her watch on the bedside cabinet. "Almost midnight."

Hayley settled across my hips, close enough for me to feel her pubic hair against my eager erection.

"The iron tongue of midnight hath told twelve," she said, in a soft voice. "Lovers, to bed. 'Tis almost fairy time. I fear we shall outsleep the coming morn as much as we this night have overwatched. This palpable-gross play hath well beguiled the heavy gait of night. Sweet friends, to bed." She pushed me back onto the pillows. "A fortnight hold we this solemnity, in nightly revels and new jollity."

"I guess that's Shakespeare?" I asked. "The only bit I can ever remember is that one about the world being a stage."

"All the world's a stage," Hayley promptly said. "And all the men and women merely players; they have their exits and their entrances, and one man in his time plays many parts."

Becky giggled. "Jeez, Hayley, you're as soft as Paul. And you've got three weeks of non-stop Shakespeare coming up."

"Details, schmetails," Hayley said in a caricature New York Jewish accent. "Is it time we got some sleep?" She stroked my chest with her fingertips and looked at me with a tender expression. "You need to rest."

I smiled up at her and squeezed her hands. "At least we've got all that out of the way this time."

"This time?" Hayley said in a mischievous tone. "He thinks there'll be a next time, Becky."

"Fine by me," Becky said. She leaned across me and dangled her boobs over my face, and I couldn't resist gripping a temptingly pert nipple with my lips. She giggled again, then leaned close to my ear.

"And if I do, I most definitely won't behave myself," she murmured.

Hayley slid off me and we all snuggled up together. "Count me in," she murmured. "And I'm not convinced Paul would mind in the least."

"I might put up a token resistance," I agreed. "I don't think you're that scary."

"Even if we told you not to come until we said?" Becky asked.

"No way," I replied, trying to ignore the nerves and excitement I suddenly felt. "I'd just have to recover quickly."

"Something to work on." Becky looked at Hayley. "He's a big boy and a genuine gentleman. Be a pity not to train him to play nicely. The needs of the many outweigh the needs of the one, as the saying goes."

Hayley giggled. "Wondering what you've let yourself in for?"

I smiled at the ceiling. "Wondering but not worried." I meant it, too. So long as my anxieties didn't resurface.

They both kissed me on the cheek, then settled under my arms. I couldn't move, but part of me didn't want to. I liked knowing that they felt so comfortable and secure with me. I turned my head and kissed Becky, then kissed Hayley. "Good night, my two lovely ladies."

I listened as their breathing got longer and slower. For the first time in ages, I drifted off to sleep feeling completely content. *They both want to come back.* I felt elated, knowing I'd not screwed things up. *Is this what happy feels like? Not sure I can remember.*

*****

I woke around dawn, rested and content. I lay still, listening to my two companions breathing steadily, the only sound I heard. After living in busy towns and cities for years, the silence here had been striking when I moved back.

I thought back over the last couple of days; what we'd done and shared, and how happy I felt about it. It felt like we'd shared more than just sex-play. I realised I'd subconsciously felt guilty about having casual sex since I moved back, so I'd treated every occasion with Hayley and Becky as special. I'd never had casual before losing Helen. Since then, I'd had what felt to me like a dozen or so relationships which only lasted one night. That might be why I'd felt like shit afterwards.

Did I have a chance to make a major change now? I felt Hayley move and turned my head towards her. She was awake and looking at me, her eyes anxious.

I rolled towards her, reached out and stroked her cheek. She put her hand on mine, drew it to her mouth and kissed it. She shuffled nearer and I put my arm around her.

"Hiya," I murmured as quietly as I could.

She reached up and stroked my lips with a finger, which I kissed. "I'm feeling a bit nervous," she said, as quietly. "About us. All of us."

"Me too, but I'm keen to work it through and see."

She swallowed. "It feels exciting and odd."

"You and me, or the three of us?"

She chewed on her lip for a few seconds. Beside me, Becky turned over, her sleeping breath rhythm unchanged.

"Maybe." Hayley paused. "I love Becky, she's almost a sister, but she does…well, take over. She likes to be the centre of attention. It's her act."

Some of the pieces dropped into place in my head. Becky being dominant was her way of hiding a lack of confidence. My act was a confident man who could perform in public, or be someone's for just one night. Like John said, if the character was in me, I could be it, at least as far as anyone else would know. I wasn't sure what Hayley's act was.

"I think she's absolutely great, but I get it," I whispered. "Maybe just you and me? For a weekend, see how it goes?"

Hayley gave me a shy smile and nodded. She moved closer and put her mouth beside my ear. "I'll talk to her. We both know you need someone. She'll sulk a little, but it'll be fine. We're not shutting her out, after all."

I swallowed a hard lump in my throat. "When?"

"Not for at least three weeks. This tour will be full-on, lots of travelling and performing most evenings, so limited chances to call each other." She must have seen the disappointment I tried to hide. "It's my career. If it's a problem, better we know soon, I guess?"

I kissed her. "Not a problem."

She wriggled and slid one of her legs between mine. "It'll be fine." Then she kissed me.

It started slowly, then got more and more passionate, and I got turned on in no time. And I got the distinct impression Hayley did, too.

Becky yawned rather pointedly. "Is that a private cuddle, or can anyone join in?"

Hayley and I stopped kissing and grinned at each other.

"Not just anyone," I said. "This club has an exclusive membership of three."

Becky giggled and leaned over me to kiss me on the cheek.

I rolled onto my back and she snuggled up under my arm. "You two whispering about me?"

"Yeah, making Hayley jealous by saying how amazingly sexy I think you are."

She raised her head and looked questioningly at Hayley. Hayley nodded her head downwards. Becky reached under the duvet and ran her fingers over my cock. "Shit, he's got another stiffy."

"Hmm, we'd better do something about that," Hayley said. "This is meant to be loving fun, after all."

"Did I hear you use the *L* word?" Becky asked teasingly.

"Oh, shit, I did. Um, well, he is kinda nice."

"Yeah. Almost cute. I'd be tempted to use it, too."

Hayley looked at me. "You don't mind if I say 'loving,' do you, Paul?"

I grinned. "It does feel that way. And I could easily fall for either of you."

"Only one of us?" Becky asked. "You're being picky."

Hayley giggled. "Surely, you could love both of us, Paul?"

"Absolutely, something new for me." *Why did I say that?*

"Live and learn time," Becky whispered.

I suddenly realised I could use my confident act and felt comfortable enough to play more edgily.

I turned towards Becky and lowered my voice to sound conspiratorial. "I have a plan."

I took both her hands and pressed them against the pillows on either side of her head. A look of surprise flashed over her face, then she smiled. "Yeah? Think you can make me behave?"

I leaned so close our noses touched. "Want a smacked bottom?"

I felt Hayley sit up beside me.

Becky giggled. "Maybe I do."

"If you deserve one, I'll put you over my knee."

I turned to Hayley. "Would you restrain Becky for me? I need to let go of her hands, but I'm not sure she'll follow my instructions yet." I looked at Becky. "She might get a bit distracted."

Hayley grinned and nodded. "Yes, sir."

I threw the duvet off the bed, then eased a knee between Becky's legs. She moved them apart and I knelt between her knees. Hayley slid beside Becky and put one arm over Becky's, holding them above her head.

I leaned down, taking my weight on my arms, and kissed Becky teasingly, making her lift her head so our tongues could meet. Then I took possession of her mouth and pushed her onto the pillow. I slid my hands down her body, over her breasts, then along her sides as I kissed and nipped her nipples. She gasped and wriggled.

Hayley giggled and kissed Becky's cheek tenderly. "Be a good girl, this once," she said. "You might even enjoy surrendering."

I slid my hands down to Becky's hips and covered her tummy with a carpet of kisses. We all knew where I was intending to stop and Becky writhed to press herself against me. "Shit, this is winding me up," she said.

"Nicely?" Hayley asked, stroking her hair.

"You wait," Becky muttered. "I'll ask dumb questions while you suffer."

I sat back on my heels and ran my hands down the front of Becky's thighs, then I traced my fingertips along the inside of her thighs, moving towards her pussy. Her inner lips were temptingly plump, and I had to resist the urge to lick them. She froze as my fingers ran along her body, as close to her pussy as I could without touching it.

"Touch me, you rotten bastard," she whispered.

"Pardon?" I asked, aiming for an authoritative tone.

Both women grinned.

Becky licked her lips. "Please, sir, touch me."

"Better," I said.

I slid down the bed and leaned on my elbows with my face inches from her. The fruity sweet-and-sour scent of her arousal was clear. I glanced up at Hayley, who watched with an expectant smile on her face. She winked at me, then kissed Becky on the cheek.

I ran the tips of my index fingers along Becky's outer lips, which made her gasp. Then I blew gently along the line of her inner lips, from where her clit was hidden down to her entrance.

"Don't be rotten to her," Hayley said. "She wants you to be *really* rotten."

Becky was about to say something, but I slipped a finger into her and her eyes widened. "Oh, fuck," she whispered. "More, please."

"How many fingers should I put into her, Hayley?" I asked.

Hayley gave me a mischievous grin. "You've got pretty big fingers, let's find out."

I slid my finger in and out of Becky, which made her writhe her legs and whimper slightly. "Certainly two. Maybe three. That'll be enough this time."

I pulled my finger out, then slid two back in and wriggled them deep inside her. She tensed her legs and lifted her hips off the bed.

"It feels like you're being nasty," she mumbled.

"You suffering?" Hayley whispered.

"I can cope."

I slowly finger-fucked and teased her until her inner muscles relaxed a little. Then I slid three fingers partway into her. Her body tensed around them and I pushed a little harder, sliding them as deeply into her as I could. I suspected I was stretching her, and felt her legs move and heard her heels sliding on the sheet.

"No more fingers, please," she whispered. "That's just on the exciting side of uncomfortable."

I carried on teasing her with my fingers and crouched down. She cried out when my tongue touched her clit.

I glanced up and saw Hayley smiling tenderly at Becky, then she looked down at me, crouching between her friend's legs and her eyes widened with excitement. I saw she'd pressed her thighs together and slowly moved one against the other.

Becky's body responded, wetting my fingers. Her aroma had developed a richer quality. I kept my fingers deep inside her and moved them in and out a little while I licked her clit. Her tummy and thigh muscles started to tremble and she pushed her hips against me, seeking release.

Hayley gave her gentle kisses on the cheek and whispered in her ear, "Let go, let it rip, Becky."

I turned my hand so my fingers hit where I thought Becky's G-spot might be, and she convulsed as she climaxed. Her back arched off the mattress, her legs clamped against me, and she let out a series of gasping moans. Her inner muscles pulsed against my fingers like a wave, as if trying to push them out. The pulses weakened as she writhed and twisted on the bed. Then she relaxed completely and let out a long, happy sigh. "Scrape me off the bed when we're ready to go. I don't think I can move."

I moved and supported my weight on my hands on either side of Becky's head. She looked up at me with what seemed like a mixture of nerves and excitement.

"Can't move, eh?" I murmured. "As in at my mercy? Nothing you can do to stop me teasing you?"

She swallowed. "Probably not, sir."

I leaned closer, pressing the tip of my cock against her hot, wet entrance. "Do you trust me, Becky?"

She nodded, her eyes wide.

I looked at Hayley and hoped I showed her they could both trust me. "You can let her arms go."

I lay on the bed, on top of Becky but keeping my weight off her. I leaned to kiss her hungrily. Her arms were suddenly around me and she writhed under me, as if trying to encourage my cock into her. I pushed my hips back and forth a few times, pressing my erection against her more firmly. I was tight against her entrance, and it would have been so easy to slide into her.

She held my face in both her hands. "Are you going to screw me?"

"Not today," I said. "If you come back, well…"

IAN D SMITH · 107

"I'll be back," she said, so softly I barely heard her. "I want you so much. Every little bit of you, right up there, inside me."

Our eyes locked and we both knew we wanted the same thing, to have our bodies locked together as we screwed. I kissed her again, then moved between the two women and we all hugged each other.

"He's a dirty, rotten teasing bastard, Hayley," Becky said. From her tone, I didn't think she was complaining.

"So are you going to tease me?" Hayley asked.

"Right now, in fact."

Becky slid off the bed, stood slowly, then stumbled around the bed to Hayley's other side and snuggled up against her.

"And she claimed she couldn't move," I said to Hayley.

Hayley shrugged. "She's a bit of a fibber sometimes."

I slid my arm under Hayley's shoulders and leaned down to kiss her. She was eager to respond and guided my hand down her body. "Please don't take the piss too much. I'm almost ready to explode."

I climbed carefully over her; she wrapped her arms around my shoulders and her legs over mine. Then she really, really tested my self-control when she lifted her hips and ground her pussy lips against my erection.

"Who's teasing who?" I murmured after a few seconds of struggling to behave myself.

She grinned and kissed me hungrily. "Better distract me, hadn't you?"

As I got to my knees, Becky slipped against Hayley's side and kissed her cheek. "For a second, I thought you were going to get what I didn't."

I explored Hayley's pussy with all my fingertips, one hand going up as the other went down. I pressed against her entrance with all the fingers on my left hand while I teased her clit with my right index finger.

Hayley writhed and gasped as Becky watched her expression, kissing her on the cheek from time to time. When Hayley half-opened her eyes and looked at me pleadingly, I slowly slid two fingers as far into her as I could. She let out an almost explosive gasp and twitched her body, her shoulders leaving the mattress for a second. Then she relaxed, closed her eyes and smiled. I finger-fucked her a few times, then leaned forward and lapped my tongue around her clit.

She arched her back a little. "Oh, shit, I'll need scraping off the ceiling too."

I glanced up and saw she was fondling one of her own breasts, cupping it and squeezing the nipple. Becky watched with interest, then glanced at me and blew me a kiss.

My tongue seemed to be having the desired effect. Hayley's hips and thighs tensed against me and her muscles trembled slightly. I changed my finger-fucking from two to three fingers and slid them all deep inside her, then looked up to see her face. Her eyes widened, then she came with a cry as her inner muscles clamped down on my fingers. She let out a long moan and tossed her head from side to side. Her inner muscles rippled against my fingers a few more times, then she lay still.

I slid back up her body to embrace her, and the tip of my cock pressed against her entrance again. She wrapped her arms around my neck. "Yes, please."

I felt her body start to open for me as she pressed back against my cock. "I've got to stop," I said, and climbed over to lie beside her. "If I do it with either of you this morning, I won't want you to go. I don't want that to be the last thing we do."

Hayley hugged me and Becky reached over her to stroke my face.

"You're worried we won't come back, aren't you?" Becky asked.

"Part of me is," I admitted. "I'm trying to ignore that voice. I've heard more than enough from it over the last year or so."

"That's the trick," Hayley said. "Ignore the voice that says you can't, it'll go wrong, or you'll make a fool of yourself. When I've walked out onto a stage to open a show, it can be the loudest thing in my head." She leaned forward and kissed me. "But, so far at least, I've got away with it."

Becky nodded. "You try keeping us away. Part of me wants to chuck it all in right now and stay here forever."

"Come on, cuddle time," I said.

I wanted to say I'd love it if they both did, but didn't dare.

12

Just as we were about to get up, Hayley looked up at me. "Is it my turn to be in charge?" she asked.

Becky grinned and raised her eyebrows.

"Go on," I said.

Hayley curled up against me in a sinuous and erotic way. "When we have a shower, I want a quick shave down there. But I want to shave your bits and pieces, too. I think it'll look great and feel amazing."

I was reluctant, but the idea of two women messing around with me like that...

Becky raised her eyebrows. "You do trust us, don't you?"

"You got all excited when we lathered you yesterday," Hayley said. "So today, we'll see just how far we can get you."

"You can be in charge again, Hayley," Becky said. "You've got a deliciously dirty mind."

It was a memorable experience. I'd never shaved a woman before, let alone two. It was well worth the odd gentle slap for getting distracted and trying to play with them.

They were gentle and teasing, and shower gel lather was a delightful lubricant. I found it difficult to stand still while Becky's hands slid up and down my shaft and Hayley knelt in front of me, but I was very aware of the razor she was running over my balls.

When she'd finished, they stood on either side of me. Hayley wanked me slowly and hugged me with her other hand. Becky cupped my newly-shaven and very sensitive balls with one hand and ran her other over my backside, and down between my legs. Her fingers teased my rim as Hayley got me closer and closer to my climax.

"You're enjoying me playing with your arse, aren't you?" Becky murmured.

"I'm enjoying what both of you are doing," I said. "You're certainly getting your own back for earlier."

"Just getting you back for being a rotten tease," Hayley said.

I felt it was time to accept the inevitable, rose a little on my toes and arched my back.

"Are you coming?" Becky asked.

"I think he is," Hayley said.

"Oh, yes," I said, through gritted teeth. It was difficult keeping my balance.

Right as my orgasm started, Becky firmly held my balls and slipped one of her fingers surprisingly deep inside me. My first shot of cum went clean across the shower cubicle and I was briefly lost in a wave of ecstasy.

*****

The time for goodbyes came far too soon. I didn't want them to leave, and the looks they gave me made me sure they didn't want to go. We had a firm final group hug, during which Becky surprised me by tearing up.

"Ring anytime," Hayley told me. "Can't promise we can talk then, but we'll ring you back, okay?"

"Either of us," Becky added, prodding me in the chest with a finger. "It's only for a month."

John, Claire, and the children joined me to wave as Hayley's car set off along the drive.

John squeezed my shoulder. "Never thought to bet on you meeting two women at the same time," he said. "You spend two years avoiding possible new partners, then two come along just as you're ready."

Claire put her arm through mine. "As I see it, you're a knight looking for a damsel to protect and rescue. My gut feeling is that Hayley needs someone to stop her from doing dumb things, and Becky needs a someone to rescue her when she does." She turned to give me a serious look. "Unless they're prepared to share you, which would be plain weird, I'm not betting either way."

"I think you should have two girlfriends, Uncle Paul," Daniel said solemnly. "They're both brilliant fun."

"I like them, too," Vicky said. "Hayley does great silly voices."

I wasn't going to argue, but I knew I had to think about what Claire had said, assuming I really did have a chance of a relationship with either of them.

Claire hugged my arm with hers. "Paul, you've let your defences down and the lovely guy you really are is back out in the open. Please don't bottle up again. Come and find me whenever you want to talk."

I felt at a complete loss for the first time in months. I tinkered with a paper I was writing, but felt trapped in my study. The bedroom seemed stark now that the scattered women's clothing had been taken away. Like Helen, it seemed my new lady friends weren't the tidiest people to share a home with, even if they didn't have much with them. But despite being a bit of a fusspot about keeping my flat neat and tidy, their clutter made it feel like home, in an odd way.

When I straightened out the pillows and duvet, I realised they'd both sprayed some of their perfumes on the bedding. That was too much for me right then. I wasn't going to start crying over women I'd only known for a few days. Not even ones I knew I was already falling for in a big way, and feared I might never see again. A lot could happen in a month.

"Grow up," I told myself. "You're not bloody fifteen anymore."

I put on some scruffy working clothes, grabbed some gloves and a few tools, scrounged a flask of coffee from Claire, then went off to repair a section of drystone wall. It was far enough away to save everyone from my increasingly gloomy mood. I thought having a job which required physical effort and concentration might help me come to terms with letting my emotions off the lead for the first time in years.

Then the silly text messages started and I spent the rest of the day grinning.

*****

The university gym was hardly used during the vacations, usually two or three early-evening users, and sometimes I had the place to myself. We hard-core regulars greeted each other with a polite nod or smile, but rarely spoke. That had been enough for me while I was getting over Helen.

That evening, I was sharing it with a young blonde woman I knew by sight. A regular who always threw herself into exercising with focussed energy, she moved gracefully, and went faster on the treadmill than me. I wasn't sure I'd even seen her break into a sweat that often.

I was a little surprised to see her there, as the week before I was sure she'd broken some fingers. I'd only just arrived and saw her hurrying into the women's changing room, clutching a hand to her chest, her expression one clearly of pain. I caught a momentary glimpse of two fingers apparently twisted into unnatural shapes. One of the other users told me her hand had been caught when something went wrong with one of the resistance machines. I helped one of the staff inspect it, and we found a securing bolt had failed. She'd already left before anyone could offer her first aid, but she seemed her normal enthusiastic self that evening, and her hand looked fine.

I guessed she was in her mid-twenties. She was good-looking, a little shorter than Hayley, with a clear complexion, striking green eyes, long blonde hair, and a physique that was both athletic and feminine.

Discreetly watching her exercise that evening, I idly wondered if she'd be interested in joining our jousting team. She had a real presence, the sort of person who'd be noticed even if she wasn't a beauty. With training, she'd probably be a competitive sparring partner. I'd read some of the recent speculation about female Viking warriors, and thought she'd be eye-catching in that sort of role.

For some reason, I simply didn't fancy her. John would probably tease me that this woman had blanked me out because she had better taste. She was always there on her own and didn't wear an engagement or wedding ring on her finger.

Although I was hoping to start a relationship with Hayley or Becky, I was still unsure where I stood with either of them. I wasn't looking for alternatives, as I wanted to see how things developed, but I wasn't sure how they'd feel if I struck up a friendship with this girl.

She left shortly before me, with a wave and a friendly "goodnight."

I finished, showered, changed, and left. I was walking over to my Range Rover when I heard a vehicle door slam close by, then a woman shouted, "That's all I fucking need."

I looked around and saw my blonde chum, now dressed in faded denims and a hoodie, struggling with the bonnet of an old Land Rover. I walked a little closer before speaking. "Can I help?"

She looked around. "Bloody thing won't start."

"We've got one like this on the family farm," I told her. "What's the problem?"

She shrugged. "Turned the key, nothing happened. Dead as a dodo."

I propped the bonnet open and had a quick look. No loose wires, no smell of fuel. "Try it again?"

She hopped into the driver's seat and I heard her fiddle with the keys. "Anything?"

"No." I thought for a few seconds. "Noticed anything different recently? Say this morning?"

She stood near me. "Bit sluggish to turn over, that's all. It was very reluctant this morning, but it was at stupid o'clock and I can't say I blamed it."

It had rained first thing and been gloomy all day, so she'd probably used the headlights and windscreen wipers. I had a suspicion. "Can you turn the lights on?"

She leaned in and flicked a switch.

The headlights came on, strictly speaking, but were the faintest of glows. "Think your battery's flat. I'll move my vehicle over, I've got some jump leads."

A couple of minutes later, her engine was running again.

"Just a flat battery?" she asked.

"Looks like it. Might be your alternator." I pointed to it. "Had to replace one on ours. I'll leave my engine running for a while, it'll help charge your battery enough to see you safely home."

"Not got that far to go." She gestured towards the fish and chip shop in the nearby terrace of shops. "Famished, can I treat you, too? As a thank you?"

Five minutes later, we were sitting side-by-side on my tailgate, eating chips.

"I'm Maggie Petherick," she said. "I'm a trainee with a law firm, doing a part-time law degree. I've had a very long 'one of those days' at work, and this was the last thing I needed. Really grateful for your help."

Her surname rang a bell, but I couldn't work out why. "Paul Torridge," I said. "Lecturer in history and metallurgy."

She looked at me for a couple of seconds. "Are you the guy in that jousting team?"

I nodded.

"Mum and Dad saw you at the Cornwall Show, said it was a great performance. I was nosey and looked up your social media and remembered seeing your name as a contact."

"Guilty as charged," I said. "My brother-in-law set it up with me."

"I can see why you train so hard, mixing cardio, endurance and resistance work. You need to be fit and strong, I guess." She pursed her lips for a second, concentrating. "Torridge... I think my parents know yours through the Commoners. Dad mentioned meeting a history lecturer called Torridge who owns a farm. I guess that's your father."

That didn't surprise me. Mum and Dad were both enthusiastic supporters of the Dartmoor Commoners, a body heavily involved in managing the moorland, which formed a large proportion of the National Park.

We ate our chips and she seemed happy to chat as we traded family backgrounds. Her dad was a former consulting engineer who had a small farm as his retirement project, her mum provided financial services for farmers and small firms, and she had a brother in the Army. I asked about her hand, mentioning that I'd heard about the machine breaking.

"Oh, it was nothing, everything's right as rain," she said casually. "Cold compress, a few painkillers and I was fine."

I felt surprised. "I was sure you'd broken a couple of fingers," I said. "I got there just as you rushed out of the gym."

She held up both hands and wriggled all her fingers. "Gave

me one hell of a fright, but I was hardly hurt."

I felt puzzled. "I thought…" What *did* I think?

Before I could ask more questions, she changed the subject. "Know anyone I can ask to look at my alternator?"

Inevitably, I ended up offering to help, and we swapped phone numbers.

Feeling curious, I rang my dad that evening and mentioned meeting her.

"Petherick? Lovely couple. He's the sort who'd soon be seconded onto the committee of anything he got involved in, and change it for the better. If this girl's anything like her mother, she'll be bright and good looking." He chuckled. "Looks like your two lady friends have a possible local rival."

"No, I don't think so. She's pretty, but I think we'll only be friends."

"Well, that's good, you've not made any new friendships since you moved down here."

I realised he was right. I'd been hiding in my shell too long.

*****

"So, how was the first night? You looked great in that photo Becky sent me. Best Hermia I've seen in ages."

"Creep. It wasn't brilliant, but not a total cock-up either. No one blanked or missed a cue, full house, perfect weather, we did well from the merchandising, and the venue made a tidy profit on catering. Already invited us back next year."

"All good news then?"

"Well…" I heard an edge to her tone.

"Go on."

"One of the guys in the cast is a complete fucking sex-pest," she whispered. "We'd been warned by a couple of the other girls. Becky and I are the only new faces around and he's totally convinced he'll be notching his bedpost before long."

I felt a cold dread. "What can you do?"

"We'll keep an eye on each other so we can politely interrupt any attempts to make a move. If he's too pushy, we'll ask the director to have a word with him. But we've both got a secret weapon, our own defence against the dark arts."

I was puzzled. "What?"

She giggled. "Remember that photo Claire took at the showground of you in your armour, holding Becky under one arm and me under the other? She sent us copies. We've told Romeo that we're both your subs, you're extremely jealous and getting court-ordered treatment for anger issues."

That picture was now the wallpaper on both my laptop and phone. "If he can't take the hint, let me know and I'll drop by. In full armour."

She sighed. "We both wish we could see you again soon. We're all over the bloody country with this tour."

I looked at the list she'd sent me. Two more days in Essex, then venues in Suffolk, Norfolk, Cambridgeshire, Lincolnshire, Yorkshire, Cheshire, North Wales, and Derbyshire. I knew it was their choice, and something many actors did, but it was beyond me. I liked being settled, even if it was at least partly from insecurity.

"Me, too," I said. I hope I didn't sound as wistful as I felt.

"We'll see you soon," Hayley said. "Come on, what have you been up to?"

"A commission to make some Roman armour and weapons for a new museum display. John's working on new routines we can show Phil, so I'm being beaten up a lot. Riding, writing a paper, going to the gym… Same old boring stuff."

"No knightly deeds of valour?" She sounded as if she was smiling when she said it.

"Funnily enough, yes. Rescued a damsel in distress yesterday evening. She had a flat battery. Well, her car did."

"A fair maid?"

"Verily," I said. "She uses the same gym as me at the university in Plymouth."

"Should I be jealous?"

"Not in the least. She's called Maggie, seems nice. I think you and Becky would get on well with her. See if I can get you all to meet up."

"Very noble, my good sir."

"Know what? I realised I'd not made any effort to be friendly with anyone at the gym since I started going there."

"Claire said you were really depressed when you moved back, so it's not surprising you were withdrawn."

I sighed. "When you two left, Claire said the old me had come out again. I think she's blaming you."

"Perfect." Hayley was definitely smiling. "Any sign of you pulling back into your shell and you'll be in big trouble, capiche?"

"Capiche."

There was a slight pause. "Paul, um, what time are you likely to be going to bed tonight?"

"Probably late. Why?"

"Well… Becky suggested we ring you and sort of, um, chat on speakerphone. When we're all in bed. We're sharing a room, of course."

I felt a thrill. "You mean a three-way, dirty phone call?"

She giggled. "Knew you were bright. Look, got to go, having a snack before we muscle down for tonight's show." She lowered her voice. "We'll ring you later for group phone sex."

*****

John and I rode side-by-side along a track on the moor. He seemed lost in thought and I left him to it for a mile or so. A second murder victim had been found, in circumstances very like the first, and now he had a bigger case to manage.

I was thinking about how to reply to the friendly e-mail Kathy had sent me. She asked some questions about our conference arrangements, and said she had viewed the video clips of our latest performances on our website. She said we were all mad, but both her children now wanted to learn to ride and joust. She'd not mentioned her close male friend, so I decided to keep it all at a polite and friendly level, and say nothing about my possible new love life.

"Sorry," he said, bringing me out of my own thoughts. "Poor company this morning."

"Want to tell me about it?"

He shrugged. "Making no progress. The second victim was another sex worker. I knew her a bit. Smart, tough kid. Ran away from an abusive stepfather. Just got over her drug habit, too. Pisses me off." He was quiet for a couple of seconds. "Unless it's a coincidence or someone with a thing about sex workers, I'm worried it's some squabble between organised crime gangs. But if that gets out of hand, we might find even more murders being committed as a way of making a point."

I knew he took all his investigations seriously. He said even a nasty villain who'd been asking for trouble was someone's son, brother, father, husband, boyfriend or friend. But he felt more urgency about those who seemed to be innocent victims.

"How's your new friend at the gym?" he asked, changing the subject. "Flat battery girl?"

"Maggie? She's fine, I think. Not that chatty, we still only really say hi." I grinned. "There was a new guy there last week, Mark, just started at the uni. I introduced myself when he asked for help with one of the bits of kit. It's quite funny as they're both distinctly smitten, can't take their eyes off each other, but I don't think they've spoken yet."

John laughed. "Reckon knightly responsibilities extend to matchmaking?"

I nodded. "I'll find some way to get them talking if he's going to be a regular."

"You should make some more friends, Paul. Do you good."

"You and Claire ganging up on me again?"

"Of course." He grinned at me. "When do the girls finish that tour? Sure it won't be long before one or the other's back."

"This week, but no firm date for another visit."

Otto turned his head to give me a glare, then tossed his head.

"Come on," I said to John. "These two fancy a gallop. Race you to the top of this hill." I shortened the reins, shifted my weight and felt Otto's back muscles flex under the saddle as he pushed himself forward. The wind in my face felt good as we charged up the hill, John's horse eager to keep up with Otto.

13

My new lifestyle meant Mondays were no longer the first of five stressful days. I'd even managed to avoid giving any lectures or tutorials on Mondays. That Monday was lovely, the countryside looking refreshed by a few days of sunshine and heavy showers. I took Otto out first thing, then went on a short, fast run.

I stopped at the top of a hill on my way back, where I could see the farm buildings and paddocks spread out on the other side of the valley, a few hundred yards away. I sat down and waited for the stitch in my side to ease. As I looked around, I realised that I felt at home in a way I'd not felt for a couple of years. These were the hills and fields Claire and I had spent our childhood exploring, our own private adventure playground. And it felt like that again.

I leaned against a stone wall for a few minutes and enjoyed the sun on my face. It was going to be a warm day, not ideal for working in my forge, but I had a promise to keep. I stood up, stretched, and set off. The replica Roman armour only needed a little more work, then I could fit it on the mannequin the museum had supplied, and arrange collection with the courier. All being well, I expected to finish it by the end of the day.

I was engrossed in my work when I heard the workshop door open. I looked around and saw Claire walk in, carrying a tray.

She'd brought me lunch; a sandwich, cake, and a huge mug of coffee. "Any chance you can take a riding lesson at four-thirty this afternoon?"

"Sure," I said. "What standard?"

"First-ever lesson. You're better with total beginners than me."

"No problem. Thanks for lunch."

She play-punched my upper arm. "You'd forgotten, as usual. It's chilli tonight, I'll be dishing up about half six."

"Lovely, thanks." I took a bite of the sandwich, which was generously filled with a strongly-flavoured cheese and Mum's home-made chutney.

"Popping over to Exeter, running some errands," she said.

"Need me to keep an eye on the children?"

"It's fine, they're coming with me."

A few minutes later, I was completely lost in my work again and stopped wondering why she'd made an effort to sound casual.

A few hours later, Daniel came to fetch me. He could barely reach the latch, so I had a second or so's warning. He leapt in and adopted a caricature fighting stance copied from some TV show he'd seen. God only knew what he'd watched.

"Mum said I had to come and get you," he announced, in a loud monotone.

"What did she really say?"

He changed his stance from left- to right-handed. "It's nearly half-past four, get your gormless uncle out of his workshop." Then he relaxed, scuffed his foot on the floor, and looked thoughtful for a second. "Uncle Paul, why haven't you got any gorm?"

"Otto ate it."

He stomped a foot. "No, he didn't!" he shouted. He loved Otto, even if he was a bit wary of him.

"I'll come right away."

He nodded. "Mum's started cooking dinner. Smells wicked." He turned and went back to the door. "We're having garlic bread," he said, with relish. He and Vicky loved the stuff.

I slipped into the farmhouse to wash and grab a cold drink from the fridge. Dinner did smell good when I sniffed the cauldron of chilli.

In the stable yard, Claire was talking to our new customer, a slim woman in new-looking riding clothes. She faced away from me, already mounted on Wally.

A good choice. A pretty coloured pony, he was patient and gentle.

I walked over and was about to introduce myself when the woman in the saddle turned around and grinned. "Hello, Paul."

My mouth fell open in surprise. "Hayley?" I looked at her and my mind went blank. "I didn't know you were here." At least I managed to say it without stammering.

Claire was sniggering behind her hand. I realised her trip to Exeter must have been to meet Hayley at the train station.

"Didn't want to interrupt you," Hayley said. "You were busy in your workshop."

I stopped beside her and patted Wally's neck, as I always did. She leaned down and kissed me, twisting so the visor on her riding hat wouldn't hit my face. I'd gone from stunned to elated in no time at all.

"I guess you're not only here for a lesson?" I asked, my heart hammering with excitement.

She wrinkled her nose. "Bit of a long way for one lesson. I fancied a few days away and remembered I've an open invitation. A tempting one. Becky sends her love, of course."

We grinned at each other for a second like soppy idiots, then my brain started working and I took Wally's bridle. "Right, let's get on with your first lesson."

Claire walked beside us and opened the gate into the outdoor school. "Dinner at half-six, so don't be late." She winked at me.

"Okay," I said, getting into instructor mode with a bit of an effort. "Basic horsemanship. Balance, centres of gravity, rhythms, and being relaxed."

She raised an eyebrow. "We're still talking about riding horses, aren't we?"

Behind me, Claire sniggered again. I guessed she'd watch for a few minutes, then slip away.

"Right at the moment, yes," I said. I had to concentrate on her riding lesson, after all.

An hour later, Hayley watched as I untacked Wally. "You'll have to teach me all this," she said. "I need to be comfortable doing it in case Phil wants me to handle any horses in the TV show."

"We'll help with the horses for the rides tomorrow. It's pretty easy. You'll get it."

We put everything away in the tack room and as soon as our hands were free, we grabbed each other and kissed hungrily. I picked her up and held her against the door. She wrapped her legs around mine, her arms around my neck. It felt fucking wonderful, with her in my arms again, her body against mine.

"Don't know about you," I said. "But I need a shower before dinner. That workshop gets hot."

"I wasn't going to say anything," she murmured, tugging at my earlobe with her lips. "I'll join you. All day, I could only think about seeing you and being together again."

I leaned back to look at her. "And?"

She grinned sheepishly and blushed ever so slightly. "Let's just say I could do with fresh panties." She raised her eyebrows ever so slightly and my body reacted before my mind consciously registered it.

After a quick clothing adjustment to hopefully conceal my raging erection, we walked over to my flat, hand-in-hand. "I've got the outline script, so we can start improvising around that." Hayley looked up at me. "Phil asked if you're free to start work next week. He knows it's last minute, but he can fit in around any commitments you've got. Two days of short scenes, nonspeaking stuff to start with, so you get comfortable with ignoring the cameras and hitting your marks."

"That's fine," I said. "Term's finished, no deadlines looming. That armour I was working on is ready for the courier."

"So, I've got you to myself?"

"Unless Becky turns up out of the blue, I reckon so."

She opened the front door to my flat with what must have been Claire's spare key. I made a mental note to find another spare for Hayley.

"Seriously, she's happy for us," Hayley said. "She'd wanted to come too, but had a fantastic last-minute offer to do styling and makeup for a prestigious fashion shoot in France. We'll all meet up again soon, but I'm under orders to catch myself a man first."

"Anyone in mind?" I asked.

She pushed the door shut behind me, stood on the second step, and wrapped her arms around my neck. "Let's get naked and in the shower." She raised one eyebrow teasingly. "I'll take my pick there."

We kissed, then she took my hand and led me up the stairs.

"Welcome home," I said, when we reached the living room.

"Thank you. It feels like that, too. I was cheeky and unpacked when I arrived." She reached up and ran a finger across my five-o'clock shadow. "You'd better shave that off, or I'll be red-raw in the morning."

"You can supervise," I said.

She grabbed my hand and walked backwards towards the bedroom, pulling me along. "And you can shave me again," she said. "But there's something we ought to do first."

"What's that?" I asked, as we went into the bedroom. I saw she'd already unpacked, as female clothes and shoes were everywhere.

She grabbed me around the waist in a tight hug. "We can do

it, here and now," she mumbled into my chest. She looked up at me, her eyes bright. "I don't give a fuck about being sweaty and yucky. I want to know what it feels like when you're inside me. Then we can do it again later, over and over again, until I get the idea."

"You have a way with words," I said, pulling off my boots. "Ever thought of acting?"

She smacked me on the backside. "Watch the cheek, or else."

"Or else what?"

"Or I'll see if Becky's suspicion's right, that you'd enjoy being spanked."

We threw our clothes anywhere, dragged the duvet onto the floor and clambered onto the bed.

Hayley rolled onto her back and reached for me. We kissed and she ran her hands over my back and through my hair, as I stroked her side with my free hand.

"I spent an hour near you, but with a horse between my legs," she said. "For days, all I've been able to think about is you between my legs."

"I've spent the last month trying not to think about that," I said. "An erection lasting that long cannot be healthy."

She grinned and stroked my face. "I know it's not very romantic, but let's just do it."

I reached over to the bedside table, opened the drawer, and pulled out a brand new box of condoms.

She raised an eyebrow. "A dozen?"

"I'll buy more tomorrow if we run short."

She laughed and I let her roll me onto my back. She kneeled beside me, unwrapped a condom and slowly unrolled it over my erection. "I've got a coil, so you can't get me pregnant, but I'd like us to use condoms for a while. Is that okay? I had a full health check recently, including STI tests. All clear."

She seemed anxious, which surprised me.

"Of course it's okay," I said. "I had the same about two months ago."

She grinned, then flopped down beside me. "Right, we can relax now."

I pulled her close and kissed her, starting off with gentle pecks, then getting more passionate as we got carried away and I explored this lovely woman's body. As I stroked and fondled her breasts and nipples, she breathed more heavily and kissed me more forcefully. When my hand strayed down her side and over her hips, she wriggled and writhed against me, rotating her hips in a rhythmic movement.

"Touch me, you rotten tease," she whispered into our kiss.

I ran my fingers along her pussy, marvelling at the soft skin there, then parted her lips and traced my fingers over the slick warmth within. I found her clit and rubbed around it for a minute or so, which made her tighten her grip around my neck and shoulders. Then I slid down to her entrance, pressed against it with two fingertips and her body opened for me. I kept my fingers shallow, just up to the first knuckle, teasing and spreading her a little.

Hayley's hip movement pushed downwards on my fingers, and they were inside her up to the second knuckle. I slid them in and out a few times, matching her rhythm, then curled them against her, searching for her G-spot. I knew I'd found it from the slightly different texture and her gentle moan. I circled my thumb as gently as I could around her clit, hoping she came before my hand got too uncomfortable from the contortions.

She broke our kiss and pressed her head against me, her eyes tightly closed. Her whole body tensed and she slowly arched her back, lifting her hips higher and higher.

Then I felt her orgasm. Her body stiffened and her arms gripped me even more tightly. Her inner muscles squeezed against my fingers in series of downward pulses. And she groaned, a single long "oh" sound.

I stopped my finger movements as soon as she flopped onto the bed, a relaxed smile on her face and her eyes half-open.

She breathed heavily and sighed. "That's so much better." She looked up at me, smiled and ruffled my hair. "Glad to see you've not lost your touch."

I pulled her against me and hugged, stroked and caressed her, wanting her to know how I felt. Touched, flattered, excited, and quite possibly falling in love. We giggled and kissed, and I felt bloody happy.

She rolled on top of me, her legs falling to either side of my hips. My latex-clad erection was between her open legs.

"Our collective turn," she whispered, then reached down, guided me into place, and pressed herself onto me. "It's been a while, so I may need a minute or two to stretch, what with me being out of practice and you being, well, a rather big boy."

"You're in charge," I said, watching her face.

She half-closed her eyes as she pressed down a little, then relaxed, and pressed down again. I felt her body open, warm and soft, letting me in to her a little more with each push she made. And then I was fully inside her. We stared into each other's eyes as she slowly worked her hips, sliding up and down my shaft.

"Oh, wow," I whispered.

"About right," she said, her breath catching a little. "It's bloody nice up here."

I held her securely against me with one hand and stroked her hair with the other. She took my hand, guided it to her mouth, then kissed each fingertip.

"Do you want to move? Can I do something different?" I asked.

"Nope and nope," she said. "I want you to lie there and let me bring you off."

"I could last for ages," I said. "This is nice."

"Relax and let go," Hayley whispered. "You've given me so much pleasure, I want to repay a little bit of it. Let yourself come as soon as you're ready."

So we lay there, me flat on my back, Hayley on top of me, pumping her hips and sliding up and down on my erection. "Come for me, Paul. Let me put that special smile on your face."

"Special smile?"

"Oh, yeah," she murmured. "You have an amazing smile when you've just come."

"So have you," I said. Things were starting to come to the boil in my groin.

Hayley looked down at me. "Smile that smile for me." She closed her eyes for a couple of seconds and let out a deep breath. "We can go at it like rabbits later."

I grinned. "Out in a field at night?"

She smiled down at me. "It's warm enough, isn't it?"

"I think we'd cope."

"Good. I'll be naked, on all fours, and you can shag me from behind. Bet I'll come at least once, with this big dick of yours sliding in and out of me."

My body was reacting without my brain getting involved. And I tried to keep it that way. Then I reached my point-of-no-return and knew I'd come in a couple of seconds.

"I'm coming," I whispered.

"Come in me, Paul," Hayley grinned and kept the same movement going.

And I came in her. I felt a single strong surge, then a wave of pleasure blossomed from the tip of my cock and washed over my body.

Then I opened my eyes and took a deep breath. "Bloody hell, that was amazing."

Hayley grinned down at me. "Good." She gave me a quick kiss, then eased herself off my slowly-subsiding cock.

I removed my condom, and wrapped it in a tissue from the box on my bedside table.

"Come on," she said. "Better jump into the shower. Can't be late for dinner."

I propped myself up on my elbows. "You expect me to move now?"

"You can soap my tits and shave my pubes again," she teased, then bounced off towards the bathroom. Her bum made that a fine sight to behold.

*****

"Hayley, will you read to me tonight, please?" Daniel was trying his *I'm quite sweet, really,* look. He'd sat next to her on the sofa and Vicky was on her other side. I'd been evicted to an armchair.

"I'd love to, thank you for asking," she said, then exchanged a brief glance with Claire. "What's your favourite TV show?"

I felt curious, suspecting some stage management was afoot.

"*Poppy and the Professor,*" Daniel said, without a pause.

I thought for a second, but couldn't remember if I'd seen the show. I wasn't usually around when the children watched TV.

"I love Poppy," Vicky said, "it's so funny."

"What's good about it?" Hayley asked.

"It's the Professor." Daniel laughed. "He gets into a mess of some sort every time and Poppy always rescues him."

"Like Mummy," Vicky said.

"Oh? How's that?" Hayley asked, looking interested.

The two children grinned at each other. "When Daddy or Uncle Paul get something wrong, Mummy fixes it for them," Daniel said.

Vicky turned to Hayley. "Mummy fixed it for you to like Uncle Paul. He's been lonely," she said seriously.

Hayley kept a straight face. "Well, I really do like him."

Claire looked like she was about to die from embarrassment and John turned away to hide his grin. I felt a huge wave of affection for my family.

Hayley changed the subject smoothly. "Did you know there's a *Poppy and the Professor* book?"

"Is there?" Daniel's eyes were wide with excitement.

Hayley leaned closer to him. "And I've brought it."

"Yippee. Can I go to bed now, Mum?" Daniel slid off the sofa.

"And me. I like Poppy," Vicky added.

"Just one story, all right?" Hayley said.

I squatted in the doorway of Vicky's room, my back against the frame, and watched two rapt children listen intently to Hayley. She was pretty bloody impressive at storytelling, making lots of eye contact with the children, using perfectly timed pauses and a variety of voices.

After two stories, she closed the book. "We'll have another story or two tomorrow."

They both thanked her politely and I tucked Vicky in, then followed Daniel into his room to tuck him into bed.

On the way downstairs, I took the book from her and looked at the cover. "Poppy and the Professor, by Anne Martin." I flipped the book to look at the rear cover. "Stories from the popular TV series starring Trevor Western as the Professor and Hayley Terence as Poppy." I looked at Hayley. "You're Poppy?"

She took the book back and opened it to show me a photo of the cast. She was instantly recognisable, despite the heavy-framed round glasses and Victorian maid's outfit. I rather liked her in that long black dress and white lace apron and hat.

I tapped on the Professor, wearing a Victorian gentleman's outfit. "I did a spot on a TV documentary he presented. Great guy. Has this dotty old so-and-so act, but he's sharp and was well-prepared. Amazing fun to be around, like Brian Blessed mixed with Stephen Fry. Loads of hilarious stories."

She nodded casually. "He's great to work with."

As we walked back into the lounge, I gestured to the book. "Where did you get this?"

"I asked the writer."

"Any other little secrets I should know about?"

She shrugged. "Possibly."

I wondered what I'd learn as we spent more time together.

We sat down and Claire passed us each a glass of wine. It was from one of the bottles Hayley had brought, far better quality than we usually drank.

"Trevor Western's one of the big names in British acting," I said. "Why's he doing a kid's show?"

"Favour to the writer. A short episode is shown as a regular part of a longer children's show," Hayley said. "We usually record six at a time over two days. It doesn't pay brilliantly, but great fun to do, and we've built up quite an audience."

John grinned at me. "So, Uncle Paul has to read stories with different voices now?"

I looked at him over my wine glass. "So does Daddy."

He sighed. "Oh bugger."

It was John's fault we drank far too much. He had the next day off and badly needed to relax. The stress from the double murder investigation was getting to him.

We'd got into bed and were giggling and cuddling when Hayley's mobile phone started playing "Girls Just Wanna Have Fun." She put it on loudspeaker.

"Hiya, Becky, John got us pissed." Hayley giggled. "How's France?"

"Hot. We're staying in a fab chateau. Photographer's a bit up himself, but gets brill pictures. The models are all eighteen or nineteen, dead skinny, cute, but really shy and no fun. Anyway, how was it?"

"Perfect, couldn't have asked for a nicer first time," Hayley replied, grinning at me. "Started off gently, then we picked up the pace after about half an hour."

"What? How long did it last?" Becky sounded puzzled.

"About an hour. Doing it again tomorrow. Made my thighs ache a bit, though."

"An hour? Jesus, you'll never walk straight."

"It was a lovely horse, too." Then Hayley rolled onto her side and had an attack of the giggles.

"I meant your first shag with yummy Paul, you plonker," Becky said.

"It was gorgeous." Hayley squeezed my hand and gave me a beautiful smile. "Absolutely lovely. And I'm rather keen to have my second any minute. Maybe two more before we get up."

"When you're sober, blow-by-blow accounts, please. And I'm not talking just about the oral. Say hi from me."

"Hi, Becky," I said.

"Hayley, you cow, am I on speaker?" Becky squealed. "Let me to talk to Paul for a second, then I'll ring off until tomorrow."

Hayley turned off speaker mode and passed me the phone.

"Hi, Becky, my sweet, how are you?" I asked.

She sounded like she was grinning. "Marvellous, but if I was with you, I'd be even better and possibly getting shagged senseless. Look, take care of Hayley, okay? Or I'll fucking kill you with unreasonable demands on your body." She paused, then continued softly. "And thanks for being so good to her. See you soon, sexy." And she rang off, leaving me puzzled.

This was totally new to me, my girlfriend openly discussing our sex life with her best mate in front of me, with said best mate then blatantly hitting on me. But I had shared my bed with both women at the same time, and we'd all indulged in some lovely sex-play.

"Have I got any secrets left?" I asked Hayley.

"I'm worth the trouble," she said. "So, have I claimed myself a man?" Her hand was making a quite specific claim upon my person at that moment, which rather derailed my train of thought.

"You have, hook, line, and sinker," I said, my erection growing fast. "Your own part-time knight in shining armour, complete with a mad family."

"You've not met mine," she said. "You've been invited over next weekend, by the way. Is that all right? I know it's short notice."

She seemed anxious, but I genuinely felt pleased.

"Delighted to accept," I said. "I guess we won't be sleeping together?"

"I've got my own flat, so yes, we will. Well, we might get some sleep." Hayley reached for the condoms and helped me put one on. She grinned and got onto all fours. "Let's practice doing it like rabbits, but indoors."

I bent down to lick her pussy and she sighed as I slipped my tongue inside her. She was already pretty aroused, which made me feel flattered and excited.

"That's lovely," she said. "Be so kind as to mount me, sir. Pray make haste. And roger me full soundly."

I grinned. "As my lady wishes." I knelt between her calves, gripped her hips, and eased the tip of my cock into her. "I am sworn to be your protector." I added, trying to sound serious.

She pushed herself back onto me and sighed again. "Pray keep your lance to hand, sir, so it may serve me royal well."

I started screwing her with a slow, steady action, pulling almost out then sinking in as deeply as I could. "My lance is yours, lady."

She lowered her head and shoulders to the mattress and sighed, then she gripped a pillow with both hands. "Fuck me, Paul," she said, her voice breathy. "Fuck me."

14

I looked around the buzzing craft market and sighed. I'd stopped to taste some alcoholic fruit cordials, and been left behind. It had only taken Claire and Hayley a few days to bond, which meant they were wandering around yakking together, and I was expected to carry everything and keep up.

I worked through the crowd in the general direction we'd been heading, trying not to get annoyed with everyone walking so damn slowly. I soon spotted Claire's shoulder-length dark brown hair above the heads of most of the other visitors, then I spotted Hayley beside her. I caught up with them without being spotted. "Ladies, perchance you invite mischief upon yourself in this market, I beseech you to remain within my compass."

Hayley turned and stepped towards me, her forehead almost close enough to bump my chin. She raised one eyebrow, and looked at me in a way that combined amusement and tolerance. "Pray tell me, Captain, art thou a mewling puppy that must trail your mistress the day long?"

"Lady, my duty is to vouchsafe your person." We were so close together that, as I looked down, her loose, low-cut top revealed an appealing aspect of the person I claimed to be so keen to safeguard. I couldn't resist taking a brief peek, which was spotted, of course. She instantly gave me an icy glare and I fought an instinct to take a step back.

"Guard that your interest in my person does not exceed your writ, sir," she said through gritted teeth. "Mayhap thou wouldst follow me to the privy, should I desire relief?"

Daniel laughed. "Uncle Paul, why are you and Hayley talking funny?"

Claire grinned. "We told you, they're practicing acting for this TV show they're doing. It's like old-fashioned English."

Vicky held up both her arms. "Uncle Paul, carry me, please."

I picked her up and sat her on my shoulders. She didn't have me wrapped around her little finger at all.

"What's a privy?" she asked.

"Old word for toilet," I said. "I wanted it to sound like we're in the olden days."

Daniel grabbed my hand and leaned back, hanging from my arm. "Say something from the olden days."

"Gadzooks, young Master Hatherleigh, thou art truly a most vile spitling."

He laughed, then turned to Claire. "Mum, I'm thirsty. Can I have a drink?"

Claire gave him her special mother's stare. There had been yet another discussion about the "magic word" not that long before.

"Please?" he added.

Hayley slid under my arm and slipped a hand into my back pocket, a lovely intimate gesture. "Becky's talked about teaching him the second magic word," she murmured.

I looked at her in surprise. "There are two?"

She nodded. "Oh yes, 'please' and 'now,' apparently."

I grinned. "She'd be in real trouble with Claire for that." I wouldn't put it past Becky. But as fond of her as I was, she could take the rap for that.

As we got to the refreshment area, a family vacated a table, and

Claire pounced. I bought drinks, then we all sat in the sunshine. The children had fun gurgling loudly through their drinking straws while the rest of us pretended not to notice.

Claire leaned her chin on her hand. "You seem to have your characters and a plausible working relationship for them. Suppose they fancied each other something rotten, but both wanted to hide it? You might worry he's not posh enough, and at the same time, he could think you're out of his reach? He'd probably feel embarrassed about his feelings and be overanxious about doing his duty without letting them take over."

Hayley nodded. "It'd fit the storyline better than only realising they fancy each other when she gets the marriage offer. And we can have some fun acting around that." She squeezed my thigh.

Claire snorted. "Acting? Try hiding it. Just remember how it felt the first day or two you spent together."

Hayley looked puzzled. "How come?"

"Jeez, you two. You were gawping at each other anytime you could."

"What's gawping, Mum?" Daniel asked. Five-year-olds can get away with questions like that.

"It's what your Uncle Paul did yesterday while I gave Hayley a riding lesson."

Hayley rearranged her ponytail. "He was very complimentary about my seat," she said casually.

Claire struggled not to snigger and I think I kept a straight face.

"Mummy, I want the privy," Vicky said.

"Kids learn too quickly," Claire muttered, then led her daughter off to the nearby row of temporary toilets.

Hayley squeezed my hand. "Did I overdo the glare earlier? You looked a bit startled."

"It was good," I said. "I wanted to take a step backwards. I'm not used to being with someone who can turn it on and off like that."

Daniel pointed to a stall about thirty yards away. "Uncle Paul, they're selling toy swords and stuff."

"I'll take him, if you want," Hayley said. "We'll only be a couple of minutes."

I glanced around, but no one nearby was obviously infirm or pregnant, so I didn't feel guilty about sitting alone at the table in the sunshine and enjoying peace and quiet for a couple of minutes. The last few days had been great fun, if slightly mad, and a nice interlude before Hayley and I started recording the first scenes for the show. I felt comfortable about the ones I'd do with my jousting display team, and improvised conversations with Hayley had been a great idea to help me to relax and get into character. But I'd started feeling more and more nervous about acting as the recording got closer.

I rummaged in a carrier bag and pulled out my purchases. I'd spotted a dichroic glass pendant which looked fabulous in the sunshine, as the colours sparkled in a fascinating way. Hayley said Becky would love it, which was all the reason I needed to buy it. Hayley had obviously admired a rather striking coloured pendant made from anodised aluminium, which I bought while Claire had distracted her. I'd wanted to buy them both nice gifts to surprise them with. No doubt Claire would tease me about being a big softie, but I could live with that. She didn't yet know I'd bought her a hand-coloured silk scarf she'd clearly liked.

I put them away and checked my phone to see if John had sent me a text. He was expecting to hear the results of his police inspector's exam today, but no news so far.

Claire and Vicky were back first. "What's he talked Hayley into now?" Claire asked.

"Looking at a stall full of toy swords. Don't worry, she won't buy him any."

Daniel ran back a minute later and climbed on his chair. "They're brilliant," he declared.

"I'll make you a wooden one."

He shook his head. "I'll wait until I'm big enough for a real one. Then I can chop people's heads off."

Claire sighed. "I've brought a monster into the world."

Hayley sat down next to me and took my hand in hers.

"Hayley, where do your mum and dad live?" Daniel asked.

"In Sussex. About four hours away in the car."

"If you're a princess, is your dad a king?" Vicky asked.

"I'm only pretending to be a princess. My parents are both actors."

She'd told me that when we first met, but always managed to evade any further questions about her family. I wasn't that bothered if she had a reason for being coy; we were still in the early days of our relationship.

"Why don't you get your real dad to be on TV with you? Wouldn't that be easier?"

"He's busy on another TV show," Hayley said. "Being very good at pretending is an actor's job."

Vicky paused, then changed the subject. "When's Becky coming to stay again? I like her, she's funny."

Claire smirked, which made me suspect she knew something I didn't. She'd clearly enjoyed the last few days, watching Hayley and I getting to know each other, our first chance to spend time together since we'd met.

"Not much longer," Hayley said. "She's working at the moment. But I know she wants to come again." She caught my eye, flicked an eyebrow upwards and gave me an ever-so-slightly-dirty smile. It left me feeling a bit nervous and excited at the same time. I'd never fancied two best friends before. I didn't know how I'd feel when we all met up again, now that Hayley and I had spent the last few days starting a relationship.

Claire collected the various bags scattered around the table, pushing the heavier and bulkier ones in my direction. "We're about done here. Next time you're visiting, we'll all go into Exeter and snigger at Paul."

Hayley looked puzzled. "Why snigger?"

Claire grinned. "He hates buying clothes."

Hayley had asked what we did for Christmas and before I knew it, we'd agreed to go out somewhere fancy, all dressed up, and I'd somehow promised to buy a dinner jacket.

"I'm only being measured up," I said. "They probably won't have my size in stock."

"Your size what, Uncle Paul?" Vicky asked.

"A fancy jacket and trousers, for when we go out before Christmas," I said. "It's called black tie."

"What's that?" Daniel asked.

"It's the most elegant way for a guy to dress," Hayley said. "Very smart."

"Uncle Paul's going to look amazing," Claire added, then gave me a big cheesy grin.

"Even better than in his armour?" Vicky asked.

Claire and Hayley exchanged thoughtful looks.

"Tough one," Hayley said. "He looks good in armour, but it's uncomfortable for cuddling."

"Black tie every time," Claire said. "Think Daniel Craig as James Bond."

Hayley grinned. "Mum worked with him, said he's a lovely guy." She turned to Vicky. "Difficult to choose. We'll have to see."

"I think you should wear your armour," Vicky said firmly. "Then everyone will want to see your shows and you can do them all the time."

"Everyone has proper jobs," Claire said. "They can only do a few shows every year."

"Can I be a princess in the show, Mummy?" Vicky asked.

"Only if I can be a knight," Daniel said.

Hayley winked at me. "We'll see. Not on this show, but maybe in another."

Claire sighed. "Be sure before you decide you want children, Hayley. They look cute, but they're actually little monsters."

*****

John came home on a high that evening, having passed his inspector's exam with flying colours, and he had been promised a promotion within his current team as soon as the paperwork was sorted out.

So, obviously we helped him celebrate.

After the last three months of limiting myself to modest social drinking, I was a little out of practice with over-indulgence. Walking in a straight line was a teeny bit challenging, especially as Hayley tried to get me to half-carry her. Fortunately, it was only a short walk from John and Claire's farmhouse to my flat.

"Were you trying to get me drunk?" Hayley giggled as we crossed the yard. "John's bad enough, but I don't think you could pour a single if your life depended on it."

"Why would I get you drunk?"

She gave me a coy look. "Um, maybe so I couldn't fight you off?"

I pulled her closer. "I seem to remember you whispered something a few minutes ago about it being time for more sensational sex."

She jabbed my side with her elbow. "What sort of woman do you think I am?"

I picked her up and put her over my shoulder, holding the back of her thighs. She batted my back with her fists. "Put me down!" she squealed.

"In a second." I looked around and spotted the door to the feed store was ajar. I carried her in and closed the door behind me. The sun had almost set, but enough milky-yellow twilight came through the skylights for me to see.

She waggled her legs and tried to tickle me under my arms. I swung her down and around so she landed softly on a stack of hay bales, with her upper body face down and her feet just touching the floor. I lifted her dress and tugged her panties down to her knees, then stroked her pussy. Her cleft was warm and slick, the outer lips already open. She gasped as I slid my fingers to her clit, then back to tease her entrance.

"You're already wet," I murmured.

She wriggled in my grip. "Well, I'm not saying no, am I?"

She kicked her panties off while I dropped my jeans and my underpants. My erection sprang up and brushed her thigh.

"Go on," she whispered. "I want you now."

"No condoms with me," I said. "I'd have to be very careful."

She gasped as I slid a finger inside her. "Well, you could always drive me mad, even if you don't come." She wriggled to get my finger further inside her. "I'll shag you senseless back in your flat."

I slid my finger out, reached round, and started rubbing it over and around her clit. She gasped, lifted her hips off the bales, then I felt her hand fumble for my cock. She reached back to stroke and squeeze me while I teased her clit, then she ran her fingers over my balls.

"I love you being bald down there," she said, sounding a bit breathless. "I was delighted you kept shaving after we trimmed you."

She guided me to her entrance and pressed herself back a little so that I just entered her.

"It was exciting when you two shaved me," I said, trying to keep my self-control and slide into her gently. "And it still feels nicely sensitive all the time."

"I'm feeling nicely sensitive at the moment," she murmured, then leaned her head and shoulders on the bale as I slowly slid my tip in and out of her. I carried on teasing her clit and felt her hips tense. I was surprised to realise she was getting close, and she came quickly, gasping loudly and shuddering.

As soon as she'd finished, she relaxed and sighed deeply. "Fuck me, please," she whispered.

"You're sure?"

She nodded. "Absolutely."

I pulled out and we both got on top of the bale. She lay on her back, I settled between her thighs, eased my tip into her and made a few more gentle thrusts before sliding easily all the way into her. I moved with a slow, steady rhythm, fully in then almost pulling out. I loved how she felt slick and open, and the way her wetness started to spread over my balls and thighs.

"Go faster," she whispered. "I love it when you go hard and fast."

I took my weight on my arms as I accelerated and felt my balls swing with every thrust. She writhed, then lay still, her head turned to one side. She'd closed her eyes, and raised her eyebrows as if surprised. *She's close to coming again.* And it brought me closer, too.

She grabbed my T-shirt and held on tightly as she came, clawing me then thrusting her hips upwards to meet me as I slid into her.

I was close myself, briefly wanted to let it rip, but I stopped and pulled out of her slowly. "I'll wait until later, when we're more comfortable. This isn't exactly the ideal setting for romantic love-making."

"Bloody perfect for some down and dirty exciting sex, though," Hayley said.

We kissed slowly and deeply.

I pulled my trousers and underpants up enough to settle beside her, lay on my back and hugged her to me. The air was full of the sweet, grassy scent of the hay, with more than a hint of sex. She slid over on top of me, and pulled her dress up so she could straddle my hips. I felt her small patch of trimmed pubic hair tickle my tummy and the tip of my cock pressed against her pussy.

"That dress is lovely," I said, trying to take my mind off the tempting idea of being deep inside her again.

"Thanks." She snuggled against me. "I like it. Nice and light for the summer."

"It's the length that gets me."

She chuckled into my chest. "It's not that short."

"No, but it's the right length to make me want to watch you all the time. A couple of inches longer or shorter wouldn't be the same. I keep wanting to lift it up."

She held herself up on her arms, wriggled her hips and my cock was suddenly against her entrance again. Her warm, wet, tempting entrance.

"You want to watch me," she whispered.

I didn't mind being teased like this, especially as it was true.

"You want to lift my dress and pull my panties down." She leaned down and kissed me, her tongue darting into my mouth. "Assuming I'm wearing any." She licked my lips. "You want to fuck me." Her loose hair fell forward, brushing my face.

"Can't deny any of it," I said, enjoying the moment.

Then she slid down onto me, taking me all the way into her in a single push. "I want to fuck you," she whispered. "And I so want you to fuck me." Then she started moving her hips, her body sliding up and down my cock. She fixed her eyes on mine. "Just like this."

We smiled at each other for a few seconds while she moved up and down on me, then she closed her eyes, leaned on my chest and hugged me tightly. I wrapped my arms around her and we screwed slowly. The evening's alcohol took over. I kissed the top of her head, relaxed, and let the moment take me over, sharing tender sex with the woman I was falling for in a huge way.

Hayley's hips moved faster, a soft warm pressure swallowing and releasing me. She moved so I rubbed against her G-spot every time I slid into her. Her grip around my neck tightened and her upper body tensed. Her expression became more determined and her breathing was faster.

"God, I'm coming again," she whispered.

She slammed herself up and down on me, then groaned into my chest and slowed her rhythm to a deliberate hard thrust every second or so. I lost control and gasped as I felt a strong surge of heat shoot out of me.

Hayley lay in my embrace, breathing deeply. "Okay, we're a bit tiddly, but I could get used to rampant sex on a hay bale in a barn." She kissed the tip of my nose. "I want us to be relaxed about sex. I've got a gorgeous hunk of a boyfriend and I want to jump you all the time. We're still new to each other, but I feel comfortable enough with you to be more impulsive and spontaneous."

I felt that we'd taken a big step in our relationship, as this meant more trust on both sides. I'd always used condoms, even with Helen, except when we were trying for a baby. She couldn't find a pill which suited her.

Hayley kissed me, then eased off. My subsiding cock plopped on my tummy.

"Any idea where my panties are? Don't want someone else finding them."

They were on the ground nearby. A little later, we were both naked and cuddling in bed.

"Can't believe I've only been here a few days," Hayley said. "It's been brilliant."

"I've enjoyed us getting to know each other."

She turned under my arm and hugged me. "Yeah, not had an argument yet. We must like each other a bit."

I grinned at her. "I like you being here."

She pouted. "That's only because I let you do naughty things to me."

"You let me? Last night you… I got detailed instructions on what to do."

"You loved it. And you were very good at it to."

"I reckon you're a sex goddess on the quiet," I murmured. "Can you remember all the details to report back to Becky, like you promised?"

She tried to look thoughtful, but her mouth gave way to a smile almost immediately. "Maybe not every detail. I get somewhat distracted."

"What distracts you?" I whispered, nuzzling her neck just below her ear.

"Loads of things." She writhed. "Say, when you told me to lie spread-eagled on the bed and firmly ordered me not to move, then you kissed and licked every single bloody skin cell on my body."

"Not being taken from behind, leaning over the sofa, while you brought yourself off with a cheeky finger? Or me giving you multiple orgasms by oral sex on the dining table? Or shagging me senseless in the feed store just now?"

She nodded. "See? Totally forgotten, so easily distracted."

"Maybe do it again, so you can take notes?"

She giggled. "You might have to help me tell tales."

I felt excited but uneasy about this. I liked Becky and felt we got on together really easily. She was bright, inquisitive, open, generous and quick-witted, with a great sense of humour, as well as the underlying anxieties I wanted to help her overcome. The two nights we'd shared my bed a month before had been the absolute erotic highlight of my life, and I'd enjoyed every phone conversation we'd had since then. I could have started a relationship just as easily with either of them, with the other as a very close friend. But I felt concerned that this openness between the women could easily make things embarrassing or complicated.

My expression must have shown my confusion, because Hayley stroked my cheek and kissed me very gently. "It's okay, Paul. We don't keep anything from each other and I'd love you to feel the same way. Yes, you'll need to get used to it, but it's bloody wonderful."

I opened my mouth, but didn't know what to say. So I shut it again.

Hayley kissed me again. "And I love it that you can both be open about fancying each other. Way healthier than denying it."

"But when we meet, it'll be different. You and I are, well, lovers."

Hayley smiled at me lovingly. "It'll be different, but we're still the same three people. It'll be fine. No, better than fine, I'm convinced. In any case, she and I come as a double-act, so you're stuck with us both." She pushed me onto my back and leaned onto my chest, smirking ever so slightly. "Anyway, aren't you supposed to be worried about meeting Mummy and Daddy tomorrow?"

Actually, I wasn't worried, more curious. She'd been rather vague whenever she talked to me about them, but I couldn't imagine they'd be anything other than polite and welcoming. "Should I be?"

She grinned. "Nah, they'll love you." She launched herself up my body and wrapped her arms around my neck. I hugged her to me.

She changed the subject. "How was your trip to the gym this afternoon?"

"Fine. I'm so used to exercising regularly that I feel odd if I don't."

"Is that girl at the gym talking to the guy she fancies yet?"

"Maggie? Yeah, she's helping him—Mark—with his fitness routine, making him work harder. Seems like a nice guy. Mostly does medical research, but he's also a medic."

She pressed a finger against my chest. "Why not go out for a beer together? It'd do you good. He'll be a bright guy and I'm sure you'll find plenty to talk about."

I thought about Mark and Maggie. They both struck me as highly intelligent, but down-to-Earth as well. He was friendly and very approachable. She'd been pretty intense when I first noticed her at the gym, but since they'd started talking, she'd calmed down and didn't exercise as if she was fighting with the apparatus. He'd adjusted his workouts, and was starting to develop more elegance in his movements. I decided that if they were dogs, he'd be a big, soft playful retriever or Labrador, and she'd be a beautiful German shepherd you'd think carefully about approaching.

"Have Claire and John been talking to you? They've been nagging me to get out and make more friends."

"We can go out on a double date together. More fun going out as a group."

I tracked Mark down on the university phone list the next morning and rang to suggest we went out for a drink the following week. He readily agreed and suggested we make an evening of it, and I could crash at his flat. I was pleasantly surprised.

15

It took just over four hours to drive to Hayley's family home, including a break for coffee and fuel. I had a distinct feeling something was on her mind, as she alternated from being excited and chatty to quiet and pensive. A couple of times, I felt she was about to tell me something, but changed her mind. I'd given up asking about her parents the day before, as she clearly didn't want to tell me much in advance.

"They'll adore you, trust me," was about as much as she'd said.

I didn't know what to expect, so when I followed the drive around a corner and saw the house, I slammed on the brakes and stared. "This is your parents' place?"

My inner historian told me it was lovely brick-and-timber Elizabethan manor house, with a Georgian extension. There were sash windows on one facade, mullioned windows with a mix of plain and coloured glass on another. My dad would drool over the chance to explore it.

Hayley nudged me with her elbow. "We call it home. Come on, you can gawp at it later. Mummy and Daddy are keen to meet you."

I parked and followed her to the stone porch on the older part of the building. The front door, ancient boards of greyish oak with rows of big black iron studs, swung open and a trim middle-aged woman wearing white linen trousers and a powder-blue polo shirt stepped out, beaming at Hayley.

"Darling, you made good time."

Hayley hugged her, then turned to me. "Mummy, meet Paul."

She held her hand out to me. "Delighted to meet you, Paul."

I recognised her immediately, but managed not to gape. Marion Terence was a well-known actress and one of the stars of a very popular period TV drama series. Mum enjoyed teasing Dad about him fancying her. Now that I saw them together, Hayley clearly resembled her mother.

I took her hand. "Flattered to be invited, Mrs. Terence."

She stretched up to kiss me on the cheek. "I'm Marion. And Terence is my maiden and stage name." She led us inside, then glanced at Hayley, who looked like she was trying hard not to squirm. "You haven't told him, have you?" Marion's voice was gently teasing.

Hayley reddened and shook her head. It looked so cute, I wanted to hug her.

"Told me what?" I asked, then immediately wondered if I should have kept quiet.

"Ah, it's my favourite sword expert."

I turned towards the sound of the rich voice and my jaw dropped open again. Aside from a neat grey moustache and goatee, Trevor Western looked exactly the same as when I'd met him the year before, talking about swords in a documentary he presented. I was sure he was even wearing the same baggy corduroy trousers, tattersall check shirt, and tan Oxford brogues.

He grinned and shook my hand firmly. "Hayley didn't tell you I'm her father, I suppose?"

"No," Hayley said, in a quiet voice. "Didn't want him to be nervous about meeting you." She grinned sheepishly at me. "I use Mum's maiden name professionally. I'm Hayley Western in real life."

"Uses a stage name to avoid sounding like that singer from New Zealand," Trevor said.

"Come through to the kitchen," Marion said. "The kettle's just boiled." She put her arm through Hayley's and they walked along the hall.

Trevor put a friendly hand on my back. "As an honoured guest, you get cake, too." His eyes twinkled and he patted his stomach. "I'm only allowed cake when we have visitors."

"Not all visitors," Marion said loudly. "His cronies don't count."

"D'you fish?" Trevor asked me. "I go sea fishing with some chums now and again."

"Enjoy it, but not done it for a while," I said.

"We usually catch enough to make it count as a fishing trip," he murmured. "More of an excuse to have a laugh and get a little bladdered."

I'd never thought about actors having an ordinary, everyday life. But chatting about everyday sorts of things over coffee and homemade fruit cake in the kitchen seemed pretty ordinary. It was rather surreal to sit there with two people I only knew from their TV work and answer polite questions about myself.

"So, your first taste of TV acting." Trevor had a twinkle in his eye. "Brought any armour and weapons?"

"A mail shirt and a sword. We're not doing combat scenes for a while yet."

"You know the drill, Daddy," Hayley said. "Start off with small scenes, people walking around, opening and closing doors, that sort of stuff. No dialogue for Paul until the second day."

Trevor looked at me. "How d'you feel about it?"

"Fine," I lied. "I hope I don't let everyone down."

Trevor and Marion exchanged smiles, and Hayley squeezed my hand. "You'll be okay, don't worry. I'm the one who's got to act, remember."

"We all feel that way, Paul," Marion said. "Every time it's our scene. And no one wants to be in one of those embarrassing outtake shows."

Trevor nodded. "Phil's a good director, I've a lot of respect for him. He wouldn't have cast you if he wasn't completely confident. Ask him what to do, then do it."

Marion put another slice of cake on my plate. "Recording a TV show mostly requires patience. Relax when you're not needed, jump when they call you. What's the title?"

"*The Princess and the King's Captain*," Hayley said, around a mouthful of cake. "I'm Princess Gwendolyn and Paul's character is Captain Rowan."

"Come on, darling, tell us all about it," Marion said. "You were still buzzing after your tour before you went off to visit Paul."

I listened as Hayley and her parents chatted about the storyline and the scenes being recorded over the following few weeks. I was grateful for being spared dialogue on the first day. Hayley's first scene was an argument with her screen father about an unwelcome but politically expedient offer of marriage.

"The main set pieces in the show are a medieval banquet, a court dance, my kidnapping and, of course, the combat," Hayley said.

Trevor looked at me. "Where's the combat being recorded?"

"A hotel near Bath." John and I had discussed the venue in a long conference call with Phil. "Their grounds include parkland, woods, a late medieval barn, some ruins, and a nineteenth century folly which looks like a castle gate and small section of wall. Three busy days for my jousting team, but with fine dining, a bar, and accommodation thrown in."

"The banquet and court dance were already being arranged for a factual programme," Hayley said. "They needed a dozen people in high-status costume for the banquet, and a dozen more for the dance. Phil offered to provide the cast and help record it. They've got experts advising on the menu, table manners, and the dancing, and already have musicians, so it'll be pretty realistic. Two birds with one stone, after some careful editing."

I wondered who the experts were, as I could have suggested a couple of strong possibilities off the top of my head had I been asked. Although my history lectures were primarily about medieval arms and armour, I was curious to know more about how people lived at the time. It would be an interesting practical insight into the period, anyway.

"Becky's been roped into a few scenes," Hayley said. "She'll be my lady-in-waiting."

This was news to me as well. "Which scenes?" I asked.

"The one in the market, where I'm being a sulky cow to everyone and you're trailing around after me, and another where I admit to her that I might just fancy you, when we watch you train some guards in swordsmanship. She'll be one of the guests at the banquet, too, and has a couple of lines in the court dance."

Trevor's eyes twinkled. "You, sulky? That'll remind us of you at the age of thirteen or so."

Marion thumped him gently, then looked at Hayley. "Ignore your father, he can't help himself."

Trevor drained his mug and stood up. "Come on, Paul, fancy a quick tour of the old place?"

Hayley put her hand on mine. "D'you mind if I stay and chat with Mummy?"

I couldn't decide if she'd sort-of asked my permission, which I sometimes felt she did, or was concerned that I'd feel uncomfortable and out of my depth.

"Of course not." I squeezed her hand.

I loved the house. It was well-maintained, and had lots of

original features, including a few panes of seventeenth century glass. It looked like modern life had been sympathetically eased into the building, too. Trevor was a good tour guide. Between his enthusiasm and my curiosity, it turned into a guy's bonding session. He was very courteous about the "new boyfriend" interrogation, too.

We were walking across the lawn when he casually changed our conversation topic. "I believe you bumped into Hayley's former squeeze."

I wondered where this was going. "Only briefly. We didn't speak." Which was true.

Trevor nodded. "We couldn't stand him. Marion was beside herself when he started taking over Hayley's life." He looked at me. "I remembered you as soon as Hayley told us your name. We're both happy for her, but we still wanted to meet you as soon as possible. Becky's been an amazing friend to her, but she's got issues too, poor girl. Yes, Hayley's an adult, but we still worry. I don't suppose your family's any different."

"Much the same," I said. "They worry and nag me nicely."

Trevor sighed. "When Hayley left him, she was like a bird with two broken wings." He held a gate open for me. "Becky hinted that you helped Hayley soon after you met her. Something about Tony?"

As conspiring with a couple of the team to spirit him away from the show venue and get him briefly arrested probably wasn't entirely legal, I considered my words. "He made a minor scene at the showground where I met Hayley. The police found him asleep in his car, in a field a few miles away. He ended up being cautioned. No doubt it was embarrassing for him."

Trevor laughed heartily. "One can but hope." He looked thoughtful for a few seconds. "Hayley's still pretty fragile and insecure. I guess that's why she didn't tell you about us. Just give her the benefit of the doubt, eh?"

I looked him in the eye. "I promise I'll do the best I can for her, and for Becky, too."

He clapped me on the back. "Pleased to hear it. Come on, time we had a little drink."

I wondered what Becky's issues were, as she seemed more confident and self-assured that Hayley. No doubt I'd find out in due course.

"Oh, one thing," Trevor said. "It's not unusual for productions to have a few people who just love to gossip and bitch about everyone else. They're usually convinced they'd do a better job than the director, too."

"Common enough in my old industry, too," I said.

"Most production companies are pretty small and recruit people for specific short-term projects, so being good at their job means egos and quirks are tolerated. If you come across it, do your best to ignore them."

*****

The rest of the day went by in a flash. I felt welcomed and accepted by Trevor and Marion, and Hayley relaxed when she realised things were going well. My gifts of Plymouth gin and Devon mead went down well. Dinner was good home cooking with tasty wine and lively conversation, followed by some excellent scotch. Hayley had prepared the sweet and seemed anxious that I enjoyed it. Marion shared some gossip about the period show she starred in. Trevor entertained us with tales about his latest project, a TV series where he travelled around Britain in a vintage car, visiting quirky little places. He quizzed me for ideas in the southwest, which they might visit in the future.

"There have been quite a few TV shows visiting the area," he said. "I'd like to visit different places from the ones they usually feature, interesting ones which might appreciate some publicity."

I thought for a few seconds, thinking about the other shows in the series which I'd seen. "How about a river trip on a paddle steamer, or a heritage tramway? I can suggest a few nice towns, too. There are a few vineyards, some distilleries making local gin and vodka, cider presses, and lots of people doing art and crafts."

"I'll get the researcher to look into all that," he said, scribbling in a small notebook. He gestured at the bottle of Plymouth Gin, which had already been opened. "That place is most definitely on my list." Hayley's flat, in a small Victorian extension at the back of the house, was small but comfortable. I had the impression she'd tidied up for my visit, as absolutely nothing was left out. But once she'd unpacked, the top of her chest of drawers was covered with neatly folded clothing, and a small chair hidden under assorted shoes.

"Mummy thinks you're rather cute," she told me. "She asked me if everyone's built like you in Devon." She grinned. "Told her I'd got the pick of the crop."

"Creep."

"You love me for it."

I raised an eyebrow and glanced at her bed. "Can I show you how much?"

She pretended to think it over for a few seconds. "Well, go on then. The mattress might be a bit soft for anything vigorous, though, but I've never shared it with a boyfriend."

I picked her up. "Better get started on sharing it then." I carried her over to the bed and gently dropped her onto the mattress. She shuffled backwards and pulled me onto the bed with her. I lay diagonally across the mattress, rolled onto my back, and pulled her on top of me. Being six foot five tall meant I had to curl up or lie diagonally across a standard double to avoid my feet dangling uncomfortably in space.

She grinned down at me. "You know you passed the Mummy and Daddy test, don't you?"

"The one I wasn't supposed to know about?"

She nodded. "That's the one."

"Do I get a prize or something?"

"The top prize; me." She leaned down and covered my face with gentle kisses, finishing on the little groove between my upper lip and nose.

I slid my hands under her tee shirt and managed to undo her bra fairly slickly. Well, for me. She sat up, wriggled, somehow removed her bra through one sleeve without lifting her top, and threw it aside. She took my hands and placed them on her breasts. Through her soft cotton top, they felt lovely in my hands and her nipples were firm little buds. She looked down at me with something approaching open lust, then shifted her hips around, teasing my severely-constrained erection.

"Can't decide whether I want to take you, or have you take me," she murmured.

"Suppose I get all overenthusiastic? You know, forceful and pushy."

She grinned at me. "You? Mister gentle and thoughtful?"

I guessed she wanted to play a little. I rolled us over so I was on top, straddled her thighs and pinned her hands on either side of her head. "Who says I can't be forceful?"

She raised her eyebrows. "Prove it, big boy."

I pulled her arms up and held both her wrists with one hand, then tugged her tee shirt up. She wriggled to help me pull it over her head, but I left her arms in it, not quite trapped, but restricted. While she giggled and struggled with that, I unfastened her jeans and tugged them down to the top of her panties, then I rolled to one side and pulled her clothing down as far as I could.

"You're cheating," she grumbled, throwing her tee shirt to the floor.

"How am I cheating?"

"I can't put up a decent fight, but I want you be all forceful and overpower me. And now I'm half-naked but you're still fully dressed."

"Let's sort that out." I jumped up and stripped.

Hayley discarded her own clothes, got into her bed and grabbed the duvet to stop me getting in with her. She didn't try all that hard, squealing when I won and threw the duvet back. We cuddled and giggled, then she stroked my face tenderly.

"I know you're conscious of being a lot bigger and stronger than me, and I love it that you try to be gentle. And you're probably trying to avoid me feeling too dominated. But sometimes I want you to be a bit rougher. Like we were in that feed room last night. I know you won't hurt me and if I want to give in to you, that's not you dominating me. Not in a bad way, anyway." She kissed me and ran her fingers through my hair, all the way from my forehead to where it was spread across my shoulders. "Sometimes, I want to feel that you're completely hugging me, every little bit of me."

I took both her hands in one of mine, stretched her arms up above her head and kissed her slowly and deeply. "Yellow for far enough, red for game over?"

She nodded and smiled shyly.

I rolled her onto her tummy, eased her legs apart and knelt between them. Then I slid a fingertip along the cleft of her pussy, which immediately spread open. She was deliciously hot, slick, and tempting. I teased her entrance and spread her wetness over her lips until I thought she was really ready. Then I moved up to stroke her pussy with the tip of my cock. She gasped and raised her hips. I took the hint and slid into her. She was so wet and open that I filled her after a couple of gentle thrusts. I screwed her slowly, pulling as far back as I could each time, then sliding as deep into her as I could.

She twisted her head and kissed me roughly. Her eyes were bright with desire and mischief. "Go on, have me. Take me."

I went faster, but still pulled almost out before sliding back deep into her. Hayley closed her eyes and relaxed completely. She made a sound like a cross between a gasp and a moan each time I slid into her. She arched her hips up off the bed, making it easier for me to pump in and out of her. Her gasping got louder and we soon both had a film of sweat over us. She climaxed loudly and suddenly, almost pulling me over the edge with her.

"You okay?" I murmured.

"Green," she gasped. "Fuck me."

I let my self-control go. My world was entirely centred around my cock sliding into the wet, soft core of the lithe, firm body beneath mine. Her gasps grew louder and she slipped her hands out of my grasp, pressing them on the bed. She pushed back against my thrusts. "Green, green, green," she whispered, then her whole body tensed as she reached another climax, crying out. That one was too much for me, and I released inside her, pulse after pulse of hot need washed through my cock to fill her.

We rolled onto one side and snuggled together; hot, sweaty, breathless and bathed in the unmistakable aroma of vigorous sex.

Hayley stroked the arm I had around her tummy. "That was rather fun."

"Bloody amazing," I said. "Remind me to be rough more often."

She chuckled. "Only when it's the right moment. Your tender, gentle approach is pretty bloody mind-blowing, too. That slow build-up makes me come harder."

She rolled onto her back and turned her face towards mine. Our noses were only millimetres apart. "And I know exactly where my G spot is now."

"Oh?"

She nodded. "I felt it every single time you slid into me. And it was heavenly." She grinned and kissed me. "Thank you."

"Thank you," I said.

"No, thank you." She giggled, then put her fingers over my mouth. "Let me have the last word. You know it's less painful that way."

I rolled onto my back and stretched my legs, which meant my feet dangled over the end of the mattress.

She snuggled up against me, enveloped by my arms. *My woman. It's so good to know that feeling again.*

16

By the time we left the following afternoon, Trevor and Marion had made me feel thoroughly accepted, which was flattering. I'd happily agreed to visit them again, as soon as we could find a suitable weekend in everyone's diaries.

Hayley and I travelled to the location where the recording would start the following morning. It was a hotel converted from an old country house, and we'd be using a wing which seemed to have hardly been touched in centuries. Phil had declared some of the original features and furniture to be perfect for production.

I felt far more nervous than I expected. Having worked once on a TV documentary helped a bit, but only with being in front of a camera and production team and ignoring the lot of them while talking to Trevor. Acting as a major character in a drama was a totally different matter. The more I thought about being a complete amateur mixing with the production team and "real" actors, the more I felt out of my depth.

And I wondered about meeting Becky again. Although we had frequent happy, cheeky, and friendly chats on the phone, I didn't know how I'd feel when I saw her, or what might happen between us. I loved those two amazing nights the three of us had shared, but now Hayley and I seemed to be well on our way to being a couple. I felt nervous, but tried not to show it, and didn't know how to raise the subject with Hayley without potentially upsetting her.

I guessed she knew I was anxious. She put her hand on my arm as we got near the hotel. "Paul, you'll be fine tomorrow. And I really do love it that you and Becky are close." She gave my arm a tender squeeze. "I'd love us all to share a bed again and, well, you know, mess about. Like we did at your place."

I felt confused and, if I was honest with myself, a little bit hurt. Wasn't I Hayley's boyfriend? "I'm not entirely comfortable about that."

"You can't behave yourself for a little while? Not even for me?"

I was still puzzled. "I'm totally lost," I admitted. "This is so weird, it's off my scale."

"Not even as a fantasy?"

I thought she was teasing me, but even so, I felt uncomfortable. "Okay, as a fantasy. But I never expected to experience it. You know the old joke, a bloke having a threesome is disappointing two women at once."

Hayley laughed. "Don't be soft. You wouldn't. And it's not going to be a threesome. Just a big cuddle."

I saw Becky's car in the car park when we arrived, and she ran out to meet us. I felt a surge of excitement and my face broke out in a huge grin as soon as I saw her. I caught her when she jumped up and slung her arms around my neck. The open and honest delight I saw in her expression overcame any idea I might have had about not showing much affection for her.

She gave me a fond and tender kiss, then looked down at Hayley from her perch in my arms. "Lost interest in him yet?"

Hayley shrugged. "Not yet."

Becky glanced at me, then back to Hayley. "Can I borrow him? Please?"

I laughed and lowered her to the ground. "Jeez, what are you like? I thought it was blokes who were persistent."

"You don't know nuthin'," Hayley said, in a New York accent. The two women hugged, then set off for the entrance, arm in arm, chatting away. I carried our luggage.

Becky's hair was longer and had been cut into a softer style, which I liked. I thought she'd lost a little weight, too. I was surprised to see her wearing a lightweight powder-blue summer dress, since her style had been far more gothic when we'd met. It looked good on her.

Becky had somehow arranged for the three of us to share the bridal suite, which, to my relief, had a super king-size bed. I left the women to unpack and chat, and spent an hour or so in the hotel's modest gym, wondering what our nights here would bring, with a mixture of apprehension and anticipation.

At dinner, Becky and Hayley seemed to be much the same as they had been when staying with me a few weeks before; Hayley a little hesitant and insecure, and Becky a bit over-the-top. But in public, they were two close friends who both flirted with me and light-heartedly teased me and each other non-stop. It felt almost as if Hayley and I being an item hadn't made a difference. No one else seemed to think it was unusual for two women to be affectionate towards the same guy, or even when I had an arm around each of them at the same time. But maybe over-the-top behaviour was normal for the entertainment industry.

After dinner, Phil gave us all a team talk, followed by separate briefings for Hayley and myself. Plans had changed a little, which Hayley accepted as par for the course. Along with the minor incidental scenes I already knew about, like striding purposefully through gates and doorways, and along gloomy corridors, I'd have two longer scenes the next day. The first only required me to walk up a long staircase into the palace, which would be the opening scene for the show. The second would be an improvised uncomfortable conversation in which Princess Gwendolyn told

Captain Rowan about the marriage proposal she'd received. Phil wanted me to show that I felt surprised and heartbroken, but trying to hide it because I was resolute about my duty.

I was wondering how the fuck I could do that when he changed the subject. "Hayley says you know a medic."

I immediately thought of Mark. "Yeah, a university colleague. He's an academic who also does emergency medicine."

"Brilliant. Look, our insurers have insisted on medical cover on-site for the combat scenes. I'm hiring an ambulance and paramedics from a first aid charity, but if he can come too, that'd be even better. If he's interested, we'll pay him a modest fee and he can have the same accommodation deal as your guys."

"I'll ask him and let you know."

He looked at me for a couple of seconds. "Come on, how do you feel about tomorrow?"

"Scared I'll let everyone down," I admitted.

He nodded. "Pleased you're honest, and that you put it that way. I find this TV production lark goes better with team players, even though everyone can come across like a bit of a diva." He leaned forward. "Look, I offered you this role because you and Hayley have a real sparkle and I know it'll come across on screen," he said earnestly. "It helps that you're close in real life, too. Imagine you've been head-over-heels with Hayley for months, but never found the courage to tell her. Then some posh nob comes along and whisks her away. You don't feel there's anything you can do. Feel that, show it, then let it go." He tapped my arm with a finger. "That's the important thing, letting it go afterwards. It's only acting. You know she's not going anywhere really, it's pretend. Okay?"

I nodded. "Thanks, Phil."

I found the women in the lobby. They seemed to be having a pretty intense conversation, but stopped as soon as they saw me, and we went into the bar together. While I waited for our drinks to be prepared, they resumed their conversation, heads close together. A couple of the women I recognised from our earlier meeting as part of the production team were chatting at a nearby table, with their backs to me while I was at the bar.

"Hayley's a good choice," one said, in a rather grudging tone.

"Phil knows her old man, Trevor Western," the other said.

"At least she can act. No bloody idea what Phil expects from that hunky stunt guy. I mean, major-league eye candy, and perfect for the fight scenes, but as leading man?"

"Hayley and that makeup girl Becky are all over him."

"Lucky bitches. Can't blame them, I'd be tempted myself. It'll be fun to watch that contest."

"Pity neither of them ever gossips. We'll have to see if he's any good on set. I'm not holding my breath though."

I remembered what Trevor had told me and tried not to feel demoralised by their comments. My drinks order arrived on a tray and I walked away, hoping I wasn't spotted by the gossips. Becky and Hayley chatted away while I sipped my beer and wondered about Becky and my developing relationship with Hayley. And despite Phil's encouragement, I felt anxious about having to act the next day. It didn't help knowing that some of the production team were unconvinced I could even do a half-decent job of it.

Becky broke my reverie by tapping my knee. "Anyone home, or did you just leave the lights on?"

"Wondering how to act. All of a sudden, I've got to do it for a TV show."

Hayley reached across and squeezed my hand. "Remember what Phil told you. We've been practicing for a few days, you're a natural at improvisation."

Becky gave me a shrewd look. "Worried what the production people think?"

"Of course."

"Fuck 'em." She sat back and waved a hand dismissively. "Doesn't matter what they think, no matter how snotty they are.

Phil's in charge, it's his decision and he'll carry the can for any mistakes. But he doesn't often make mistakes, because he's a sharp cookie." She leaned forward. "Like Hayley said, you're a natural." She tapped my knee with her index finger. "Relax and let it happen."

Hayley looked at Becky and raised an eyebrow. "Are you… talking about the acting?"

Becky shrugged. "Of course."

I looked pointedly at Becky, who blushed. "*Mostly* about the acting," she mumbled.

We both grinned at Becky for a few more seconds while her blush deepened.

Hayley gathered our empty glasses. "My round," she said, then walked over to the bar.

"Paul, please don't think we're messing with you," Becky said. "We're not. I don't want to come between you and Hayley, but I don't want to lose you or her either. It's only for a couple of days. Surely I'm not that scary?"

"No, you're not scary at all. I'm just, well… confused." I sighed. "This is a totally new situation for me, exciting and terrifying at the same time. I don't want things to blow up and leave someone hurt."

"We've all been hurt," Becky said. "Me and Hayley have both been let down big-time in the past, and you lost your wife, which is way tougher. I don't think we'll hurt each other, none of us want that. In fact, I think we can all help each other. Give it a chance?" She leaned even closer and looked at me with obvious pleading. "Please?"

I knew I couldn't do anything I thought might hurt her, so I nodded.

She relaxed and hugged my arm. "Thank you. Odd as it sounds, being with you two helps me. Hayley's my closest friend and I feel I can really trust you." She paused, then carried on in a quieter voice. "I've had some bad experiences, ones I've kept to myself. When I feel ready, I'll probably open up about them." She sat back in her chair and suddenly looked small and vulnerable, totally unlike the confident woman I usually saw. "Please, for now, just don't do anything which makes me feel I'm being forced out. I want to feel like I'm loved, I suppose."

Hayley returned then, bearing a tray of drinks. She smiled warmly at Becky, who immediately returned to her normal bouncy self. I envied her that ability to switch on an act.

By the time we retired, we'd had quite a lot to drink. Hayley hugged me on the stairs. "Sure you're happy about this?" she whispered.

I squeezed her and nodded, even though I felt nervous and uncertain. "Just cuddles?"

Hayley smiled at me. "Nothing wrong with cuddles, and maybe more, if we're all up for it?"

"We'll see how it goes," I heard myself say.

Becky opened the door, ran across the room and jumped onto the bed. "Bliss. All big and bouncy."

Hayley went into the en-suite and I turned off all the lights except those on the bedside cabinets.

Becky kicked her shoes off and rolled on her side, facing me. "I've missed you," she said. "Phone calls, texts, and e-mails are lovely, but being with someone's much better."

I sat on the bed and leaned down to kiss her. She put a hand around my neck and pulled me on top of her. We both giggled, then kissed deeply. I'd missed her, too. I liked being with both of them.

The mattress bounced as Hayley climbed onto the bed. "Snogging my guy, eh?"

We stopped snogging. "She started it," I said.

"He was there, tempting me," Becky said.

Hayley leaned closer and grinned at me. "I'm not saying I mind." Then she kissed me on the lips. "So long as I can join in."

"Kissing me or kissing Becky?" I teased.

She paused for a fraction of a second, then raised an eyebrow.

"Now that would be telling. Get ready for bed, mister."

Without knowing why, I suddenly felt far more relaxed and happier. A fair few drinks had helped, I knew, but I was sure the three of us would be fine.

"I think we should both watch him undress," Becky said. "As a punishment for snogging me without permission."

"You dragged me on top of you," I protested.

Becky sat up and shrugged. "So? I'll do a striptease, too."

"Sounds like a fair deal," Hayley said. "As the injured party, I'll sit here and smirk."

Becky snorted and Hayley hit her with a pillow. Becky grabbed another pillow and they had a short tussle that involved more giggling than fighting, while I took my shoes and socks off. Then they sat primly on the edge of the bed, side by side, and watched me undress. I took my time, folded up my shirt and put it aside, then hung my trousers in the wardrobe.

I was about to slip my underpants off when the women started a slow handclap. "Off, off, off," they chanted.

I turned my back to them and tried to wiggle my backside seductively, but that only made them laugh out loud. The next thing I knew, I'd been grabbed and hustled onto the bed, where my underpants were tugged down my legs by two grinning women.

Becky straddled my thighs and glanced at my growing erection. "Don't give up the day job yet, Paul. We need to teach you the art of sexy stripping first. Now, pay close attention."

I made a huge effort to keep my eyes on hers, but my gaze kept flicking downwards to watch as she slowly unfastened all the buttons down the front of her dress. She shrugged it off her shoulders and smirked at me. "Like my all-over tan?"

I cleared my throat. "Can't see enough of you to be sure."

Hayley, who'd been watching my reaction with amusement, reached across and unfastened Becky's bra. Becky wriggled and her bra fell forward, releasing her breasts. She grinned at me and leaned forwards. "Better?"

I nodded. Her breasts were the same healthy tanned tone as the rest of her upper body. She slid off me and stood on the floor. She pushed her panties down and did a quick pirouette. "See, an all-over tan."

She looked absolutely lovely. I was sure her hipbones and ribs were a little more obvious than I remembered and briefly wondered why she had lost weight.

"I guess the weather was good in France?" Hayley said, grinning. "And you had plenty of privacy."

"The only guy around was the photographer," Becky said. "Gay, sensitive and totally lovable. The girls were sunbathing nude all the time, we all came back with all-over tans."

Hayley jumped off the bed and undressed. I slid under the duvet as Becky got back onto the bed and lay beside me on my right. Then Hayley snuggled up against my left-hand side. We were all naked. And I had a rock-solid erection. Becky leaned on my chest, her face close to mine. "So, still fancy me then?"

I couldn't help but grin. "Yeah," I said. I ruffled her hair. "I still fancy you."

The two women exchanged a glance across my chest.

Hayley kissed me. "Enough to be naughty with both of us?"

Becky wrapped her hand around my cock. I closed my eyes for a second, enjoying the warmth and pleasure from her small fingers.

"Naughty I can cope with," I murmured, perfectly honestly. "More than that... Can I say stop without upsetting you?"

"Of course," Becky said.

"Just like we can," Hayley added.

She and I kissed tenderly and slowly while Becky wound me up, then they swapped roles. I held both women as best I could, despite the distractions.

"Will you kiss my pussy?" Becky murmured into our kiss. "I'd love to kneel over your face."

I had always enjoyed giving a woman oral attention, and was happy to do as Becky asked. "You bet." I replied, then gasped and lifted my hips as Hayley's teasing fingers closed around my cock and triggered a wave of pleasure. Hayley giggled as Becky and I tried to arrange ourselves. My feet ended up over the edge of the bed, of course, but Becky distracted me from even noticing. She knelt on the bed and leaned on the headboard to support herself. She was wet and open, hot and salty. And from the way she pressed herself against my lips, she wanted a lot of contact from my tongue.

Hayley got to her knees and started working my erection with both hands. Her small hands were warm and exciting. I hoped I could keep enough self-control to give Becky the attention she wanted before I came myself. She made it quite clear where she wanted my tongue by moving her over my mouth. She came by fingering her clit while I pushed my tongue as far into her as I could.

Becky climbed off me and flopped onto the bed. "That was worth waiting for," she said, breathing heavily.

"My turn," Hayley said eagerly.

"Allow me." I pulled her down onto the bed and rolled over to lie diagonally across the bed, my head and shoulders between her legs. Becky shuffled over to hug her. I slid two fingers inside Hayley, enjoying the texture of her body, and then found and teased her G-spot. Becky hugged her across her tummy and kissed her cheek, then grinned down at me. I slowly licked up and down Hayley's inner lips, then around her clit. Her flavour and natural scent were very like Becky's. Hayley's climax built more slowly than Becky's had, but her release seemed to be more intense, too. She tensed, lifting her hips from the bed, then bucked so much I almost lost contact with her. She rolled her head from side to side, eyes shut and mouth open, then relaxed completely, letting out a long sigh.

She panted loudly. "Fuck me."

Becky winked at me. "Fine, so long as I can watch."

Hayley laughed and slapped Becky's arm gently. "Jeez, that was so powerful."

I climbed up the bed and they slid apart so I could get between them.

"This might sound weird," Becky said. "I've got an idea."

"Try me," I said, hugging them both.

"I've never watched a guy toss himself off. Not in real life." She looked at me pleadingly. "Would you?"

I liked the sound of that. I kissed her forehead. "Well, you asked nicely."

Hayley got up onto one elbow and smiled at me. "I'd love to watch you, too."

I looked from one to the other. "I'll ask for the favour to be returned sometime."

Becky got up onto her knees. "Tomorrow morning, if you want. Mind you, there's an early start, so we'd have to wake up at stupid o'clock. Anyway, come on. I might learn something sneaky about how to touch you and then you'll be in real trouble."

I stroked myself to climax with two lovely women watching me. They stroked my thighs, hips, tummy, and balls, and occasionally kissed me. I had a powerful climax, then opened my eyes to see them grinning at me. They helped me clean up, then we curled up together in a big, snuggly cuddle. We chatted for a short while, then they both drifted off to sleep, one on each side of me.

I liked having them both in bed with me. I hadn't realised how much I'd missed it, despite only doing it once, over a month before, and it felt right somehow. I wondered if I could happily live with this as an occasional part of my relationship with Hayley.

17

"The staircase is kinda long, but it'll look great." Phil was clearly doing his best to encourage me. "Just follow the camera drone up, it'll keep pace with you."

I knew he was being a bit evasive and couldn't resist teasing him a little. "Kinda long?" I asked. "Not short, but not long?"

He looked a little embarrassed. "About a hundred steps, with a landing half-way up. I asked you to wear chain mail and carry a sword as Rowan's come back from an official errand. Is that okay? It might need a few takes, what with the weight you're carrying, but that's fine."

I kept a straight face. "Yeah, it's okay."

He looked surprised. "You sure?"

I nodded. "Let me have a quick word with the drone operator."

The drone operator's eyebrows went up when he heard my suggestion. "Well, yeah, if you're sure."

I knew I was showing off, but couldn't resist it. When Phil called, "Action," I jogged up to the landing, with the drone hovering a few feet in front of me. I stopped in front of the young actor dressed as a man-at-arms standing guard, sighed, shook my head sadly and straightened his tunic. He grinned. I gently punched his shoulder, then jogged the rest of the way up. And I managed it without getting breathless. Just.

Phil loved it, but we had another two takes before he was happy, then I was asked to pose for the stills photographer for a few minutes.

"Great improvisation," Phil said. "Lovely little gesture with the guard, wish I'd thought of it."

John had suggested it; one of a few things he thought might show my character was a natural leader. I'd asked him, thinking his police experience gave him insights I'd never get in my own life.

But I was still worried about how to look like a plausible hero. I'd never even seen anyone doing anything heroic in real life.

The afternoon recording with Hayley was good fun, at least partly because she had an attack of the giggles before we started. But it was also a bit spooky. The script we had was a storyline to improvise around, which at least saved me from having to memorise lines. But as soon as we started, I heard myself say things I'd not even thought about, but it felt that was what my character would probably have said if it was really happening. It just felt real for those few seconds. Uncomfortably real.

After our first take, Hayley gave me a hug while the camera and lights were moved. "That was weird," she said. "I'd thought about what to say, but it came out totally different. And better. You were great."

"Thanks," I said. "It felt like my character took over. Is that normal?"

She shook her head. "It can feel a bit like that when you really know the lines, but nothing like this. Bit odd, but it felt like it worked well."

When we'd finished, I couldn't actually remember what we'd said, which made it odd to watch the first edits that evening. I watched Rowan take the news about Gwendolyn's marriage proposal stoically, with a brief change of expression showing that he was upset, which he quickly hid. Hayley was utterly convincing as Gwendolyn, even managing tears when she turned towards the camera after dismissing Rowan.

Becky slung her arms around our shoulders. "Convinced me you fancy each other, guys."

Phil was happy and the editor gave me a nod of approval. I began to feel that I might not be letting everyone down quite yet.

Phil ran through the plans for my next scenes; another uncomfortable conversation between Rowan and Gwendolyn, the banquet, and then the dance, all being recorded the following week at another location. Even as a first-time actor, I knew recording would be out of order with the storyline, but arranged around the availability of locations and cast members.

In bed that night, I decided to take charge a bit. We all hugged, kissed, and cuddled, which resulted in an exciting, complex writhing mass of bodies, arms, and legs. Becky untied my ponytail, so my hair was loose, like Hayley's. Eventually, I rolled Hayley onto her back, spread her legs gently and crouched between them to use my fingers and tongue. She pushed my hair back from my face, so we could see each other's eyes. Becky lay beside me and squeezed and stroked my cock while I teased Hayley to her climax.

From the way Hayley arched her back, tossed her head around, and threw her arms wide, it seemed to be a powerful orgasm.

"Come and give me a hug, Becks." She took in a couple of deep breaths, then pulled Becky towards her.

It was lovely to see the two of them embrace. And a bit exciting too, even if it was just a loving thing between two close friends. They murmured and giggled, then Becky lay on her back on top of Hayley, letting her legs fall open across Hayley's thighs. I was struck by how intimate this seemed.

"I'll hug and hold her in place while you sort her out," Hayley said.

I squatted on the mattress between Hayley's legs again, while Becky put her own legs over my shoulders. I kept my gaze on Becky's eyes as I leaned down and ran my tongue up her pussy lips. She closed her eyes and gasped, rolling her head back so her cheek was against Hayley's. I got to work. She came surprisingly fast, letting out a series of loud moans as I licked her clit. Her inner muscles squeezed against the three fingers I had deep inside her, and I felt her heels press against my back.

When Becky recovered, I lay on my back and was slowly wanked off by two pairs of hands interlinked around my cock. They kept the same steady pace all the time, which built me up and up until I was almost having an out-of-body experience, then I felt an all-too-brief and intense wave of delight, and felt cum splash across my tummy. To my surprise, they both leaned down and Becky licked the splashes off my skin while Hayley took me in her mouth to clean my cock. I pulled both up and gave each of them a deep kiss, tasting myself. It complemented the flavours of my two lovely ladies lingering on my palate.

We lay together on the bed, me in the middle with an arm around each of them, as was becoming our habit.

"Think we got him, Becky?" Hayley asked, in a stage whisper.

"Hope so," Becky replied. "He didn't half get me."

Hayley giggled. "Yeah, he's rotten like that."

"Complaining?" I asked.

"Not as such," Becky said.

I grinned at the ceiling. "Good, otherwise I'd have to really sort you out."

"You've already done that a few times," Hayley murmured.

Becky stretched up near my ear. "Yes, please," she whispered. "Put my ankles on your shoulders and fuck me hard till I squeak. While Hayley cuddles us both."

I said nothing, but immediately liked the idea and felt my cock start to stiffen again. Then I felt uncomfortably guilty.

*****

The next morning, my ladies took turns to bring themselves to climaxes, after I'd been firmly told to watch, but not touch. Then they ganged up on me again, watching me bring myself off. It was a great way to start the day.

Hayley had a couple of short scenes to record, and Becky was busy doing make-up. Once the recording session had finished, they were both going to stay with Hayley's parents. We had a private smoochy goodbye, and I drove away, thinking about my odd situation with them, but feeling comfortable about it too.

I knew we'd have to sit down together and discuss it like grown-ups at some point, but, with me being me, I decided to let things roll along rather than bring them to a head. When I unpacked, I was missing a couple of tee shirts, which I suspected had been "borrowed." The women had both sprayed perfume on some of my other clothes, which made me smile. I remembered Helen doing the same sort of thing at the start of our relationship.

Of course Claire wanted to hear about Hayley's parents and the recording. Once her curiosity seemed to be satisfied, I spotted a mischievous gleam in her eye.

"How was Becky?" she asked, in a conversational way.

I shrugged. "Her normal self. New hairstyle, which I thought suited her."

She looked at me for a second. "Nothing else?"

I felt puzzled. "She seemed to have lost weight."

"Did you have a proper talk? Like a heart-to-heart?"

I didn't feel comfortable sharing what Becky had told me, as it felt a bit too private. "We talked a lot, but nothing that deep and meaningful."

Claire poured us another cup of coffee. "I know you too well, Paul. Please don't scuttle back into your shell if you feel insecure. You know I'll keep your secrets."

I looked at her. "I know you often chat with them. Have I missed something?"

"I don't think so." She sipped her coffee. "Look, you and I know each other in a way no one else will ever understand, Paul. For one thing, we both feel we need someone to look after. We've got Mum and Dad, and each other, like we always have. I've got John, who thinks he's looking after me, and we've got the children. We really appreciate your help with them, especially when he's working silly hours on a case. Although you had your ups and downs, you and Helen both looked after each other without even thinking about it." She paused for a couple of seconds. "You know I think Hayley's a good potential partner. I can see why you're attracted to Becky as well. She's full of fun and life on the outside, but I think she's bottling something up. But if you're thinking of looking after both of them, who'll look after you?"

I stared into my coffee for a minute, thinking things through. "I don't know what it is," I said. "I could so easily fall for either of them and really love the other as a good friend. But…"

"But you can't choose?"

"I thought I had, or at least that Hayley had, by coming to see me again. But they don't make it any easier by being exactly the same as they were when I first met them."

"Is Becky being a tease?"

I shook my head. "Doesn't feel that way. They both flirt and tease me, but in a nice, fun way, like before Hayley and I became a couple. It's more like neither of them can say what they really want."

"Now who does that remind me of?"

I stuck my tongue out at Claire, who grinned.

"So, you feel completely comfortable about starting a relationship with Hayley rather than Becky?"

I felt a twinge of unease, which surprised me. I spent a few seconds trying to order my thoughts. "I think I could have started a relationship just as easily with either of them," I admitted.

"So if Becky had come back here first, she'd be your lover and Hayley would be the mutual friend?"

I thought about that. "Probably, yeah."

She looked at me. "It sounds more like you've met two possible girlfriends and they're waiting for you to make a decision."

I wanted to say Hayley was my girlfriend, but realised she had a point. It didn't feel as if Hayley and I were totally committed to being a couple, as we both wanted Becky to be with us. And if she was, then I'd find it hard to be the only one saying no to any sexy play. I knew I wanted her as much as I did Hayley, but the idea of sharing a three-way relationship seemed bizarre.

Claire looked at me thoughtfully for a few seconds, and clearly decided she'd given me enough to think about, as she changed the subject. "Off to the gym later?"

"Yeah. Be back about half six."

She nodded. "I think John needs some time to sit and chat. His case is getting weirder." She looked into her coffee mug. "They've found another dead girl," she said quietly.

My heart sank. I didn't like the idea of people being murdered, but even more than that, I didn't like the way it got to John. He was leading a large team working hard on these cases, and he felt they were his responsibility to solve. While he didn't quite seem to take the murders personally, they seemed to eat away at him until they'd caught the people responsible. "Where is he now?"

"He came back a while ago, said he needed to get away from work and let his head clear. I think he's in the greenhouse."

He was. This year's tomato plants were getting unruly and John was trimming wayward stems.

"How was it?" he asked.

"Hayley's parents were great; the recording was interesting."

"You'd met her dad before, of course."

He'd clearly done what I hadn't, and searched for information about Hayley.

"Yeah, that documentary about swords." I pulled a few handfuls of trimmed stems out of the greenhouse, to clear the floor. "How are you?"

He looked at me. "Honestly?"

"Of course."

"Really pissed off." He sighed. "Three murders we're sure are probably linked, but no-one's talking to us. Two girls injured, too."

"What makes you say they're linked?"

"For one thing, they were all sex workers. We think they're all protected by the same crime gang."

"Any chance it's turf war?"

He shrugged. "Might be, or what the business world would call an unfriendly take-over bid."

"You said 'for one thing', what else?"

John thought for a few seconds. "This is strictly only for you. The third one's formally a suspicious death, because her body was too decomposed to confirm a cause. The two survivors said they were attacked by a huge dog, which was consistent with the two dead girls' injuries, and we found dog hair at every scene."

"Must have been a fair-sized dog, even if it was aggressive. Might be a good lead. Any witnesses see it?"

He snorted. "If they were attacked by a dog, then it was a bloody werewolf. All the girls lived in upper floor flats, sharing with another worker. The dead and injured ones were discovered by their flatmates. Our crime scene guys did an awesome job in every building. DNA from hordes of people, what you'd expect in a busy sex worker's cheap, short-term rental flat. But the only signs of a dog anywhere were in the rooms they were attacked in."

The mention of rental properties rang a bell, but I couldn't remember why. "The suspicious death, how long had she been dead?"

John pulled a face. "From the decomposition, the pathologist guessed at least four weeks in a hot flat, but a witness swore blind she saw her a week before." He paused for a few seconds, looking out of the glazed wall, but I don't think he was paying the garden any attention. "We found another woman's DNA and clothing, probably a flatmate we've not traced. The other girls' flatmates all vanished within a day or two. Hopefully they've done a runner and got well away. All but one were from eastern Europe." He turned towards me. "But we found some weird stuff, too. A kitchen knife covered in blood, a man's clothing soaked in blood, with tears and stab holes in it, and bloodstains on the floor. All the same blood, from an unknown male. But the clothing was stuffed full of dust."

I stared at him for a couple of seconds. "What?"

"Twenty kilos or so. Forensics said it seemed to be a sort of blood and bone meal fertiliser."

It made no more sense to me than it did to John.

"Come on, tell me about the recording you did," John said. "I need to stop thinking about work for a while."

*****

Mark and Maggie were exercising together, as usual, and greeted me when I entered the gym. Something seemed a bit different, but I didn't figure it out until they were about to leave and I overheard Maggie say something about Mark meeting her parents the following weekend. She looked rather embarrassed, which seemed kind of sweet.

I felt a huge grin take over my face. *Great, they're together at last.* "So, Mark and Maggie are an item?"

Mark grinned happily, but to my surprise, Maggie blushed deeply.

"I'm really happy for you both," I said.

Maggie gave me a shy smile. "Thanks."

"I met my girlfriend's parents for the first time a few days ago." I felt a slight anxiety, as if I was overstepping some mark. But as Hayley and I were starting a relationship, it seemed a suitable description.

Maggie looked at me, and I saw her eyes sparkle with mischief. "You've actually got a girlfriend?"

I was impressed. It was perfectly timed, and Hayley couldn't have deadpanned a punch line any better.

Mark looked surprised, as if he'd not realised she was teasing me, then seemed relieved when I laughed. "Really pleased for you, Paul," he said. "Hope it works out well."

Maggie smirked. "So, when are we going to meet Miss Wonderful? Maybe a double date sometime?"

I just about managed to keep a straight face. "I'll suggest it. Who knows, the idea might even be acceptable to Miss Wonderful."

Mark put an arm around her. "Come on, Maggie, time I bought you some dinner. Get your blood sugar level back under control." He grinned at me. "And say hi to the boss for us."

Maggie gave me a lovely warm smile. "I hope you're happy together, Paul."

"Thanks," I said, flattered by their reaction. "You, too. It's going well so far."

Mark gave me a big grin and a thumbs up. Maggie rolled her eyes, then smiled as she left.

Mark was definitely good for her. And he seemed happier, too.

I was surprised when Maggie rang me the next morning to apologise. "Sorry if I came across as rude last night," she said. "I got a bit, well, flustered. I hate the girls at the office going on about their love lives and asking me when I'm going to get a boyfriend. I like to keep my life private."

I hadn't thought anything of it, but was touched by her call. She even asked me to look after Mark when I went out drinking with him a couple of days later.

*****

It was the sort of summer day that holidaymakers dread; grey, blustery, cool, and wet. I sat on the wide window ledge in my living room and watched the rain splash in the puddles on the paved yard below. It was a good spot to sit and admire the scenery on a good day, and coincidentally where I got the best mobile phone signal in my flat.

"Paul, I don't want you to feel uncomfortable around Becky," Hayley said. She sounded concerned. "I'm sorry you felt I was teasing you about it."

"Look, I really do like her, but I thought you and I were an item now."

"We are, as far as I'm concerned. Why d'you think I wanted you to meet Mummy and Daddy? But I don't want to push Becky away. She's helped me so much over all the time we've been friends. I really owe her and feel it's time I repaid some of that. She's had rough times she's never opened up about. She tended to big-sister me when we first met at university. I picked up the pieces for her a few times, but I'm sure she's kept things from me, for some reason."

"I don't want her to feel unwelcome in any way. It's just that…" I paused to try and think what to say. "The only times I've ever shared a bed with two women have been those nights with you two. It's great fun, but really weird as well. Maybe I feel a bit inhibited, but there's a limit to what I feel comfortable doing."

"We don't have to bonk," Hayley said. The tone of her voice made me think she was smiling.

"I agree. But bonking you is rather bloody lovely."

She chuckled. "So you wouldn't mind bonking me if she was there?"

I opened and closed my mouth a couple of times, not knowing quite how to respond. I wasn't entirely sure Hayley was joking, and suspected Becky wouldn't actually mind if Hayley and I screwed like rabbits, so long as she didn't feel left out. But rampant sex felt like something we should only share as a couple.

"Look, can we all sit down and talk about it next time we meet up?" I asked. "It's not something I want to do over the phone. It's too personal."

"So can I conclude that you wouldn't mind Becky watching while we bonked?"

I felt sure Hayley was teasing me. "Maybe if we tied her up and gagged her."

Hayley laughed. "She'd love that. Maybe make her sit on a vibrator while you hump me silly."

"Interesting imagery," I said, then enjoyed hearing her giggle for a few seconds.

She cleared her throat. "So, you're off drinking dirty beer with your mate tonight?"

"Yeah. With Maggie's approval, so long as I look after him."

"Good, pleased to hear it. I expect a full and frank account. Or, if it's a really good night, send me a copy of the police report and any CCTV recordings featuring the two of you."

*****

I parked near Mark's flat, and dropped off my overnight bag and sleeping bag. We'd just set off for town when I heard a squeal of car brakes and a revving engine. I turned to watch a big black Lexus reverse into a space at the side of the road, and a short wiry guy got out of the passenger side before the car had finished moving. He had an oddly pale complexion, sunken eyes, and a shaven head. He glanced at us, his expression arrogant, cold and dismissive, then walked over to a people carrier further up the road and got in. Something about him made me shudder.

We stopped off in a fancy-looking hotel up the road. Mark was likeable and good company; bright, chatty, full of funny stories, and I felt he was truly interested when he asked me about myself. It was rather sweet that he got embarrassed when I hinted he was good for Maggie. But I'd probably have squirmed too if anyone said the same about me and Hayley.

I found out we had something surprising in common; his last girlfriend had died. It had been almost a year earlier, during a trip to Romania.

"How?" I asked, hoping it came across gently.

He shrugged. "No idea. She disappeared with three other women, their remains weren't found for a couple of weeks, but they were too badly decomposed to get a cause of death. That didn't make sense, given the time and weather, but I couldn't fault the pathology reports, and the police drew a blank despite thorough investigations."

I felt surprised, and remembered what John had said about the most recently-found victim he was investigating. "You saw her post mortem report?"

He nodded. "Her parents asked me to look at it, for their peace of mind. First time I met them was at her funeral."

"Must have been bloody awful."

"Well, yeah. We'd only been going out a few months, still at the mad-keen-on-each-other stage. Not like with you and your wife, years of a shared life."

We looked at each other, each knowing something of how the other felt. Helen and I had still been very keen on each other when she died. And we were both over the moon about her pregnancy.

The emotional intimacy of the moment was broken by the door opening and banging against the wall. It was the bald guy we'd seen near Mark's flat, followed by two pretty young women, both wearing short, low-cut dresses. He looked around the bar, spoke curtly to the women as if giving them instructions, then left. The two women clearly relaxed and ordered drinks. They then started smiling at a group of middle-aged men in smart-casual clothing, who I guessed were working away from home, and having a Friday night on the town.

Mark nodded towards the girls. "I'm upset they don't reckon we're worth buttering up."

A little later, I raised the subject of the TV show and he happily agreed to provide emergency medical cover. To celebrate, we visited a few more pubs and an Indian restaurant. Mark handled his drink rather better than I did, but maybe five years at medical school and two older sisters who sounded very like Claire gave him an unfair advantage.

It was getting late when we wandered past the hotel again, on our way back to his flat. I looked through the huge windows into the bar, wondering if the girls we'd noticed earlier were still there. I couldn't help wanting to be a knight in shining armour, even when I was in denims and a polo shirt, and a bit drunk. I felt a bit concerned about them. A lot of the sex workers in Plymouth were on the game directly or indirectly through drugs, but somehow those two didn't look quite right. They both looked unhappy and almost resigned... I tried to remember my impressions of them and the bald guy I assumed was their pimp.

I almost jumped out of my skin when a woman screamed nearby. It was unmistakably a scream of terror.

18

Mark took off down a service alley beside the hotel, towards the source of the scream. Considering his usual performance on the running machines in the gym, and his heavy leather boots, I was amazed at his turn of speed. He stopped near a woman in the alley, who was near a wall-mounted light. She grasped his arm as if he was saving her from drowning. As I caught up, I saw she was one of the girls from the bar, and she was clearly absolutely terrified.

"Please help," she mumbled, in accented English. "My friend… a man"—she gestured down the alley—"he is killing her, please help."

Mark took off again and I barely kept up, leaving the woman stumbling after us. In a dimly lit area ahead, I saw a girl sat on the ground, slumped against a wall, with a tall skinny guy holding one of her arms. He looked at us, dropped the girl's arm, turned, and ran. Mark dropped to his knees beside the girl and I went after the guy, even though I had no clue what to do if I caught him. But, despite the guy's very clumsy-looking running action, he easily outpaced me. By the time I got to the other end of the alley, he'd vanished down any of four nearby side-streets.

When I got back to Mark a few seconds later, he knew both the girls' names, had calmed down Magda, the scared one, and now held a tissue against the unconscious Ola's neck. "Can you call an ambulance?"

He pulled the tissue away and I saw it was dark with blood. Before he replaced it with a fresh one, I glimpsed a narrow arc of red marks with puncture wounds at each end. *Shit, looks like a bite.*

My hand was shaking as I pulled out my phone. I speed-dialled the emergency number and asked for an ambulance, saying it was for a woman who'd been attacked. I knew the control room would contact the police themselves.

Then I rang John's mobile, as I knew he was on duty in the city centre that evening. "John? I'm with a woman who's been attacked. Looks like she's been bitten in the neck."

"Fuck. You sure?"

"Yeah, called an ambulance—"

He interrupted me. "Just had a shout about that. Stay put, we're on our way."

"Okay." I felt surprised by his abrupt and emphatic tone.

I squatted beside Mark and the two girls. "My brother-in-law's a detective sergeant, he's on duty tonight. He'll be here in a minute."

"No police," Magda said.

"My friend will only want to help you," I said. "Nothing else is important to him."

I heard an ambulance siren getting louder and went to meet the paramedics, then helped them get their kit and a trolley along the alley. Mark gave them a rapid and incomprehensible briefing, then stood back while they took over. Ola was wrapped in blankets and on the trolley with a drip in her arm almost before I knew it.

"Got a container for this?" Mark asked the paramedics. He held up a syringe I'd not seen before. "I think her attacker was injecting her with it."

I thought I saw movement in the corner of my eye; I turned and glanced back up the alley. Something bulky and low moved slowly. *Is that a dog?* It certainly wasn't the guy I'd chased.

A car screeched to a halt at the kerb and two men jumped out. Both wore jeans and baseball caps, stab-proof vests labelled "Police" and equipment belts. They headed straight for us. I breathed a sigh of relief when I saw John, and introduced him to Mark. The other guy, round-faced and a bit overweight, introduced himself as Pavel. He hurried over to the ambulance and started chatting with Magda, who immediately looked relieved.

John nodded his head in Pavel's direction. "Polish and Russian parents, a degree in Eastern European languages. Speaks more of them than I knew existed." Then he looked from Mark to me. "So, what happened?"

We told him, then he repeated into his radio our description of the guy who'd run off and asked for patrol cars to start searching.

He turned to Mark. "Paul said the wound looked like a bite. What d'you reckon?"

"Maybe... right size and shape for a human jaw, but with unusually long and sharp front teeth. Oh, it looks like she was being injected with something. I gave the syringe to the paramedics. If she's been drugged, it'd help to know what with."

"Okay, thanks." John seemed far more alert and focused than I'd ever seen him before. "Paul's got your number?"

"I'm staying at Mark's tonight," I said.

"Right, no point you hanging around here. I'll be round first thing tomorrow for statements." He lowered his voice and looked serious. "Don't breathe a word about this to anyone for now."

He went over and talked to Magda and Pavel for a few seconds, then the ambulance left. Pavel and Magda got into the car John had arrived in, and set off after the ambulance. Three more police vehicles had already arrived, and officers stood around, waiting for orders.

John hurried over to a group of six wearing black jumpsuits, body protectors and riot helmets, and carrying batons and small transparent shields. After a quick briefing, they broke into three teams, which set off in different directions.

I looked around and saw two armed police officers watching the alley entrance, their military-style rifles held ready. Beside them were two very alert dogs and their handlers. On John's signal, they headed into the alley together. I was surprised to see the dogs advanced in low crouches, their ears flat back on their heads, as if they were expecting a fight, rather than loping off up the alley.

I'd not seen John at work before. Although I knew he was tense and concerned, he seemed calm, confident, and completely in command of the situation. Everyone looked to him for leadership. Not quite heroic, but damn impressive.

I looked around when I heard a car squeal to a stop behind me and saw a tall, lanky and obviously senior officer in uniform jump out of it. "Where's DS Hatherleigh?" he shouted, in a rather high-pitched voice. My immediate impression was that he was well outside his comfort zone.

Suddenly feeling overwhelmed by everything, I let out a long breath and tried to calm down. "Plymouth isn't usually this lively until the nightclubs kick out on a Friday or Saturday and there's a Navy ship in port."

"I had hoped for a bit more excitement than Cambridge when I moved here," Mark said, apparently quite relaxed.

Rattled, I stuffed my hands deep into my pockets and looked at him. "Leave it to the professionals?"

"Yeah." He looked around thoughtfully, then turned to me and grinned. "Since I've sobered up all of a sudden, it's a good job there's a bottle of nice Scotch back at my place."

I looked at him, bemused. We'd suddenly found ourselves in a weird and scary situation. This nice, rather geeky guy had outrun me, helped an injured woman and calmed her near-hysterical friend in next to no time, and stayed calm and professional. And now he was cracking jokes.

Big tough me needed a big drink to stop my hands from shaking.

*****

As a practical joke, John had set "Yakety Sax" as the ring tone for his number on my mobile phone. I'd left it as I couldn't be bothered to figure out how to change it back, and it was kind of amusing. Usually.

But it seemed a spectacularly crappy choice when his call woke me up far too early the next morning. My head hurt, my mouth tasted disgusting, and I felt like crap. Mark and I had watched *Dog Soldiers* on DVD and drunk rather a lot of excellent whisky. I'd arranged his sofa cushions on the floor and slept soundly in a sleeping bag.

"Hung over?" John sounded far too bright for my liking.

"Possibly," I croaked.

He laughed. I wasn't up to swearing at him. Telling him Mark's address was hard work. I let my head sink back down as soon as the call ended.

Mark opened the door and stuck his head in. "Morning, sleeping beauty."

I was face down on the cushions, with my hair all over the place. I lifted my head and glared at him with one eye. "Fuck off," I mumbled. "I hate cheerful people when I'm dying."

Encouragement, a shower, delicious hot coffee, and some painkillers revived me in time to talk to John. He was tired, but relaxed. All he'd tell us was that Ola was in the intensive care unit and Magda was safe. He swigged coffee and stuffed his face with the bacon sandwiches Mark produced. I wasn't quite up to eating then, but suspected my stomach might recover eventually. Say in a week or two.

After getting our statements, John looked at each of us in turn. "The guy who got away… could he have had a good look at either of you?"

Mark shook his head. "We were probably against the light. He might have seen Paul more clearly at the other end of the alley."

"No sign of him when I got there," I said.

John sighed. "Reassuring."

My brain had started working. "You're linking this with these other attacks, aren't you?" I asked John. "And if it's gang-related, we might get caught up in attempts to scare witnesses."

John nodded. "If he didn't see you clearly, I'm not too worried." He looked at Mark. "But no harm in keeping an eye open, especially when you're alone or not in a well-lit area."

I hoped he was right and we didn't need to be concerned.

John picked up another sandwich. "These are wicked," he said. "I'll have to pop round here again."

"Don't answer the door to him," I whispered to Mark. "You'll never get rid of him."

John nodded towards the DVD case still on the coffee table. "Now this sort of horror I can cope with. Not crap like we've had in the city recently. Not got any of the *Buffy* TV series I can borrow, have you?"

I wasn't really at my best, but it struck me that I might be able to talk to John and Mark about how to look as if I were doing heroic leader things. They'd both looked the part the night before.

But I desperately needed another mug of coffee before I did anything else. And those bacon sandwiches did smell rather good.

*****

John asked me for a lift back home. He'd been on duty all night and dozed off in the passenger seat, then went straight to bed. Claire asked me to take the group ride out that morning, as she had to take Vicky for a medical appointment. The fresh air helped clear my head and it was good to be out on the moors with Otto. There were about a dozen riders with me, all female, ranging from early teens to late middle age. I enjoyed the moorland scenery and did my best to let their endless chatter wash over me.

"Did you hear about all the police in Plymouth last night?" I heard one say. I automatically tuned in.

"My oldest is on the door of a pub there," someone else replied. "Told me they had machine guns and dogs and everything."

One of the local girls escorting the group with me joined in. "Reckon it's to do with them women what was murdered. Eaten alive by huge dogs, I heard."

"One had been dead for ages," said another woman. "I work at the hospital. Heard the mortuary technician say she was badly decomposed."

"Let's hope they catch whoever it is quickly. Not sure I feel safe in Plymouth of an evening."

"Maybe it's the Plymouth Ripper?"

Some of the group laughed nervously.

"People on social media saying it's to do with gangs from Eastern Europe."

"Well, I dunno about that. There are loads of Poles, Russians and Romanians where I work. They're all real nice. Can't think it's one of them."

We arrived at the hill we usually cantered up. Otto shortened up and tossed his head around excitedly, expecting a bit of exercise. "Everyone ready for a canter?" I asked. "Don't get too close to each other and don't overtake me."

When we settled down to a gentle walk again a couple of minutes later, thankfully the conversation changed to holiday plans.

When I got back to my flat, I rang Mark, who said he was fine and asked when we could go out again.

Then I called Hayley, who was shocked at my news, but glad we'd been able to help the two girls. She asked me how Mark was, and made me promise to ring Becky to tell her all about it.

Becky was delighted to hear from me, alarmed by my news, but wanted to know everything, asking me some very perceptive questions.

"You sound a bit like a journalist," I said.

"I've done some freelance work," she said. "I write fiction and nonfiction, but make most of my living from styling and make-up work at the moment. This sounds fascinating, aside from the scary stuff, anyway."

"Maybe I can find out a bit more from John and you can write a story about it."

"I'll give it a shot," she said, then paused for a second. "Hayley said you felt confused after we met up."

"A bit," I admitted, wondering what to say. "I think we need to talk about things."

She sighed. "I don't want to come between Hayley and you, but I love feeling close to you, and I do want us to be good friends. And if you feel upset, just say."

"Okay."

"You mean that? I mean, you're a guy and you've kept yourself bottled up for a couple of years. It can't be easy opening up now."

"I will try," I promised her. "I want us to be good friends, too." *And I like sharing a bed with the two of you, even if it is bloody confusing.*

*****

Late that afternoon, John wandered into my flat, looking refreshed. He carried a box of bottled continental beer and both the family dogs followed him. They jumped up onto the sofa, John flopped beside them and looked at me with obvious concern. "You okay? Really okay?"

I nodded. "Yeah, I think so. I mean, it was scary at the time, but I didn't feel in any danger. Someone needed help."

He grinned. "A classic damsel in distress."

"Two damsels, but definitely in distress. The one who got bitten, how's she doing?"

"In intensive care. All they'll say at the moment is she's poorly and being treated for a nasty infection. She needed a major blood transfusion, too. Mark's quick thinking about the syringe must have helped. Magda's with her all the time she can be. We've sorted out temporary safe accommodation near the hospital. Poor kids deserve a break after what they've been through." He looked around. "Got Mark's *Buffy* boxed set here?"

"In my overnight bag. I'll get it."

By the time I got back, he'd opened two bottles of beer and put the box on the floor where he could reach it. One of the dogs lounged across his thighs, the other lay on its back beside him, while he scratched its tummy.

"You said 'after what they've been though.' What did you mean?"

He pulled a face. "Trafficked from Romania. They've both got qualifications and could easily get jobs in hospitality here. Crooks promise transport, jobs, and accommodation, to be repaid once the girls are earning. The crooks keep their passports, subcontract them as cheap labour, keep almost all the money, put them in shitty, crowded flats, and terrorise them into staying silent. These two were promised good hotel work, but it turned out to be menial stuff and they were paid so little it would have taken them years to pay off the gangsters. Or a year on the game."

I felt horrified. "What can you do?"

"Our damn best to arrest the gangsters and rescue all their victims. Assuming we can find them, of course."

I fed the first DVD into my player and started the first show. We both drank some beer in silence, watching the opening sequence.

"So how are things with your lovely ladies?" He didn't look at me, a hint that this was a serious talk.

I decided to cut to the chase. "A bit confusing. At first, I fancied them both. Then when Hayley came back and…"

He raised an eyebrow and grinned at me. "I get the picture."

"I thought it was me and Hayley, with Becky as a good friend. But it doesn't seem to be as clear-cut as that, at least as far as the girls are concerned."

"So?"

I sighed. "I'm confused."

"I don't think they'd mess you around, don't seem like the sort. They both clearly like you. Competing with each other, maybe?"

I shrugged. "They're women, so if they are, it'll go over my head."

He laughed. "Don't be so sure. Claire and Helen trained you pretty well." He sat up. "Look, here's what I think. They're both still getting over shit in the past. If you want a serious long-term relationship with either of them, you'll probably have to help them both, and deal with some fallout."

"Hayley said her ex, Tony, was domineering."

He nodded. "She shows some classic signs; bit hesitant, eager for your approval, always says how long she'll be when she leaves you, stuff like that."

I looked at him in surprise. I'd sort of noticed Hayley doing that. "What should or shouldn't I do?"

"Don't lose your rag or boss her around. She could retreat into her shell and need ages to recover her confidence afterwards. I guess her parents and Becky did a good job getting her where she is now."

"How do you know this stuff?"

"You do know I'm a detective, right? I have to talk to victims, witnesses, and suspects. If they've got serious issues and we screw up, we get nowhere, can't help anyone, and they're in an even worse state."

He sipped his beer and thought for a few seconds. "Becky's different. I wonder if she'd been abused when she was younger. Seeks approval, wants to be the centre of attention, clowns around, tries a little bit too hard. Incredibly protective of Hayley. And smitten with you, which proves she needs help."

I ignored his little jest. "Any suggestions?"

He shook his head. "Depends what she suffered, and assuming I'm right, of course. Press the wrong buttons and you'll know it. She's a bright girl and does her best to come across as confident. Might have compartmentalised it and learned to get by." He looked at me. "I guess you've done an internet search on them?"

It simply hadn't occurred to me. "Why would I?"

"They're both public figures to some extent. Claire looked them up. Hayley's been acting professionally since her mid-teens. Becky's developing a career writing. You know she writes *Poppy*?"

I looked at him. "You mean Becky's actually Anne Martin?" I thought for a few seconds. "Why change her name?"

He shrugged. "Ask her. Let's just watch *Buffy*."

So we watched more of the show and drank more beer, and John visibly relaxed.

After a while, he turned a cheeky grin in my direction. "Suppose things get hot and steamy with you and the girls? Up to a threesome?"

"I could probably manage." I didn't want to admit we'd already shared a bed a few times.

John nodded. "Don't tell Claire for God's sake, but I had a threesome once, before I met her. Two women, me, and too much to drink one night on a training course. I mostly remember lots of arms and legs. But we all felt really awkward and embarrassed the next day." He sighed. "Pity. I fancied my chances with one of them. But you introduced me to Claire soon afterwards and there we go."

He opened a couple more bottles of beer and passed me one. "How about a three-way relationship?" From the way he looked at me, I thought it was a serious question.

What? I shrugged. "Dunno." I hoped I'd sounded casual and quickly thought about it. "Be a bit weird. And I can imagine all sorts of tensions creeping in. Particularly as we all live some distance apart."

"The three of you need to sort it out soon. If you don't, you're soft enough to let it drift on and on, and that'll screw you up. I'm not at all sure you could handle the emotional turmoil of a three-way thing going wrong. I know these happen, but I've never come across it. Hayley and her parents clearly make an effort to keep their lives private, but the gossip columnists and bloggers always love something salacious." He paused for effect. "Want your name splashed around in the media for the wrong reasons?"

I felt a cold shock and wanted to scratch the back of my neck, my own personal lifelong anxiety tell. John was talking sense. The media had messed up plenty of peoples' lives "in the public interest." If I was honest, it felt like we were on the way to starting an unusual relationship, even if I didn't know quite how it would develop, and it was far too personal for me to want to talk about it in detail with John, or even Claire. I wondered how I would tell my parents about it, the guys in the jousting team, or Mark and Maggie. And if it became gossip, what would the effects be on my family? John's career? Claire's business?

On my TV screen, Sarah Michelle Gellar efficiently despatched a vampire after some energetic and well-rehearsed hand-to-hand combat.

Keen to doing or saying anything which might make him suspect that the three of us had already shared some sexy times, I tried to change the subject. "Some of the women on my ride were talking about the incident last night and the murders.

Rumours are starting about a serial killer."

"We're wondering about that too, but we still think it's gang-related."

I remembered that glimpsed movement in the alley the night before. "Right before your guys went up that alley with the dogs and guns, I thought I saw something move up it, away from us. My first guess was that it was a dog, probably a largish one, crouching and moving cautiously."

He shrugged. "Could be. Our dogs scented something, they got really wound up and aggressive, but we didn't find anything."

I thought back over what he'd said. "That girl who'd been attacked. She'd lost a lot of blood?"

"She was given three units at hospital while Pavel was there."

"I don't remember seeing any blood at all where we found her. Mind you, I was a bit rattled."

"We only found traces." He shrugged, but I knew he was puzzled, too. He always said the more evidence he had, the quicker he could figure it out.

"Maybe the guy who bit her drank it," I joked.

He shuddered. "Not funny."

But where did her blood go? One of the dead girls looked like she'd been dead for weeks, but supposedly seen a few days before she was found. I remembered Mark saying his last girlfriend's body had decomposed very quickly. Was the Romanian link just coincidence?

I didn't want to be disloyal, but decided I had to tell John, even if it damaged my developing friendship with Mark. It might save lives. I took a deep breath. "Mark told me his last girlfriend was one of a group who died in mysterious circumstances in Romania about a year ago. Their bodies were far more decomposed than expected, given the time and weather."

"Was he there?"

"No."

He nodded thoughtfully. "Thanks. I'll keep him out of it as much as I can. I know he's a mate of yours, and I liked him, too. Seems like a sound guy."

On my TV screen another vampire crumbled to dust. I remembered John telling me about the dog hair found at the scenes of the attacks in Plymouth, and his quip about it being a werewolf, the clothing full of dust which seemed to be fertiliser, and Ola's unexplained blood loss. I opened my mouth, then closed it again. I remembered what Kathy had said about the original myths and legends about vampires being turned upside down for modern entertainment. *Werewolves and vampires are just myths*, I told myself. *There's bound to be rational explanations for everything.*

19

Later, I looked up my new lady friends on the internet. I felt uneasy about poking into their lives, even if only public-domain information.

Hayley and her parents had definitely kept their personal lives private. Her online biographies all mentioned her parents, but were otherwise entirely professional, and her social media presence was very professional, managed by her agent, I suspected. They were all mentioned in a lot of show-biz articles, but I found nothing about their personal lives.

I learned that *Poppy* had won a TV award earlier in the year for best children's show, with photos of Hayley and Trevor with the trophy on-stage at a glitzy event. The media were far more interested in the pretty and well-built actress from a popular soap opera who had an embarrassing wardrobe malfunction, revealing enough for uncensored photos to be blocked. It seemed clear she'd worn nothing under a very slinky designer dress. There were vague hints about bad blood between Hayley and this actress, but no details.

Becky's social media was strictly professional, with photos of models and actors as examples of her styling work. She had a different, equally professional profile as Anne, clearly an emerging writer with a number of publishing credits to her name, including the scripts and the first spin-off book for *Poppy*, and teasers about the show I was involved with.

Becky obviously had her reasons for keeping her different working identities separate, and for the lack of personal accounts. I supposed a lot of people in the entertainment industry did much the same. If John was right and she had suffered abuse, I'd wait for her to tell me when she felt ready.

I knew my own social media posts were limited to Knights Errant performances, the things I'd made for museums, and my academic career. Helen had created lively accounts for us as a couple, but I'd deleted them when she died. I didn't want all those reminders of what was lost forever.

*****

A few days later, I was in the gym with Mark and Maggie. As usual for the early evening, we had the place to ourselves. They'd both noticed the small bag I kept close to me all the time. I wondered how long it would take one of them to ask me about it, and who that would be.

As it turned out, Maggie asked me when we'd all finished.

"Come on, Paul," Maggie teased. "You've kept that bag by your side for the last hour. What's in it? The Crown Jewels?"

"Just a teaching aid."

Maggie bounced over and tried to grab the bag. "Wanna see, wanna see," she giggled.

I was struck by how happy and relaxed she'd been since starting her relationship with Mark. The change was striking.

"No, can't play—my toy," I said, standing up to hold the bag out of her reach.

After she jumped almost high enough to grab it, I gave in gracefully.

I opened the bag and carefully unwrapped the sheathed dagger inside. I was rather pleased with it.

"It's a copy of an Elizabethan knife on display in a local

historic house," I said, sliding it out of the leather sheath "I made it for a lecture on historic metal-working. Got my sister to video all the key steps."

"Can I see it?" Mark asked.

I passed him the knife and he carefully tested the edge with his thumb. "Razor-sharp."

"That's why I kept it safely wrapped up," I said. "I needed it as sharp as I could get it for some testing we did today. I brought it in here as I didn't want to leave it in my Range Rover."

He passed it to Maggie, who was fascinated. "It's amazing, Paul." She angled it so the blade caught the light. "How long did it take?"

"A few days of pottering," I said. "I don't get as much practice as a blade-smith from the good old days."

Mark pointed at the rippling dark lines on the silver-grey blade. "How'd you get this pattern?"

"Pattern welding. Heat steel ingots, twist them together into a spiral and then hammer out and shape the blade. An acid wash reveals the pattern."

"I'd love one like that," Maggie said. "Smaller and not as sharp, of course. Maybe a letter opener." She passed it back to me.

"Give me a couple of weeks." I re-sheathed the blade and wrapped it up carefully.

We all left the building at the same time. Outside, we lingered in the lee of the building while the elderly security guard locked up behind us. Our cars were over a hundred yards away, and it was raining again.

"We'll only get wet," I said. "Race you."

Maggie tried to shelter under Mark's waxed cotton jacket, which appeared waterproof, but I guessed it was more of an excuse for a cuddle. I was thirty yards ahead of them, walking fast, when I heard Maggie shout in alarm.

I turned around and saw Mark face down on the ground, with a monstrous shaggy dog standing on his back. Maggie was few yards away, frozen in fear, staring at the animal in horror. The dog stared back at her, teeth bared, ears flat, and growling loudly. I felt a sudden cold shock. I knew that dog was going to attack her next, and there was nothing she could do.

As the dog moved off Mark, he rolled aside, sprang to his feet, and quickly moved to put himself between the dog and Maggie. He held her hand and they slowly backed away, facing the animal.

"Mark, Maggie, get over here," I hissed, and wondered what I could do. My instinct to panic certainly wouldn't help. As I watched the dog, I remembered what John had said about the women killed and injured by dog attacks.

Mark seemed amazingly cool and kept his eyes on the dog as they both moved backwards towards me. He was rummaging in his bag without looking. "Paul," he called out. "That knife of yours?"

Thank fuck someone's thinking clearly. It was bundled into my gym clothes inside my sports bag. My hands shook as I unwrapped the knife and pulled it from its scabbard.

"Distract it for a few more seconds," I shouted.

With the dagger in my hand, I dropped my bag and ran towards them. Mark had wrapped a towel and sweatshirt around his left forearm, which he held out in front of him. He passed his bag back to Maggie, then stepped forward, shouted, and waved his padded arm in front of the dog. The dog sprang up, knocked him to the ground and gripped his arm firmly in its mouth.

The next couple of seconds seemed to last forever. Showing way more guts than sense, Maggie shouted at the dog, kicked it hard in the ribs, and swung both their sports bags at its head. Mark gripped the animal's throat with his free hand while its teeth tugged at his padded arm.

All I thought about was that my friends were in danger and I was the only one who could help them. I punched with the dagger, felt it break the dog's skin and stop when the finger guard hit its body. I pulled the knife back and struck, and again. Warm wetness gushed over my hand and, as the blade scraped against the dog's ribs, I wanted to throw up.

The dog made a loud cry of pain, let go of Mark's arm, and stumbled clumsily away in the opposite direction.

"Maggie, run," I shouted. "My car." I triggered the remote lock on my fob, then grabbed Mark with my left hand. I pulled him to his feet in one movement, one of those moments when one doesn't know their own strength. "Come on."

Maggie had grabbed all our bags and leaped into my Range Rover almost before I knew it. Mark and I piled in; I dropped my dagger into the footwell and started the engine. I floored the accelerator and we left with squealing tyres while Mark was still pulling his door shut.

"My place," he said. "I need a fucking big drink."

Somehow we made it without having an accident. Mark helped Maggie in and put her on the sofa. She was as white as a sheet and trembled like a proverbial leaf. I stared at the dog's blood, still red and wet on my right hand and forearm, and sat down heavily.

"Better call John," I mumbled. "He's on the late shift again today. I'd be bloody surprised if it's not linked to the other shit going on."

Then I started shaking and felt a wave of nausea. At least I got safely to the bathroom before I threw up. I remembered to wipe my hand with tissues to give the police a sample of the blood before I washed my hands and face.

Mark had changed his sweatshirt and T-shirt by the time I got back. He gave me a glass with about three fingers of scotch inside it.

"John's on his way. They're looking for that dog." He put his hand on my shoulder. "And thank you. You showed a lot of guts."

Oddly, I immediately felt better, despite just having emptied those very guts down his toilet.

He sat next to Maggie and held her tightly against his side. She was starting to look a little more human. I was amazed how calm

Mark seemed in yet another mad situation. Medical training clearly had something to be said for it.

A few minutes later, the doorbell chimed. Mark answered it, and came back with John and a young, anxious-looking uniformed officer.

John was in work mode again; in command, brisk, efficient, and matter-of-fact. We each told him in turn what had happened. Mark showed him the bruises already developing on his arm, and the torn, blood-stained towel and sweatshirt he'd wrapped around his arm. I took John out to my Range Rover, where I'd left the dagger. We didn't touch it. The light from the torch on his mobile phone showed hairs and blood stuck on the finger guard.

"I'll need the knife for forensic tests," John said. "I'll get it back to you in a day or two."

I stared at him. "Why? I stabbed a dog."

He paused, muscles in his jaw clenching and relaxing. "Just go along with me for now. There's... well, it's a bit messy."

A middle-aged crime scene officer arrived, put my knife and the tissues I'd wiped my hands with into plastic evidence bags, scraped out some of the dog's blood which was still under my fingernails, took photos of Mark's arm, and DNA swabs from all three of us for elimination purposes.

Elimination? I thought. *DNA from dogs and humans must be easy to tell apart.*

After she left, John looked at Mark with interest. "Good trick with the dog. Where'd you pick it up?"

"My dad," he said. "He's the first-call vet for the police and military dogs in his area. He's had a lot of experience of dealing with large, angry, upset animals who've all been trained to grab arms."

Then John's mobile phone rang. We sat silently as he listened, grunted a few words, and looked increasingly puzzled. He rang off and thought for a few seconds before speaking.

"Pavel. They found blood, even with the rain. One of our dogs tracked it to a nearby road, where it abruptly stopped. Probably had a vehicle waiting." He looked around at all of us.

"Which makes it sound like a planned attack," Mark said quietly. "Someone knew we'd be there and set the dog on us."

John nodded. "Strong possibility."

"But why?" Maggie's voice trembled a little.

John shrugged. "We need to figure that out." He sighed. "Look, I believe you. You were attacked by a dog and defended yourselves by sticking it with Paul's knife. But a minute or so before you rang it in, the hospital reported that an unknown man was dumped at the accident department with multiple knife wounds to the abdomen and chest. We're going as fast as we can to figure out what happened. It's almost certainly a coincidence, but we need to establish the facts."

I nearly threw up again. *But I stabbed a bloody huge dog.*

Mark's eyes went wide; Maggie's face went white and she visibly shook again.

John rubbed his hands over his face and pinched the bridge of his nose. "I sent someone down to the hospital, just waiting to hear from them, and the car park you used is covered by CCTV. We just need a few minutes to review the evidence."

His phone gave an alert sound and he read something on the screen. "The guy at the hospital was dropped off wearing jeans and a sweatshirt," he said, clearly relaying what he read on his phone. "No tears or cuts anywhere in his clothing. He was basically dead when he was dropped off. The rain made the CCTV footage too blurry to get the vehicle registration number, but we know it was a medium-sized white van."

We all sat in silence for a minute. I felt awful and confused. Maggie fidgeted with Mark's sweatshirt while he held her. John was almost completely immobile, leaning forwards with his elbows on his knees, staring at his phone, but I'm not sure he saw it.

We all jumped when his phone rang.

"Hi." He listened intently for a few seconds. "Thanks." He cut the connection and looked at us. "CCTV confirms exactly what you've told me; you defended yourselves from an attack by a very large dog, which went off in the direction of the scent trail we found."

John leaned forward and rested his head in his hands, thinking. No one moved or said anything for about twenty seconds. I held my breath.

He looked at us again and I knew from his expression he'd reached a conclusion. "Okay, what you told me corresponds exactly with that CCTV recording. You called me at almost the same time that guy was dropped off at the hospital. I'll report your incident exactly as you described it. Probably stay unsolved unless we find that dog or the bastards who set it on you. Unless someone can convince this cynical copper that you were attacked by a shape-shifter, our unknown dead man's a separate crime and the timing's coincidental."

John leaned back in the chair and. "I enjoy horror films, but here the real world, I don't believe in werewolves or vampires. But I'm buggered if I can think of another explanation." He let out a long breath. "It all stinks of organised crime, which is outside local police force work. We'd already decided to hand this case on to the National Crime Agency, which is what they were set up for."

His phone rang again, and he raised his eyebrows when he looked at the caller ID. He sat up straight as he answered. "Sir." He listened for a few seconds, his face as immobile as a sculpture, then he suddenly looked surprised. "Not a problem, sir. I'll cooperate fully, of course." He paused. "Yes, I'll see everything is passed on to them."

He cut the connection, put his phone in his pocket, leaned back, his head on the top of the cushion. He was silent for a few seconds, and the three of us stared at him. "Slight change of plan," he told the ceiling. "The NCA are being bypassed and I've been ordered to pass this on to the Weird Shit Squad."

"The what?" Maggie asked.

"Their official title is the National Investigation Task Force." He looked at me. "That's the bunch Greg said had talked to Hayley's ex. I asked around and one of the older sergeants called them the Weird Shit Squad. All he knew was that they're a specialist national team who take over any Mulder and Scully cases. They're already in the loop on this one, according to my Superintendent." He pulled a sour face. "Nice to know big brother's been looking over your shoulder."

We all sat in silence for what seemed like an age, but was probably only thirty seconds. The doorbell rang. "That's for me," John said. He went out and came back with several pizza boxes.

"Should help your shock," said John. "There's a good delivery place near here. I'm bloody famished." He looked at the uniformed officer. "Get some plates and a knife from the kitchen, eh?"

Maggie started giggling and Mark looked at John in disbelief. I grinned. My brother-in-law had his own ways of doing things and that was good enough for me.

While everything was sorted out, Maggie took her phone into the hall and had a brief and hushed conversation with someone. I couldn't understand the little I overheard, as it was in a language I didn't recognise. Some of it was clearly very emphatic, from her tone of voice.

I hadn't wanted to eat at first, but Mark put his hand on my shoulder as he passed me a plate, and I realised I felt hungry. Maybe doing something so everyday grounded me, and I soon felt calmer and enjoyed the pizza. I was still feeling rattled, though, but I felt as if the incident had happened a couple of days earlier, not an hour or so.

We all gave John our statements, and he and the uniformed officer left. Then we had another drink or two and talked about it between ourselves. I'd soon drunk far too much to drive home safely, and still felt shaken, so readily accepted the offer to sleep on Mark's sofa cushions again.

I kept waking from a recurring dream in which Mark and I were trying to protect Maggie, Becky, and Hayley from a pack of circling dogs, which got closer and closer, but I always woke up before they attacked. While the dogs circled, I was vaguely aware of someone watching us and directing the attacks, but could only see a vague figure.

Mark and Maggie both seemed to be in good spirits the next morning. I noticed Mark watching me carefully, and I wondered if he was checking to see if I was still in shock. They both made a point of thanking me, and I got a tight hug and a kiss on the cheek from Maggie before I left for the farm.

I rang Hayley to tell her about the dog incident, but had to leave a voice mail. It was the day to set off for the recording of our medieval feast, the court dance, and a few other scenes. I exercised Otto for half an hour in the sand school, doing some dressage exercises which did us both good. I packed everything I needed to take in my Range Rover. As I had nothing tempting in my fridge to eat on the trip, I wandered into the farmhouse to see what I could steal from Claire's kitchen.

When I opened the kitchen door, she was pouring steaming water from the kettle into a large cafetiere.

"John told me about last night," she said. "I was about to come and find you. Sure you're okay?"

"Yeah, bit rattled and not quite sure what to make of it right now."

"Not surprising. John's sure you saved Mark and Maggie from being badly injured."

"Where is he?"

"Taken the kids to the beach for the day. Do him good as well." She passed me a mug of coffee and leaned back against the counter. "So, you're off to be an actor for a couple of days.

Anything about that bothering you?"

"I think I'm okay with pretending to be a leader. I simply have to think 'what would John do' and do it. He's given me a few nice pointers. But I'm still worrying about being a hero."

She shrugged. "Why not think 'what would Mark or Maggie do' instead? From what John told me about last night, they were both bloody brave."

Why didn't I think of that? "Good idea, thanks."

"Or remember how you felt when you dived in yourself." She tapped me on the chest with a fingertip. "You saved them, so that makes you the hero. I'd have run a fucking mile." She paused and pulled a face. "No, I'd have whimpered, curled up and wet myself."

I laughed. "You? No way. You'd be in there like a shot."

She pointed at me. "Like you were. We're the same, remember? Identical twins and all that?"

She had a point. "Fair enough."

She grinned. "Big sisters are worth all the trouble they cause, eh?"

"About fifty-fifty," I mumbled into my mug. "And you're only a few minutes older than me."

"Now tell me what's really worrying you."

I was going to deny that I was worried, but she held up a hand. "Come on, we always know when something's wrong with each other. You've been unusually quiet for a few days."

I sat silently, wondering what to say.

We looked at each other for a few seconds, then Claire sighed and sat down next to me. "Look, I know you fancy both Hayley and Becky, and they're both attracted to you. For what it's worth, I'll say again that I think Hayley probably suits you better as a partner. And I think you find Becky fascinating, because she's different and a live wire."

"I'm getting more and more confused," I admitted. "I want to focus on Hayley and develop our relationship, but it's like Becky's orbiting both us and every time I'm with her, everything gets fuzzier.

They get on so well; I'd feel guilty if I came between them." I paused for a couple of seconds. "The simple truth is, I don't know what to do."

"Have you asked them what they want?"

I looked at Claire, feeling surprised.

"Look, Helen was amazing and we all loved her," she said. "But of all the adjectives I could use for her, 'tactful' or 'subtle' wouldn't be high on the list."

I grinned. "Yeah, she could be a bit blunt."

Claire squeezed my hand. "She was the only woman you've had a long relationship with. If something bothered her, she came out and told you. She was direct, had a short fuse, and didn't even notice when she'd hurt someone. You've never learned about a more typical woman, the sort who expects guys to figure it out without being told, and who simmers quietly without you realising it."

"We've all agreed to sit down and talk it through," I said.

"Will you?"

Could I really come out and ask Becky and Hayley what sort of relationship they wanted the three of us to have? Or was I quietly hoping they'd tell me first?

"I'll try, but it's pretty scary," I admitted. "I might not like the answer."

"Worse than fucking big dogs attacking you?" She grinned. "Just think, 'what would someone brave do' and give it a try." She patted my hand. "You need to sort it out, figure out who you're going to look after. You can't look after both of them." She took my empty mug over to the sink. "Now bugger off and act for a couple of days. Then come back and tell your big sister all about it."

"Yes, dear," I said. *Well, maybe edited highlights.* I wasn't sure if the three of us would share a bed again, but part of me hoped we would. While I didn't know for certain what we'd get up to, I hoped Hayley and I could find a bit of time alone for sex.

She pointed at two garment bags hanging from a coat rack. "The outfits we lent Becky and Hayley for the jousting show. They asked if they could borrow them again. I've tweaked them a bit, so they look a little more courtly."

20

When I arrived, neither of the girls' cars were parked outside the venue. Hayley had told me when she thought they'd arrive, which wouldn't be for an hour or so.

Originally a stately home with a Georgian frontage, it was now a hotel which hosted banquets, events, conferences, weddings, and was the location for the odd TV or film recording. Phil had told me the hotel had restored a sixteenth century hall during renovations, which we'd use for the banquet and dance. Across the manicured gardens, I spotted the tower of a medieval church, which I knew we would use as the location for a scene set on a castle tower.

The receptionist told me that the production team was in the conference suite, so I dropped everything off in my room. The super king-sized bed made me feel a mix of anticipation and nerves. I rang Mark to ask how he and Maggie were and, reassured that they were both fine, went to see what was going on.

Phil was in the middle of briefing the technical team on the shooting plans. With the documentary team there as well, it was a far larger group than we'd had at the first location. A production assistant passed me several pages of notes, which I scanned while Phil ran through his slideshow presentation. When he'd finished, he introduced the expert he'd recruited to advise us on the banquet and dance.

A woman in the front row stood up and I recognised her immediately. Kathy looked exactly how I remembered her from the conference a few months before. I wondered if I could sneak out without being spotted, in case she felt embarrassed about meeting again. We'd exchanged polite, professional and friendly emails, but a surprise face-to-face meeting was a different matter. I felt happier when she caught my eye and flashed me a warm smile.

I was actually really pleased to see her again, as I'd enjoyed our conversations even before we ended up in bed together. She would have been on my shortlist if Phil had asked me for some names. There weren't many people as familiar with medieval domestic life as she was.

She briefly described typical late medieval high-status formal meals; seating, food, service, and etiquette. Then she went on to talk about court dances. All the participants of both events would be coached as necessary the next day, with the help of a group of dedicated reenactors who enjoyed dressing up and living in the past for a while.

As soon as the meeting broke up, Kathy walked over and gave me a warm smile. "Paul, lovely to see you again. I recognised your name, of course."

"Delighted to see you again," I said, meaning it. "Fancy a drink?"

She nodded. "Please. I'm interested to hear how you got yourself involved in this delightfully madcap venture."

We sat and chatted; two academics who knew and respected each other, rather than two people who'd spent an enjoyable night together in bed. She laughed when I told her how I'd ended up being the leading man on the show.

"Other stunt performers became well-known actors, but probably not quite so rapidly. How are you finding acting?"

We chatted for a few more minutes, then she leaned a little closer, as if about to share a confidence. "I got home from your conference feeling very, very happy and, well, a little naughty," she murmured. "My children weren't due back from my parents until the following day, so I decided to visit the male friend I told you about. The upshot was that we're now spending a lot of time together. It's lovely to relax and let myself enjoy it, and he gets on well with my children. You seem to have helped release some hidden reservoir of passion in me."

I grinned. I didn't mind being accused of something like that. "Thanks. Hope things go well for you. I've turned over a new leaf since then."

"You've met someone? That's wonderful." She looked at me thoughtfully for a couple of seconds. "Not the actress playing the princess, by any chance?"

I hoped I didn't look too surprised. "Yes. How did you guess?"

She shrugged. "The way you talked about her when you told me about being recruited for this show." She reached forward and patted my hand. "She's a pretty girl and a talented actress. My children adore that *Poppy* show she's in. I do hope it works out and you're happy together."

Behind Kathy, I saw Hayley and Becky walk into the bar, clearly having a serious conversation. When they spotted me, they smiled, waved and walked over. They both seemed surprised to see Kathy. I kissed them each on the cheek, then made a three-way introduction. We chatted politely for a couple of minutes until Kathy was asked to meet the catering team leader for a discussion.

"An old friend?" Hayley asked.

"We met at an academic conference earlier this year," I said.

"Leading expert on medieval domestic life."

"Big tits, too," Becky said, pointedly.

Hayley nudged her sharply. "Don't be bitchy. She's tall and well-built." Hayley looked at me. "A bit like Helen, I guess."

I nodded. "Yes, very like Helen. Apart from being alive and a mum." I immediately felt uncomfortable, as I'd spoken more sharply than I'd meant to.

Hayley bit her lip, looking embarrassed. She leaned closer and squeezed my hand. "Sorry, shouldn't have a go. It's my insecurity. I'll get some drinks."

When she'd walked out of earshot, Becky leaned close. "Claire hinted that you'd had a wild night at a conference earlier this year."

I looked at Becky. "And?"

She briefly chewed a fingernail, then studied it. "With cuddly Kathy?" she asked in an off-hand tone.

"Does it matter who? That was before I grew up and met you and Hayley."

She looked at her fingernail for a couple more seconds, then up at me. "She any good in bed?"

"How should I answer if someone asked me that about you or Hayley?"

She shrugged, but I spotted a flash of insecurity in her eyes too. "That we're the best you'd ever had the honour to fuck, of course."

I was tempted to point out that she and I hadn't actually gone that far, but I remembered what John had said to me. I didn't want to push any buttons by mistake.

Becky sighed, leaned back in the seat, and stretched her legs out, wrapping her calves around my ankles. "Sorry, don't mind me. I'm knackered. No excuse for being a cow. Long drive and I need an early night."

Hayley came back, balancing a tray of drinks. "This is tricky. If I ever need to work as a waitress, I'll be hopeless."

Becky immediately went back to being her normal chatty and

perky self, which left me with a vague feeling that there was something in the air. We all chatted away for a few minutes, which eased my anxieties. I spoke on the phone with Hayley almost every day and Becky nearly as often, but as before, it felt far more real and intense when we met up.

Hayley skimmed her production notes. "Bloody hell, that's not fair." She held the offending sheet up so Becky could read it. "Only one early morning in this whole production and it's tomorrow. So early it's probably still night-time."

"The dawn scene?" I asked.

Hayley nodded. "I'm never at my best first thing in the morning."

Becky tried to hide a smirk. "I dunno. From what you've told me, Paul seems to like you then."

Hayley slapped at Becky's leg. "You know I don't mean that. Mind you, he'd jump me any time of the day."

Becky put on a pout. "You get all the luck."

Hayley raised an eyebrow. "I think Paul would be perfectly happy to jump you."

They both smirked at me while I tried not to look flustered. "Look, I'm doing the same scene," I said, trying to divert the conversation's direction. "So it's an early morning all round."

Hayley leaned forward. "So come on, tell us about this dog attack. It sounded absolutely terrifying on your voice mail. You're sure your friends Mark and Maggie are okay?"

Half an hour later, Phil wanted to run us through the next morning's scene. "You'll be on top of the tower," he said. "If we're careful with the angles, it'll look perfect. The scenes we're doing tomorrow will be the most challenging for you, Paul, but I'm sure you'll be fine."

"My character's upset about the princess marrying, isn't he?" I asked. This would require me to truly act, which I was quietly dreading. The coaching Hayley had arranged wouldn't start for a couple of months. I'd have to rely on winging it, on-the-spot direction, and inspiration.

Phil nodded. "You're upset and confused, but doing your best not to show it. You've been on duty all night, not sleeping for worry. You're heartbroken because you feel you can't compete and are about to lose her forever."

"So when I go up to talk with him, I feel guilty when it's obvious he's hurt?" Hayley asked. "The script has me saying something which gives him hope, but leaves it to me to improvise."

Phil nodded. "You challenge him to admit his feelings and make an offer to the king for your hand."

"So what about the banquet and the dance?"

"You're both still upset and avoiding each other in the banquet," Phil said. "Hayley's waiting for you to decide, which you'll do by the time you dance together."

"So lots of hurt and anxious glances, but not talking to each other?" Hayley said. She turned to me. "How do you feel about it?"

I nodded, hoping I looked confident. "I'm sure we'll convince the audience." *Fingers crossed.* It sounded odd with Phil talking about us as if we really were our characters.

"But during the dance, we sort of fix things?" Hayley asked.

"How about this?" Phil asked. "You'll already have told the king you expect Rowan to ask for your hand and you're more than happy about it. During the dance, he'll realise it is what he wants to do. Of course, you'll be kidnapped the next morning and he has to do the heroic big rescue thing before the wedding plans are sorted. We'll record your heart-to-heart with the king later, I've got a great location for the Royal Apartments."

Hayley and I nodded at each other. "Okay," she said.

At least one of us feels confident, I thought. I knew I was probably still unsettled by the previous evening's events, and a poor night's sleep.

Phil rubbed his hands together. "Let's go up the church tower now, so we can get the angles and marks sorted out."

On the way over, Phil coached me quietly. "Paul, I know you're worried about this scene tomorrow morning. Look, imagine you've been awake all night, stewing over what you can do about Gwendoline. You've convinced yourself you can't compete with the visiting lord. But she'll make you think you've something to hope for. You come to believe that and get your confidence back during the banquet and the dance. Okay?"

The winding stairs and narrow doors on the way up to the top of the tower looked a bit tricky for Hayley in the long dress she'd be wearing. The top had a wide walkway around a low, leaded roof, giving plenty of space for the production team and us, and the parapet crenellations made it a good stand-in castle tower.

The camera operator looked around and asked where the sun would rise. The assistant director struggled opening a large map in the breeze.

"Sunrise will be over there." I pointed out across the countryside.

Everyone looked at me in surprise.

"How'd you know?" Becky asked.

"It's late in the day, so the sun's in the west now." I pointed along the church roof. "Churches are aligned east-west with the altar at the eastern end."

There was a brief discussion about camera angles to get the dawn sky without including anything modern. Parked vehicles, the hotel, a nearby mobile phone mast and distant power lines would rather spoil the effect.

Dinner was noisy and fun. The two production teams chatted away. The actors playing the king and the visiting noble bad guy both made a point of chatting with Hayley and me for a while, which I certainly appreciated. They struck me as friendly, intelligent, and professional. The extras playing the banquet guests enjoyed the meal and the chance to talk to the more established actors. But I thought Becky seemed a bit subdued, and was sure she didn't eat all that much. So I made sure to give her as much attention as I could, in case she felt left out.

"Seem like two decent guys," I said.

Becky nodded. "We hoped Trevor could play the king, but he's already committed."

I frowned. "We?"

She grinned sheepishly. "Well, yeah. The story and the outline script you're using are mine. My big chance to show I can write a longer show with more drama in it."

"Really?" I stared at her, feeling surprised, and a little bit upset that she'd not mentioned it before. I'd already teased her about not telling me she had an alter-ego who'd written *Poppy*.

She shrugged. "My full name's Rebecca Anne Martin. I'm still self-conscious about being a writer; Mikey tended to poo-poo anything I did, so I've used a sort of pseudonym."

"You know I'll do my best not to blow it. Any other successes?"

It was the first time I'd seen her look bashful. "A few ideas in development, but nothing else you'll have seen," she said. "Hayley and Trevor insisted on working on *Poppy* as a favour."

"You'll be working on the scripts for the other shows if this one goes down well?"

She shrugged. "Wait and see, but I hope so."

I grinned. "Always happy to help if you want to bounce some ideas around."

I felt her hand squeeze my knee. "Just ideas you want to bounce?"

I leaned close. "Now you're asking for trouble."

"That's not what I'm asking for at all," she whispered.

Thanks to the direct look she gave me, and my dirty mind, I got an uncomfortably solid erection.

Becky smirked at me, sipped her wine, then casually slipped her hand onto my lap and patted the firm bulge in my trousers. "Now that's something I wouldn't say no to."

After our long journeys, a good meal, and a fair few drinks, we were all tired by the time we went to bed, so with the alarms on all our phones set early, we opted for chit-chat, kisses, and cuddles, until we drifted off to sleep.

It was pitch dark when I woke, feeling groggy and befuddled. Hayley was stroking my cock, which was already rock-hard. She'd rested her head on my chest, close enough for me to smell the last traces of the scent from her shampoo. "Becky's fast asleep," she murmured into my ear. "Screw me very slowly from behind."

I felt excited at the thought, as I'd never done anything like this before. But I also felt guilty about Becky, as if we were cheating on her.

I rolled onto my side and Hayley tucked her back against me, her head resting on my left arm. She guided my cock to her pussy, which felt hot and wet. I slid into her as far as I could, while she reached down to grasp my thigh with her right hand. Hoping we didn't make the bed move and wake Becky, I steadily eased in and out, her body a hot, yielding pressure around me. She took my left hand in hers and nibbled and licked my fingertips. I fondled her breasts with my right hand and gently pinched her nipples.

She twisted her face so close to mine that I felt her heavy breathing. "You're hitting my G-spot with every thrust. I'm almost there." She moved her right hand to her clit and, through my cock, I felt her body move as she stroked herself. I lifted my head and kissed her deeply. Her body tensed and she gasped into our kiss as she climaxed.

"Wow," she murmured. She sounded a bit breathless. "How close are you?"

"Nowhere near. I'm happy to wait until tomorrow."

She kissed me again, running her fingers through my hair. "Thank you. I'll return the favour then."

As I eased out of her, she rolled towards me and snuggled up, hugging my left arm. A couple of minutes later, her breathing was slow and steady.

I couldn't get back to sleep right away, but felt happy and relaxed. A few minutes later, Becky rolled over beside me and lazily slid an arm across my chest. I leaned across and kissed her gently on the lips. She surprised me by responding with a long, slow, and very passionate kiss, and writhed, her legs and hips moving sinuously against me. My erection, which hadn't totally subsided, was suddenly fully revived. She lay partly on her front, her right leg across mine, and guided my right hand under her and against her pussy. It felt awkward, but I didn't want to spoil it for her. I ran a finger along her cleft, and found her warm and wet. My fingertip slid easily inside her. She sighed so softly I felt her breath on my chest more than I heard her.

On my other side, Hayley rolled over, let go of my left arm, then lay still. I gently rolled to face Becky. I'd felt guilty about secretly having sex with Hayley not long before, but now I felt guilty about playing with Becky with Hayley asleep beside me. But I was only going to touch Becky. So long as I kept my self-control, anyway.

I found Becky's clit and rubbed it steadily with a fingertip, and I made good use of my long arms, reaching my left hand down between her legs to tease her entrance with my fingertips. She pulled a pillow under her face and squeezed my right arm even more tightly.

Becky pushed herself back onto my fingers at her entrance, so I eased two of them into her, and started a slow in-and-out movement, reaching as far inside her as I could. It wasn't comfortable, but no worse than messing about with girls in a car when I was younger. I tried to reach her G-spot as I teased her clit with my other hand. I felt her tense her body for a few seconds, then she relaxed again. A few seconds later, she tensed and relaxed once again. I wondered if she was getting close, but felt inhibited with Hayley sleeping beside us. I slipped both fingers out of her and slid three back in as deeply as I could manage. I only pulled them back half an inch or so before pushing deep again. I kept this up for a few more seconds, then she tensed and lifted her hips off the bed. I felt her whole body tremble, then soften as her orgasm released her tension. She groaned once, her voice muffled by the pillow, then relaxed completely, breathing deeply.

She lifted her head, kissed me lovingly, then rolled over and tucked her back against me. I wrapped my arms around her, and nuzzled the back of her head. I was sure she and Hayley had used the same shampoo that morning. She pulled one of my hands to her mouth and gently bit each of my fingertips. Then she reached down and tucked my cock between her thighs, pressed firmly against the wet, hot, open pussy I'd teased with my fingers only a few seconds before. From the feel, I was sure my tip was right against her entrance. I knew if she gave me the slightest encouragement, I would have slid deep into her and worried about feeling guilty afterwards. She wriggled against my erection, took my hand and interlinked her fingers between mine. A little later, Hayley rolled against my back and slid her thighs up against mine. She wrapped an arm around my waist, then was still.

I lay there, feeling something unique for me. I was in bed with two women I felt strongly about. I was spooning one while the other spooned me. It felt absolutely lovely, their thighs against mine, Becky's back against me, her backside in my lap and my rock-hard cock pressed against her pussy. Hayley's arm was around me and her breasts pressed against my back.

As I lay there, I couldn't help wondering about timing. Had Becky been awake while I was screwing Hayley? Had Hayley still been awake while I was playing with Becky? Had they plotted this? I certainly didn't have the confidence to ask them.

Too alert to get back to sleep, I thought about the emotional scenes I'd be recording in a few hours. Hayley had said many actors drew on their own experiences to create the emotional response the audience recognised. I'd never been told I was being dumped for another guy, and had only had a few serious girlfriends before meeting Helen. Since her, there had been a dozen or so women, who all only wanted one night with me before returning to their normal lives. They'd all told me they were single before things had got interesting, as I wouldn't have wanted to be involved in helping anyone cheat. I'd not properly thought about that string of one-night affairs, but now I was starting a hopefully serious relationship with Hayley, my self-control was off-duty.

How did I feel about those other women? Grateful for the brief reminder of happiness they gave me, if I was honest. The colour and feeling each had briefly brought into to my grey, numbed life. I felt grateful for the affectionate fun we'd shared through uninhibited sex. Each time, we'd each known it was a one-off, so I couldn't blame them for anything. The confusion I felt after each occasion was entirely of my own doing.

How would I feel if Hayley walked away from me? We were still in the early stages, but she was great company, we got on well together, and I felt optimistic about life for the first time in a couple of years, with optimism starting to replace the dark feelings I'd felt shrouded with.

Would Becky still want to see me if it didn't work out with Hayley? I felt much the same about her, despite spending less time together. But these two women were best friends and I suspected that if I lost one, the chances were I'd lose them both.

I didn't think I'd fall back into the deep depression I'd struggled out of, but it would knock my confidence. More to the point, I knew I didn't want to lose either of them.

I held Hayley's arm, and relished the feel of her soft, warm skin against my backside and back, at the same time I felt Becky's hair tickling my chest. Being with the two of them felt incredibly reassuring. At least when I wasn't feeling confused about my strong sexual interest in both.

21

I woke from a nightmare. All the women I'd slept with since Helen died were there, saying I was ideal for a sneaky night away, but not relationship material. Then Becky and Hayley appeared and argued with them, saying I was a keeper. But they were both eventually persuaded by the other women. Then they all looked at me appraisingly, turned to each other and nodded in agreement. For some reason, I couldn't say anything in my own defence. The alarm sounded from Becky's phone before I could get back to sleep, so the memory of the dream left me feeling disturbed.

It was far, far too early for me and I felt detached and distant from lack of sleep. It was still dark, and we all struggled to get up. Hayley was grumpy as she stumbled off to the shower, which was new for me. Becky seemed to be on autopilot as she pottered with her makeup kit. I made us coffee while Becky showered. When she came out and sorted out Hayley's hair and makeup, I shaved, showered, and got into costume. Becky brushed my face with something or other, then helped Hayley with her costume.

"You're a right grump," Becky told her.

"Too bloody early." Hayley looked a bit sulky. "Told you I hate really early mornings."

"Don't think we ever got up together this early before."

I wedged our door open with a shoe, to stop the clunky lock disturbing anyone sleeping in nearby rooms. I looked down into the lobby and saw a couple of the production crew. They seemed subdued, so I guessed they didn't like early starts either.

I went back to our room and opened the door. I glanced across the room and froze. Hayley had stood up and Becky was hugging her from behind. In the mirror, I saw Becky's hands cupping and fondling Hayley's breasts. Hayley had leaned her head to one side and Becky was nuzzling her neck. I heard Hayley sigh happily and I saw her slip a hand down and stroke Becky's pussy through her clothes. Then they turned to face each other, hugged, and shared an intimate lover's kiss, with Hayley's hands cupping Becky's bottom.

I felt something like vertigo, and stepped back out into the corridor, feeling incredibly hurt and confused. The only two women I'd trusted to get close to me in the last two years had deceived me. I leaned against the wall, took a few deep breaths and struggled to keep control. I realised I was still far too close to the deep, self-destructive depression I'd slowly escaped from. *They're playing games with you,* an inner voice told me smugly. *All the women you meet now only ever want to play games with you.*

I took a couple more deep breaths. *You can do this. Get through today, do your best for this show, but walk away from this fucking weird set-up.*

I took a final deep breath to steel myself, checked that my hands weren't shaking, then pushed the door open again. Hayley had picked up her handbag and Becky was checking the huge shoulder bag she used for carrying her makeup kit.

"Ready?" I asked.

Hayley nodded, then looked at me and frowned, but didn't say anything. I guessed I hadn't managed to hide my emotional state as well as I hoped.

Thankfully, no one in the lobby seemed keen on the usual chit-chat. I couldn't have managed small talk right then. We all made our way to the top of the tower, where the cameras, microphones, and lighting had already been set up. Hayley and I had radio microphones tucked inside our costumes, then I stood on my mark, on the side nearest the sunrise, which was already filling the sky with colour, and waited while Phil, and the sound and camera operators sorted themselves out.

Phil ran through the scene again with me and Hayley, she gave me a look which I thought combined puzzlement and anxiety, then it was time to perform.

I pretended to survey the distance for attacking Vikings, Orcs, shuffling zombies, flying dragons or whatever. I heard a door creak behind me, then Hayley's footsteps on the wooden boards as she walked around the edge of the tower. It struck me that the scenes I'd dreaded most might not be too difficult. I didn't have to act feeling hurt and confused, but my problem might be not showing too much. I knew what the script had outlined, but I didn't know what I'd actually say in a few seconds.

"Captain, hast thou stood watch this long night?" Hayley asked. She sounded hesitant and uncertain.

I didn't turn towards her. "I have, my lady."

She walked closer and stopped a few feet away. "You took no rest?"

I shook my head. "Sleep would not come. Better one of the guards slumber since I could not."

She turned towards the sunrise and waited a few seconds. "A fair morning."

"That it is."

Out of the corner of my eye, I saw her bite her lip. "Captain, have I done you some hurt?"

"Highness, your protection is my duty and my honour. When you wed, I will proudly continue to protect the king, your father."

She turned to me and glared. "Why dost thou speak in riddles? Have I wronged you or no?"

I turned to look at her and let my self-control go enough to feel some of my pain and confusion. "If you have, my lady, it was my weakness."

She looked genuinely puzzled. "Weakness?"

I shrugged. "If I am wronged, I allowed it."

I was stunned to see tears in her eyes. "You allowed it? Rowan, thou art a good and brave man, but your life holds much more than your duty and sword. Surely you know your own heart? There are times when you must hear it."

"My duty calls on my sword, not my heart."

She reached out and covered my hand with hers. "Why can you not let down the guard around your heart?" she said in a quiet, gentle voice. "Pray, tell me what ails you?"

I paused for a couple of seconds, then pulled my hand away. "It is not my place, my lady."

Hayley's expression changed from concern to frustration. "You good, foolish man. Who else might you tell? You spend all your days at your duties and see no other woman more than you do me. I entrust you with my life, Rowan. Pray, why not entrust me with your concerns?"

As I heard her last sentence, I knew we weren't talking purely as our characters. At least that explained why my throat suddenly hurt. "Lady, please hold that I am not a man who opens his heart with ease. To do so would leave me disarmed."

She looked at me, her face immobile for a few seconds. "It is the prospect of my betrothal, is it not? Captain, I am of age, with no other offers." She looked down and traced her fingers across a stone block in the wall. "It would be wise for me to accept Duke Roland. He is powerful, wealthy, and his lands adjoin our realm. You must know of him, as your fellow countryman. This small kingdom needs such men as friends, not foes."

I looked at her and saw tears run down her cheeks. I pulled a plain, linen handkerchief from a pocket and pressed it into her hand. "Lady," I said, "I am your servant. Your choices are yours to make and I am sure you will choose well."

She wiped her face. "You have the king's high regard." She took a deep breath, collected herself, passed my handkerchief back, and gripped my forearm with her hand. "Talk to the king," she whispered. "He is my loving father as well as your liege lord."

I looked down for a second, then turned towards Hayley. "Lady, I am but the man you see. No great titles, no land, no treasures. Naught but my honour and foolish pride."

Her lower lip trembled until she bit it. "Sir, you have a true noble's bearing, manners, and education. You would bear the responsibilities of high title as easily as if born to them, be a fair and just lord, and a wise treasurer if the chance fell to you. Your honour counts for far more than what you might now own."

I swallowed hard. "A wise man knows his place, lady," I said, almost in a whisper. My throat burned, as if I was on the verge of tears. "Such chances do not fall to a man like me. The dice have fallen and I must accept my loss."

We stared at each other for a couple of seconds. I thought Hayley struggled to keep her face under control. She turned away and walked over to the door, her tread slow and heavy, as if wearing weights on her feet.

"I will tell my father to expect you," she said, without turning to look at me. "Not the king, but my father. Please do this for me." She paused. "He trusts and respects you as he would a lifelong friend. He will know my mind and my heart, and should you seek his blessing, be certain that he would be generous to ensure my happiness." She stepped through the door and pulled it closed. The click of the latch was incredibly loud in the cool, quiet morning air.

I looked at the closed door for a few seconds, folded the handkerchief carefully and looked at it. I wiped my own eyes, then put it away. Then I leaned on the wall and looked away into the distance again, surprised to see the camera drone hovering a few yards away. I'd honestly forgotten all about the cameras, lights, microphones, and the small production team a few yards away. The drone drifted further away, while I stared at it, without seeing anything.

"Cut," Phil said. "That's a wrap. No second take; you'd never top that." He walked over and patted me on the back. "Bloody amazing, Paul. I really felt you were heartbroken. Great work."

Hayley came back out onto the roof, and Phil went over to congratulate her, too. She still seemed upset. There was little conversation among the production people, probably because they were tired. Among them I spotted one of the women I'd overheard bitching about me before our first recording session, staring at me with what looked like open disbelief.

Becky came over. "You okay?"

I nodded. "Sure. Why?"

"You don't need to hide it from me, Paul," she said. "If something about that scene upset you, let's talk about it. It's bloody obvious to me you let something personal out. Something important."

I squeezed her arm. "Thanks. But I've got to stay focused for this afternoon."

"No, you don't." She frowned at me. "That's not healthy. You said Phil told you to feel it, then let it go." She gripped my arm. "Talk to us if something's bothering you. That's what our relationship's all about, isn't it? Trust?"

Trust, yeah, right. I managed not to snort. "Maybe later. I need some coffee."

I felt like a shit, walking away while Becky was so obviously worried. I was sure she and Hayley didn't know I'd seen them kissing. In fact, I hoped they didn't, so I wouldn't have to face talking to them about it.

The restaurant had opened early for us. I wasn't hungry, but forced myself to eat some toast. The objective, sensible part of my brain reminded me this was how I'd been when I'd moved into my flat and was still grieving for Helen. Claire had thrown a first-class hissy fit when she discovered I was largely living off sandwiches, take-aways and cold food out of tins. She insisted I joined her family every evening, to eat healthily and spent some time in company. I still appreciated that gesture, and the love that motivated the well-deserved arse-kicking she gave me.

Hayley and Becky sat with me, both looking anxious.

"Paul, you were amazing," Hayley said. "I've never known a scene like that to be done in one take with no rehearsals. But you really must get out of that head-space."

"I'm okay," I said. "Just overtired."

I couldn't run away, not while I was supposed to be a grown-up. I felt tired, confused, and hurt, but didn't feel I could talk to them about it. A day of real-life armoured combat would be less scary than talking about my deepest feelings.

Before they pressed me again, Phil saved the day.

"Paul, the documentary crew's just about ready for you. Their idea is a how-to-do-it spot where you learn how to make manchet bread. I think it's brilliant."

Hayley looked puzzled. "What's that?"

"Apparently it's a luxury medieval white bread," Phil said. "They've got a genuine sixteenth century recipe."

Becky grinned at Hayley. "Maybe we could persuade them to let you do that, and Paul could do your session, dressing up in multiple layers of rich lady's frockery?"

Thankfully, Phil preferred his idea. Which gave me a perfectly good reason to hide for a while.

The hotel kitchen was hot, noisy, busy, and full of amazing aromas as I was guided through. Behind it was the original Georgian kitchen, restored for use in this documentary to look like a late medieval one. There was a small raised dais in the middle, with a wooden chair from which the chef could supervise people working at a huge wooden table and the cooking fires. Firewood was being fed into the crackling glow inside a bread oven set to one side of a traditional open wood fire. That had been lit, but the chimney wasn't drawing properly yet, so there was a smell of wood smoke. Kitchen staff in costume were cutting and chopping vegetables and fruits, preparing various joints of meat and poultry and arranging them on spits, ready to be roasted. Two camera operators were busy recording close-ups of the action.

Kathy was delighted I'd agreed to her idea to add a bit of fun to the documentary. She gave me a sharp look when I arrived, then introduced me to the director and the master baker. She excused herself to go and help Hayley dress up like a genuine late-medieval princess for the other session being recorded.

The documentary director took charge and it turned into a fun morning. The baker and I hit it off and exchanged good-natured banter and teasing while he coached me. In time, I even managed to clumsily knead and shape two small loaves of bread at once, one with each hand. They weren't brilliant, but it all took my mind off things for a while. The director was delighted, which was a bonus.

Kathy came back just before we finished, and caught my arm as I left. "Paul, what's wrong? When you arrived, I was sure you were trying not to look upset."

How do women do that? "Had a bit of a surprise this morning," I said. "Not sure what to do and I'm still worrying about it."

"If you want to talk about it, let me know, okay?"

I nodded. "Thanks."

She looked at me seriously. "No chocolates this time, just talk. I mean it."

I grinned, remembering the chocolates we'd eaten off each other. "I could get the hotel to order some in," I murmured. "But only as a thank you."

She slapped my backside and gave me a half-grin, half-glare. "Bugger off, you big hunk. My briefing on medieval dining etiquette is in the banqueting room, twenty minutes."

I found Phil and described an idea I'd had a little earlier. "At the end of the show, how about a light-hearted scene, showing the princess has mellowed? She visits the palace kitchen and gets teased into having a go at making bread."

The twinkle in his eye showed he liked it. "That'd be perfect for the end credits, something to smile at. And a nice contrast from the 'snotty princess in the market' scene we'll have early in the show. Thanks."

Hayley arrived in a fabulous multi-layered outfit of rich fabrics, a bejewelled coronet and a golden necklace. It was clearly rather restrictive, as she didn't move around with her normal easy grace. The briefing was immediately followed by the recording, which provided thirty-odd of us with a substantial and alcoholic feast. The seating arrangement had me at the other end of the table from Hayley, but we both caught each other's eye from time to time and briefly exchanged awkward looks. Becky, who sat beside Hayley, gave me a couple of meaningful glares.

We were in groups of four, each with our own set of serving dishes from which we cut or picked out small pieces at a time, using only knives and spoons. The selection of joints, fowl, potage, pies, and vegetables was fascinating, mixing the familiar with things I'd only read about. Fortunately, it had all been prepared for modern tastes, with no weird seasonings or dishes full of offal. I liked the manchet bread; tasty, denser than most modern forms, and still warm from the oven. Kathy recorded a few short pieces to camera for the documentary with us in the background, but mostly it was just us chatting, pigging out, and ignoring the cameras, lights, and overhead microphones.

The final course, which I had learned was called the banquet, was selections taken from trays of dried and sugared fruit and other sweet delicacies set out on a separate table. They were fabulous and I decided to do some research for recipes and recreate some for my family at Christmas.

The recording and the meal finished in the mid-afternoon, and I wouldn't be required until the briefing for the court dance early that evening. Hayley and the actors playing the king and the visiting noble had a couple of scenes to do, which kept Becky occupied, too. I slipped outside, found a comfortable bench in a quiet corner of the gardens, and tried to let my mind empty.

Which it flatly refused to do, of course.

What I'd seen that morning completely explained the close affection Becky and Hayley shared, and their comfort with being naked with each other. Although I was very hurt they'd kept it secret, I honestly couldn't say how I'd have reacted if they had told me. My first reaction had been total surprise and shock, before my self-confidence crash-dived. I didn't want to walk away from either of them, but I had to know where we could go from here. I had to believe I could trust both from now on, and that they would trust me.

The only positive was that I hadn't had an anxiety attack like the one a few weeks before, when I mistakenly thought I'd blown it with both of them.

A cheeky rabbit was grazing the lawn about ten yards away. "What the fuck am I going to do?" I asked it.

It looked scared and ran away.

Very tempting.

22

A little while later, and still confused, I was surprised when Kathy sat beside me. She had two mugs of hot coffee and passed me one.

"Nice view," she said casually. "Good to sit and stare, sometimes."

"Yeah," I said. "It can help."

"But not when you need to talk," she said, in the same no-nonsense tone Claire used for delivering advice. She sipped her coffee. "I might be wrong, but I suspect Hayley's scared stiff she's losing you and is trying hard to hide it. Your feelings for each other were perfectly clear when I saw you together yesterday."

I started saying something half-hearted about acting, but she held a hand up and interrupted me.

"Whatever, as I hate my children saying. Look, I know when people are feeling hurt and confused. That would be you and that pretty blonde actress." She looked at me. "We chatted this morning; a lovely girl, bright and cheerful. But I'd have expected you to fancy the makeup artist. Becky, isn't it? Seems bouncy and a bit off the wall, more the sort of challenge I'd have thought you'd go for. And she's a bit down in the dumps, too."

I sighed. "I was getting confused, but things got way more complicated earlier today. And I honestly don't know how to deal with it."

She tucked a foot underneath her on the bench and turned to face me. "So you're out here, stewing about it, your mind going around in ever-decreasing circles?"

"Well, I watched a rabbit on the lawn a while ago. But, yeah, mostly stewing."

She put her hand on my arm and squeezed it gently. "Perhaps your choice is remarkably simple. Worry about it, or know for certain."

"You should meet my sister," I muttered. "You could gang up on me."

She smiled. "Or you could talk to Hayley. Or Becky. Or both of them."

"I could."

"So will you?"

How come everyone but me can do common sense? I nodded. "Yeah. I'd rather know, one way or the other."

"Good. Don't avoid feelings. They do need to be confronted sometimes." She squeezed my hand again. "Remember when we met for dinner after the conference?"

I nodded. "Of course."

She licked her lips and let out a breath. "I'd felt flattered by the interest you showed in me and my work, you'd listened carefully to my presentation, and you showed me that you found me attractive in a respectful way. I was nervous about our dinner date, it was my first in a couple of years, but your quiet confidence and impeccable manners helped me relax." She paused to sip her coffee. "From what I gather, acting is all about being confident that you can realistically portray your character. You helped me admit to myself that I rather liked the idea of sleeping with you, just that once. After I discovered my husband was unfaithful, a painful divorce and three years of being single, I probably needed reassurance that I'm still an attractive woman, not merely a divorcée and the mother to two wonderful children. Our delightful little interlude gave me that." She leaned back and thought for a few seconds. "From what the production people said, your performance in the scene recorded first thing this morning was one experienced professional actors would be proud of. From what you've just told me, I suspect you didn't have to act, you expressed exactly how you felt."

She looked at me questioningly and I nodded.

"Undoubtedly this story will have a happy ending," she said, "your character overcomes today's doubts and anxieties, and wins the fair maid's hand, and they live happily ever after, once he's indulged in some family-friendly mayhem and violence?"

I nodded again.

She grinned at me. "So what's the problem? You can clearly do heartbroken, you know you'll defeat the bad guys, you only have to deal with your own self-doubt and confusion, then you can show us all a real-life happy ending as well as a fictional one."

We looked at each other for a few seconds while I tried to work out what to say.

Kathy held up a finger. "There are two young ladies worrying themselves sick over you, ones you obviously care for deeply and find very attractive." She looked me up and down. "And you're not a bad catch, I suppose. Polite, well-mannered, hunky, decent looks."

I laughed and she grinned again.

"I won't ask about my performance in other respects."

Her lips quirked as she suppressed a smile. "It was, um, perfectly acceptable."

When I raised an eyebrow, she looked down into her lap and blushed.

We were quiet for a few seconds, then she looked at me. "So?"

"If I want to carry on getting to know two attractive and fascinating women, I do the scariest thing I know, and ask them what they're thinking."

"And what would be the ideal outcome from your perspective? Your immediate reaction, please."

"We deal with the confusion and give things a chance to develop."

"Good. I knew you were a bright chap. It's what my new man and I are doing, and it's been delightful so far." She nudged me with her elbow. "This conference I'm arranging next year… could I persuade you to present? And by all means, bring your lady-friend with you. Or both of them, if that's how things work out."

"Thank you, I'm flattered."

She stood up, ruffled my hair, and grinned again. "First things first. You've the minor matter of facing your personal dragon. Wait here, please."

She took both the empty coffee mugs and walked back to the hotel.

A couple of minutes later, Becky and Hayley found me. I saw that they were both worried. They were both wearing the costumes I'd brought from home, which reminded me of when we first met and how excited I'd felt at the time. Claire and Libby had done a beautiful job of embellishing them both with rich details in lace and silver thread.

"Paul, please tell me what's wrong," Hayley said. "I know something's upset you."

I took a deep breath and jumped off the high board into the darkest, deepest water I'd ever faced. "The only thing I really want to know is what you want. For you, Becky, and me."

They exchanged an anxious look, then sat, one on each side of me. "To put it simply, we both want to be with you," Hayley said. "And we both hope that's what you want."

What? "As in two relationships, one with each of you?" *Where was this going?*

"One relationship," Becky said quietly.

"All three of us," Hayley added, almost in a whisper.

I honestly didn't know how to react and looked from one to the other a couple of times. "But isn't three a recipe for disaster?" I asked. "One feeling jealous about the other two?"

"Not if we're open and honest," Becky said. "We all have some deep-seated insecurities, of course. But if we admit when something feels off, we can deal with it together."

I thought for a few seconds. "We all need to be completely open and honest from now on to get anywhere."

I looked at Hayley, then at Becky. I thought they were both holding their breath.

"You didn't know that I saw you kissing this morning," I said. "I was surprised, and hurt that you'd kept that from me. Now I've thought about it more, I think I can understand why. Not an easy thing to slip into getting-to-know-you conversations."

Hayley wrung her hands in her lap and looked upset. "Look, Paul, we didn't want to hit you with everything all at once, it would have been too much. Yes, Becky and I love each other and, well, everything that goes with that." She looked at me, her eyes pleading. "But we both want you as well."

"We've been best mates since we met at university," Becky said. "We only fell for each other after Hayley left Tony. We both needed affection and comfort at a shitty time in our lives, and there we were."

I leaned back. "I'm confused, too. To be completely honest, I fell for both of you when you stayed with me. But now I've slept with Hayley, things seem different."

They both slid beside me. Hayley hugged one of my arms; Becky lifted my other and put it around her. That contact reassured me.

"We, um, had thought about that," Becky said, sounding a little sheepish. "We sort of hoped you might give in to my charms tonight. I lost my bottle last night."

"You had a plan?" I asked.

Hayley shrugged. "Well, like last night, only pushing a bit more. We've been trying to figure out how to overcome your gallantry and gentlemanly reserve. We wanted it to feel like a natural step we all took together."

"Last night was a set-up?"

"No, it was spontaneous and absolutely bloody lovely," Becky said. "You've no idea how turned on I felt knowing you were doing it with Hayley, right next to me. All I wanted to do was hug you both."

"I couldn't help myself from hugging you after you sorted Becky out," Hayley said. "I was really tempted to suggest you did it with her, too."

"But if I'd had sex with Becky last night, I'd have felt guilty." I squeezed Hayley. "I already felt guilty about what we did last night with her there."

"Even if I'd encouraged you? I'd have been hugging and kissing you like mad the whole time," she said. "You'd have realised straight away that it was exactly what I wanted you to do. Hell, it would have turned me on again."

Things had gone too fast, so I needed to put that on my mental back burner for a few seconds. I rewound our conversation. "So, this shitty time you were both having at the same time? What happened?"

"Hayley had escaped from arse-wanker Tony," Becky said. "She was in a right state, no self-confidence at all."

"And Becky was heartbroken after finally being dumped by Mikey," Hayley added. "I always reckoned it was an abusive relationship. Becky was smitten, but it was a convenient on-off affair for Mikey when other women weren't on the scene."

"Why didn't you tell him to fuck off when you found out about the other women?" I asked. "You've never struck me as lacking self-confidence."

"Mikey's short for Michaela. She... I dunno, bewitched me." Becky let out a long breath. "I've had major emotional problems since my early teens. They keep me off-balance and looking for security, which I've never found. All the guys I dated hurt me, mostly sooner rather than later. The only caring relationships I've ever had were with girls, mostly really close friendships."

I realised John had been right. There was a lot of background I needed to get to grips with to understand Becky well enough to avoid accidentally pressing the wrong buttons. And I needed to understand more about Hayley's history with Tony as well. But could I maintain a three-way romance? I'd only ever considered monogamous relationships.

I hugged both to me. "Look, I'm genuinely flattered that you both want to be with me, but it's pretty damn confusing."

Hayley leaned her head against my shoulder. "So you're thinking about it?"

Becky wove her fingers through mine. "And maybe give it a try?"

I grinned and heard myself say, "Yes and maybe." *Shit, I really mean that, too.*

Becky shuffled on the seat, got onto her knees and nibbled my ear, which made me squirm and grin. "What can I do to make you say yes and yes?"

Hayley giggled, then kissed the hand I'd wrapped around her shoulders. "There's no excuse for Becky. Tactless is her only setting."

"You've no idea how hard it was for us not to touch each other when we were in bed with you, Paul," Becky said. "It was so exciting being there together."

"I need some time to process it," I said, wondering if I was making the right choice. Or was I already committed without knowing what was coming?

Becky jumped to her feet. "No, we all need a drink. I'll get them." And she picked up her long skirts and scampered off towards the hotel.

"Sure you're happy about it?" Hayley asked.

"I'm so confused, it's pushing me right up to my limits," I said. "But it's what you both want and I really don't want us to walk away from each other. You know I think Becky's great, but I'm worried we won't be able to stop it blowing up and hurting us all."

Hayley slid onto my lap and hugged me. "You and Becky need a little time together," she said. "Like you and I had."

I wrapped my arms around her and nuzzled her hair. Her costume carried the scent of Claire's fabric conditioner, which reminded me of my home and family. "It'd feel weird, like I'm running around with two women and cheating on you both."

She kissed my cheek. "We'll have you and me time, you and Becky time, me and Becky time, and all of us time. And we'll all be open about it. No cheating, no secrets. Well, apart from nice surprises."

"I need to know more about Becky, so I don't do or say something stupid and upset her."

Hayley nodded. "I don't know all her story and I don't want to push. She hardly ever talks about her parents, but I know her dad died when she was eleven or twelve and her mum a few years later. I suspect something else upsetting happened in her early teens. And I'm convinced she had a rough time at university before I met her. If she doesn't want to talk about it yet, well, I'll be there for her when she does. She was a bloody angel in my hour of need with Tony. She literally rescued me."

Becky reappeared with a pint of beer and two glasses of wine on a tray. "Hey, don't wear him out, we've a scene to record."

We settled ourselves with our drinks and something seemed to click into place. We all relaxed, as if a crisis had passed. The tension I'd felt faded away and things seemed... normal.

Becky sipped her wine and grinned. "You two were fucking amazing this morning. The whole production team stood there with their mouths open. They were totally convinced Rowan was heartbroken about the idea of Gwendoline marrying that other jerk, and that she was desperate for Rowan to propose so she could say yes."

"Me, too," Hayley said. "It was amazing to act against that. But I couldn't have done another take." She nudged me with her elbow. "If you'd looked any more hurt, I'd have ignored the damn storyline and bloody well asked you to marry me there and then."

Becky squeezed my thigh. "That was probably the toughest bit of acting you'll ever have to do."

I grinned at her. "Probably, only the easy bits to do now. Defend the king, chase down the bad guys who kidnap the princess, kill them all, rescue her, then defeat the evil, scheming duke. Oh, and do a formal court dance." I sighed. "I'm honestly hopeless when it comes to dancing. Two left feet, no coordination, no sense of rhythm."

Becky snorted. "Yeah, right. We've seen you fighting, remember? Those routines were far more complicated than any dances we'll do here."

I couldn't argue with that. I knew my lack of confidence about dancing came from anxiety about making a fool of myself when I was a gawky teenager, but that was deep-seated now.

Hayley slid a hand under my tunic and jabbed me in a ticklish spot. "Not a bad day's work so far," she said. "I feel stuffed after that meal. I'm grateful the dancing will all be pretty slow."

*****

A group of enthusiastic medieval dance reenactors had been recruited for the documentary, who had their own costumes, as did the musicians playing lutes, recorders, drums and percussion instruments. The "proper" dancers, the other lead actors, Becky and some of the extras were all involved. Kathy had asked to join in, too, and she clearly relished swanning around in a fetching period costume.

One of the reenactors explained how the dances would be performed and they demonstrated the steps. I was relieved to see it was slow, measured, and surprisingly similar to things I'd managed to blunder through at barn dances.

We ran through the first dance a couple of times while camera positions were sorted out, and those acting could figure out when and for how long they could speak to each other.

"Come on, Paul," Becky teased, as I turned the wrong way yet again. "It's not that difficult."

"I hate dancing," I said, almost tripping over my feet. "I'll figure out a show-jumping course on one walk-through, or a complex fight scene after a couple of practices, but dancing's a total bloody mystery to me."

Fortunately, everyone else was more than competent enough to cover for me. And hopefully the camera angles would keep my feet out of sight.

In the first dance, we started in couples, changed partners in turn, and bowed or curtseyed to each other a lot. Even I found it fairly easy to follow most of the time. Once we'd sorted everything out, those with lines had radio microphones fitted, and we started recording. I hoped I wouldn't make a total hash of it while thinking about dialogue as well as where my feet were supposed to be.

Hayley and I started the dance as a couple. She looked a little anxious as we approached each other. "Captain, have you spoken to my father yet?"

"Duke Roland is his constant companion, my lady. My personal concerns are scarce a matter of state."

"But you will speak to him, sir?"

"When chance permits, my lady." The dance drew us apart. My partner after next was Becky, cast as one of the princess's ladies in waiting.

She looked at me coolly. "Sir, would you so carelessly reject the hand my mistress offers?"

"My lady, I have naught to offer to compare with Duke Roland."

She gave me a pitying look. "How can you know any woman's true desires, sir?"

I hadn't expected that line, so didn't need to fake a dumbfounded expression.

Becky looked me in the eye. "Captain, do not let a golden prize slip your grasp."

I wondered whether we were in character or talking about real life again, but the dance moved on. I had a minute or two of concentrating only on the dance, until it ended and I returned to Hayley.

She smiled at me gently. "So, Captain, this dance is done. Where do we stand?"

I knew what the outline script said, but I didn't say that. When I opened my mouth, I said what I really wanted to. "We stand a man and a woman, my lady. A man who would ask you to share his life."

She swallowed and I saw a tear run down her cheek. "So you will speak with the king?"

"I will speak with your father, my lady."

Then we parted with a courtly bow on my part and a curtsey on hers. Hayley turned and caught Becky's eye. As the group milled about, a camera operator moved close to me. *Something new and improvised.* I felt a hand on my arm and turned to see Becky standing close to me.

"Sir, should the king demur, my family would rejoice to have me wed to such a fine gentleman." She gave me a cheeky grin and slipped away.

That wasn't in the script either, but I felt that I'd been given a broad hint about something other than acting, which I didn't want to think about too much right then. Hose and a tunic were comfortable to wear, but concealing an erection would need some discreet rearrangements.

Becky and I joined in more dances, and I just about managed to avoid making a complete prat of myself. Hayley had some scenes with the king and Duke Roland, while the rest of us were dancing and making merry in the background. At one point, Kathy and I were partnered for a while.

"Come to any decisions?" she asked me.

"Only one," I said. "To see where things go."

"Is that genuinely your own decision?"

"Yes, it's what I want to do."

She grinned at me. "Good. It's the brave choice. The worst that can happen is you lose eventually, but the easy choice means you lose immediately."

"Fingers crossed we all win."

She paused for a second. "So, my conference next year?"

"I'll even do the after-lunch session, if you want."

She wrinkled her nose. "The graveyard slot? No, I'll leave that for some terrified postgrad. Fancy being the keynote speaker? Maybe the realities of medieval arms, armour, and combat? And perhaps we could do an after-dinner double act about working on a documentary and a historical TV show?"

A lot of work, but flattering. "Count me in."

Phil and his assistant were very complimentary about my work during the day, which I took as attempted confidence-boosting flattery. But I won't deny that it gave me exactly the welcome boost I needed.

The schedule required me to do a couple of scenes with the king the next day, both from earlier in the storyline, one including Hayley as well. My asking for permission to marry the princess would be recorded later. Duke Roland would throw a hissy fit at that point and have the princess abducted, while he and some of his men-at-arms provided noisy distraction. I would set off in hot pursuit, deal with the kidnappers, rescue her, defeat Roland's men-at-arms in a minor battle, stuff him in a joust, marry the princess, and presumably live happily ever after.

A buffet had been laid on for the dance re-enactors, the production team, and anyone who wasn't still feeling stuffed after the banquet earlier in the day. It was rather fun to see the bar full of people wearing clothing from the mid- to late-Middle Ages mingling with others in modern dress. There was a cheerful atmosphere, friendly conversation and lots of photos and selfies were taken. I was pleased to see Becky eating well from the buffet. I had a nagging feeling that she'd lost weight through worrying about how our relationship would work out.

Those who'd had an early start were the first to leave the bar. I felt a mixture of excitement, nerves, and curiosity as I followed the ladies upstairs. Things had changed between the three of us and I guessed we all felt much the same.

23

I followed the women in and closed the door. Becky hugged me tightly while Hayley turned off all the lights except those on the bedside tables.

"Stand still and close your eyes," Becky whispered. "We'll undress you."

It felt pretty weird, but exciting in an edgy way. At least I kept my balance, which wasn't a given after our evening at the bar, and the assorted garments that made up my costume.

"Keep your eyes shut," Hayley whispered.

I heard clothing being removed, hushed whispers and giggles, then I was led by both hands over to the bed, and pushed onto it so I sat near the edge with my feet on the floor. One of the women climbed onto the bed behind me and the other sat astride my lap, with her arms around my neck. Whoever was behind me wrapped her arms around my chest and I held the woman on my lap. I felt their breasts against me, and knew they were both naked.

"Open your eyes," Hayley whispered. From behind me.

Becky looked nervous, but she gave me a shy smile. I ran my fingers through her hair. "Fancy you," I murmured.

"So I see." She wriggled a little and I felt her tummy against my erection, which stood up between us. I was very aware of both her perfume and the scent of her arousal.

"We don't need to do anything new tonight," I said.

She nudged my nose with hers. "True, but I want to."

"What do you want?"

She swallowed. "I want to feel you inside me," she said. "Just a couple of minutes of me moving up and down on you, slowly and gently. Will you let me be in charge?"

I felt a mix of anticipation and anxiety, as I wanted our first time to be special for Becky. This was also our first step into what looked like being a full-on three-way relationship.

"Of course," I said. "Better put a condom on."

She shook her head. "If you want to, that's okay. Hayley and I both had the same health check, and she told me about yours."

"But—"

"And no, you can't get me pregnant," she said. "I've had contraceptive implants for years. Unreliable periods used to drive me mad." I thought it would feel odd using a condom with Becky, but not with Hayley, and might make Becky feel I didn't trust her somehow. "Well, in that case, it's okay with me."

Hayley slid one of her hands down my body and gently gripped my cock. Then she did her best to distract me by nibbling and licking one of my ears. Becky moved up and Hayley wriggled my cock around until it was pressed against Becky's pussy, which felt invitingly hot and wet. Becky moved a little and I was wedged firmly in her entrance. Hayley let go of me, then Becky took a quick breath and pressed down onto me. Her body resisted for a second, then the soft pressure and heat of her body surrounded my tip.

I kissed her deeply as she moved up and down, taking more of me into her with each downward push. Then she broke from our kiss and pressed her face against my chest. She seemed to be holding her breath.

Hayley pushed my loose hair away from my neck and planted

soft, wet kisses just along my hairline, which tickled enough to make me want to squirm a little. She moved backwards and pulled me down on the bed, and I held Becky as she followed me down. Hayley moved to one side, and hugged both Becky and me as best she could.

My instinct was to push upwards and get deep inside Becky, but I resisted and let her move how she wanted. She took about half of me on her deepest pushes, then slowly relaxed her grip around my neck and breathed deeply.

"You okay?" I asked.

"Bloody silly question," she whispered. She raised herself off my chest for a few seconds by taking her weight on outstretched hands. "I've wanted this since we first met. I had a nice day-dream about screwing in your truck at the show, with people outside not knowing what we were doing."

She lowered herself back onto me and seemed to completely relax, and I put my arms around her. She slid gently up and down my erect cock, breathing deeply and threading her fingers through my hair.

Hayley stroked Becky's hair and back and looked incredibly happy. She saw me watching her, grinned, and leaned over to kiss me passionately.

"You two snogging?" Becky mumbled into my chest.

"You're busy with one end of Paul, I'm distracting the other," Hayley mumbled into my mouth.

Becky chuckled, which made her inner muscles tense against my erection. "Bet this is more fun."

Hayley turned Becky's head to face her. "You should try both of us at the same time." Then she leaned in and kissed her friend softly and slowly on the lips. Becky pulled Hayley closer and their kiss intensified. It was beautiful to see. I wondered how I'd react when I saw them truly together, and what I'd learn about how they liked to be touched.

They bumped their foreheads together and giggled. Then Becky stretched up and slid her tongue deep into my mouth as if taking possession of me. It was easily the most assertive and demonstrative kiss she'd given me.

She pulled back and gave me a beautiful smile. "Not bad for a first time," she whispered, then slid off my cock, which plopped onto my tummy.

She changed position to sit astride my thighs, then ran her fingers along my erection. "She grinned and wrapped all her fingers around me "You're wet from being inside me."

"And being in you was utterly lovely," I said.

Becky raised her eyebrows, gave me a rather dirty grin, then started wanking me slowly. Hayley distracted me up by kneeling over my face and lowering her pussy onto my mouth. From her aroma, I knew she was already aroused. I teased her with my tongue and she moved to get my attention where she wanted it, back and forth from her clit to her entrance. She almost covered my ears with her legs, but I could still hear her sigh happily.

Becky moved and slowly guided me back inside her, but deeper this time. It was lovely to feel her body surround more of me. After lifting and pressing down a few times, I felt as if I was filling her. She stayed with me like that while she rotated her hips and fiddled with her clit, which I felt as a rhythmic movement around my cock.

Hayley came unusually quickly for her and was more vocal than usual. Her thighs trembled as she held her position with her clit over my tongue and she twitched and gasped.

A few seconds later, Becky stopped swivelling her hips and her thigh and hip muscles tensed. The pace of her clit-fingering increased, then she gasped as her climax arrived, her inner muscles squeezing my cock.

Both women flopped onto the bed, one each side of me, and let out satisfied sighs. Then they both reached out and hugged me.

"Wow," Hayley whispered. "That was powerful."

"Best I've had in years," Becky murmured. "I feel all stretched inside, too."

"I just had two women come on me." I was amazed at how natural it had felt.

Hayley reached out and wrapped a hand around my cock. "You made him all wet, Becks."

Becky's hand joined Hayley's. "He smells and tastes of me, too."

They started wanking me. First Becky, then Hayley, wrapped one of their legs over mine, and snuggled up tightly against me. Which felt a bit weird, but in a nice way. They took turns to kiss me, then they both slid down the bed and the hand-job became far more oral. They took it in turns to take the first inch or so of my cock into their mouths for a few seconds, while the other licked and stroked my shaft. Becky pressed her tongue around the rim of my tip and it wasn't long before I arched my back and my self-control started to give. I instinctively tried to hold back, as Helen hadn't liked me coming in her mouth, but my two lovers were persistent, and their occasional giggles were distracting.

"Come on, Paul," Hayley whispered. "Let go." She took me into her mouth.

"You know you're going to," Becky said. "We want you to let rip."

I guess my gasping, wriggling, and tensing-up gave the game away, because they were sharing my cock when I felt hot pulses run up it and the nerves in my tip went into meltdown. I think they both licked up some of my output, then shared a slow, sloppy kiss. They slid up the bed, eyes gleaming, and each shared a brief, sloppy kiss with me. I tasted myself on each of them and felt like the luckiest man in the world.

Hayley turned out the bedside light on her side of the bed. The other created a gentle warm glow while we snuggled together in the warm nest of love we'd created.

"Tonight's the first time a guy let me be in control," she said. "Others just fucked me and assumed I'd come from being screwed. But I don't. Never have. It left me feeling frustrated and used. And hurt." She paused and Hayley reached out to reassure her friend.

"I've not slept with all that many women," I said. "But I think maybe only half came while we were bonking. So you're perfectly normal."

Becky ran a fingertip in a tight circle on my chest. "That's what I've heard, too. But I wanted our first time to be special. I suppose I wanted to give myself to you, in a way. And I know you can make me come with those wicked fingers and that evil tongue of yours."

I kissed the top of Becky's head, and Hayley leaned across me to kiss her on the cheek.

Becky sighed. "I'm not saying I won't want you to fuck me like a steam engine next time, but it was lovely to be in control."

"Say what you want," I said quietly. "Every time."

"My last two guys were..." She took a deep breath. "Well, ones I want to forget about."

I was tempted to ask why, but remembered what John had said about being careful with her in case I pressed the wrong buttons by mistake.

"What was your first time like, Paul?" Hayley asked.

I smiled at the memory. "I was eighteen. Lovely girl, but we never fell in love. It was a close friendship, curiosity, and too much cider at a party."

"Mine was a get-it-over-with opportunity at a summer vacation drama course before I went to university," Hayley said. "Both virgins, hadn't got a clue, and it lasted about two seconds, but it was okay. Then I met a nice guy at university and we worked it out."

Becky took a deep breath. "After Dad died, Mum had a string

of blokes. There was one who seemed keen to make friends with me. He… One day, when I was fourteen or so, he persuaded me to wank him off. I was totally innocent, hadn't got a clue what to do. This carried on for a while, the old 'our little secret' and 'your mum won't believe you' crap, classic gaslighting. Mum knew something had happened, but I wouldn't tell her anything. She somehow arranged for me to go to a boarding school, no idea how she could afford the fees."

I obviously knew abuse like this happened, and it always made me feel angry to hear about it. But I'd never known anyone who'd experienced it. My first instinct was to track this monster down and make him pay, but I didn't think Becky would tell me who it was, even if she could remember.

"Anyway, at school, I developed a crush on one of the teachers. She was like a big sister, absolutely nothing inappropriate. I suffered a bit of bullying until one of the older girls started paying me a lot of attention. I was flattered, she seduced me and I found out sex could be fun."

She paused and sniffed a couple of times. "Then at university, there were all these boys. I spent the first month letting anyone do whatever they wanted to me. As this included giving me an STD, I decided to stop and think. Hayley came along and I had a steadying influence at last. But every guy I dated must have seen 'mug' tattooed on my forehead, they all used me or cheated on me. When I met Mikey, she seemed to offer the comfort I wanted. But I still wanted to be normal and have boyfriends."

I felt flattered that she wanted to share this with me, as it was so intimate and personal. It made me determined to protect and help her in any way I could.

"You could have told me this years ago," Hayley said. "You know I'd have done anything for you."

Becky rolled onto her back and stroked Hayley's face. "I know you would. But I was a screw-up, especially after Mum died. It took me a few years to find my feet. I'm terrified about having children, in case I screw their heads up. Your mum's the most positive role model for a mother I've had by miles." Then she turned towards me. "Then I finally find a guy I fancy, like, and feel I can trust."

I kissed her. "I'll do my damn best never to make you feel you can't, not even for a moment." I hoped she realised how strongly I meant that.

"And my best mate felt exactly the same about you," she said, turning to grin at Hayley. "And you asked to see her again before I got your attention, you bastard."

"The nearest we've ever had to argument," Hayley said, hugging Becky. "All over some silly boy."

"Hey, watch it," I said. "Who are you calling silly?"

Hayley touched the tip of my nose with her index finger. "You. And your sister called you that, too."

Becky laughed. "Yeah, I'd forgotten that. She told us to grow up and let you choose. Only we hoped you'd like us both, even if it made the choice more difficult."

"Why me?" I asked.

Becky rolled towards me and Hayley wrapped her arms around her. "You and the guys looked so amazing at that first show," Becky said. "Realistic but theatrical enough to be entertaining. But we'd watched how you all worked together, and saw you running around all the time, checking everything and everyone, especially the horses. Everyone obviously likes and trusts you. It's like John's the director and you're the natural star of the show, partly because you worked hardest at it."

"I was so jealous of Claire until I realised she wasn't your girlfriend," Hayley said. "Then I was struck by how much she obviously loves you. So you couldn't be all bad."

I felt a bit embarrassed. "But why try to get this three-way thing going?"

They looked at each other. "We both fancied you," Hayley said. "And you seemed to fancy both of us. Or at least couldn't decide between us. When we were talking in bed about you that first night in your flat, while you were asleep on the sofa, we'd drunk enough to think *why not have some fun*? I didn't realise how natural it would feel for it to be three of us."

Becky reached out and stroked my shoulder. "Does it feel natural for you?"

"It does, even though it's all new."

She swallowed and I felt her tense. "Something you could get used to?" she asked in a near-whisper.

They were both looking at me intently, which made me feel my answer was important. I wondered if they both felt the only future option with me was the three of us. "Yes," I said, and hoped I could.

Becky swallowed and curled up under my arm. "Remember those two guys I wanted to forget?" She started trembling. "Those were both date rapes who thought a nice meal out deserved repaying. I said 'no' but they just forced me."

Her body shuddered as she sobbed. I gathered her in my arms, and Hayley jumped out of bed, ran around and climbed in behind her. While Becky sobbed, we each held, hugged and kissed her, and stroked her hair.

I felt helpless, as there was nothing I could do to take her memories away. And I felt so angry at those two selfish bastards taking advantage of a sensitive and vulnerable woman. I knew John had investigated crimes like this, and I wondered how he could stay objective and professional while he did. "I'm here for you, Becky," I whispered, "just like Hayley is. We're both here whenever you want us. You're safe with us and always will be. We'll do whatever we can to help you be happy."

When Becky felt calmer, she wiped her eyes and sighed. "Thank you both. It means so much to know I can trust you and stop worrying all the time." She leaned across and kissed Hayley. "My best friend's utterly fantastic." She twisted to kiss me. "And our awesome boyfriend's got a real suit of armour."

We cuddled for a while longer and Becky fell asleep lying between us. Hayley reached across and stroked my face. I nuzzled her fingertips and she giggled quietly, then she snuggled up against Becky. I heard Hayley's breathing slow as she fell asleep too.

I'd expected my early morning and long, intense day to catch up with me fast, but I stayed awake, thinking over everything which had happened that day. I'd been on the point of walking away from these two ladies, and now we were starting a three-way romantic affair. And Becky had opened up about some of her past, which must have been painful and incredibly hard for her to do. I still felt unsure about how things would play out and hoped none of us would get hurt.

I seemed to be on the point of falling asleep when I saw Helen standing at my side of the bed, wearing what I remembered were her favourite top and skirt. Considering she'd been dead for over two years, she looked really well and happy.

She gave me her beautiful smile. "So, it takes two women to replace me, eh?" she said quietly. "Never thought I was that much trouble."

"You were never trouble," I murmured. "Just full of life."

She grinned. "Yeah, yeah. I know I could be a pain at times, and I'm sorry that I hurt you sometimes without realising it. I didn't handle stress well, did I?" She and looked at Hayley and Becky as they slept. "Good choices, Paul." She leaned on the mattress beside me, which sagged slightly, reached across and stroked Becky's cheek, then Hayley's hair. "They both need you more than they'll ever let you know, and you know you need them, too. You made a good start today. I know you'll do your best, so keep on paying attention and make sure you all communicate. Take care of each other and you'll all be happy."

I reached out with my spare hand and took hers. It felt firm and warm, like it had in life. "Are you real?"

She gave me an amused look. "You think I'm here, so I'm real enough, aren't I?"

She shifted on the edge of the mattress, which moved again. "I'm so sorry I couldn't stay with you any longer, but I didn't have a choice and I've missed you as much as you've missed me. Mum and Dad said to say hi, too." She looked away for a second. "I know things will pick up for you now." She ran her fingers through my hair. "These violent incidents you've been involved with, the dog thing, the woman in the alley... It's not over yet, but you and your friends will be okay. There'll be more odd experiences, but nothing you can't cope with. I don't know any more than that. You've got way more guts than you think you have, as well as that half-decent brain between your ears." She stroked my cheek. "Take care of these two and of yourself, lover."

Then she stood up and walked around the bed. "Oh, and Paul... please don't hang on to my jewellery. Claire always loved some of those pieces, and I'm sure Becky and Hayley will, too." She switched off the dim light on the far side of the bed and I couldn't see her. "Now get some sleep."

24

The next thing I knew, it was early morning and I felt relaxed and refreshed. Bright sunlight shone around the thick curtains. I must have dreamed about talking with Helen. But it had been so vivid and realistic, just like the dream I'd had about us having sex in the bed in the horse transporter cab.

Hayley yawned and stretched her arms. "I slept like the dead."

Becky rolled over and threw an arm across my chest. I rolled towards her and stretched an arm over her to reach Hayley. "Morning, lovers."

Becky stretched and wriggled between us, then yawned. "Let's make a habit of waking up early."

"Any particular reason?" I asked.

She rolled onto her back, glanced at Hayley and then at me, and gave me a cheeky grin. "A couple come to mind."

Hayley kissed Becky's cheek, then rolled over and scrabbled on the nightstand for her mobile phone. "Fuck, it's after seven. We've got to get ready for this morning's scene."

Becky rolled towards me and snuggled up in my arms. "You mean we don't have time for more rampant sex with our super-stud boyfriend?"

Hayley launched herself across both of us. "Not unless he can sort us both out in five minutes. You'd feel short-changed if he did."

We all had a quick kiss and cuddle, then Hayley sat on the edge of the bed and stretched her arms out. I loved the way the soft light fell on her back, showing the muscles moving under her skin. "Funny, I'm sure we left a bedside light on last night."

I felt a sudden shock as my vivid dream resurfaced in my mind. My dead wife had walked around that side of the bed and turned the light off. In the dream...

Becky slid out of my arms and stood up beside Hayley. "Come on, if we can't bonk, let's have a fondle in the shower."

They grabbed me and tried to drag me across the bed. I gave in gracefully. A shower with the two women I was now sharing a three-way relationship with seemed like a decent way to start the day, especially as it would almost certainly involve intimate shaving. I could think about that dream later.

During breakfast, Phil joined us to discuss a new scene, the one I'd suggested and Becky had now scripted an outline for. "Okay, I know it's a bit silly, but it's fun and light-hearted, too," he said. "Be perfect to use with the end credits. We'll almost certainly have music, but improvise some dialogue; someone's bound to lip-read you."

Hayley gave Phil a puzzled look. "I'm really going to make some bread?"

Becky grinned. "Yeah, the ice maiden princess has thawed under the influence of true love. This is set after you're married."

Hayley looked at me, then at Phil. "And I get to drag Paul in with me?" She paused and looked thoughtful. "His costume's black and I'll have flour and dough to hand." Her grin held more than a hint of mischief. "This is going to be fun."

Just then, my phone started playing "Yakety Sax," so I stood up and walked a short distance away.

"Hi, John, what's up?"

"Hot news." He sounded excited. "Remember the national task

force that took over that investigation?"

"Oh, yeah, the Weird Shit Squad?" I knew he'd felt frustrated that he'd not been able to solve it and someone else whisked the case away.

"All I can say is they're well supported and don't mess about. They've done comprehensive DNA tests on the blood from the dog which attacked Mark and the hair samples found at the scenes of the other attacks. Results were a perfect match. They've concluded that you almost certainly killed the dog involved in all those attacks." He paused for a second. "Paul, you're a hero, mate. In real life."

"You're taking the piss." In my surprise, I must have spoken more loudly than I expected, as a few people turned to look at me.

"No, dead serious." John paused for a second. "Oh, the guy leading the task force asked if you'd make him a dagger like yours."

I smiled to myself. I knew that knife was a decent piece of work. "Better set a price, I guess." I remembered the odd skinny guy, the one I chased, who attacked Ola. "What about that guy Mark and I stopped behind the hotel?"

"They think he's linked with the Romanian criminal gang. Seem confident they'll sniff him out, though. Anyway, that's all I can say now, so go off and act, then tell us all about it when you're back."

When the group discussion had concluded, we left to get into costume.

"Any news?" Becky asked. "That phone call?"

"It seems I'm a hero of sorts."

The two women exchanged a glance. "And that's news?" Hayley said.

"The dog, which attacked Mark, had been used by gangsters to attack other people," I said quietly.

"And they reckon you killed it?"

I nodded.

"So, you don't need to worry about acting the hero now, do you?" Hayley hugged my arm. "You know what it feels like."

"Yeah," I said. "You get stuck in and do what you need to." *Even if you feel guilty and throw up afterwards.*

An hour later, the scene started with Hayley pushing the door open and dragging me in to the kitchen. She casually waved aside the fussing by the chef and cooks, stopped by the baker and asked what he was making.

"Bread, highness." He was in medieval dress and looked the part.

"Pray show me, good master," Hayley said. She watched carefully as the baker demonstrated kneading, then tried her hand at it, working enough dough for a single loaf on the table top. After a short while, she paused for breath and wiped her face, leaving flour on her cheek. "Master baker, this is fair hard labour."

I watched from the other side of the table. "You're scarce started, madam."

She gave me a mischievous grin. "Your point, sir?"

"The magic of bread needs time and sweat."

The baker, who stood beside Hayley, nodded. "True, highness," he said, "then time to let it rise also."

"All arts need practice," I said. "The making of good bread is truly an art."

Hayley gave me an overdone glare, a clear challenge. She lobbed the lump of dough onto the table in front of me. "Many hands make lighter work, do they not, my liege?"

I dusted my hands with flour and started kneading it one-handed.

Hayley watched for a few seconds, then stared at me in amazement. "Sir, you mock me."

"Indeed I do not, my lady." I took a second lump of dough, then kneaded them both at the same time. I was slow and clumsy, but I did well enough to make the baker smirk.

Hayley stood with her fists on her hips and pulled a face. Then she picked up some small pieces of dough and flicked them at me. I gave her a "watch it" look. She picked up a lump of dough and was clearly thinking about throwing it at me. I held up my two lumps of dough in a "go on then" gesture. She pinched her lips and glared at me, then grinned, put the dough back on the table and wiped her hands on a cloth.

"Master, my thanks for your time and courtesy," I said to the baker. "We shall delay you no longer." I wiped my hands, walked around the table, took Hayley's arm and urged her towards the door.

She reached out and snagged a small cake from a side table. "We thank you," she called back over her shoulder.

Watching the playback, I couldn't remember how or when I might have acquired a small floury handprint on my backside, but it was a safe guess either Becky or Hayley knew.

*****

Hayley and Becky both had a few day's work arranged over the next week or so, so we'd next meet shortly before filming the outdoor scenes on Dartmoor. I unpacked and breathed in the perfume they'd sprayed on some of my clothes. I found the T-shirts I'd missed after the previous recording freshly washed and neatly folded in my bag. I appeared to have lost another two, but no doubt I'd see them again eventually.

Claire had called me earlier to say she was treating John to a night in a hotel on the outskirts of Plymouth as a break from his work stress, and had arranged for Daniel and Vicky to stay with our parents. So I popped in to have a chat before she set off for their night of passion.

She gave me a hug, then plied me with coffee and fruit cake.

"So?" she demanded.

"Filming went better than I expected."

"You can tell us all about that tomorrow. What about Hayley and Becky?"

Oh shit, here we go. I took a deep breath. I was worried about her reaction to the news, and while I wasn't looking forward to telling her, it wasn't fair to hide it. I expected to be told I was being ridiculous to even consider it. "We've agreed to see how things go between all three of us."

She raised both her eyebrows. "So my little brother is in a ménage?"

I was puzzled. "A riding arena?"

"No, dumbass, a ménage à trois."

"Oh, right. Yeah, looks like it."

"You're happy with that?"

I nodded. "It feels like the right thing to do. And no, I don't expect it to be easy."

She looked thoughtful for a few seconds. "What are you going to tell other people?"

"Not sure, but I'll have to at some point."

She studied my face for a few seconds, her expression giving me no hint about what she was thinking. "I'll tell John, but we won't tell Mum and Dad or the kids yet. And if you must have two girlfriends, at least you picked two we like." She looked into her mug for a few seconds. "I can't say I'm not worried... It could all blow up really easily. You all have insecurities I can see developing into destructive jealousies."

I couldn't argue with her point.

She took our mugs and plates over to the sink. "And I'm bothered you'll get wound up because you won't express your own needs." She gave me a meaningful look. "Remember how stressed you felt at times with Helen?"

I nodded. I'd hated working in a noisy open-plan office for an unpleasant team leader, so wanted to chill and forget about the day's shit when I got home. But Helen often came home wanting to vent to deal with her own work-related stress. Which left me feeling stressed because I felt I had to be supportive even though I needed some quiet time.

"I'll do better this time, promise," I said. "I don't think either of them are like Helen when they get stressed."

"I don't think so either. But even so, I think you're all bloody mad for even thinking about it."

I hadn't fancied an evening in my flat as I knew I'd feel restless, so I'd already asked Mark if he fancied meeting that evening. He and Maggie met me for dinner at a pub on the outskirts of Plymouth, and they wanted to hear all my news. I didn't talk about my love life, as I wanted to get used to it myself.

When I said I was getting a dinner jacket, Maggie gave me a mischievous grin I suspected meant trouble. "Get Hayley down, and Becky too, we'll all dress up and go out together somewhere fancy before Christmas."

I sighed and got kicked under the table. Mark rolled his eyes and got an elbow in his side.

"It's not too bad an idea," he said thoughtfully. "Assuming the girls are up for it."

"They will be," Maggie said.

"How can you be sure?" he asked.

Maggie shrugged. "What woman wouldn't want to dress up and go out with two good-looking men in black tie?"

Mark pretended to be puzzled. "Well, I'm one," he said slowly. "But who's the other?"

Maggie made him buy the next round of drinks for being rude.

While he was at the bar, she showed me a photo on her phone. It was of her looking fabulous in an elegant evening dress, arm-in-arm with an army officer in dress uniform, wearing a few medals. "The only time I've really dressed up was for a formal regimental dinner as my brother's guest. His rig tops black tie. Just."

"What regiment's he in?"

"He was commissioned in the SAS, but he's commanding a small ceremonial unit at the moment," she said casually. "No one's ever heard of it."

"Has Mark met him yet? Making a good impression on a brother can be hard work."

She grinned at me. "Don't tell him that. I've still got to meet his sisters, which is even worse. So when are we going to meet Hayley?"

"I'll arrange an evening out when she's visiting." *How am I going to introduce the idea of having two girlfriends?* Claire seemed to be reluctantly prepared to see how things developed, and I suspected John would be too. Eventually, anyway. But other people?

Mark arrived with the drinks, which meant a change of subject. "So, how's acting?"

I thought for a second. "It's weird, to be honest. I've no idea what I'm doing, but when I'm on set, something seems to take me over." I sipped from my bottle of alcohol-free beer. "But the director's happy. Almost everything has been done on the first take so far."

Maggie grinned at him. "Looking forward to seeing it. Mark asked if I can tag along when you do all these action scenes and the producer was quite happy about it."

*****

John and Claire both looked relaxed and cheerful when they got back the next morning. Claire went off to collect the children from our parents, and John suggested we went for a ride together. Something about his manner made me sure he wanted to talk privately, and I was worried in case it was a grilling about my unorthodox romance.

"Nice hotel?" I asked, as we went side-by-side along a track.

"Fab. One of those country house places, fine dining and a great bar. Nice old building, too. Sort of place your dad would love."

"If it's fairly local, he's probably already had a look around it."

"True." He paused for a second or two. "I don't want to be nosey, but..."

My heart sank. *Here we go.* "But?"

"Mark and Maggie. How well do you know them?"

I was surprised by his question, which wasn't what I'd expected. "Not that well, yet, but I like them a lot. Both clearly bloody bright. He's a really likeable guy, seems to be settling in here okay. She's more reserved than him, probably fitter than me. She was pretty wound up when I first met her, but is far more relaxed now Mark's with her. Why?"

"When I requested the file about that thing in Romania, someone in the Cabinet Office rang and asked what my interest was, in a polite and conversational sort of way. When I said there may be similarities to recent cases here, I quickly got a brief report which told me what you said Mark had told you, and that the Coroner's court returned open verdicts."

"Odd," I said.

"Then, the day after the dog in the car park thing, I asked for a routine background check on both of them, just in case it gave any clues about possible motives for the attack. From the CCTV, the dog clearly went after him, but something about her made it hesitate."

I remembered how the dog had stared at Maggie. "So what did you find?"

"Electoral registration records, car insurance and registration, and driving licence details."

I turned to look at him. "What? Surely you get sight of all sorts of stuff?"

"Normally, yeah. But... well, the Weird Shit Squad are running it now. After a phone call from someone in Whitehall, my gut is telling me that if I dig more, I'll feel heavy breath down my neck."

I felt astonished. They were both people I instinctively liked and trusted, and seemed to make a lovely couple. "But he's a university researcher and she's a trainee lawyer. They only met a few weeks ago at the gym, and I'm sure they genuinely didn't know each other."

"That's what puzzles me. Her law firm, Harker, Murray and Seward, is rock-solid, founded back in the mid-nineteenth century. Very discreet and efficient, specialising in civil work; business, property, family law, stuff like that. Any idea what his research interests are?"

"Genetic diseases and disorders. He said his research is partly supported by a private institute."

"Yeah, that's in his profile on the university website. But I couldn't find out anything else about them beyond their own website, which is top-class vague."

"Probably helps them filter suitable applicants for funding."

"Maybe." He chewed his lower lip for a couple of seconds. "Believe it or not, the guy leading the Weird Shit Squad is Maggie's brother, Tom Petherick. He's an SAS major on secondment. Very professional, bit quiet and reserved, and very focused, but sound. Claire said she met their parents a while ago, some Commoners social event she went to with your mum."

I remembered Maggie has said Tom commanded a small ceremonial unit, which I now guessed might be cover for the task force. "Dad knows them a bit. So why's a police unit being run by an SAS officer?"

"They're not police. Only met a few, but I'd bet they're either current or former military. Tom was rather vague and said they operate under special authority, with more freedom than we have. They clearly have friends in very high places; never seen my Superintendent be so deferential before."

"Maybe it's Maggie's connection to Tom which rang alarm bells at Whitehall?"

He shook his head. "Doesn't seem likely. I've been told to liaise with Tom on anything to do with these cases, and daren't do any more digging." He paused for a second, as if wondering whether to say more. "It's just me puzzling over loose ends, don't let it affect your friendship with them in any way. I'm looking forward to meeting them both again socially."

I thought about it and couldn't figure out how Mark and Maggie might be even unwittingly involved in something which was some sort of state secret. The simplest answer was Maggie's brother Tom being involved in secret work.

25

Phil asked for some Dartmoor locations where he could get outdoor shots of me riding off to rescue Hayley, and of us returning together to the palace. He wanted to get both in the can on the same day, and, as his other commitments meant it had to be a weekend, the Knights Errant team could show him John's ideas for combat scenes, too.

After some good-natured discussion, we agreed on a few places with a suitable landscape free of modern life, and where we and the camera crew could get to easily with the necessary vehicles. I duly took photos and video at each and sent them to Phil.

Hayley said she'd travel down on the Friday before the shooting, after finishing some voice-over work. Becky wanted to visit sooner and arrived late on the Wednesday afternoon. I felt excited about spending some one-on-one time with her, as I had with Hayley. And I tried my best to keep my anxiety under control. I wasn't sure how things would go with my family, although I was sure they'd be polite.

I heard Becky's car when she arrived, but the children had already reached her by the time I got down from my flat. She had Vicky in her arms, Daniel had wrapped his arms around her legs, and the two terriers were running around, jumping and barking in their excitement.

"It's Becky, Uncle Paul," Daniel shouted.

Becky grinned at me. Her hair was now a rich shade of auburn and styled into a neat bob, which framed her face nicely. I got her bags while she and the children enjoyed their group hug.

"Go tell your mum," I told the children, who ran off together, shouting happily.

Becky launched herself at me, jumped up, and grabbed me around the neck. I held her up while we grinned, then shared a brief and deliciously sloppy kiss.

"Wotcha," she murmured.

"Wotcha right back. You okay?"

She nodded. "Yeah. Bit nervous."

"What about?"

"Well, it's our first time. You know, without Hayley. Maybe we won't get on."

"Don't be daft." I lowered her to the ground and picked up her bags. "Let's drop these off, then say hi to Claire."

She scampered around my flat like an excited child, stopping only to look out of my bedroom window at the view we'd all admired together on her first visit. I put my arms around her and looked over her shoulder.

"Tomorrow morning," she murmured. "Can we cuddle here and watch the sun rise?"

"I could be persuaded," I said.

"Maybe this will persuade you." She reached round and put her hand on my cock, which had already started paying attention. "It'd be way too early for breakfast, wouldn't it?"

"We could arrange to be up that early."

She turned around and we kissed as if we'd not seen each other for months, rather than the ten days it had been. Phone calls can't match a good kiss. I was tempted to suggest we take things further right then, but I wanted Becky to feel completely in charge of our first time together as a couple.

"Come on," I said. "If we don't stop now, Claire might get the wrong idea about you."

Becky gave me a saucy grin. "Oh, she knows I'm here to bed her baby brother."

As soon as we walked into the farmhouse, Claire gave Becky a huge grin and a warm hug. They chatted away like old friends over mugs of tea and a plate of fruit scones.

Claire glanced at me. "So, how are things with Paul and Hayley?"

I bit into a scone. *Don't mind me,* I thought.

Becky smiled. "Pretty bloody excellent, I think."

"Pleased to hear it. Now, what did you think about my tweaks to your costumes?"

Even if it was only in front of me, Claire seemed prepared to accept our unusual romantic arrangement without comment, but I still felt relieved. I wondered if there had been conversations between the three women I'd never know anything about.

John still hadn't said anything about it to me yet, which wasn't really a surprise. We had a good friendship based on shared interests, but feelings weren't something we aired much. While I wanted to know what he thought, I wasn't going to ask him; he'd let me know when he was ready. I just hoped he and Claire were at least prepared to let the three of us work it out in private. If they weren't willing to tolerate it, I'd feel uncomfortable when either or both the girls visited.

John was openly welcoming when he got back from work, giving Becky a quick and friendly hug. We chatted over dinner; family news, what Becky had done lately, the recordings which hadn't involved me, and the next weekend's scenes.

"Daddy, will you and Uncle Paul pretend to fight on TV?" Vicky asked.

"We all will," he said. "We'll change our clothes and pretend to be different people, so it looks like there are lots of soldiers."

Vicky looked at Becky. "Will you pretend to fight, too?"

Becky shook her head. "Not in this story. But I'll be in a few scenes. One's a dance with Hayley and Uncle Paul. We recorded that a couple of weeks ago."

"Bet you'd be great in a fight," Daniel said, with a little too much glee. "And Hayley, too."

"Definitely think about that for another show," Becky said solemnly.

"Any other ideas?" John asked.

"Yeah, loads. I've started sketching them out, but it's still early days. We need to get *The King's Captain* aired first."

"You mean *The Princess and the King's Captain?*" I asked.

She gave me an embarrassed smile. "That was the original title, but, well, Phil had a rethink after seeing the material he's already got. A very plausible hero, he called you."

Shock filled me. "But Hayley's the star. I'm not even an actor."

"Phil thinks you are. And now you'll get equal billing," Becky said.

I rubbed my face. "If anyone at university sees the show, I'll never hear the end of it."

"They may well have seen the social media stuff already." Becky put her hand on my shoulder. "Teasers, photos, a few very short clips."

"I've seen some of that," Claire said. "Getting lots of positive reactions. Even if I didn't know about the show, I'd be interested."

"Bugger." I leaned my head on the table.

"What's wrong, Uncle Paul?" Vicky asked.

"I'm all over the internet," I mumbled.

"I know, Mummy showed us."

Thankfully, only being three, Vicky had a butterfly's attention span. "When's Hayley coming?" she asked. "I want her to read *Poppy and the Professor* to us."

"Friday," Claire said. "But we've got a few recorded if you want to watch them again."

"I'd love to read to you, if you like," Becky said. "There'll be a box set coming out in time for Christmas, on Blu Ray and DVD. The show's turned out to be a bigger hit that we imagined. I'll get you a copy as soon as I can."

"I think Uncle Paul should be on it," Daniel said. "If he's Hayley's boyfriend in one TV show, why can't he be her boyfriend in *Poppy*, too?"

"They finally figured out that Poppy's actually Hayley," Claire said.

Becky looked at Daniel. "That sounds like a fun idea. We'll talk about it later."

He beamed at her.

I wondered where this would end up.

*****

That night was the first Becky and I spent together without Hayley. Becky seemed nervous. I was, too.

She put her arms around me and held me tightly. "Did Hayley ring you?"

"Yup. Gave me a firm but polite talking-to. I'm absolutely not allowed to feel I'm cheating on her. You and I are to feel every bit as happy about being together as we are when it's the three of us."

"I got the same talking-to." Then she looked up at me. "The hardest thing I've done in years was not lose it when Hayley came to visit you on her own," she said quietly. "I was terrified I'd lost you."

I kissed the tip of her nose. "And now?"

She bit her lip and suddenly looked anxious. "Now I'm scared I'll lose Hayley."

"And I'm not worrying, too? It feels like if I lose either of you, I'll lose you both."

She bumped her head against my chest a couple of times, then looked up at me. "I'm scared of that, too. And I think Hayley is, too, behind her super-cool act."

"So, do we let our insecurities win, or trust Hayley and each other?"

She giggled. "You wouldn't believe my insecurities. But they've ruined enough of my life."

"So?"

"So…" She swallowed. "Take me to bed, eh?"

It felt as if a weight had been lifted off me. I smiled at her. "I was about to suggest that."

"Come on, get 'em off." Becky was naked in seconds and jumped onto the bed.

I followed her example. We cuddled and kissed while I stroked her side, back, and bottom. I took my time. I nuzzled her collarbones, then moved down over her breasts, tummy, hips, and inner thighs. I made a point of going slowly and when I finally lay between her legs and planted my tongue on her pussy, she arched her back and moaned with pleasure. She came quickly, her body almost pushing out the fingers I had inside her. Then she pulled me up to kiss her. As I did, she reached down and guided my cock inside her.

"Fuck me, please," she murmured. She looked deep into my eyes as I slowly eased into her, a little at a time, until I felt surrounded by her soft warmth. "That's better," she said.

I set a slow, steady rhythm, pulling almost all of the way out of her and sliding fully inside with every stroke. She writhed underneath me and sighed happily. She wrapped her legs over mine, stroking my bottom with both hands as I moved in and out of her.

"Watch out," she murmured. "I'm getting a taste for this."

"Me, too."

She gripped my bottom more firmly. "Come on, let's go for

it, hard and fast, get this bed rattling. I'm planning to shag you as often as I can over the next couple of days."

"Hard and fast?"

She nodded.

I took my weight on outstretched arms and made a point of slamming harder every time I slid into her, which made her breasts sway enticingly and our bodies slapped together.

She closed her eyes, reached up and gripped my forearms. "Oh, fuck, that's so good." Then she started writhing beneath me, pushing back against my thrusts and breathing heavily. I felt her pubic bone against mine every time I slid deep into her.

She gripped my arms more tightly and grinned up at me. "I want to watch your face when you come inside me."

"You mean I can stop struggling to hold back?"

She grinned. "Excited, eh?"

"Just a bit."

"Well, hold on a little longer, please. I'll tell you when." She released my arms and slid her hands over my chest, then gripped my waist firmly.

Trying to hold back my climax wasn't new, but being asked to wait was new to me.

A couple of minutes later, we were both clammy with sweat and I was very aware of the scent of hot sex. I was struggling to hold back, but didn't want to change what I was doing. Everything I felt was exciting; her hands on me, the way my balls swung back and forth, the way her small breasts moved, her body reacting to mine...

"Come inside me," Becky whispered. "Slam in all the way and let rip."

I let my self-control go. A few seconds later, my moment arrived and I pushed as deep into her as I could. Intense warmth flowed up my cock, then a wave of intense pleasure washed over me as I shot into her.

I opened my eyes to see her grinning at me.

"I like your sex face," she whispered. "I plan to see it a lot more often."

I withdrew my softening cock and lay beside her. "You don't scare me with your talk of seeing my sex face more often."

"No?"

"No."

She wriggled against me teasingly. "Good."

*****

Becky got her wish of watching the sun rise the next morning. We cuddled in front of the window, and I nuzzled her neck and shoulders. She wriggled her bum against me until I was rock hard and feeling randy.

"When we looked out of here that first morning," she said, "Hayley whispered that she'd like to finger me until I went pop, leaning against the windowsill."

I reached around and slid my hand over her pussy. "I'm probably not as good as she is yet," I said, "but practice makes perfect." I dipped my fingertip into her soft, warm entrance, which opened immediately, then drew back up between her lips until I found her clit.

She sighed happily. "Practice all you want."

I seemed to do pretty well for a first time, as she tensed then shuddered in my hug, crying out as she came, then leaned on the window ledge to get her breath back. "Not bad, I suppose. Now it's your turn."

She grabbed my hand and pulled me back to bed, then rode me hard, swivelling her hips around as she slid up and down my cock fast. She leaned back enough for me to watch my cock vanishing into her, and I was struck by how slender and fragile she seemed, and how fat my cock seemed compared to her waist. I loved seeing her hips moving over mine, her taut tummy muscles and firm thighs, her clearly-visible mound, accentuated by her patch of fine pubic hair.

She came while I was inside her, from her own finger. She came a second time from my tongue, after I'd come. I loved tasting myself and her at the same time as she clawed my scalp in her climax.

Becky had a riding lesson with Claire that morning. It was clear she'd ridden quite a bit in the past and quickly remembered everything. I felt confident she'd soon be more than capable of joining one of our faster moorland group rides.

I did an hour or so's archery practice that afternoon, using my most powerful longbow and some war arrows I'd made. John's idea for the big rescue scene involved me shooting a couple of dummies before engaging in hand-to-hand combat with everyone else. I needed to get used to how these heavier arrows flew so I had a good chance of hitting the dummies with my first shot. Phil was keen to get the whole combat scene recorded in a single take, and had talked about recordings taken from a drone and hidden static cameras, then mixing the best views in the finished show. I couldn't work it out, but he was the director and had his "vision", as Becky put it.

When I got back, Claire casually mentioned Becky had chatted with Daniel and Vicky, then sat down to type away on her laptop. Becky admitted to working on an idea for *Poppy*, but wouldn't tell me anything else.

John was chatty and happy over dinner that evening, teasing Becky in a friendly way, which me feel confident that he liked and felt comfortable with her. I had a feeling he wanted to try to get her to open up, but was restraining his inner inquisitor to avoid a telling-off from Claire. He was rather vague about what he'd been doing at work recently, in a manner which I felt meant he couldn't tell us, rather than because he didn't want to. I suspected he was still working with Major Tom's mysterious task force.

Becky wanted us to try doggy-style that night, leaning over the sofa in my flat as soon as we got back. It was great fun and I loved watching my cock slide in and out of her. While I held her hips, I was struck once again how slim and fragile she seemed. I guessed it was at least partly my need to have someone to care for and look after, but she was by far the slimmest lover I'd had, and Hayley wasn't much better built.

"Fuck me harder." She gasped every time I slid into her. "Make me feel like I'm really being taken. Make my tits wobble."

I held her firmly and thrust more forcefully, moving her back and forth across the cushions. She reached down with one hand and brought herself to orgasm, which I felt as a soft rippling around my cock as I slid in and out of her.

"My knees have gone all weak after that." She panted a few times. "Can we finish off in bed?"

I picked her up, carried her into the bedroom, and laid her on the bed, then knelt between her spread legs. She grinned up at me and stroked my erection. "Put this big, hard thing back inside me and fuck me until you shoot."

So I did as my lady asked, which involved both of us gasping, groaning, and giggling, and sharing a lot of close hugging.

The next morning, I woke when she slid down the bed to give me a blow job, which was a great way to start the day. I still felt I had to hold back from coming in her mouth, but she told me to give in gracefully.

When I got her back, she scratched my shoulders with her fingernails when she came. "Fucking hell." She let out a long breath. "Scrape me off the ceiling, please."

26

For the first time I could remember, Hayley didn't let me know her anticipated arrival time. I hoped this meant she was starting to work past her Tony-related anxieties. I heard her car in the yard in the mid-afternoon and we went out to meet her. As soon as she parked, she jumped out and hugged Becky, then me. "God, I've missed you two," she said. "I can't wait to get into bed together."

As it turned out, we all had to wait until she and Becky had each read a bedtime story to Daniel and Vicky, and enjoyed a sociable evening's drinking with Claire and John.

John and I had finally had "that" conversation in the kitchen, while getting more drinks.

"I'm convinced you're asking for big trouble," he said. "Claire's worried you'll get hurt, but told me to keep my nose out and let you figure it out between yourselves."

"Only way to see if it works," I said.

He sighed. "Look, I like them both. Either would be a great for you. But both at the same time? I think you're all fucking mad. Just don't come crying, okay?"

I felt a flash of anger. "Have I ever done that?"

He pursed his lips. "Well, no, not even over Helen."

I let out a breath and let my anger fade. "Look, I'm incredibly grateful for everything you both did to help after I lost Helen, and I will be for the rest of my life. But that's the worst thing I'll ever go through by a fucking long way."

"All I'm saying—"

"Is that you don't think it'll work," I interrupted. "Like I've not thought about that myself?"

"Suppose it doesn't? Then what?"

"Worried I'll go back to being a selfish, self-destructive shit?"

He sighed. "No, I don't think you're that person anymore. But I'm concerned, okay? You're my best mate as well as family."

I looked him in the eye. "John, I'll cope. I don't know how things will pan out, but if it crashes and burns, I'll sulk for a while, get over it and carry on."

He held his hands up in mock surrender. "Just don't drift into it without thinking carefully, all three of you could end up hurt."

"I don't want to end up again like I was two years ago. We'll make no promises and no commitments until we all feel we're on really solid ground."

"Okay, you're keeping your eyes open. They're lovely girls helping you try something adventurous, which is great; until you moved back here, you'd always struck me as being rather cautious." I couldn't deny that. But when Helen died, I'd stopped caring about myself enough to think about the consequences of a decision. "Taking this risk may or may not bite me, but I won't know until I take the chance, will I?"

He thought for a few seconds. "Just remember that a relationship isn't defined by the 'yee-ha' good times, but by how you cope with the crap, how you support each other when the shit hits the fan. And you're now in two long-distance relationships, which aren't easy."

He had a couple of good points there. I was certainly in the excited-about-a-new-relationship stage, and I knew from experience that long-distance relationships could be difficult.

"We'll just have to see, won't we?"

"Suppose it does work out? Your flat's too small even for a couple to live full-time."

He had another good point. We were pretty isolated, so finding a larger home would mean moving away, even if only a couple of miles. How would that change the relationships I'd come to cherish?

He passed me a tray of wine glasses. "Said what I wanted to, subject now closed." He gave me a pointed look. "Even if it goes tits up."

*****

We were all slightly drunk when we went to bed, which left us giggly and relaxed.

"That bed's calling to me," Becky said.

"Strip off first," Hayley said. "Lie still in the middle of the bed." She grinned at me. "Just follow my lead."

We all undressed and Becky climbed onto the bed and lay down in the middle. We lay either side of her. I watched Hayley and tried to follow her lead. We each nuzzled Becky's neck and shoulders, licked and kissed her collarbones then moved down her body, across her breasts and then swirled our tongues around on her nipples.

"That's evil." Becky laughed.

"Want us to stop?" Hayley mumbled into Becky's breast.

"Not right away," Becky murmured. "But remember, I'll get you both back."

"I'm already terrified at the thought," I whispered.

Hayley grinned at me and stroked Becky's tummy with her fingertips. I slid further down the bed and nuzzled Becky's hip bone. Hayley followed suit and we locked eyes as we kissed and licked our way down towards Becky's pussy. Becky sighed and wriggled a little, spreading her legs further apart.

Hayley took one of my hands. "We'll have to take it in turns here." She guided my fingers along Becky's cleft, already open and slick. "What can we do?" She clearly had a good idea, as she guided two of my fingers to Becky's entrance.

I slid them as deep inside Becky as I could, paused for a second, slowly pulled them almost out of her, then kept this up. Hayley watched my fingers for a few seconds, grinned, then leaned across and kissed the front of Becky's pussy. I was in an excellent position to watch Hayley's tongue tease Becky's clit. Becky let out a long sigh and lifted her hips, pressing against my fingers and Hayley's tongue.

"It feels amazing, but it's almost distracting having two of you down there," Becky said.

"We'll get better with practice," I said.

"And that's going to be bloody good fun," Hayley mumbled, her face pressed against Becky's pussy. "I've got an idea. If you screw Becky from behind, but sort of lie to one side, I can tease her."

Becky's grin suggested she thought it sounded like fun. I certainly did. She lay on her back beside me and rested one of her legs over mine. Hayley guided the tip of my cock into place and opened Becky's inner lips, then Becky eased down onto me as I slid into her. I leaned back a bit, and held Becky as I slowly moved in and out of her, trying not to make her body shift too much. I couldn't fill her from that angle, but it felt lovely all the same. Hayley cuddled and kissed Becky while fingering her clit and pussy and my cock and balls, then she slid down Becky's body. I felt Hayley's breath on my cock as she licked Becky's clit, which made her gasp and sigh from time to time.

Then Becky tensed in my arms. "Fuck, I'm coming any second," she whispered.

A few moments later, she almost screamed as she came. Panting, she rolled off me and lay limp beside me.

"He's all yours," she told Hayley. "Make the bastard suffer."

IAN D SMITH · 285

Hayley climbed on top of me, slid herself right down onto my cock, then sat up and rode me enthusiastically. After a minute or so, Becky straddled my legs behind Hayley and reached around to fondle her breasts. Hayley leaned back against Becky. I'd enjoyed watching her breasts bouncing around, but seeing Becky's hands cup them was erotic as well as sexy. Then Becky slid a hand down Hayley's tummy. I felt a wriggling as Becky's finger worked Hayley's clit. "Come on, Hayley, come for me," Becky whispered, but her eyes never left mine.

Hayley leaned her head back on Becky's shoulder, and came, gasping nearly as loudly as Becky had a few minutes before. A few seconds later, I reached the point where I knew I could come, or hold back if I made an effort. I let go and came, my climax a hot surge from within me, followed by intense pleasure.

When I opened my eyes, my girlfriends were both grinning at me.

"Gotcha," Hayley said.

They lay one on each side of me, as usual, and each put an arm across my chest.

"We okay, then?" Hayley asked.

"We're fucking marvellous," I said, still feeling a bit breathless.

I've got two girlfriends. This only happens in stories.

"You know we'll make more unreasonable demands on you in the morning, don't you?" Hayley asked.

"I certainly will," Becky mumbled.

"Oh well, if you must" I said.

*****

A few days before the recording session, I'd had an idea and discussed it with Becky, who called Phil, and he came back with an even better one. "Don't say a word to Hayley," he said, "but brief your guys. She'll be surprised, but then play along perfectly."

In the first session of the day, I was in hot pursuit of the princess and her kidnappers. I had to look like a seriously pissed-off man on a mission. I wore a mail vest, carried my sword and a couple of daggers, held my unstrung longbow as if it was a lance, and had a quiver of arrows tied to Otto's saddle.

Otto was a total star. He gave the camera drone a suspicious glare, snorted at it, then completely ignored it. Several long clips were recorded in which we cantered steadily along isolated tracks and across open moorland, jumping the odd low stone wall and splashing across streams, with the drone flying in front of us.

Once everyone was happy with the recordings, we relocated and set up for the second shot, where I'd escort Hayley back to the castle after rescuing her.

I gave Hayley a leg-up and she settled herself in the side-saddle posture she'd quickly been coached in by Claire. I gave her a woollen riding cape to wear, which swallowed her completely.

"It's far too big," she grumbled. She tilted her head back so she could peer from under the rim of the hood. "And hot."

"In the story, it'd be mine, remember, so it's bound to be kind of large. You'd want something to disguise yourself a bit," I said. "I think you look cute in it, too."

"Okay, guys," Phil said. "Up this track and over the top of that rise, nice and steady, please. We'll start with the drone, then the camera crew on the other side will take over. Your mics will be live the whole time. I'll give you a wave when we're ready to go."

When we set off, I walked beside Otto. Hayley held his reins, but in reality, he followed me like a big, soft dog, his leather tack creaking quietly with every step. It only took a minute to reach the top of the hill, the drone moving almost silently ahead of us.

At the top of the rise, all we could see was open moorland sweeping away in front of us, with scrubby bushes, the odd grey boulder, and a tor on a nearby hill. The only modern thing was the camera crew thirty metres or back from where our track met another. Oddly, the group of mounted knights riding along the other track looked anything but anachronistic. Their armour and colourful livery were eye-catching in the bright sunlight, and their progress was clearly purposeful.

As soon as she saw them and realised she had to improvise, Hayley looked shocked. "Captain, what does this mean? Are these knights errant, or are we undone?"

"We need not be fearful, my lady. I know and trust these noble gentlemen from before my service with your father."

"They are from your country? What is their purpose?"

"They are, but we must ask."

We all stopped where the tracks met, and the knights took their helmets off.

Hayley cleared her throat. "My lords, I am Gwendoline, the king's daughter, and I bid you welcome if your intent is peaceful."

The warriors bobbed their heads politely. No one had actually volunteered to do dialogue, but David and John needed suspiciously little persuasion.

"We thank you, highness," David said, confidently and clearly. He was the herald at our shows. "Indeed we ride in peace." He gestured towards me. "We seek this gentleman, on a matter of great import."

"How fare my father and brother?" I asked.

David looked down. "Our nation mourns both their king and his heir."

I looked down at the ground for a few seconds, took a deep breath, then looked up. "This came about how?"

"The prince fell from his mount at a tourney. The king took ill with a fever."

Hayley stared at me, surprised. She knew nothing about this little twist, but her professionalism shone through. "You are a royal prince, Captain Rowan?"

"No, Highness," David said. "He is now our king."

John dismounted, bowed his head and handed me a large signet ring. "Your seal, Majesty."

I looked at it, then looked up at Hayley. "I regret I must leave your father's service, my lady. But hold that you and he have my full support and friendship at all times."

I turned to the knights. "I will see the princess safe with her father, then deal with Duke Roland, who abducted her."

"Duke Roland seized the princess?" John asked, looking surprised. "He must have loyal men here. We will escort you, sire, our swords yours to command."

"Roland's title and lands are forfeit," I said. "He will be exiled."

Hayley turned to the knights. "Your company is most welcome, sirs. We are but two hours from my father's palace."

Everyone but Hayley dismounted and we all walked with our horses towards the camera team. John walked beside me.

"Sir, you know your king well?" Hayley asked John.

She'd obviously decided to continue improvising, with a plausible question for her character to ask. I wondered how John would respond, and if Becky had primed him with some ideas.

"We learned and served together as young men, highness. His friends grieve that he found no place in our kingdom after the old king named his brother as heir."

Becky and John have definitely been scheming.

Hayley grinned. "Sir, pray tell me tales of his youth."

John laughed. "I dare not, Highness. My loyalty is to my king."

"Sir, your king will formally ask for my hand this very day. I would know the man I will wed."

John grinned at me. "Sire, this is true? We congratulate you. Our nation will have a good queen and you a fine wife."

I looked from one to the other, raised my eyebrows and sighed. I guessed the camera had zoomed in on me for that reaction.

When Phil told us the scene was over, Hayley looked around. "Whose idea was that thing about Paul being a bloody prince?"

I held my hand up. "I suggested Captain Rowan was secretly rich enough to provide for her, Becky suggested he inherited a title, but Phil said it would be even better if he was royal."

She grinned. "Well, it worked well. But it was a rotten trick to spring on me."

Back at the farm, we ran through the combat scenes we'd worked out. Phil had recruited a couple of dozen battle re-enactors to act as men-at-arms in the more general fighting scenes, but only our team would engage in the more vigorous, and potentially dangerous, hand-to-hand combat. John would play the duke in the final joust, being replaced by the actor once he'd lost. The poor guy could barely sit on a horse and had been very relieved when he heard the plans.

We put on a barbecue, then enjoyed a balmy evening once everyone had left. John and Claire both shared little family anecdotes—embarrassing ones about me, needless to say. When I hinted I knew plenty of comparable tales about Claire, she glared at me and John looked intrigued. But it stopped the embarrassing stories. Best of all, it had felt very relaxed and natural.

*****

We lay together in a slightly sweaty heap after a lively three-way sex session, and I was very aware of our intertwined arms and legs. I smiled when I remembered what John had said about his only threesome.

"You know what?" Becky said. "This three-way stuff seems to work best when we don't worry about fucking."

"I love all the cuddling and touching," Hayley said. "It's sort of erotic and exciting."

"I like it all," I said. "Just going for sex play is great fun. And not knowing, or caring, who does what is amazing."

Hayley leaned on my chest. "I know what you mean."

"If anyone's inside me, I know whose willy it is," Becky mumbled.

Hayley winked at me. "Well, Paul's not met our sex toy collection yet."

Becky sat up. "Now that will be fun. For us anyway."

"What makes you think I won't enjoy it? Zapping a woman with a vibrator's good fun."

Becky put an arm around my neck. "Suppose we zapped you with one? Or if I wore a strap-on?"

I looked from one to the other and wondered how best to respond. "Get me drunk, be gentle, and talk me into it."

They grinned, then Hayley looked at Becky. "And if you got rough and damaged him, he knows a doctor who'd quietly sew it all up again."

Becky laughed. "How are your chummy lovebirds? We'll meet them at the hotel for the combat scenes, won't we?"

"You will yes," I said. "They seem very happy, but Mark's a bit low because Maggie's away, visiting some family in Wales."

"She'll be back soon, won't she?" Hayley asked.

"Yup, and we've all been invited to dinner so you can all meet," I said.

"All three of us?" Becky asked.

"Of course. Why wouldn't it be?"

She sat up and looked at me. "You're going to introduce us both as your girlfriends?"

"Well, I wasn't going to blurt it out, but I do want us to be comfortable going out socially together. We're working together on this show, after all."

"I'm not sure," Becky said. She bit her lower lip. "Look, I'm totally over the moon with our relationship, but I'm not at all happy about it being public knowledge. I'm cool about you two being the couple as far as the rest of the world's concerned. The last thing I want is to be a public figure. And don't forget, the media would kill for a lesbian sex romp story involving a popular actress."

I sat up and wrapped my arms around Becky. She snuggled up against my chest. "I'll go along with whatever you want," I said. "But I'd love us to be able to go out together anytime, with anyone, anywhere. We can behave ourselves in public, after all. We have around here, and did at the location shoot."

Becky looked uncomfortable. "It's honestly not you two. It's me. I want to keep my life private. I'm sure I'll be comfortable with Mark and Maggie, but I'd like to be Hayley's best friend and the show's writer as far as they're concerned." She glanced at Hayley. "You happy about that? You're not hurt?"

Hayley ruffled Becky's hair. "Daft sod, of course I'm not hurt. But I don't want you to feel under pressure. Just tell us, okay?"

I felt there was something more behind Becky's anxieties, and wondered if it had anything to do with Mikey rattling her self-confidence. As I thought about it, I remembered seeing Becky in only one of the general photos I'd seen of the TV awards ceremony, and she hadn't joined Hayley and Trevor on-stage when they collected their award, even though the whole idea was hers. I knew she wasn't shy, but if she was reluctant to share the spotlight, there was a reason. I'd respect her wishes, and hope she felt able to explain why at some point in the future.

27

As it worked out, both Becky and Hayley were still with me when Mark rang to say Maggie was on her way back from Wales. He wanted us all to meet at a restaurant. As he'd drive past the farm, I suggested he leave his car there for a day or two, and I drove us all.

Like me, he usually wore jeans or chinos and polo shirts, but we'd both had hints about dressing up a little. My ladies both looked very fetching; Hayley in a slinky navy-blue dress, Becky in a white blouse and black trousers, and they'd even put on some make-up. I suspected they wanted to put on a bit of a show.

Mark was soon having a lively and friendly conversation with both Becky and Hayley, and I enjoyed listening as they chatted away. I parked next to Maggie's beaten-up old Landrover in the car park and we hurried in through a light shower.

Mark beat us to the bar, where we found him holding Maggie off the floor and exchanging happy-to-see-you kisses. He put her down, and they both looked slightly embarrassed as we walked over. Maggie looked striking in a classic little black dress which fitted her like a glove.

"A natural beauty," Becky murmured. "She'd look good in a sack, never mind that dress."

Hayley grinned. "They're clearly smitten with each other."

"I did warn you they're embarrassingly soppy," I said, loudly enough for them to hear over the buzz of conversation.

Maggie and my ladies gave each other a lightning-fast once-over, then shook hands. They seemed to like each other well enough to start chatting away immediately, picking on Mark and me as safe subjects to start with.

"No doubt Paul's told you a bit about me," Maggie said.

Hayley smiled. "Well... he's not bad for a guy, but, you know."

They nodded in agreement, then looked at Mark. "Mark's pretty good, actually," Maggie said.

"Pretty good, or pretty good for a guy?" Becky asked.

"For a guy."

I looked at him and sighed. "This is a mistake, we're out-gunned."

"I love your dress," Becky told Maggie.

"Borrowed it from my mum," Maggie said. "I've nothing this nice in my wardrobe."

Hayley's eyebrows rose. "Your mum still has the same figure as you? She must diet like mad."

"Your mother's still in good shape, Hayley," I said. Marion had admitted she exercised regularly and was careful about her diet.

"Yeah, but she'd kill for the figure she had when she had at my age."

While Mark went to the bar, I looked at our ladies. Seeing them side by side was interesting. Hayley's natural grace was clear, and she seemed to be very relaxed and self-confident. Becky seemed to feel a bit on edge, but was trying to hide it. Maggie had an elemental, natural beauty, an air of energy and strength, and some quality which eluded me. I was still trying to put my finger on it when Mark came back with our drinks.

"You are bringing Maggie to the recording session, aren't you?" Hayley asked him.

"Of course," he said.

Maggie nodded eagerly. "Looking forward to it."

"We'll be near Bath," Hayley told her. "Everyone says there are some fab shops there. Becky's our make-up artist and stylist, so we could have a girlie day out while the boys are doing their rough and tumble stuff."

"Shit, then we'll really be in trouble," I murmured quietly to Mark.

I was surprised when Maggie grinned at us. *She heard me over all the background conversation?*

For a first joint outing, we all got on well. Mark was, as usual, good company. Becky, Hayley, and Maggie seemed to enjoy getting to know each other. I got the impression my ladies made a particular effort to make friends with Maggie. We had a nice, relaxed meal and a happy, rambling conversation, with lots of teasing and laughter, and were almost the last guests to leave. I insisted on paying, and thanked the manager for a great evening and promised to be back.

The earlier showers had turned to steady, heavy rain. I hurried over to bring my Range Rover near to the front door while everyone else sheltered in the porch.

I parked, grabbed a large umbrella and Mark's rucksack, and joined them in the porch just as the rain really intensified. I hefted the umbrella. "I'll give you a lift to Maggie's wreck."

"I'll have you know it's a timeless classic," Maggie said, clearly trying to sound offended.

"Bet it leaks in the rain," I teased. Mark shrugged his rucksack over one shoulder and looked at the rain.

Maggie guided his other arm through the strap "What's in there? Seems heavy."

"Some clothes, my laptop, and review copies of a couple of textbooks."

"Any good?"

"Both are, actually."

We all looked out onto the rainy street, now almost deserted.

"Wait a minute, or run for it?" asked Maggie.

I looked around. For some reason, my attention was drawn to a medium-sized white van, about thirty yards away, in a disabled parking area. Then a taxi arrived and we stood aside to let the last of our fellow diners scuttle into it.

"It's not too far," Mark said. "We'll be sheltered by the building most of the way." He and Maggie stepped to the entrance to the porch and looked towards the car park.

Becky nudged me. "What's that?" Her urgent tone alarmed me.

I looked up and saw a horizontal line of what looked like dancing red dots stand out against the darkness. I glanced at Maggie and noticed a single bright red dot move across her body and stop on her chest. I glanced to my left, back along the line of red dots and saw a short, stocky man standing by the white van's passenger door. He faced us, hunched over something in his hands.

At that instant, I realised it was a laser gun sight and lunged forward. Mark also reacted, pulling her into a shielding embrace and crouching over her. I heard three incredibly loud bangs in rapid succession. Mark was punched forwards and fell. I heard his head hit the stone porch with a stomach-turning thud.

Becky and Hayley both stepped forwards, obviously wanting to help, and I saw the red dot swing around wildly and settle on Hayley, but only for the fraction of a second it took me to get in the way.

"Take cover," I shouted, pushing Becky behind me. My mind was in a whirl as I tried to process what was going on and how to react. From the line of red dots where raindrops hit the laser beam, I was sure the gun was aimed at me. *He might shoot*, I decided, *or he might not.*

I set off like a rocket, ignoring the rain and the slick pavement, with a vague idea about protecting everyone by distracting the gunman. I heard someone shouting in a language I couldn't understand, and the gunman jumped into the van, which sped away. I got close enough to be sure of the make, model and some of the vehicle registration.

I ran back when I heard Maggie's despairing scream. "Don't die, please don't die." She grabbed Mark and rolled him onto his side. "Don't you dare die," she shouted. "It's all my fault, stay with me."

Hayley was trying to pull Maggie into the porch, while Becky had one of Mark's rucksack straps and was struggling to move him. Something clicked in my head and everything seemed crystal-clear.

"I'll get him out of the rain," I said. "Get the police, an ambulance and a first aider if you can." I grabbed Mark's rucksack straps and was about to drag him into the restaurant when someone stopped me with a hand on my shoulder.

"Don't move him." It was the restaurant manager I'd been talking to a couple of minutes before. "I heard shooting," he said, "one of my staff is calling the police."

"What do we do?" I asked. I was way out of my depth here.

He turned towards the restaurant door, where a young waitress stood, her hand over her mouth. "A really sharp knife, lots of clean towels, the first aid bag and some umbrellas," he shouted.

The waitress nodded and ran inside, Hayley right behind her.

The manager leaned in close to Mark's face. "Breathing but unresponsive."

Twenty seconds later, Becky and the waitress held umbrellas over Mark while the manager cut through his rucksack straps. Maggie was just inside the restaurant with Hayley's arm around her. They were both white-faced, clearly shocked and scared.

I took Mark's rucksack, which had some ragged holes high across the back, like Mark's jacket. The manager quickly cut Mark's jacket and shirt with some scissors, then squirted some sterile saline from a plastic bottle across the holes in Mark's skin, washing away the blood. He put a couple of folded cotton towels over the wounds. "All we can do is try to stop the bleeding," he said. "Press firmly. We'll change them if they get sodden, change it."

"Ambulance is five minutes away," someone shouted from the restaurant door. "Police are on their way, too."

Maggie knelt beside me. "Please don't die, Mark," Maggie said, her voice trembling. "It's my fault, they know who I am."

Hayley put her arm around Maggie. "Give them space," she said gently. A waitress draped a blanket across Maggie's shoulders, and she stood a few paces away, with Hayley's arm around her again.

"See who did it?" the manager asked.

"Saw their van clearly," I said.

"Tell me what you remember and I'll pass it on," Becky said, pulling her phone out of her handbag.

While I did that, the manager quickly changed the towels on Mark's back and I pressed the new ones firmly.

"Not bleeding too badly," he muttered, inspecting the towels he'd removed. "No sucking wounds, either. Can't say anything about internal injuries, of course."

"Didn't cover gunshot wounds on my first aid training," I said.

The manager grinned. "We did in the Navy. No major bleeding I can see, don't think he's got a punctured lung."

A police car arrived a few seconds before the ambulance, with a second pulling up while the paramedics were hurrying to help. They were calm, professional and efficient as they examined Mark and questioned us. One of the policemen asked us more questions, noting our answers. I must have been in shock, as I lost track of time, but the paramedics suddenly had Mark on a trolley and were wheeling him out, and Maggie was already on her feet.

One of the policemen moved forward, clearly intending to stop her.

I grabbed her arm. "Maggie, I'll take you. There's nothing you can do at the moment."

Hayley wrapped an arm around Maggie. "He's right."

"I'll drive," she said, fumbling in her handbag.

Hayley took her hand. "No. We're taking you, don't be silly.

Becky put a hand on Maggie's shoulder. "And we'll stay with you."

Maggie let me put my arms around her and she trembled against me. "It's all my fault," she sobbed into my chest.

What? She said that before. "No it wasn't," I said.

"It is," she sniffed. "They know what I am."

Becky and Hayley exchanged puzzled looks, then looked at me questioningly. I gave them my "beats me" expression.

I made a point of thanking the manager for his help, then we followed the ambulance. My ladies both seemed pretty calm, at least compared to Maggie. I dropped them off, parked, then rang Claire as I hurried back to the hospital, to let her know what had happened, and reassure her as best I could.

"John's already been called," she said. "He flew out shouting about finding a van. He didn't know who was involved, though."

I found Maggie sat between Becky and Hayley in the accident department, all watching the medical team clustered around Mark. All three looked pale, and Maggie was trembling slightly.

"They're talking about scans and emergency surgery," Hayley said. "They don't think he's bleeding internally, but don't want to risk it."

I had to bodily pick Maggie up to stop her following Mark into the operating theatre, after she barged a rather large, and very surprised, security guard out of her way.

We sat and waited in a bland but comfortable relatives' room, and tried to comfort Maggie, who alternated between wringing her hands and bouncing around like a fly trying to head-butt its way through a window pane.

"Why not tell your parents?" I suggested.

I didn't understand a word of what she said, as it wasn't in

English. I remembered Mark had mentioned that her mother was Swedish, so I guessed that was what she spoke.

Much to my surprise, the first person into the room was an Army officer, wearing a camouflaged combat jacket and trousers, with a rolled-up maroon beret sticking out of a chest pocket. Maggie immediately squealed with delight, jumped to her feet and threw herself at him in a single blur of movement. He was significantly taller and heavier than her, but still took a step back from the impact.

"I'm Maggie's brother Tom," he told us, over her head. "Mark's fine; he was blood lucky. The stuff in his rucksack saved him. Stopped two of the bullets and slowed the third so much it only just broke his skin. Almost all his wounds are from fragments from his laptop. He's almost certainly got a concussion, too."

He kissed the top of Maggie's head. "Once he's out of theatre, he'll be put in a private room. An armed policeman's already here to guard him. Now, tell me all about it."

Whatever personal authority is, Tom had way more than his fair share. My first instinct was to do whatever he said. So we told him and he listened carefully, his face set. "The police found that van abandoned in an industrial estate," he said. "Stolen, of course. It's being examined for any evidence." He looked at me. "Someone needs to tell Mark's family; would you be willing?"

"Of course."

"We found their number on his phone. The doctor wants to brief you first on what to say."

We stopped a short way along the corridor, and he held his hand out. "Thank you," he said. "Mark means a lot to Maggie, and I'm so grateful that you helped them both. I'm sure it scared the shit out of you, but by running forward, you protected everyone else and were able to tell the police more about the van. That's the sort of presence of mind we look for in the military."

I shook his hand. His grip was firm and dry.

"It sounds like he aimed at Hayley as well," he said. "He was probably just told to shoot a blonde woman, he didn't know Maggie by sight."

I felt a cold shock as I remembered the red dot settling on Hayley. It hadn't occurred to me that the gunman was actually aiming at her. "You're sure Maggie was the target?"

He nodded. "Can't say why, but yes."

"Not a chance it's anything to do with Hayley's ex?"

Tom shook his head. "He's all mouth, hasn't got the balls to do more than be pushy in business dealings. He'd wet himself faced with the sort of criminals who run around with automatic weapons."

"Didn't your team interview him?"

Tom paused, as if considering his words. "We did. His being detained was just opportune. He'd had a business meeting with someone of interest earlier in the day, but it turned out that Tony isn't relevant to our investigation. We got the police to let him go in case our subject heard he'd been detained and vanished."

"Okay."

He grinned at me. "I was impressed with the way you got him out of the way."

I wondered how he knew. He might have figured it out, of course. I was sure David said no-one had seen him and Libby, but I vaguely remembered something about a dog walker…

I probably only had a couple of minutes, so pressed ahead with something I wanted to ask him. "Maggie said the attackers knew who she was. Any idea?"

He shrugged. "I'm involved in an investigation into people-smuggling from Eastern Europe, one with national security angles. The gangsters involved are pretty nasty bastards. We suspect they know she's my sister and wanted to threaten me by attacking her."

"That incident Mark and I were involved in by the hotel, and the dog thing in the car park?"

"Possibly connected, but that's only a theory. No evidence either way." He tapped my chest with a finger. "You were bloody lucky not to be shot last night," he said firmly. "If anything like that ever happens again, duck."

I knew he was right. Running towards the gunman could easily have been the last thing I ever did.

I felt a chill as I realised something. "They knew we were there… Maggie had only just got back in the area, so did they follow Mark?"

Tom shrugged. "Probably. But I don't think for a second that there's any risk to you, your family or your friends. You were just caught up in a botched attack."

"Okay, thanks. That's good to know." I was briefed on what to tell Mark's family, then spoke to his father, who had a lovely soft Scottish accent. He courteously thanked me, asked me to thank the medical staff on his behalf, then asked about hotels near the hospital.

Mark, still unconscious, was in his own room within an hour, with a large, cheerful and well-armed police officer outside the door. Maggie understandably wanted to sit with Mark, and Tom kept her company for a while.

Becky, Hayley and I sat in the corridor nearby. Now that some time had passed, we all felt badly rattled by our close touch with sudden violence and talked quietly together about it. Yes, even I talked about how I felt. Eventually, they dozed off, one against each of my shoulders. I stayed awake for a while, aware that the armed policeman pointedly ignored two young men in civilian clothes who sat quietly in chairs further along the corridor. I suspected there was more going on than I knew, wondered how the gangsters might know about Tom and that Maggie was his sister, and what she'd meant when she said they knew what she was, rather than who.

28

I woke with a start when someone nudged one of my feet. I felt confused, and looked around, wondering where I was. My legs and back were stiff and aching, and Becky and Hayley were both slumped against me and fast asleep. Then I remembered the evening before, which seemed like it had happened years before, not a few hours.

"Come on, sleepy-heads," Claire said, nudging my foot again with one of hers. She had a couple of bags on the floor by her feet. "I've brought you all a change of clothing and a flask of coffee. John's back home, exhausted but anxious to hear all about it."

Hayley sat up and yawned. "Hey, Claire. What's the time?"

"Just after five."

I introduced Claire to Maggie, then we each freshened up and changed in the nearby public toilet. Maggie said Tom had left once she felt more settled, promising to be back later during the day.

We had a different armed policeman on duty, with two women loitering along the corridor now, and, as before, they all ignored each other.

Around seven, Maggie's parents arrived with a change of

clothing for her. They both made a point of thanking us all profusely for helping the evening before.

As soon as I met them, I knew what Dad had meant. Her father had even more personal authority and presence than Tom. They both seemed fit and energetic, and I thought they looked around a decade younger than my own parents, even though they must have been of similar ages. Maggie closely resembled her mother, who was an eye-catching woman in her own right, with a quiet charisma.

"Now, Margaret, you must eat," her mother said, in a no-nonsense tone. "That restaurant by the hotel up the road does a decent full English breakfast."

"I'm not going anywhere," Maggie said, firmly.

I'd have stopped arguing at that point, but her mother was made of stronger stuff. She reminded me of my own mum in wearing-down-all-opposition mode. "Mark will recover fully, he is in no danger and is being protected. You can leave him for an hour, and you are perfectly safe."

She gave Maggie a rather pointed stare, and I decided that I'd been right to guess the men and women nearby were for additional security, probably from Tom's team. Something made me think that the armed policeman was little more than a highly obvious gesture.

Maggie's dad caught my eye, then joined in. "You know she's right, Maggie. You need to keep your energy up. It's been a long and stressful night."

I glanced at Becky and Hayley, who came to the rescue.

"We'll stay with him," Hayley said. "I couldn't face breakfast. We'll let you know when he wakes up, promise."

"The very second," Becky said.

I saw Maggie was wavering and joined in the peer pressure. "Come on, I'm gagging for a bacon sandwich and decent coffee."

Maggie let out a breath. "Okay." She gave both Becky and Hayley a hug. "Thank you."

On the way to the car park, she grinned up at me. "You kept that quiet."

"What?"

"Your throuple with Hayley and Becky."

I'd not heard the word before, but the meaning seemed clear. I decided to play dumb all the same. "A what?"

"A throuple. Like a couple, but three. Mark guessed it last night, too, during dinner. Don't worry, we won't tell anyone. At work, we never mention our three senior partner's relationship."

I was amazed that she'd worked it out in next to no time, but it left me lost for words. "Er..."

"I wondered from how you talked about them both. When I saw you all together, your body language and behaviour gave it away. It's lovely to see, you're all obviously really close and affectionate."

"Thanks. It's... well... I'm still getting used to it."

She squeezed my hand, which surprised me. "They're both lovely. You have good taste. And, well, I guess they could have done worse than you."

I grinned. Then I took a mental breath and asked a question which had been on my mind for hours. "Maggie, last night you said the people who shot Mark know who you are. What did you mean?"

"That I'm Tom's sister," she said, her tone just a little too casual.

"So they know he's after them? It was a sort of threat?"

She shrugged. "Guess so."

"And you said they knew *what* you are."

"Like I said, Tom's sister." Her expression and tone were bland.

Whatever the truth was, I suspected I wouldn't get any different answers from Maggie.

In the restaurant, we were guided to a small area well away

from the few other patrons, aside from a young couple who casually watched everything going on while they drank coffee and nibbled croissants. It made me wonder how many people Tom could call on at short notice. The restaurant was comfortable, the staff efficient, and the food was fine. Thankfully, the call that Mark was awake didn't come until Maggie had devoured a substantial breakfast and calmed down a little.

When we got back, he was groggy and in pain, but thanked us for helping him and looking after Maggie all night.

I left Maggie and her parents with him, and took my ladies home.

"It's weird," Becky said. "Last night, I remember feeling really scared, even after we knew Mark would be fine. And the attack was bloody horrible. But now…" She pursed her lips, as if trying to find the words.

"It's like it happened a year ago," Hayley said. "I can remember it all, but the feelings have sort of faded."

I realised I felt exactly like that, too. I remembered either a fragment of a dream, or a woman with intensely blue eyes waking me during the night. "Hello, Paul," she'd said in a soft voice. "Could you tell me about the attack, please?"

I decided it was a dream. It had been a stressful night.

Claire and John were anxious, but happier once we brought them up to date and talked about the more dramatic parts of our evening. John had a quite chat with each of us, too. I thought he was worried we might be trying to hide some trauma, but I don't think he felt anxious about us afterwards.

"Do you know what sort of gun they used?" I asked. "Tom explained about his rucksack saving him."

He shook his head. "Not for sure, but it was one of the nine-millimetre machine pistols which fire three-round bursts. Mark was bloody lucky, leaning forward at just the right angle for the bullets to hit the stuff in his rucksack." He chewed his lower lip for a couple of seconds. "Probably best to keep quiet about this, okay? There's talk of a police statement suggesting he was badly hurt. Don't want to tempt the crooks into having another go."

That made sense, but I and my ladies carried on talking about it between ourselves for a couple more days.

Mark made a rapid recovery, thankfully, and we all visited him several times, which he and Maggie clearly appreciated. I briefly met his family, who'd travelled down from Yorkshire and Scotland to see him. His two older sisters reminded me of Claire in her bossy loving mode. They were all lovely, and made a point of thanking me, which I felt touched by.

When he was discharged, I drove him and Maggie back to his flat. He felt safe there, as the police had increased their visibility in his area. I was sure that others would also be discreetly watching over him and Maggie. I wasn't too surprised that the whole incident was scarcely mentioned in the local news, and we were never asked for statements by the police.

*****

A couple of days later, John had a quiet word with me before he set off for work. "I'm bloody impressed by how you all responded when Mark was shot. You all kept your heads, followed the restaurant manger's instructions, did everything you could to help Mark and Maggie since, and the three of you have supported each other. Normally, I'd have encouraged you to contact a victim support therapist, but you're there for each other and you're talking about it."

"Thanks. I was struck by how calm the girls were at the time. I think they helped Maggie a lot."

"Sounds like you found your inner leader, too." He grinned at me. "And your inner dumb fuckwit, charging at a man with a bloody machine gun."

Becky and Hayley had plotted with Maggie to make a surprise

visit to put on a barbecue in Mark's garden early that evening. During the afternoon, I exercised Otto with Claire's help, and finished the session by popping him over a few show jumps, which he enjoyed nearly as much as jousting.

My ladies were perched on the post and rail fence with Vicky and Daniel. One of his milk teeth was close to coming out, and, as I rode past, the women watched with morbid fascination as he showed them how loose it was.

Claire was adjusting one of the jumps. "One metre forty?"

"Please. Then we'll call it a day."

She set the pole, then stood back and watched while Otto cleared it effortlessly twice from each direction. She took the jump down while I walked him round to cool off, then walked beside us for the last circuit of the school.

"John and I are relieved how things seem to be working out," she said. "You and the girls seem right together. I'm enjoying getting to know them better, too, we're becoming real friends. But I'm still worried," she said. "You're always putting everyone else first. I think they're both a bit insecure and want your attention and approval." She looked up at me. "Never thought my dopey brother would turn out to be some sort of alpha male with a bloody harem." She patted Otto's neck, then looked up at me. "If you decide to move in together, you'll have to find somewhere bigger than your flat."

"Still early days," I said.

"Uncle Paul," Vicky called out. "Can we ride Otto?"

The children loved sitting on Otto while I walked him around. He was always a total angel with both of them. I guided him over to them and dismounted. Claire held his bridle while I lifted the children down, and helped them put riding helmets on.

"Are you going to help us down, Uncle Paul?" Becky teased.

Hayley grinned at her. "Wimp. Just jump."

They sat side by side on the fence, so I put an arm around each and them and pulled them towards me. They giggled as I held them off the ground. "I've got you both," I said.

"Yeah, but who's got you?" Becky said.

"We all have," Daniel said. "Mummy said we all need to look after Uncle Paul."

"That's right," Vicky said.

I tried to ignore the sudden lump in my throat. I put the women down on their feet, then swung Daniel up and onto Otto's saddle. I put Vicky in front of him and gave her the reins. "Come on, you can ride Otto over to his paddock."

I took his bridle and led him towards the gate. Claire walked close enough to grab the children if they lost balance. Becky and Hayley followed us.

"So, everyone's looking after Paul?" Hayley asked the children. "Can we help?"

"If you want," Vicky said. "But you'd better ask Mummy."

Claire laughed. "Of course you can. More the merrier."

Becky ran ahead and held the gate open as we walked Otto through it. She and Hayley exchanged grins. "We'll look after him, Claire," Hayley said.

"You can trust us," Becky added, pulling the gate shut.

Claire looked at me questioningly.

"Don't worry," I said quietly.

She held a hand so only I could see she'd crossed her fingers. "Thank you," she called out. "I know I can. He might be a big, grumpy sod who thinks he's independent, but he'll always be my little brother."

I grinned at her.

"You're going to let someone else take care of you?" she said more quietly. "This I must see."

"I'll try, but you know me."

"I should by now. You only let me look after you when you moved here and were on your knees, and then only after a fight."

"I'll be okay, even if it all goes horribly wrong."

She looked at me. "Know what? You've come out of your shell, you're the old Paul again. And with Becky and Hayley, you're happier than I can remember since Helen's accident. John said the same thing last night."

She was right. "Hopefully that'll carry on," I said. "No doubt we'll have our ups and downs, but I think I'll be okay now."

"Every relationship has those."

"John still thinks we're all asking for trouble, I suppose?"

"Of course, but he's not as worried now he's seen you support each other. The real test will be coping with a threat to your relationship, of course. I'm always here if you need to talk, you know that."

"That's what a big sister's for," I said.

"Yeah, you need some sense knocking into you from time to time."

"Remind me never to train you how to use weapons."

"Too late. I've just about persuaded John to let me join the team, doing the equestrian stuff to start with."

"That's great." She was an excellent rider, competitive, taller than three of the guys, and physically strong and fast. "Weapons and combat?"

"You'll both teach me, of course. And you'll be making my mail and armour."

Bloody hell. "At least the girls will be watching my back."

"Fair enough. That'll make three of us."

"Four, Mummy," Vicky said. "I'm watching his back, too."

"Four's a magic number," I told Vicky. "It means everything will work out fine."

Otto nickered, a lovely deep throaty sound, and turned his head slightly.

I looked around, curious about what had caught his attention. Helen was leaning against the fence beside the gate into Otto's paddock.

"Make that five," she said.

Then she wasn't there. Or maybe I just couldn't see her.

"Is five an even more magicker number?" Daniel asked.

"Oh yes," I said. "Even more magicker than a totally magical thing."

"Good, 'cause I'm watching, too, Uncle Paul."

Despite not knowing *exactly* what Tom's National Intelligence Task Force was or how Maggie and these strange attacks fitted into anything yet, I knew one thing for certain… I was surrounded by people who loved me, who would all help me make a new start. I was sure I felt a hand rest briefly on my back. It felt reassuring.

TRADEMARKS

ACKNOWLEDGEMENT

The author acknowledges the trademarked status and trademark owners of the following wordmarks mentioned in this work of fiction:

A Midsummer Night's Dream: written by William Shakespeare (Act V, Scene I)

As You Like It: written by William Shakespeare (Act II, Scene VII)

An American Werewolf In London: Universal Pictures Inc

Girls Just Wanna Have Fun: written by Robert Hazard

Range Rover: Jaguar Land Rover Limited

Buffy the Vampire Slayer: Twentieth Century Fox Film Corporation

Dog Soldiers: Pathé

James Bond: Danjaq, LLC

Lexus: Toyota Jidosha Kabushiki Kaisha (as trading as Toyota Motor Corporation)

Land Rover: Jaguar Land Rover Limited

Yakety Sax: composed by James Q. "Spider" Rich and Homer "Boots" Randolph III

ABOUT THE AUTHOR

I'm a professional scientist with a career spent primarily in health care, and I live in the south-west of England.

Writing is one of my creative hobbies, and a fulfilling outlet for my overactive imagination. I'd love more people to read and hopefully enjoy my stories, even if writing never becomes a full-time activity for me. I'm an active member of the Erotica Readers and Writers Association, currently the editor of one of their website galleries for highlighting members' stories.

Some of my work has been published in anthologies and I'm revising more with a view to publication. Thankfully, my muse keeps on whispering other story ideas, so I've plenty to write yet.

Where possible, I like to use my own experiences to add a bit of realism to my writing. I've been a horse rider for years, spent a day learning the basics of jousting, I enjoy archery, and have practiced a number of martial arts. I've also flown in a balloon, in gliders, helicopters, light aircraft and a supersonic RAF aircraft, driven a tank and a hovercraft, and been underwater in a submersible craft… maybe these will be helpful in my writing at some point.

I'd love to forge my own knife one day, just because I can.

CPSIA information can be obtained
at www.ICGtesting.com
Printed in the USA
FSHW010625271021
85725FS

9 781948 780322